The Pipp

Book 3

The Matchgirl
And
The Magician

By

L. Palmer

Copyright

The Matchgirl
And
The Magician

Chapter 1

Frigid air gusted down the alleyway, blasting through Adeline's threadbare dress and shawl. Clouds heavy with snow shadowed the moon. Most of Pippington's citizens were bundled in their homes, sitting by warm hearths. The child huddled against a brick wall, cradling the crate of matches in her slender arms, her legs shaking. Tears threatened to come. Adeline had never been so cold in all her nine years. But she swallowed back her tears and clamped her chattering teeth together.

Too many matches remained unsold. She had done her best, singing to catch the attention of those passing by as she walked main boulevards. A few shouted her away. Others smiled sadly, bought a few matches, and said, "Poor child," before walking on and forgetting her.

As evening came, she shuffled her way back to Mr. Torvald's and her bed of a moth-eaten quilt. He grumbled as she poured the few coins onto the table, adding up to only a few skoons. She cringed just before he slapped her jaw. His face was red as he grabbed her by the arm and tossed her down the front steps.

"This is no charity house. Come back when you've sold enough."

Hours had passed since and her face and arm still throbbed. She had sold a few more matches, but they wouldn't be enough.

Rocking, she tried to rub the cold from her legs. She couldn't go back and so had come here, across the street from her father's statue.

His bronze eyes watched over her, his metal face strong and heroic. She lit another match and sang into it. Perhaps, with enough magic, she could turn the statue into her father.

He would lift her up and laugh. They would waltz around the square and he would take her home.

The match's flame disappeared and, wishing she knew how to conjure fire, she lit another.

Only a few months before, she had stood beside her mother as the statue was unveiled. Women in furs and silk handed them a mountain of flowers, pouring out condolences. She posed as her mother told her to, trying to understand the crowd and ribbons. When she asked one of the women what these decorations were for, they pinched her cheek and tapped her nose.

"Your father was a brave, brave fire brigade officer and saved many lives."

Adeline knew why her father was gone. She didn't understand how flowers and ribbons would stop her mother from weeping every night.

During the ceremony, Adeline's grandfather stood apart with her two uncles, taking in speeches about her father's final heroic deeds and thank-you's for funding the statue. Her grandfather and uncles said nothing to her or her mother. Once the ceremony was over, Adeline's mother said, "We are better off without their help."

A shudder of cold ran through Adeline, bringing her attention back to the alleyway. Her hand shook as she lit another match. Images of monsters rose in the illuminated shadows. Adeline sang, focusing only on the flame and its small warmth. It flickered in the wind. She held her hand over it, the flame biting her skin. The fire spread out with her song, as if carried by the soft notes. Her mother had taught her this trick one night when there was little wood for the fire. They had huddled together as their songs carried magic into the flames, helping them grow.

Horse hooves echoed down the street. Adeline blew out the match and huddled in the darkness.

"Never show anyone your magic," her mother had said. "They don't believe in it and won't understand."

Adeline waited till the carriage passed and the echoes were far away. Taking in a few breaths, she took another match from the pile. She shouldn't use what she was supposed to sell, but the warmth was so inviting.

Striking the match against the wall, she sang and focused on the fire. A feast of goose, potatoes, rolls, pie, and everything delicious arose in the flames. Her mother was at one end, her cheeks pink and full as they had once been. Adeline's father sat at the other end, tall and proud. Her parents smiled at her before disappearing in the smoke of the burnt-out match. She flicked the splinter of wood away. Flakes of ash floated, mingling with the falling snow.

The alleyway seemed darker and emptier. She struck three matches against the wall. Her voice shook as she sang out the melody. She had to recapture her father's smile. The flame flickered, revealing an image of her parents lying in caskets, their faces pale and stiff. She tried to sing the illusion away, but her teeth chattered. The flame started to move, flickering with images of her mother and father dancing. Her mother wore a fine dress with feathers and glittering jewelry. Her father was in a suit, his hair smooth, his face handsome.

Her father had promised always to protect her but had chosen to save others instead. He had gone into the flaming building one last time and it collapsed in a cloud of sparks and ash. Months passed, and winter came and stole her mother away. Adeline shut her eyes, trying to forget waking to her mother's still face only a few weeks before.

The chill settled deeper into Adeline's skin as she curled up on the cobblestone, her cheek to the pavement. Her eyelids drooped. If she fell asleep, she would wake in her parents' arms, wrapped in a thick quilt as they sat by the fire. They would laugh and sing, telling her stories of far off adventures. She would be far away from the frost stiffening her clothes.

The matches burnt out and the warmth of her dream left. She shut her eyes tight, trying to grab onto the dream instead of the pain tingling in her fingers. She sang, her voice little more than a whisper. The song would keep her warm as she faded into rest.

Footsteps crunched in the alleyway and Adeline tried to open her eyes. Hands wrapped her threadbare shawl around her quivering frame. The stranger rubbed her hands between his until her fingers uncurled. In the dim starlight, he pulled one of the matches from her crate and struck it against the wall.

Her eyes opened. The stranger's face was warm-brown, like earthen clay. Snow weighed on his dark hair and goatee. His kind eyes reminded her of how her father had looked at her.

"Little One," he said, his Sandarian accent coloring his words with the warmth of far-off deserts. "What are you doing here alone?"

Her jaw was frozen. The Sandarian removed his overcoat, revealing a layer of jackets and scarves beneath. Taking the crate of matches, he wrapped his coat around her.

He pulled her slender body into his arms, cradling her like a bird with a broken wing, and held the crate by its strap. Though he was a stranger, she nestled her face into the warmth of his shoulder.

Her face began to thaw as they entered the street. They passed the echo of people singing in a bar and the clatter of hooves from carriages. Her head fell as sleep overcame her. She woke as a rush of warm air hit her. The click of silverware against plates and a rumble of voices marked a full dining hall.

"No room."

They returned to the freezing night air. Another street was passed and another building entered. Adeline absorbed the heat until "no room" was repeated. The Sandarian walked on. At the fifth place, a Sandarian woman said, "There's space by the fire."

She led them to a table.

"Poor child," she said with a warm smile before stepping away.

The man gently pulled his heavy coat from Adeline's shoulders, but left his scarf around her. As he sat, the woman returned and set down plates of steaming food.

The man broke his bread, indicating to Adeline to use it with a spoon to scoop up the pile of rice and chicken. She followed his example as best she could with her small, shaking fingers. Once she shoved food into her mouth, her senses were filled with the warm spices and rich aroma. She had never tasted anything like this in her nine years.

"Madame Pomray makes a fine curry, does she not?" He smiled at Adeline. "I am Rompell."

Eyeing his gloved hands, she said, "Adeline Winkleston."

He touched his forehead and made a bowing motion with his arm. "I am blessed to meet you, Miss Adeline."

Adeline tried to hide her blush as she pulled his scarf tighter around her slim shoulders.

"And why is a little one like you wandering the streets on a night when fire might freeze?"

She looked at her small crate of matches. Though she was warmer, she trembled. She glanced at the fire and envisioned Torvald's red, fuming face.

Rompell picked up a few matches from the crate and held them between his fingers. "You are selling these? For how much?"

"A penny for three." She prodded her food with her spoon as she yawned. The fire was warm and she was so tired.

Rompell held the matches on his palm and closed his fist around them. He waved his other hand over it and opened his palm to reveal a penny where the matches had been.

"I seem to have lost them," he said. She gaped as he dropped the penny into her hand. "That is the price, is it not?"

She nodded. The penny felt whole and real. She put it into her money sack. The coin clinked against the floor. Tears welled up in her eyes as she stared through the bag and the hole at the bottom.

"May I see?" Rompell said.

She handed him the bag. He poured out the few remaining pennies on the table. "And how many matches have you sold?"

"I—I don't know." She wiped her face with the napkin, trying to hide her tears.

Rompell pulled out a handkerchief and set it on the table in a pyramid shape. He slapped his hand down, crushing it. Coins showered from the cloth onto the table.

She stared at his gloved hands. It appeared to be magic, but she didn't sense the tingling on her skin like when her mother had used her powers.

Laying out the cloth, he said, "I'll tell you what we will do, Miss Adeline. I will give you this handkerchief to carry these coins in return for a joke."

"A joke?"

"You do know one, don't you?" He raised his eyebrows. "I should warn you, I expect it to be a good one. What say you, Miss Adeline?"

She stared at him. Her father always told jokes, but the memory flitted away every time she tried to think of one.

Rompell's eyes softened. "We will wait on the joke. Let's finish eating and get you home. I am sure your papa and mama are looking for you."

Adeline stirred her curry, trying to hide fresh tears. She looked at Rompell's warm face. "They cannot."

Rompell's smile disappeared. "Are they gone?"

Adeline's throat clenched as she nodded.

"What was your father's name?"

She licked her lips. "Conrad."

"A brave name."

Adeline nodded.

"And your mother?"

Her shoulders shook as sobs threatened to take over. "Mariana."

Rompell set down his spoon. "How long have they been gone?"

Tears streamed along her cheeks. She fought through a few hiccups to say, "Father's been gone months, but Mother—She was right beside me, and then she was taken—taken away."

She crumpled in her chair, all her fear, all her loneliness collapsing in on her. Rompell knelt beside Adeline. His gloved hand wiped away her tears as his eyes remained steady and calm.

"Your parents can never be taken away." He pressed his palm to her shoulder. "They are always with you if you are willing to remember them." He waved his gloved hand in the air. "I believe I saw them watching over you as you sang in the alleyway."

Her eyes widened and she went still. She had hidden her powers, just as her mother had taught her. He shouldn't have seen it.

Rompell leaned forward and whispered, "Those who have been touched by magic can see far more than those who have not."

He rolled his fingers and a flash of flame followed.

"Eat, Little One."

Her tears ebbed and she devoured the plate of curry. Once finished, she wiped the sides with her piece of bread, gathering the last drops. Madame Pomray stopped by and cleared their dishes. Rompell touched the woman's arm and spoke softly in Sandarian. She smiled and gave a quick nod.

Minutes later, she set a small chocolate cake in front of Adeline, steam rising from the plate.

"My gift for your company," Rompell said.

Adeline hesitated before digging her fork in. Molten chocolate spilled onto the plate. Her stomach was nearly full as she took the first bite. The rich chocolate was sweet and powerful. In moments, the cake was gone and she stared at the chocolate residue.

"Go ahead," Rompell whispered.

She licked up the final crumbs. Madame Pomray returned and laughed.

"Enjoy it, did she?"

"It was excellent, Madame." Rompell laid cash and coin on the table. "Thank you for your kindness and warm room."

He led Adeline to the door and knelt beside her. "Little One, where do you call home?"

Adeline shook as her lip quivered again. "I—I don't have—"

"Do you have family nearby? An aunt or uncle? A grandparent?"

She shook her head. "He doesn't want me."

"Who?"

"Grandfather—my father's—"

"But he must be worried."

She shook her head as she wiped her eyes with Rompell's scarf.

"He hates me and Mother. He says we're why Father—"

Rompell squeezed her arm. "Then, not there. Where have you been living?"

"I can't—" She swallowed back a sob. "Mr. Torvald—he'll be angry."

"Who is Mr. Torvald?"

"Mom needed a room for us." Adeline forced herself to finish, "He lets me stay there, if I work."

Narrowing his eyes, Rompell said, "Is he the one who sent you out to sell matches?"

Her throat too tight to speak, she nodded. She wiped her nose on her sleeve and the thin fabric fell back. Rompell's smile turned into a hard line as he rolled back the sleeve further, revealing dark bruises along her arm.

Coldness overtook his eyes. "Was this Torvald's doing?"

"He just—I—"

"A child should not be painted by such foul colors."

"I don't want to go back." The words barely pushed past the

thickness filling her throat.

Rompell dropped his gloved hand as a softness filled his eyes. "I am no more than a street magician, but I will find you a better place."

He held out his palm. Adeline swallowed before taking it. His grip was sure and strong.

"First, is there anything of yours at Torvald's?"

"My mother—her chest. It has pictures and—"

"We will collect what is yours, Little One."

She clung to his arm as he led her to the exit. The wind blew with fury and ice as they stepped outside. He wrapped a scarf around his own head before bundling her in his coat. Gripping her hand, he led her into the street. She nearly fell into the slush, but he grabbed her arm and pulled her to safe ground.

Shutters clanked in the wind as they walked the dark streets. At last, they reached Mr. Torvald's house and Rompell pounded on the door. Cursing sputtered on the other side as a light turned on. Adeline jumped as Mr. Torvald slammed the door open and glared at Rompell.

"Good evening, sir." Rompell's voice was warm and booming. "I am Rompell, Master Magician and Traveling Wizard." He bowed with a flourish.

"What are you bothering me for?" Mr. Torvald said.

"I was passing through the street, when I found this remarkable girl. I need such a child for my act. She says you have her possessions."

Mr. Torvald's bloodshot eyes glared at Adeline. "She's got nothing. In fact, she owes me."

Rompell flipped a coin in the air. "If I pay her debt, will you give me her mother's chest?"

"That's mine, along with the girl." He moved toward Adeline, but Rompell stepped in his way.

"I will pay a handsome sum for her, along with her mother's chest."

Mr. Torvald scratched his bulging stomach and eyed Rompell. The

Sandarian smiled as he raised one hand and poured coins into the other.

Mr. Torvald watched the shower of gleaming coins adding until Rompell clapped his hands together. His hands spread apart and the money was gone. Adeline scanned the air, looking for hints of his magic. He kept it hidden better than she could.

With a grunt, Mr. Torvald said, "Come inside."

Adeline wiped her face with her sleeve and tried to keep calm. She clung to Rompell's hand as he led her inside.

The room was dark, as always, and Mr. Torvald's wife snored upstairs. Adeline shook at seeing the stairs leading to the attic where her mother had died. Sitting on a cluttered shelf by the mantle, was her mother's chest, no longer than Adeline's forearm. The wood was scratched around the latch where Mr. Torvald had tried to open it.

"She's a dear child," Mr. Torvald said as he went to a cabinet. "I can't imagine parting with her."

Rompell kept his face interested but unimpressed. From his pocket, he pulled a hefty stack of cash, adding up to at least a few hundred macs. Adeline stared at the money. His clothes were patched and worn, giving no sign of having so much.

"Will this ease your pain, sir?"

"Won't it be suspicious," Mr. Torvald said, licking his lips as he slowly opened a drawer, "if the police hear of a Sandarian man running about buying children."

"You wish me to buy your silence?"

Rompell stepped back as Mr. Torvald ripped a pistol from the drawer. Adeline squealed and hid herself against Rompell's leg.

"I think you'll hand over all the money you carry and leave."

Rompell held his palms in front of him. "I did not come for trouble. I can pay you double, if you wish."

Mr. Torvald jabbed the pistol at Rompell. "Turn out your pockets."

Adeline took a breath. This was her only chance. She sang out a quiet note, sending a chair falling into Mr. Torvald. He yelled and shoved the chair away. Rompell took the distraction to grab the man's arm and shove him against the wall. Twisting Mr. Torvald's wrist, Rompell forced him to drop the gun. Mr. Torvald snarled and fought against Rompell's grip.

"This child is under my protection," Rompell growled. "Do not come near her again."

Mr. Torvald cursed at Rompell before saying, "I'll find you and rip your hide."

Rompell jerked Mr. Torvald's arm back. Adeline cringed as a crack echoed through the room. Mr. Torvald let out a wheezing whimper.

"I have only dislocated your shoulder. Any doctor will be able to assist you."

Mr. Torvald's legs began to slump. Rompell slapped his hand across the back of Mr. Torvald's head. The middle-aged man's face knocked into the wall. Rompell stepped back, letting him collapse onto the floor.

Adeline stared at the sinews on Mr. Torvald's arms as he lay still, waiting for him to rise again. Rompell slid the coins and money into his pocket.

"Where is your mother's chest?"

Adeline pointed. Rompell grabbed the chest and held it under his arm before offering his gloved hand to her. She shook as she stared up at him.

"We must go, Little One."

Adeline swallowed before taking his firm hand. He led her outside, keeping an arm around her to stop the gale of wind from knocking her over. The dark streets blurred together as he led her closer to the wharf near Lake Chalice. He took her to the side entrance of a warehouse.

Holding out his hand, he whispered a few words. A spark of light flared and the chain blocking the door fell open.

"We can't—" she whispered as she glanced down the street for guards.

"It is mine." He opened the door and motioned for her to enter.

Inside were a few large crates illuminated by the street's gaslights gleaming through the dirty windows. Adeline kept close to Rompell as she shivered, the stone walls seeming colder than the wind outside. He led her to a corner closed off with old blankets hanging from ropes. He pulled back a blanket and bowed to her.

"Tonight's palace, Little One."

Worn silk cushions covered the floor, the embroidery faded. Several thick quilts were piled in a corner near a small warming stove. Rompell placed a few pieces of coal in the stove along with some rolled up papers. He waved his hand over the papers as a fire flared from his wrist.

Adeline's eyes drew up to his face, her mother's bedtime stories of magic and sorcery running through her head. She felt she should be nervous, but the warmth in his eyes calmed her. Rompell gave her a quick smile before patting the cushions. Adeline curled up beside the stove and watched the fire grow. He breathed on it and shut the grate. He helped her pull off the coat and her shoes before wrapping her in one of the thick blankets.

As he turned to leave, Adeline said, "I know who you are."

His back went stiff and he turned around, his face shadowed.

"And who am I?"

"You are a genie."

Rompell laughed. "You have found me out, Little One." He leaned closer, his voice turning to a whisper. "And as mistress of my secret, I must grant you three wishes."

Her eyes widened. Rompell pulled a tarnished coin from his pocket and placed it in her hand. On one side was an eagle. On the other, was an engraving of Rompell's face as a younger man.

"When you are ready to make your wish, rub the coin and sing my name three times." He pulled his gloved hand away. "Now, young mistress, what is your first wish?"

She held the coin tightly. "I can wish for anything?"

"Within reason. I am not a powerful genie."

Her tongue pressed against her teeth as she thought. Once her wish was carefully chosen, she shut her eyes and ran her thumbs over the coin. "Rompell, Rompell, Rompell."

"What is your command?"

She opened her eyes. Rompell knelt on one knee as he bowed to her. She held the coin tight to her chest as she said, "I want a home."

Rompell arched his arms over his head and ran his hands through a series of shapes and secretive motions. He held his palm to his mouth and blew. A cloud of glitter flew over Adeline. He cupped his hand to his ear as if listening to something.

"The Powers have agreed to your wish, Miss Adeline, but on one condition."

"What?"

"You must answer this riddle: Why is the sky so happy?"

Looking down at her hands, she said, "Because it is beautiful at sunrise and sunset?"

Rompell smiled as he shook his head. "It is a good answer, Little One, but not the right one." He leaned toward her and whispered, "It is because both the sun and moon beam.

"The sun will keep you warm on the coldest of days and the moon will guide you to home and safety." He rubbed his gloved hands together. "Fortunately, the Powers are merciful."

He stood. "Sleep well, Miss Adeline. Tomorrow, I will grant your wish."

With a flourish, he stepped out and closed the moth-eaten curtains. Adeline smiled as she snuggled into the cushions and blankets. She was here, safe with her genie. Shutting her eyes, all of the pain of the past few months ebbed away as she fell to sleep.

Chapter 2

Adeline held out Rompell's warped hat as the small crowd clapped at the show of sparks and smoke. She watched the specks of light, trying again to sense his power tingling on her skin as she had when her mother did magic. As the crowd gasped at Rompell's tricks, she sensed nothing.

He must be a master at hiding his secret talent.

Rompell finished the show with a bow and the spectators tossed coins into the hat.

As they cleared, Rompell took back his hat and slipped the collected skoons into his pocket. "A few more appointments and then we'll go to your new home."

"Where?" She hurried to keep up with his swift stride.

"Where would you like it to be?" Rompell shifted the bag carrying her mother's wooden chest.

Adeline's forehead wrinkled as she tried to picture where she wanted to go. All she knew were the small apartment she and her parents had lived in and Mr. Torvald's attic. Her father had once taken her past his own father's estate. The mansion and grounds had been grand and beautiful but closed off by towering fences.

She looked up at Rompell. "Could I live with you, in your real palace?"

"My real palace?" He smiled. "I am sorry, Little One, but I must keep it hidden. There are too many secrets inside."

Adeline nodded even as she imagined the marble halls and gilded chandeliers a man with such magic must have hidden.

"I am taking you to a place where you will be cared for and protected," Rompell said. "It is no palace, but it is safe."

The morning wore into afternoon as Rompell stopped to perform his tricks. At several street corners, Rompell met children dressed in rags similar to Adeline's. Each performed a song or a trick and received a few coins in return. With each trick, she looked for a secret pocket in his coat where he hid all his money. However, this remained as mysterious as his magic.

They left the main thoroughfare on Carter Street and rode in the new horse-drawn trolley to a quiet row of shops along Dabbler Street. Rompell removed his bent hat before leading her into a storefront.

"Welcome to Talbot's Boots," said a balding man, streaks of white hair combed over his head. He looked up from the counter. "Mr. Rompell, you're bringing another one?"

"The usual, Mr. Talbot."

Mr. Talbot walked around the counter. "Peter!"

A boy in his teens climbed the stairs, his body holding the awkward squatness of growth yet to come. He mumbled for her to sit, pulled off her shoe, and took measurements. Her stomach grumbled and she pressed her hands to her cheeks to hide their redness. She had last eaten that morning when sausages and sweet rolls had appeared in Rompell's warehouse. The day had been full of too many wonders to remember to eat.

Peter's eyebrows scrunched as he mumbled something and walked away.

As she waited, Mr. Talbot said, "Where'd you find this one?"

"She floated to me on a cloud," Rompell said. "How was your daughter's wedding?"

"Nice affair, though it tugged on my wallet more than I would like. Not all of us have your employer's wealth."

"I think there would be more trouble if we did," Rompell said.

Adeline frowned, wondering if Rompell had an employer, or if it was a lie to hide his magic.

Mr. Talbot chuckled before saying, "Have you bought her new clothes yet?"

"That is our next task."

"If you can take some business over to Mr. Chancey's, it'd be a mighty help. Seems he's an eye for my Molly. If I can get both girls out of the house, my boy and I might have some peace."

Adeline began to pull on the tatters of her shoes. Peter returned with a pair of boots and a half-sandwich. He set the sandwich beside her and said, "The boots are a bit large, but the closest fit we had."

As he helped her pull on the boots, Adeline stared at the sandwich, her stomach grumbling louder. It was meant as a kindness, yet she felt too guilty to touch it.

"Go on," he said. "Just a bit of ham and mustard."

Adeline took a bite and he smiled. She found herself returning a small smile before running to join Rompell by the door.

Their business done, Rompell flipped a roll of cash through his fingers before setting it on the counter.

"Not so much, Mr. Rompell." Mr. Talbot tried to hand the money back. "You can't do all this good work on your own."

"It is my employer's money."

"Take a bit to buy yourself a new coat, or—"

"Consider it a gift for the wedding."

Mr. Talbot grinned. "That I'll accept."

Rompell turned to Peter. "And for you, good sir—" He flicked his fingers and purple smoke rose. In the haze, Rompell's fist punched forward and dropped a few skoons in Peter's hand. "Buy yourself something nice or a treat for a girl you like."

Rompell winked and Peter blushed.

Adeline took Rompell's gloved hand and they left the shop. The soles of the shoes were stiff, but her feet were warm. She finished her sandwich as they walked down the street toward *Chancey's Fine Dresses*.

They entered, the shop smelling of new paint. She stared at a dress made of pale blue fabric, lace at the collar, the sleeves puffed. Her fingers curled, wanting to touch the fabric. However, she couldn't smudge it with her dirty hands.

A muted giggling was followed by a thump. Rompell pulled aside a curtain, revealing a young man and woman leaning against the wall, their lips engaged in impolite activity.

The man snapped away. The young woman kept hold of his hand. "But Albert—"

She stopped, following the track of his pale-faced stare.

"Mr. Chancey," Rompell said. "Molly Talbot, I presume?"

The curved young woman gave a brief curtsy, her face red from the discovery. Adeline clung to Rompell's hand and pressed to his leg.

"Mr. Rompell," Mr. Chancey said as he straightened his coat and smoothed his hair. "What can I do for you?"

"This young lady needs a few dresses."

Molly raised her chin as she looked down at Adeline. "There's a second-hand shop around the corner. I am sure those dresses are better suited for the girl."

Adeline hid herself behind Rompell's long coat, feeling the layers of dirt ingrained in her skin and clothes.

"It's all right, Molly," Mr. Chancey said. "You'd better run off. Mary'll be looking for you."

Molly gave him a lover's smile before exiting. Once the door closed, Mr. Chancey said, "Usually, you bring them washed."

Rompell squeezed Adeline's hand. "Things were more immediate today."

"Well, if the children must be brought in this state, I'd be better pleased if you used the back door. Molly was just mentioning ill rumors running about. I know you're an honest man, but it's the appearance of things."

"Do any of your other clients use the back door?"

"No, but—"

"Then, we will enter by the front door, whether it is yours or another shop."

Mr. Chancey ran a hand through his hair. "Well—Right." He tugged the measuring tape hanging around his neck. "This way then."

Rompell knelt beside Adeline. "Go on. I'll be right here."

Adeline joined Mr. Chancey behind the curtain. He hardly seemed to see her as he wrapped his measuring tape around her and wrote the measurements on a notepad. As he pushed her out of the curtained area, Mr. Chancey said, "She's a bit slim for our ready-made dresses, but I've one or two that'll do."

Mr. Chancey pulled dresses from drawers in the far-corner of the small shop and laid them on the counter. Adeline stood on her toes, looking at the new fabric and lace collars as Mr. Chancey wrapped the dresses in paper packages. Rompell held one out to her. She ran a hand over the paper and clutched the package to her chest.

They returned to the horse-drawn trolley and rode across the city. Light snow began to fall and the sky turned gray before they reached a wrought-iron gate below a sign reading, *The Bradford School for Girls.*

Rompell led her into the schoolyard. The sloped roof and tall spire shadowed the brick courtyard lined with shrubs. They went up the precise brick steps of the main building's back porch and Rompell knocked.

The door opened and the warm smell of fresh rolls and roasted chicken wafted out. A round, red-faced woman came to the door, an apron stretched across her girth. Without looking, she said, "No beggars."

Rompell removed his hat and she grunted in recognition.

"Good afternoon Mrs. Meriben. I'd like a word with Mrs. Hunter."

Mrs. Meriben shook her head with a grumble and slammed the door. The wind picked up as they waited. Rompell stepped behind Adeline and put his coat around her. She stared at the door and dark walls. This was far from the palace she had hoped for.

The door opened. "This way."

Adeline kept tight hold of Rompell's gloved hand as they entered the warm kitchen. She lingered as they passed rolls fresh from the oven. Rompell's hand flashed out and he handed her a roll.

Mrs. Meriben turned around. "Are you taking food again?"

"Only for the girl," Rompell said.

The cook glared at him before leading them into a narrow hallway. "Don't know what you think you teach these children."

Portraits of stern-faced women and rotund men lined the hallway. All glared down at Adeline, disapproving of her appearance. She clutched the package tight to her chest as if it would protect her.

They entered an office and Adeline faced a large oak desk. The woman sitting behind it leaned back in the armchair like an empress in repose.

"Mrs. Hunter, thank you for seeing us."

"I have told you before, Mr. Rompell, this is not a charity school."

"As always, my employer will provide for whatever she needs." Rompell pulled a stained envelope from his coat pocket.

"We have a waiting list already full of families of good repute."

"Even with the new wing?"

Mrs. Hunter raised an eyebrow. "A lady who graduates from the Bradford School must be a perfect mix of talent, intelligence, and poise."

Rompell held up a gloved hand. "Ah. Talent. That the child has." He knelt beside Adeline. "Do you mind singing for the lady?"

Adeline looked up at him, her tongue clamped to the roof of her mouth. Even if she wanted to, she was sure her voice wouldn't work.

"Just a little song, like the one you sang to the matches."

Adeline shook her head. Mrs. Hunter wouldn't understand. She would be afraid and toss her out.

Rompell lowered to his knees and looked her in the eye. "The greatest gift I can give is for you to learn from Mrs. Hunter. She knows far more secrets than she lets on." He rolled his fingers and a coin appeared. "First, you must give her a reason to teach you."

Adeline looked into Rompell's warm brown eyes as she sang. The melody was weak and quiet, but the light in the gas lamps grew with her song.

One day I sat beneath a cloud, but it became cold and rained,
The sun came and warmed the sky but drove my cloud away.
I sit beneath the willow tree, for my friend I watch and yearn.
Clouds come and go as they please, but mine has not returned.

The melody ebbed away and she could feel the magic she had gathered fading. The lamps returned to their usual glow.

Rompell smiled and squeezed her shoulder. "Wonderfully done."

Mrs. Hunter stood from her desk, her eyes now on Rompell. "Where do you find these children?"

"My employer pays me to watch and listen. Once they are found, I make sure they are safe. This one is an orphan and cannot go back to the false charity she has been living in."

Mrs. Hunter walked around the desk and stood over Adeline. "We expect the best conduct from our students. There is a strict schedule and little tolerance for nonsense. In return, our graduates go on to greatness. Do you believe you have the determination to succeed here?"

Adeline looked up at the stern woman. She was slightly less cold than the portraits in the hall. Rompell gave her an encouraging tip of his head and Adeline nodded.

"What is your name?"

She swallowed to wet her dry mouth. "Adeline Winkleston."

Mrs. Hunter frowned. "Are you related to Spencer Winkleston?"

"He is my grandfather."

Mrs. Hunter's eyebrows rose. To Rompell, she said, "Is he aware of the child?"

"She says he turned her away, but my employer is making inquiries. For now, she needs an education and a warm bed."

"She is in greater need of a bath." Mrs. Hunter's eyes turned to Adeline. "And what of your mother, Miss Winkleston? What was her maiden name?"

"Dumond," she whispered, trying not to see her mother's fading eyes the night before she died. "Her name was Mariana Dumond."

Mrs. Hunter's eyes widened, but the flicker of surprise was soon cloaked by her composure. "Was she from the Surris Mountains?"

Adeline nodded. Her mother hadn't spoken much of her childhood home in the mountains along the frontier far to the west of Pippington. From the few stories her mother had told, it seemed a dreary place.

"And you have heard nothing from her family there?" Mrs. Hunter said.

Adeline shook her head.

"You have a perplexing heritage, Miss Winkleston." Mrs. Hunter picked up a massive ring of keys. "However, we will make a place for you here."

Adeline clung to Rompell's gloved hand as Mrs. Hunter opened the door. Rompell gave her his warm smile as he handed over her mother's wood chest.

"Where will you go?" Adeline said as she clung to the chest.

He brushed a frightened tear from her cheek. "I am your genie, am I not? I must return to my lamp and prepare for your next bidding." He walked to the door and gave her a deep bow. "It has been an honor to assist you, Miss Adeline."

Tears poured down her face as she held back a hiccup. He couldn't disappear just as her parents had. She moved to run to him, but a plume of blue smoke appeared in front of him. Mrs. Hunter groaned. Once the smoke cleared, there was no sign of Rompell.

Adeline stared even as Mrs. Hunter touched her shoulder.

"Come along, Miss Winkleston."

Following Mrs. Hunter out of the main hallway, she went up the stairs and to the dorm rooms, Adeline looked over her shoulder. If she glanced one more time, he might return and take her somewhere better than these dark, cold halls.

Rompell shook snow off his coat as he entered his warehouse. The empty space was colder without Adeline's presence, but this was no place for a child. She was better off at the Bradford School. He wished he could give her a softer home, with parents who would make her part of the family. However, they wouldn't understand her magic. Once she went through the growing pains of her maturing power, they would be frightened by what they didn't understand. She would be treated as if diseased or possessed instead of nurtured and protected.

Mrs. Hunter would provide safe shelter. Few in this blind city understood magic better than her. Only a handful of girls at the school had magical talent and Mrs. Hunter took special precautions to hide and protect them from the public eye and those who would abuse their magic. The nation of Barthan had no official laws banning magic and those with power hid behind society's ignorance.

It was a strange nation, but one where Rompell could hide and be forgotten.

Raising his sleeve, he tapped the fuel reservoir for the spark lighters hidden at his wrists. He would have to restock the fuel and smoke snaps. First, he had to change his costume and perform one more trick to help Adeline.

As he pulled off his layers of coats, his eyes were drawn to the pile of pillows where the girl had slept the night before. A weight hung on his shoulder where her head had rested after he lifted her from the snow. Cradling her had brought a wholeness, carrying memories of holding his sons and daughter.

He rubbed at his chest, trying to push away a pang. His hand drifted to a hidden breast pocket and pulled the photograph his brother Solvan had sent months before. Rompell's jaw trembled and he swallowed to hold back his tears.

His sons were lost, but his daughter, Tamina, was safe in Solvan's care. She was nearly four now and had her mother's dark, loose curls.

Resting his head against the large crate, he shut his eyes. Inside were the few relics from before he lost his family and entered exile.

For over a year now, he had wandered Pippington disguised as a vagrant street magician. His charm mixed with his worn appearance led orphans and widows to trust him. Helping them eased his loss but it was no cure.

Sitting across from Adeline, watching her eyes widen at his tricks, comforting her as she wept for her parents, was the first time the hollowness had ebbed away. He had found other children with magic, but they only had a few sparks and their parents cared for them. Adeline was as alone as he was, in a world which could not understand her.

But, he was too dangerous. Instead, he would work from a distance to set things right for the girl.

He washed himself and put on a fine suit with gold buttons and crisp lines. The appearance of wealth opened doors often slammed in the face of a beggar.

Once fully polished, he set out for the ornate offices along the north end of Carter Street. A few coins passed to messenger boys led him to a dining room full of businessmen making deals between puffing on cigars. Rompell passed a few macs into several hands and was led to Spencer Winkleston's table.

Mr. Winkleston had all the appearances of a revered hero in his later years, with thick white hair and a noble face. Rompell doubted the veneer matched the man's character but had to hope otherwise.

Setting down his cigar, Mr. Winkleston said, "Men rarely spend so much to meet me."

"I have found something I fear you have lost." Rompell pulled Adeline's birth certificate from his pocket and set it on the table. He had taken it out of her mother's box the night before.

Mr. Winkleston's glare would have bored through weaker men. "This child is nothing to me."

"I found her last night, dying in the snow. She's been left in the care of a boarding school, but I am sure she needs her grandfather's love and protection."

"No respectable school would take in a maid's daughter."

Lines of bitterness marred Mr. Winkleston's features, revealing the wrinkles shadowed by the dim light. Rompell forced his own face to remain calm while his gloved fingers closed into a fist beneath the table. He knew too much of men caught up in the whims of society and position. He had to play to what this man valued.

"What about the granddaughter of one of the wealthiest men in Pippington?" Rompell said.

Mr. Winkleston leaned back with a tight smile. "There's the game: claim to want to help this child and pocket the money. Did her mother help plan this scheme?"

Rompell's cheek flinched but he kept his gaze steady. "Her mother passed on."

"A poor fate, but not my concern." Mr. Winkleston swallowed his drink.

"You would abandon your son's only child?" Rompell said.

"Abandon?" Mr. Winkleston's eyes narrowed and he jabbed his finger against the table. "Her mother stole my son. That child is a result of her lies and is no relation of mine."

Rompell wished he could grab the man by the lapels and shake him, shout at him and tell him he had the chance to build his family once more, to have a piece of his son back. However, none of that would change the man's mind.

"I once was a father," he said, forcing his voice to remain level, "but my children are lost to me now. I would do anything to bring them back. You have that chance with Adeline."

"I have lived without my son for ten years and that child is only a reminder of his foolishness." Mr. Winkleston snapped to a waiter. "My other two sons live up to our family name, sir, and there is no need to bother them about the girl."

Rompell rose and pressed his palms on the table. He looked into Mr. Winkleston's cold blue eyes and dropped his voice into a growl. "She is better off without you."

A pair of waiters moved to escort him out, but he shoved past them. He breathed deeply once he was outside, taking in the crisp air. Turning up his collar, he marched down the street.

He knew too well the sort of men trading millions, ignoring the fate of a child. If his life had gone as once planned, he would have been comfortable among them. Shaking snow off his coat, he was glad he had left behind the man he once had been.

The First Tale of the Magician

Many Years Before, In the Deserts of Sandar

Rompell panted as he fell to his knees. Pressing his hands to the tunnel floor, he tried to center himself in the endless darkness. The roar of the sandstorm echoed through the passage, giving some hope of escape from this maze of caverns and tunnels. However, the opening he had fallen through had collapsed and there was no going back.

Shaking away his tiredness, he pushed himself to his feet. He was the third son of the King of Gathray and would find a way to rejoin his caravan.

A bat's chitter echoed off the tunnel walls, reminding Rompell of the Emperor's Court's laughter only a few days before.

The burr of anger still rubbed at him, grating on his thoughts. They had come for the sake of their people. This year's harvest had been ruined by blight, leaving little flax to weave into linen. Without fine cloths to trade for food from other kingdoms, Gathray was starving.

His eldest brother, Ferrab, had groveled at the feet of Emperor Kaloman XV of Sandar. He raised his jewel-covered hand in dismissal. His teenage daughter, Princess Favay, started the laughter which soon filled the court.

Ferrab led them out with his head high and back straight, ignoring the whispers of, "Look at the beggar princes."

Rompell reached for the pistol and sword at his belt, but his second-eldest brother, Solvan, tapped his wrist. "We will find another way."

They traded what remained of their fine carpets for bushels of wheat and left Alqon, the capital of the Sandarian empire. Their small caravan appeared poorer than the merchants passing them.

Rompell's brothers would search for him but could not delay their journey long. There was not enough food nor water. Once they reached Gathray in a few days, it would be a week or longer before their small army could be sent to find him.

If he did not escape on his own, he was likely to end up a forgotten corpse.

His boots splashed into a stream. He crouched and cupped water to his parched lips. It was sweet, despite the minerals.

He reached down to scoop more water but stopped as a faint gleam broke the blackness around him. A smile spread, despite the cracks in his lips and he stumbled forward, hoping the gleam would lead to sunlight. The glow brightened as he walked, illuminating the stone around him.

His mouth hung open as he exited the tunnel and entered a cavern almost as grand as the steps of the Emperor's palace. Stone pillars and smooth walls marked the hand of man in its creation. A ring of glowing rocks edged the ceiling, their light reflected in the pool at the room's center.

An energy pulsed through the air as he walked further. He stopped beside the water and shivered as a cool breeze rushed past. There was a feeling of haunting ancientness despite the cavern's beauty. He would be glad to return to the world above.

His eyes drew to the pool. Beneath the surface glimmered golden statues and treasures half-buried in sediment. The statues were made by a true craftsman, the details of faces, hair, and folds of clothing perfect. He stepped closer to the water, holding his breath as he quieted a flicker of hope. If he could bring home a few of the treasures, his whole kingdom would celebrate, and the gold might feed his kingdom. He would convince his father to use some of their new wealth to raise the station of their royal house to match the wealthiest kingdoms in Sandar. The next time he and his brothers traveled to the Emperor's Court, they would be the envy of the whole palace.

He knelt beside the water, looking for anything small enough to carry. There was a chest toward the edge which might hold some jewels.

Remembering the warnings of his father's sorcerer, he dipped his knife into the water.

It remained steel.

Good. No treasure was worth a curse.

He waded into the waist-deep water. Using all the strength of his worn body, he hauled the chest out of the sediment. It was larger than expected, requiring him to pull harder to drag it to shore.

Once on solid ground, he dropped beside it and panted. The chest was large enough to serve as a narrow bed. He stretched his back before rising to his knees and digging his knife in the wax seal along the edges. Air hissed out as the seal broke. He raised the lid and drew back as he stared at the bounty of his efforts.

Where treasure should be was a man. His hair and skin had the lightness of far-off lands, but he wore Sandarian robes. He was young, his face firm and body appearing strong. The slight rise and fall of his chest indicated life.

Rompell glanced at the tunnel he had come through. The man could be innocent, or he could have been trapped there for a reason. However, the law of the desert was to not leave men to die in a wasteland.

He touched the man's arm.

The stranger's eyes opened. Rompell jumped away, his hand going to his sword hilt.

The stranger's hands shook as he grabbed the sides of the chest and sat up. His blue eyes stared at Rompell.

Reaching his hand out to Rompell, he said, his voice hoarse, "Help me stand. Please."

Rompell grabbed the man's arm. It took his full strength to pull the stranger to his trembling legs.

Stepping out of the chest, the stranger collapsed on the ground. His body shook as he breathed, "I owe you my life."

Rompell raised his head and folded his arms behind him. This man did not yet know he was addressing a prince. "What is your name?"

"It is better left behind," he said. "However, for you, I will give it." He rolled onto his knees and raised his head. "I am Benjamin Stiltsken, once from Barthan."

With a tilt of his head, Rompell frowned. Barthan was far away, across oceans. He had seen a few Barthanians before at the Emperor's Court. They all were as pale as this man. Rumors said the people of that nation pretended magic did not exist. It was a strange homeland for a man locked away by a spell.

"I am Rompell, Third Prince of Gathray." Rompell sat on a nearby rock as if taking a throne. He pressed his forefinger to his forehead and twirled his hand in formal greeting. "How does a Barthanian end up in a box in a Sandarian cavern?"

A heaviness filled Stiltsken's eyes as he raised his hand. He hummed and a blue light flickered across his palm. Rompell sat up. This was no ordinary man.

"I escaped from Barthan and came to Sandar to learn about my power. When I trained with sorcerers in Davron, I discovered some of their secrets. Last I remember, they put me under a sleeping curse." He glanced up at the pillars. "They must have dropped me here to rot."

"What sort of secrets?" Rompell said.

Stiltsken's eyes lit up and he grinned. "Mainly, the chieftain's daughter."

Rompell laughed. As a prince, though barely seventeen, he had played similar games himself.

"I do not know how long I've slept." Stiltsken's smile faltered. "Tumnah VII was Emperor when I was cursed."

Rompell's back straightened as a chill ran across his spine. "He died over a hundred years ago."

Stiltsken ran his hand over his hair and stared into the pool, his cheeks taut.

"Was she worth a hundred years?" Rompell could not give him revenge on men long dead, but he could give him friendship.

Stiltsken gave a half-smile. "Almost."

He rested his hands on his knees before pushing himself to his feet. Standing in front of Rompell, his head raised, he said, "Prince of Gathray, if you had not come, I might have slept for a thousand years more." He held his fist to his chest. "I owe you my breath and my life. What can I give you in return?"

Rompell rose from his makeshift throne. If this man could help him, he was worth far more than a chest full of jewels.

"I am trapped here myself," Rompell said. "Can you and your magic help find a way out?"

With a smile, Stiltsken whistled and turned his hand. An orb of light formed over his fingers. "Of course, but, I can do much more for you, if you wish."

Rompell stepped forward, his eyes drawn by the orb. In his mind, he saw again the court laughing at him and his brothers. He looked into Stiltsken's eyes. This was the face of a man he could trust, a man who would deliver on his promises. However, Rompell's true desire was beyond any man's ability.

"I want to become the greatest man at the Emperor's Court," Rompell said. "But, I will not hold you to so grand a wish."

"I am your servant, sir," Stiltsken said. "I will make sure it is done."

Rompell gripped Stiltsken's shoulder and returned his smile. "I'd be lucky to have so great a servant, but none of that matters unless we escape this cave."

Stiltsken clapped his shoulder. "Do you have anything from home?"

Rompell pulled off the ring his parents had given him when he had come of age just a few months before.

"Place it in the orb," Stiltsken said.

Rompell dropped it into the glowing orb. The ring spun and a bluish light shone from it, pointing toward the far wall.

Stiltsken waved his arm. "Lead the way, Your Highness, and guide us home to Gathray."

Chapter 3

Adeline laughed as rain poured down and she jogged hand-in-hand with her friend, Serena Quinn. When she had started at the Bradford School two months ago, she felt alone as everyone stared at her. Becoming best friends with Serena, however, had only taken ten minutes of giggling together as their history teacher's toupee kept flopping off his head. Today, they followed the double-line of girls hurrying toward the Bradford School, their day at the park cut short by the sudden downpour.

Mrs. Hunter would tsk over the runs in their stockings and grass stains on their dresses, but it would be worth the games they had played. Adeline had caught Serena three times during Chase the Dragon Tail and they had laughed through their game of croquet. That was until Serena tripped, bruising her knee as she fell. Fortunately, Miss Appleton hadn't seen her. She would have forced Serena to sit down and then the fun would have been over.

The trail of girls began crossing the street. A cart and horse came rushing toward them. The driver shouted and waved his arms, his horse charging forward with madness in its eyes. The girls scattered, bounding left and right. Adeline lost hold of Serena's hand at the panicked tide dragged her away. She shouted for her friend but couldn't find her in the rush of people.

Pushing out of the crowd, she climbed up on a wood box and looked for her friend.

Across the street, threading through the growing crowd, was Rompell.

He was nearly unrecognizable in a long, dark cloak. A wide-brimmed hat was pulled low over his forehead and a maroon scarf around his chin. However, Adeline would know her genie anywhere.

Many nights, she had lain on her hard cot in the room she shared with Serena, rubbing her thumb over the coin he had given her. She whispered her day to him, picturing his warm smile. On bad days, it was good to know he was listening from wherever genies hid.

She called out to Rompell, but her voice drowned in the spatter of rain. Jumping off the crate, she moved to run after him. Miss Appleton caught her arm.

"Where are you going?"

"I just—" Adeline started to point, but Rompell had disappeared. She dropped her arm. "I'm coming, Miss Appleton."

The teacher raised her rounded chin and ushered Adeline back to the group of girls. Serena gripped her hand. They kept close to each other as the group of girls hurried back to the school. Wet shoes slid on tile floors as they rushed inside. The girls stopped in the common hall as if hitting an invisible wall. Mrs. Hunter stood, pocket-watch in hand, her dark eyes scanning the crowd of sopping hair and muddy clothes.

"A Bradford Girl is always presentable." She shut her pocket-watch and the girls snapped to attention. "Classes resume in one hour. I expect you to look your best."

Adeline moved to scurry with Serena to their shared room.

"Miss Winkleston, a word, please," Mrs. Hunter said.

Serena squeezed Adeline's hand and gave her an encouraging nod. Adeline marched after Mrs. Hunter, ignoring several girls' smirks.

The headmistress had spoken to her a few times in the past two months, her eyes always measuring. Adeline often stared up at the tall, lean woman, waiting for her to point to the door and pronounce her a fraud among these daughters of business owners, politicians, and other important people.

Once inside the headmistress' wood-paneled study, Mrs. Hunter motioned for Adeline to sit in a red armchair by the fire. Adeline pulled herself into the chair, her calves barely reaching the edge.

Mrs. Hunter handed a teacup to Adeline. She went to sip, but the cocoa inside was cold.

Taking her own cup, Mrs. Hunter sat in the opposite chair and stirred with a small spoon. "Why don't you taste it?"

Adeline took a sip and tried not to scrunch her face.

"Is there something wrong?"

Keeping her eyes down, Adeline said, "It's cold."

"Then warm it."

Adeline looked at the fire. Was she supposed to put the cup in there?

"Do you know why Mr. Rompell brought you to me?" Mrs. Hunter said.

Adeline shook her head, her hands clamped on her cup.

"Most girls he brings are unremarkable and I quickly transfer them to more appropriate schools," Mrs. Hunter said. "But you, Miss Winkleston, are a remarkable child."

Mrs. Hunter's face was as cool and stern as ever, the praise clipped off as a matter of business.

"Do you know why?"

This was Mrs. Hunter's most common question, bringing dread into the hearts of many Bradford Girls. Lessons did not end until someone ventured a respectable guess. Their only reward was Mrs. Hunter's sharp nod and expansion on the topic. Adeline frowned, wondering what she was supposed to understand.

"What did Mr. Rompell have you do when you first arrived here?"

Adeline searched the floor for her answer. "I sang."

"You did more than that."

Adeline sank in her chair, wishing she could melt into it. She had only shown her magic because Rompell had asked. Mrs. Hunter hadn't said anything about it since and Adeline hoped she had forgotten.

Mrs. Hunter held out two fingers toward the fire. She sang a few notes, her voice a cobblestone of vibrato. Her tone cleared and a flame floated to Mrs. Hunter's outstretched fingers. The flame rotated just before she flicked it away. It arched across the room and landed in Adeline's cup. The liquid sizzled before letting out a spout of steam.

"You may want to wait a moment before drinking it."

Adeline stared at the warm liquid, her skin tingling with the sense of Mrs. Hunter's power. She had felt a similar tingle many times while walking the halls, but she had thought the sense of magic came from Rompell's coin.

"Mr. Rompell brought you here because he thinks I can teach you." Mrs. Hunter pulled the fire poker out and shifted logs on the fire. "However, I can only teach those who are willing to learn."

Adeline sat up, forgetting about the hot cocoa until a drop spilled on her leg. She wiped it off and set the cup down.

"Your magical talent is remarkable, but I had to be sure the rest of your potential was worthy of the Bradford School." Setting down the fire poker, Mrs. Hunter looked at Adeline. "Your growth is impressive, though your edges are still a bit rough."

She folded her hands into her lap and tilted her head. "How does magic work, Miss Winkleston?"

Adeline thought through everything her mother had told her about magic. It really wasn't much. Just a few songs here and there, as well as some flicks of her wrists to help a spell along.

"It works when I sing."

"Why?"

Shifting in her chair, Adeline watched Mrs. Hunter. The headmistress would give no hints.

"Singing helps it along?" Adeline cringed at her own answer.

"An excellent guess," Mrs. Hunter said. "Many will tell you foolish tales making magic seem an illogical mess of emotions and miracles. Over the centuries, those with magic have been called mages, witches, warlocks, and sorcerers. Such things exist, but those of us who have mastered our craft and understand the science of it call ourselves Illuminators."

Adeline's breath stilled and she leaned forward. Mrs. Hunter opened a drawer in the table beside her and pulled out a thin red book.

"Magic works much the same as the light and sound waves you've been learning about in science. There are a few like you and I, with the natural talent to manipulate the waves of magic filling the world. For us, music is the simplest and easiest tool and flame is simple to manipulate, since it is made of light. There are much more complex methods and devices, but they are best left for later discussion."

Adeline took the offered book. The title read, *Curing Warts and Other Household Remedies*. She frowned and opened it, releasing the smell of old paper. The words inside were densely packed and matched the cover's mundane promise.

"The true text can only be read with a spectroscope." Mrs. Hunter held out what appeared a jeweler's monocle.

Adeline took the spectroscope. Under Mrs. Hunter's expectant gaze, she raised the plain steel and glass cylinder to her eye. The room erupted in color. Glowing lines arched around Mrs. Hunter and her teacup, swirling brightly. Adeline gasped as she looked down at the book.

It now appeared gold. She flipped it open. The cures for everyday maladies disappeared, replaced by densely-packed text giving a history of magic, followed by pages of categories and spells and more than Adeline had ever thought had existed.

Adeline's heartbeat quickened as she held tighter to the book. She was on the edge of something vast which she had always known was there but couldn't quite see.

These past few months, with her mother gone, she had felt alone with her magic towering behind her. She hadn't dared use it and instead had tried to tuck it away. Now and then, it flared out. A few days before, one of those flares had knocked over Miss Appleton's chair. Adeline had joined in the giggling while she sat on her hands and tried to quiet her magic.

With this book and Mrs. Hunter's lessons, she would begin to understand this strange part of herself. Flipping through a few more pages, she wanted to try everything as fast as she could.

"With enough practice, you will learn to see some faint lines of magic without the spectroscope," Mrs. Hunter said. "However, even the most skilled need the device for more complex spells."

Adeline lowered the spectroscope and the room grew duller in color. She clutched the cylinder, running her thumb over the smooth metal.

"The lessons will not be easy," Mrs. Hunter said. "You will be exhausted after each one and must keep up with your other studies." She nodded to Adeline. "Do you wish to learn, Miss Winkleston?"

Adeline's head bobbed up and down. "Yes."

A slight smile crossed Mrs. Hunter's lips but disappeared before Adeline could be sure it ever existed.

"Before lessons begin, I need your promise to continue keeping your magic secret."

Adeline's hand tightened around the spectroscope. This promise meant she couldn't tell Serena anything.

Forcing herself to look Mrs. Hunter in the eye, Adeline said, "From everyone?"

"Everyone you do not have magic lessons with, including Miss Quinn."

Adeline sank deeper in her chair. "But, Serena—"

"Must remain ignorant," Mrs. Hunter said. "It is acceptable to use your power when alone to mend a tear or stop something from falling.

However, if magic were practiced openly, we would have widespread panic and every problem blamed on magic."

Her eyes turned grave as she added, "And, there are those who, if they found out you have magic, would twist your powers to dark purposes. To keep yourself safe, you must manage your abilities properly."

"I will," Adeline said, holding the red book to her chest.

"I look forward to teaching you, then." Mrs. Hunter stood. "There are still a few minutes until classes resume. Plenty of time to return to your best appearance."

Rising from the chair, Adeline tried to ignore the damp spot her wet clothes left behind. She clutched the spectroscope and book while hurrying out the door. As she stepped into the hallway, the walls seemed stranger and yet more familiar than a moment before. Reaching into her pocket, she rubbed her thumb along Rompell's coin.

"Thank you," she whispered before running up the stairs.

Chapter 4

Adeline sat cross-legged, her head pressed against the banister overlooking the Bradford School's entryway waiting for the end of the monthly visiting day. All the other girls laughed and played with their parents, the girls proudly demonstrating their latest skills from music and language classes.

No one would come for her, yet she looked to the door each time another set of parents entered. She pictured her mother and father arriving, her father grinning as he lifted and twirled her, her mother kissing her cheeks and asking to meet her friends. Then, she envisioned Rompell in his worn clothes, his tall figure looking down at her with a warm smile.

Hiding from her loneliness, Adeline had spent most of the day behind Serena and her parents. Serena's mother and father welcomed her, just as they had one afternoon last month when they brought her to visit while Serena stayed home with the flu. The week Serena stayed home and recovered left Adeline feeling almost as alone as the month just after her mother died. Today, at least for a few hours, she felt included as Serena's parents asked the teachers about her as well.

Then, Serena's parents began discussing their summer plans with Serena, of traveling from Pippington to the eastern shores far across Barthan. As the conversation wore on, Adeline retreated to this spot on the balcony, hoping to hide her tears. Serena's family would travel to grand adventures, while Adeline remained here, alone with only

Mrs. Hunter and her lessons.

Most of Mrs. Hunter's sessions had been on history from centuries ago when magic was practiced freely by the ruling class of Illuminators. Part of Adeline wanted to see a time so full of wonders, before they were exiled and a spell was placed over Barthan, making those that remained ignorant of magic. However, when Mrs. Hunter mentioned cruel acts of magic, like transforming people into frogs for their own amusement, Adeline found herself preferring the modern era of factories and steam engines.

The best but most rare lessons were spent practicing magic. Each one was challenging but drove Adeline to learn more. Afterward, Adeline's head throbbed, and she fell asleep on her textbooks. As her grades slipped, she was almost glad she had no parents to disappoint. Mrs. Hunter's frowns were intimidating enough.

If only she could have her mother and father instead of a summer here, alone.

The chimes sounded, marking the visiting day's end. Younger girls wept as they clung to their mother's skirts. Adeline hid her face against her sleeve, covering her tears.

Serena waved and called to Adeline from the entry hall, her other hand holding her mother's. Adeline wiped her face with her handkerchief and ran down the stairs to her friend.

Once close enough, Serena hopped as she grabbed Adeline's hand. "Mother, can I tell her?"

Mrs. Quinn laughed. "Of course."

"Oh, Adeline, isn't it wonderful? You get to come!"

Adeline tried to smile. "To what?"

"For the summer, my dear," Serena's mother said. "Since you've no family to stay with, we'd like you to come with us."

Adeline's smile came freely as she nodded. She laughed and hopped with Serena. They spun in a circle, their chatter melding together as they spoke of all the places they would go.

"Miss Quinn, Miss Winkleston."

Both girls stopped immediately under Mrs. Hunter's firm tone. They turned as the headmistress touched Mrs. Quinn's arm.

"While your offer is generous, I am afraid it will be impossible for Miss Winkleston to join you. She is behind on her studies and will be part of a special class I am conducting."

"We can hire a tutor," said Mrs. Quinn.

Mrs. Hunter looked down at Adeline. She wished she could sink into the floor and hide.

"As Headmistress, I cannot, in good conscience, grant permission."

Mrs. Quinn bent down and hugged Adeline. "Mr. Quinn and I will see what we can do."

The Quinns were whisked away with the rest of the parents, leaving the Bradford School filled with more echoes and silence than before.

That evening, Adeline was grateful to hide in her room as Serena chatted with girls down the hall. With the door shut, she lit the candlestick on the dresser. She sang and waved her hand as Mrs. Hunter had shown her. The flame formed into ships before collapsing into the figure of her mother and father dancing. Adeline leaned against the bedpost, watching their ghostly images twirl.

If they were here, they would let her go with Serena. Maybe Adeline could hide in Serena's trunk with a few sandwiches until they were too far away for Mrs. Hunter to drag her back.

The doorknob turned and Adeline blew out the candle. The smoke danced as her parents' forms dissipated. She dropped onto her bed and pulled the blankets over her.

Serena sat on the edge of Adeline's bed. "Mother and Father will make things right. They always do."

Adeline pressed her lips together. Serena was trying her best but couldn't keep this promise.

"Mrs. Hunter can be so mean," Serena said. "I don't know how you can stand her lessons. What do you learn from her in your special classes?"

Adeline turned away. "Nothing."

"Tell me," Serena whispered. "We've taken the Oath of Cymbeline."

Adeline glanced at where she kept the lock of Serena's hair from when they had made the oath to be true friends for life. Even then, she had kept secrets from Serena.

"Why won't you tell me?" Serena said.

"Mrs. Hunter told me not to."

"Mrs. Hunter's an old grump. She always gets mad at me when I skip to class."

Adeline's jaw firmed as she pictured Mrs. Hunter's cool glare, squashing a whole dream of a summer abroad.

"Light the candle," Adeline said.

Serena giggled as she struck the match and lit the wick.

Sitting up, Adeline held out her pinky. "You can't tell anyone."

Serena nodded, her eyes wide as she wrapped her pinky around Adeline's. With a deep breath, Adeline sang out a few notes. Serena frowned until a hot air balloon made of flame and smoke rose from the candle. It floated around the room, soon followed by an elephant tossing its head, just like Adeline had seen when her parents had taken her to the circus. The objects made of flame turned in a grand parade, hovering through the air.

Serena gaped. Then came a warning bobble just before Serena's legs collapsed and she fainted. The balloon and elephant wavered as Adeline grabbed Serena, protecting her head from the bedpost. The hot air balloon wisped into smoke, but the elephant touched the curtain before disappearing. Acrid smoke spilled out as flame rose up the cloth and charged toward the ceiling.

Adeline shouted as she slid Serena onto the floor. She should have been more careful. Serena was still weak from her flu and had fainted at least twice since returning to school.

Leaving her friend, she grabbed the water pitcher and tossed the liquid. It splashed, sprinkling into steam over the flames. The fire spread, heating the rafters.

Crying for help, Adeline grabbed Serena by the legs and dragged her into the hall. Her hands threatened to slip. Other girls opened their doors and screamed at the billowing smoke. An alarm bell rang. Miss Appleton ran down the hall, her hair in curlers.

"Be calm girls!" she shrieked.

Girls spilled into the hall. Adeline held onto Serena as flames scorched the ceiling. Adeline shut her eyes, wishing it would disappear. Then approached the steady of clomp of heels coming the opposite direction of the fleeing girls.

"Miss Winkleston, I need your help." Mrs. Hunter did not wait for an answer as she stepped into the burning room. Her hair hung in a thick braid, her shoulders covered in a worn shawl. Adeline looked down at Serena.

"Leave her. She will be safe."

Adeline followed Mrs. Hunter, her mouth dry. The wallpaper cracked and wrinkled in the intense heat. Mrs. Hunter grabbed Adeline's hand.

"Sing with me."

Adeline swallowed and forced herself to join the song. Mrs. Hunter held out her hands, shaping an invisible box. The flame spiraled from the curtains and walls and was drawn into the invisible box. Mrs. Hunter's arms shook as she held the cube of flame, all fire inside. She pushed her hands together and the box of fire puffed into smoke, a dusting of ash fell to the ground.

Mrs. Hunter leaned against the bedpost, her face pale with exhaustion. Her mouth hardened as she stood.

"This way."

Adeline stared before following Mrs. Hunter to the bathroom. Her stomach clenched as she waited for the lecture.

Mrs. Hunter filled a bucket with water and handed Adeline a pitcher before leading her back to the room.

"Sing with me."

Mrs. Hunter sang out a few roughshod notes and Adeline joined the song. Orbs of water formed and rose from the bucket, spreading through the air like a raincloud. Mrs. Hunter pointed her fingers forward in a pinching shape before snapping. The water orbs exploded, splattering through the room.

"That will have to do." Mrs. Hunter wiped an ash-streaked arm across her forehead. "Come along."

Once in the hall, Mrs. Hunter knelt and waved her hand over Serena's face. She hummed a brief tune and Serena yawned as she woke.

Stretching, she said, "What's going on?"

"You fainted again and knocked over a candle," Mrs. Hunter said. "Everything is safe now, but you shall have to be more careful."

Adeline looked at the wall, wishing she could blend in with it and disappear.

"You should be grateful to Miss Winkleston," Mrs. Hunter said. "She was brave and pulled you from the room."

Adeline's throat felt thick as tears fell. If Mrs. Hunter had not been here, Adeline could have burned the whole school down.

"It is late. Both of you will sleep in my study." Mrs. Hunter turned her hard eyes on Adeline. "Miss Winkleston and I will discuss her reward in the morning."

With a yawn, Serena nodded.

Adeline kept her head down as she followed the headmistress. They were almost to the stairs, when footsteps pounded up. Mrs. Hunter pulled Adeline to the side as firefighters ran past. There was a pause before a pair of police officers ran up.

"Margaret!" said the female officer, her gray-blue eyes scanning the mess. "I came when I heard the alarm was from the Bradford School."

"It's been managed, Gertrude," Mrs. Hunter said. "Thank you for your concern."

Gertrude sniffed the air. "I see." She frowned as she looked at Adeline. The girl lowered her head, hoping she could become invisible.

Holding out her hand, Gertrude said, "Officer Gertrude McCay. And you are?"

Adeline stared at the offered hand, wondering how quickly the officer would discover the truth.

"Pardon us, but Miss Winkleston and Miss Quinn need rest," Mrs. Hunter said.

Officer McCay dropped her hand. "I've got to write a report."

"I trust you will make your best judgement."

"I didn't mean to knock the candle over," Serena said in the midst of a yawn.

Officer McCay raised an eyebrow while keeping her eyes on Adeline. "And I suppose Mrs. Hunter put it out with a teaspoon?"

"Miss Winkleston was quite brave and brought water to help." Mrs. Hunter gave her a pointed look before grabbing the two girls' hands. "If you'll excuse me, I must get these girls to bed. It has been too exciting of an evening."

"I'll manage the report." McCay tipped her hat. "There shouldn't be too many of the wrong questions."

Mrs. Hunter kept a firm grip on both girl's hands as they went to the first floor. They reached the door to her study as a fire brigade officer came down the stairs. Adeline watched him, wondering if he had known her father.

He stopped in front of the crowd of girls filling the dining hall. "Everything's clear. You may return to your beds."

A stampede of girls surged down the hall and toward the stairs. Miss Appleton waved her arms as she blocked the stairs, trying to create some form of order. The girls pushed past her.

"Now, ladies," she said. "Really, I—"

Mrs. Hunter bit back a groan and pointed at Adeline and Serena. "Stay here."

They nodded automatically while Mrs. Hunter stepped past Miss Appleton and led a herd of pin-curls and nightgowns up the stairs.

Adeline's heartbeat thundered as the girls left her and Serena behind. She looked up at the door and listened to Mrs. Hunter's calm voice cutting through the giggles of excitement. Serena slumped against the door jamb and dozed off, letting out a soft snore.

Adeline rubbed her hands over her face. The whole school could have burned down, along with her best friend. She tried to swallow back tears. Mrs. Hunter's fury in the morning would be unbearable, but she would be right. Adeline had broken her promise and risked everyone's lives.

Mrs. Hunter would expel her and Officer McCay would return with shackles. The other girls would discover what she had done and rumors would spread. They would mock her as she was led away to prison.

She was better off alone, unable to hurt her friends.

The second floor grew quieter as doors shut and girlish voices faded. Hesitating another moment would end her chance.

She hurried to the entry hall, watching for Mrs. Hunter to come after her. The entry hall was lit only by the streetlamps gleaming through the window. Adeline snuck along the wall until she reached the coatroom. With the light off, she took her coat from its hook and pulled on her hat and boots.

Scurrying as silently as she could, she went into the kitchen. She took a few rolls from the counter before slipping out the door. Outside, the spring air was cool but not chilling.

She moved along the side of the main building. A few fire brigade and police officers stood around the gate, holding back the growing crowd. Adeline tied the belt of her coat and stuffed the rolls into her pocket. Though her hands shook, she climbed up the oak tree in the corner of the yard near the back alleyway. She had seen other girls climb it when Mrs. Hunter was away.

Adeline stretched over the longest branch as it creaked. She pulled herself past the iron spikes on top of the fence. Her hands and arms shook as she let herself hang over the edge and the bushes lining the fence. She shut her eyes as she made a quick prayer. The branch cracked, dropping her to the ground.

With a cry, she landed side-first in a bush. She rolled off the bush and fell onto the cobblestone.

Her arm throbbed, but nothing seemed broken. She stumbled to her feet and ran down the alleyway to the street. There, she joined a crowd moving away from the school. Once clear of the main avenue, she wandered, unsure where to go.

She dodged a pair of drunk men and ducked into an alleyway. Huddling in a cold doorway, watching the silhouettes of passersby move across the wall, she shuddered as she remembered the night Rompell had found her freezing in the snow.

Reaching in her pocket, she pulled out the coin he had given her. She sang a quiet song and it glowed an iridescent blue, the light forming a small arrow. Adeline held her breath as she stared. She would find her genie and he would take her somewhere safe.

She rose, holding the coin tight, and followed the path through dark alleyways and shadowed streets. Her shoes echoed on the cobblestone until she reached a warehouse. It had to be Rompell's, but it looked the same as all the others. A light flickered on inside and she jumped back.

Taking a breath for courage, she climbed a stack of crates near a window. The window was clouded with grime, but a hole lay in the glass, just large enough to peek through.

Rompell sat on a narrow cot beside a small stove. The rapid pounding of her heartbeat slowed and she raised her hand to knock on the glass. She hesitated as he ran his gloved hands over his face, exhaustion betrayed in the furrows and lines of his forehead. He stared into the flame of the stove, his eyes bearing the weight of dark years. Adeline had seen a similar pain in her mother's eyes toward the end.

He glanced up as a small owl fluttered in through a hole near the ceiling and landed on the clothesline above his bed. Lifting a bucket full of ash, he set it on a crate beside him. Delicately, he rolled a glove off one hand and set it aside. He rubbed his hands together before breathing into them. With his palms pressed together, he shut his eyes, a wince of pain crossing his face.

He reached into the bucket with his bare hand and stirred the ash. As the gray powder sifted through his fingers, it became glittering and gold.

Adeline held her breath. There was no tingle of magic, but the transformation was real.

Rompell shook off the flecks of gold and blew on his hand. The specks floated and gleamed in the air. With a flurry of hoots, an owl dove toward the glittering metal. Rompell waved his arm, trying to bat it away. His bare fingers struck the bird in its breast. It let out a pained squeak and thumped onto the crate.

Lying with its wings still in mid-flight, was a pure gold statue of the owl.

Adeline jerked back and from the window. Her feet slipped and her arm hit the window pane. She held onto the wall to steady herself as her heart rammed against her ribcage.

Glancing down the alleyway, she climbed down. The crates shook, but she made it to the ground safely. She crept around the corner, keeping each step as quiet as possible.

"What did you see?" Rompell's words snapped in the air as he stepped in front of her.

She wanted to cry out as she stared up at him, but her mouth clamped shut.

Here was her genie, but he was not what he appeared.

Backing away, she said, "I didn't mean to see anything. I'll tell no one. Please—"

She moved to run but his gloved hand grabbed her shoulder. Shutting her eyes, she waited for the cold creep of metal as her skin turned to gold, just like the poor owl.

Rompell's grip loosened as his gloved finger touched her cheek.

"Adeline," he said, his words firm. "What did you see?"

Staring at his gloved hands, she shivered. "The owl—is it going to be all right?"

"No. It cannot be saved."

Rompell pulled a handkerchief out and wiped her tears from her face.

"What are you doing here?" he said. "You should be at the Bradford School."

Adeline shook her head. "I can't go back."

"Why not? There is nowhere better for you."

Her lips trembled as she stepped away. He approached her and she ran. As he sprinted after her, she sang a quick note and shoved her hand toward him. Her wave of magic shoved him back into a stack of crates. As he shouted, she sprinted out of the yard.

She did not watch where she was going. She only ran, getting away from him and his hands.

After a while, the buildings thinned and she stumbled into a meadow. Everything was dark around her, the moon a sliver in the sky. She wheezed as she tried to keep running, but her lungs burned and her legs were tired.

She slowed, concentrating on putting one foot in front of the other. Her next step, however, had no ground beneath it.

Her stomach lurched as she fell. She smacked into cold dirt, her entire body stinging.

Digging her fingers into the hard earth, she pulled herself up. She reached as high as she could and tried to jump, but the opening was too high. Letting the tears drop down her cheeks, she huddled against the side of the pit.

Her whole body shook as she pressed her head to her knees.

There was no going back.

Mrs. Hunter wouldn't let her into the Bradford School again. Serena would find out the truth and hate her. And Rompell—She shuddered, picturing the golden owl lying on the shack floor.

She had nothing to go back to and nothing to go forward to. The rest of her days would be lived in this pit and she would be forgotten.

These thoughts crowded her mind until sleep came in small fits of nightmares full of fire and turning into gold. The nightmares gave way as the sun rose at last, but the edges of the pit hid its warmth from Adeline. She called out for help until her mouth was dry and voice hoarse.

She fell back in the tight space and shoved her hands in her pockets. Her fingers brushed Rompell's coin.

She knew his secret. He would not come.

Yet, she touched her cheek where he had wiped her tears away.

Looking up at the patch of sky above her she pressed the coin between her hands and shut her eyes. Though he was dangerous, he was her only chance to escape.

She breathed in before whispering, "Rompell, Rompell, Rompell."

Chapter 5

Rompell held the boy's gaze as he tossed his ball at the jacks. As he had planned, the ball hit a few jacks before bouncing from the circle. It would be enough to appear he was trying. The boy picked up the ball and rubbed it between his hands, his eyes squinting as he considered his next toss.

Trying not to tap his fingers as he waited, Rompell glanced at the sky. The morning was disappearing as swiftly as the night. Adeline was lost out there, afraid of him and far from safe. He had almost not kept his appointment with the boy. Now, as he waited for the boy to throw, Rompell wished he had continued his search. He would have found another way to deliver money to the boy and his widowed mother.

The boy finally threw and Rompell forced himself to join in laughing.

"An excellent throw." Rompell lifted the ball and breathed on it. "For the game."

As he slung it with a twist of his wrist, a child's voice lilted in his mind, *Rompell, Rompell, Rompell.*

Adeline's voice tugged at Rompell's chest, beckoning him. He raised his head, seeking the source.

The ball skipped across the side of the circle, bouncing onto the walkway.

The boy tittered with laughter, pointing at Rompell as he fell back.

"Your winnings," Rompell said with his practiced grin. He waved his hands over the circle of jacks, scooping up most of them while making the boy's winnings appear. It would be enough to feed his six siblings and widowed mother for a week. Longer-lasting solutions would have to wait. "Congratulations."

He dropped a smoke snap and used the yellow cloud from the simple parlor trick to disappear around the corner. His step quickened as he followed the pull of Adeline's voice. Turning into a quiet alleyway, he removed a pouch from around his neck. One of the coins inside glowed blue. He lifted it and stared at the line of light.

He had suspected this was how she had found him last night. For months now, he had heard her voice each night as she whispered her day to him, telling him of her lessons with Mrs. Hunter, her games with Serena, and of her childhood dreams. He had tried to ignore her voice coming from the coin but found himself going back to it.

After the first few weeks, he began to look forward to hearing her voice. He would find a quiet spot where he could sit, his smile growing as he listened, picturing himself sitting at her bedside, tucking her in for the night's rest.

It was a foolish notion and the tie between him and the coin had brought her to him at the worst moment. His mind flashed to the golden owl, lying on the ground, never to breathe again.

Every time a living creature fell to his cursed touch, a light inside him dimmed. Helping orphans and widows did little to balance the life lost.

Yet, she called to him. Or, at least the coin called for her. The sorcerer back in Sandar had been unclear how much power the coin had on its own.

She was a precious girl and had to be found. Even if she ran from him again, he needed to know she was safe.

Rompell tracked the beacon, jogging along streets and following her winding path to the city's edge. The city's buildings became more spread apart, leading to a large meadow. Huffing in air, he stood in the field, searching for a sign of her. The open land was broken by the orchards leading to Craggsville and the rising scaffolding marking the beginnings of the dragon racing stadium. He raised the coin, hoping she hadn't tried to hide in the construction.

Hearing voices, he closed his hand to cover the light. A young couple glanced at him as they walked by and he nodded as he continued as fast as he could without gaining notice.

The beacon led to the edge of a pit, dirt mounded around it from an abandoned project. He held his breath as he squatted and looked inside.

Huddled in the corner was Adeline.

A weight evaporated from him and he dropped into a sitting position. His throat clenched and he shut his eyes. Clutching his gloved fist to his mouth, he forced himself to take deep breaths.

He had told himself she was just another child, even when listening to her nightly stories. Yet, sitting here, looking down as she whimpered and held her knees to her chest, he did not know what he would have done if she was not alive.

He made a silent prayer of thanks before leaning over the opening and stretching out his arm toward her.

"Adeline."

She started as she looked up, her blue eyes wide, her skin ashen. He could feel her fear and doubt. Despite the heavy beating in his chest, he forced a soft smile.

"I heard your call."

Moving stiffly, she rose and reached her arm up. Her fingertips nearly touched his gloved hand, but she drew back.

"As long as my gloves are on, my hand is safe." He forced his eyes to be calm and sure.

She rubbed her wrist before stretching her hand toward his. He pushed himself further over the pit and reached as far as he could. Her palm pressed against his and he got a steady grip. He pulled swiftly, her body light for her age. Once she was high enough, he wrapped his other arm beneath her shoulders and lifted her the rest of the way.

Her whole body shook as she clung to his neck and sobbed into his shoulder.

"I can't go back," she whispered between sobs. "The fire—I could have burned the whole school. Mrs. Hunter—she'll never forgive me."

Keeping his voice soft, he said, "What happened?"

He held her to his chest as she spoke between whimpers, the story of last night gradually unfolding. Many details remained vague, but it was clear Mrs. Hunter had failed to protect Adeline from herself.

There was no one better for Adeline to learn from. Anyone else he took Adeline to would fear her magic and not understand it. If her magic was discovered, she might become a target for those who would steal her power for their own.

However, the Bradford School was not a home. She needed somewhere safe, somewhere to be accepted for all she was.

He knew he could give her such a place. Yet, there were his gloved fingers, so close to her soft cheek. A single slip and this sweet girl would be lost.

He set her on her feet and brushed back her hair. "Come, Little One. We must return."

She shook her head, her eyes wide. "No. Mrs. Hunter will—"

"She will forgive you." His gloved fingers trembled as he touched her cheek. "And, if she will not, I will make sure you are safe."

Adeline clung to Rompell's gloved hand as they walked to the main entry of the Bradford School. A shiver ran through her as she looked at her room's burnt window.

Rompell squeezed her hand. "Courage, Little One."

Looking up at him, she wondered how she had been so frightened. His touch was dangerous, and the owl was lost, yet the warmth in his eyes made her sure of her safety.

She jumped as he rang the bell.

Footsteps pounded toward them and the door flung open. Mrs. Hunter panted as she looked down at Adeline. A few strands were loose from the bun, dark circles hung under her eyes, and a streak of ash marked her forehead. She lay her hands on her skirt as if steadying her composure. Adeline pressed herself to Rompell's leg, wishing his coat would hide her.

"Where has the child been?" Mrs. Hunter said.

"She was captured by a dragon and placed in a tower," Rompell said, keeping one hand touching Adeline's shoulder.

Mrs. Hunter's bloodshot eyes glared at Rompell. "Miss Winkleston, follow me please."

"She is under my protection. I will have a word with you before she returns to your care."

"I thought she was a ward of your employer."

Rompell's jaw was firm as he held her gaze. Mrs. Hunter raised an eyebrow. "This way, Mr. Rompell."

The hall was longer than Adeline remembered. Girls peeked up from their desks as she passed open classroom doors. Her slender fingers clung more tightly to Rompell's as the whispers crowded on top of each other. Rumors of what she had done had surely spread. Adeline kept her eyes straight forward and concentrated on the swishing of Mrs. Hunter's skirt.

Once at Mrs. Hunter's study, Rompell motioned for Adeline to sit on the wood bench outside. He crouched beside her and said, "Stay here while I have a word with Mrs. Hunter." His gloved hand cupped her cheek. "Everything will be made right."

Her wide eyes followed him as he and Mrs. Hunter entered the office. The door shut, leaving their voices a dull murmur. Adeline pulled her knees to her chest and stared at the muddy toes of her boots.

"I brought her here to keep her safe!"

Adeline jumped at Rompell's raised voice, the door barely quieting the sound.

"She endangered the other girls."

"They are safe, are they not?"

"Yes, but—"

"She will have learned from this one mistake. Much can be forgiven on such a merit."

"The amount of power she used, Mr. Rompell, is enough to catch the attention of those I must hide the girls from."

There was a long pause as the voices became muffled again. Adeline leaned closer, but the sound was no clearer. Giving up, she counted the slats of wood in the floor.

Once Rompell came out, she might convince him to take her away. She pictured him taking her to a palace hidden in the clouds. They would ride on the wind and he would make her a princess.

"Adeline!"

She jumped. Serena ran to her, pigtails bouncing. Before Adeline could move, Serena threw her arms around her.

"Where'd you go last night?" Serena said. "I couldn't sleep. Mrs. Hunter—" Serena's eyes widened. "She marched the whole building looking for you. She left Miss Appleton in charge while she and Officer McCay went to find you."

Adeline tucked her hands in her coat pockets, trying to hide their shaking. She pictured herself in a cement cell, staring out at iron bars. She shouldn't have come back.

"I was scared," Adeline whispered.

"It was my own fault, for fainting and hitting the candle." Serena looked at her hands. "You saved me, Adeline."

A hiccup burst through Adeline as she sobbed again.

"Don't cry." Serena hugged her. "The fire crew got here in time.

No one was hurt."

Adeline hugged Serena back as she wept. This needed to be goodbye.

Once Adeline let go, Serena handed over her handkerchief. "It's all right. I'm so sorry—"

She broke off as Mrs. Hunter's door opened.

"Adeline," came Rompell's gentle voice. "Come."

Her whole body ached as she shook. Guiding her inside, Rompell kept a firm hand on her back. She stepped on the now-familiar carpet and was led to one of the hard-backed chairs in the study. Mrs. Hunter rubbed her temple as she leaned against the desk. Rompell squeezed Adeline's shoulder before sitting in the chair beside her. Stretching herself into a proper posture, she waited for her sentence.

"Miss Winkleston," Mrs. Hunter said. "Mr. Rompell and I have been discussing your future at the Bradford School."

Adeline pushed herself to her feet. Keeping her eyes down, she said, "I know the fire was my fault. I didn't mean to—I just wanted to show Serena—I'm sorry." She took a wheezing breath. "I—I know you'll have to lock me up now. I've made myself ready to go. I've said goodbye to Serena."

Rompell leaned forward, his hands resting on his knees. Mrs. Hunter rubbed her cheek as she stared at Adeline. Holding fingers to the bridge of her nose, she shut her eyes and said, "You are not going to prison, Miss Winkleston."

Adeline dared look up. "I'm not? But, Serena said Officer McCay was looking for me. She—"

"You were a missing child." Mrs. Hunter opened her eyes and glanced at Rompell. "Mr. Rompell and I have come to an agreement that will allow you to stay at the Bradford School. We both agree this is the safest place for you. However, there are conditions. Mr. Rompell has agreed to his part, but now it is up to you."

Adeline sat in the chair, keeping her posture as she waited for her sentence. She hid the shaking of her hands by tucking them into her lap.

"You are welcome to remain friends with Miss Quinn, but you will have your own room and will not be permitted to let other girls visit.

"You will continue your studies with me, but we will meet daily. If you demonstrate your powers without permission again, I will be forced to expel you. I would rather help you hone your gifts, but I cannot have you endangering other girls."

Adeline glanced up at the dark wood ceiling. If it meant staying here with Serena, then she would make sure this was the only room she ever used her powers in again. The daily lessons would be dreary, but they were worth the cost.

"If you do not agree, Mr. Rompell will find another boarding school for you. I warn you, however, that most headmistresses are stricter than I am and few have any inkling magic exists.

"Do you agree, Miss Winkleston?"

Adeline looked to her genie. There were probably many places he could take her, but he had chosen this school. She watched him, waiting for a confirmation. All he did, however, was run a hand over his goatee, his eyes focused on the desk.

She swallowed before nodding.

A hint of relief relaxed Mrs. Hunter's cheeks, though her face remained stern. Gesturing toward the door, she said, "Mr. Rompell would like a word with you. May I suggest the garden?"

Adeline frowned as Rompell stood and opened the door. His eyes avoided hers as they left the study and walked to the garden behind the school. He led her to the small pond, where koi fish gleamed in the sun. However, she didn't feel much of the sun's warmth.

They sat on the bench. Her throat clenched at the grayness in his face. In her heart, she knew he was leaving and would not come back. She had seen his secret and being near her would be too dangerous.

"Mrs. Hunter said you pulled Serena from the fire," he said.

Adeline's brow furrowed as she wondered why that mattered. "But I started the fire."

"And saved your friend." He looked out at the pond as he pressed his hands together. "Such an act is one of a bold heart and Mrs. Hunter would like to present you a medal at the next Visiting Day."

Adeline felt as if the garden were pressing tighter around her. She shook her head. "I don't deserve it. I—"

"It takes courage to face what we have broken, forgive ourselves, and remember the good we have done." He placed his gloved hands on his knees. Staring down at them, he said, "Mrs. Hunter has asked me—"

He swallowed and a tear broke, falling down his cheek. Adeline stared at the drop of water until it disappeared into his goatee.

"I would like to be there," he forced out, "to stand in place of where—"

His jaw clenched and Adeline's breath was still as she waited for him to finish.

"To stand in place of where your parents should be." He spoke quickly to get the words out.

Adeline's eyes widened, remembering wishes she had tried to hide from herself. Her throat felt thick as she trembled, unsure if this moment were real. "You will be my papa?"

"Yes," he whispered, "if that is what you wish to call me."

She sat up, her hand touching his arm. "And we will live in your palace?"

"Palaces are not so pleasant as you think." A sad smile crossed his lips. "But, in a few weeks, I will take you to a home worthy of you."

Her own smile formed even as tears fell down her cheek.

He wanted her as his family.

The memory of months of feeling alone, even with Serena's friendship, softened as she threw her arms around his neck. She longed for her mother and father, but the strength of Rompell's arms around her quieted the sorrow. For months, she had felt like a lone flower lost in a field but holding tight to Rompell brought her to the warmth of home.

Adeline leaned against him and he put his arm around her. Shutting her eyes, she let the quiet sounds of the garden and murmur of the girls in the classrooms fade away as she enjoyed sitting beside her new papa.

The Second Tale of the Magician

Hidaya watched through the red silk curtain, counting the rhythm of the drumbeat as she waited for her entrance. Her heart leaped along with Rompell, Prince of Gathray, as he somersaulted through rings of fire spread across the open floor of the Emperor's Court.

Yesterday's practice had ended with his ankle catching on an unlit hoop and him pounding into the practice pad. She had stepped forward but stopped herself. If alone, she would have run to his side and gripped his hand. With his father and brothers standing near, she could do nothing but watch Rompell's valet Stiltsken help him off the floor.

Rompell had limped a little, but bowed to his father and said, "Tomorrow will be better."

Tonight, she had no need to worry about the performance. The evening's grand spectacle was moving with the clockwork precision her father, Terrivan, had planned for the past two years. Rompell was landing each trick and the dancing elephants, acrobatics, plumes of fire, and flashes of illusion, were all met with cheers.

Her gaze, however, kept drifting to Princess Favay, the emperor's daughter, the woman all of this splendor was meant to impress. The princess sat on the Emperor's dais, leaning on her elbow, her beaded veil doing little to hide her boredom.

Six princes had performed for Princess Favay and been dismissed. Each of their nations had spent at least twice what Gathray had on this spectacle, and Gathray had sacrificed more than they could afford. Rompell's failure might break the small kingdom. To maintain his kingdom's honor and protect his people, he had to be chosen.

Yet, if Rompell succeeded, Hidaya would lose him.

Hidaya's throat clenched. A year ago, she would have been happy to let Rompell go. At first, his warm smile and longing glances were false. In practice sessions with her father, he stole moments to whisper florid words his father's poets had written for Favay. Too often she overheard Rompell laughing as his valet, Stiltsken, told of his latest romantic conquest.

As months passed, something about him softened. Rompell began to laugh and joke with her father. The men and women of her troupe warmed to him. She found herself often sitting near him as he waited to practice his next trick, joining the laughter.

A few months ago, he had kissed her hand in secret. That led to other stolen moments, his arms wrapped around her, her head leaning on his chest. There, taking in his warm scent, sharing their whispered conversations broken by brief kisses, she could almost forget he was a prince. Potential futures together began to form in her mind, but they broke every time Stiltsken snapped to Rompell warning someone was coming. Stiltsken glared at her before escorting Rompell away.

During the week-long journey here to the capital, she felt Rompell's gaze following her, but she ignored him. They were approaching the end and she was not foolish enough to believe he would give up his position nor the hand of Princess Favay for a traveling performer's daughter.

Hidaya's eyes turned back to the spectacle as Rompell grabbed a rope with one hand and the hidden crew raised him to a platform overlooking the crowd. He danced, pretending to conjure something and smoke boiled through the arena.

This was her cue.

Hidaya ran to her seat on the large platform, her gold and red dress matching the curtain hiding her. She checked the mechanisms in the spinning wheel and the gold thread looped through the spindle. She tugged a little, testing the spool underneath her seat. Everything was in place.

The platform shuddered as a pair of elephants wearing red and gold headdresses pulled her to the court's center. Almost a thousand royalty and nobility from around the empire lined the hall.

A shower of sparks erupted around her platform and the curtain fell.

Her heart jolted as her eyes met Rompell's.

She forced herself to smile and look out at the crowd. Her gaze turned to Favay. The Princess sat up, her eyes bright with interest for the first time that evening. Hidaya bit back a curse. After everything her father and Rompell had done for tonight, she may have ruined it with one stray glance.

The musicians began playing. She had to do her part to end this wretched evening.

Her foot pumped the lever spinning the wheel and she sang the legend of Gathara, the goddess who weaved the tapestry of the sky. Deftly, she picked up strands of straw from a basket and fed them into a hole hidden beside the spindle. In the straw's place, gold thread appeared, filling from the spool hidden beneath her seat.

The full troupe, now dressed in gold robes, filled the arena and joined her song. The music swelled as the lamp was lit inside Hidaya's seat and the light reflected on mirrors hanging from the canopy, creating a bright glow. It was a beautiful sight even from the center. This had to please the princess.

Hidaya pulled the skein of gold thread from the spindle and raised it. She slipped it onto a hook hanging from a hidden wire. The wire pulled the skein up, making it appear to be flying. At the apex of the room, the skein exploded into sparks and smoke. In the haze, a tapestry emblazoned with a sun in gold thread fell from the ceiling, appearing as if by sorcery.

The crowd cheered and the troupe, Hidaya, and Rompell bowed themselves to the floor. She took in several deep breaths, but this did little to slow her heartbeat. The crowd's cheers quieted and Hidaya shut her eyes. She prayed silently. Everything they had done and worked for had to succeed.

The chatter in the arena hushed as Favay rose, the jewels on her robes clinking. Hidaya raised her head just enough to view the princess.

With a flick of Favay's hand, her spokeswoman rushed to her side. There were a few whispered words before the spokeswoman said, "The Princess asks if this thimbleful of gold is all she is worth."

Rompell rose to his knees and gave Favay a forced smile. "Her Glorious Highness is worth a thousand palaces full of gold."

Favay spoke to her servant. Several courtiers were called and each nodded as the princess gave commands. Hidaya glanced at her father standing at the rear edge of the troupe. His face was taut as his eyes remained on the ground.

The spokeswoman stepped forward. "The Princess is ordering a room be filled with straw. If your dedication is true, this woman will turn all to gold by morning. If not, then you have lied to us and she will be beheaded."

The warm brown of Rompell's face washed away to paleness. A shudder forced its way through Hidaya. She raised her head and glared into Favay's eyes. The princess's eyes bore a smirk.

Rompell bowed his head and said, "If it is her will, it shall be done."

She knew neither he nor she could do anything as guards marched toward her platform. Still, she wished he would shout, speak up against the princess, or fight the guards. She would join the fight, but there would be no opportunity for escape. Gathray was Rompell's home and she would not betray his chances to do what was best for his people.

Keeping her head high, she stepped down from the platform,

keeping her grace and dignity. She held her palms out to the guards, though it took concentration to keep from shaking. Favay wanted fear and despair from her, but Hidaya would not give it.

The guard clasping iron cuffs on her wrists bore an apology in his eyes. Another guard grabbed her by the arm and shoved her forward.

Her troupe, her lifetime friends, parted, their heads bowed, almost hiding their fear. Hidaya tried to give her father a smile, but the tears wetting his beard brought a thickness to her throat.

The intricately carved, massive doors to the Emperor's Court shuddered closed behind her as she entered the hall. The guards led her through dark and narrow servants' corridors. Whispers of her proclaimed task and fate echoed around her as the servants watched from doorways.

Her path ended at a large room in one of the smaller towers at the rear of the palace. Straw already filled a quarter of the floor and a spindle sat with the tools placed on the stool. The thick wooden door slammed shut and Hidaya fell to her knees. The pile of straw loomed over her as she pressed her hands to her face and finally allowed herself to weep.

Stiltsken waved away Rompell's other servants as he followed the prince into his suite. This conversation had to be done alone. The young man needed to clear his head and focus on what mattered. As his valet and friend, Stiltsken had to prevent Rompell from ruining everything they had worked toward for two years. No pretty face was worth losing an empire.

"How petty can she be?" Rompell ripped off his silk turban and tossed it onto a sedan. He ran his hands through his thick hair as he faced Stiltsken. "It was clearly an illusion and now she's playing—"

Stiltsken gripped Rompell's shoulder. This young prince had saved his life, but there were so many times his youth and narrow vision were apparent.

"Keep your focus on your future empress," Stiltsken said. "I will make sure Hidaya is safe."

"What must I do?" Rompell raised his hand. "And don't tell me to forget her. I know my duty and will perform it, but I will not let Hidaya be sacrificed."

"Sentiment only weighs down greatness."

Rompell opened his mouth to argue, but Stiltsken inched closer.

"Favay would not focus on Hidaya unless she was interested in you," Stiltsken said. "You have her attention. At tonight's feast, you must deepen her interest."

Shoving off Stiltsken's hand, Rompell strode across the room. "I know how to smile and flatter. But, what good is any of this if Hidaya dies?"

Hidaya's execution would do no good for anyone. Rompell's affection for the young woman would become the great tragedy he wallowed in. Favay was only playing a game of who would flinch first. Rompell was no match for the princess' cunning, just as he was no match for the rest of the court games he sought to play. It was often exhausting moving pieces, making promises, and betraying allegiances behind Rompell's back. However, Stiltsken would keep his promise, even if he had to be the true power and Rompell merely the façade.

Stiltsken's jaw flexed. Rompell would make a poor front tonight if he was busy worrying about Hidaya. A plan formed in his mind. He whispered it as he helped Rompell into his robes for the feast and fireworks.

Rompell slapped Stiltsken's shoulder and grinned. "We will win, won't we?"

Stiltsken forced himself to return the smile. He bowed as he opened the door to where Rompell's father and brothers waited.

Rompell's step was light as he joined them.

Once Rompell and the other royals were gone, Stiltsken went through the servants' passage to the grounds where Terrivan and his troupe had set their tents. He gave a warm smile to several female servants who had melted under his charm. A dark corner and a few strategic kisses often gained more information than a month of spying.

Angry voices rumbled through Terrivan's tents. Stiltsken entered the room packed with the troupe members and all went silent.

"Have you come to gloat?" Terrivan said, rising to his full height.

"I have a plan to save your daughter," Stiltsken said. "And I need your help."

Rompell rubbed his cheeks as he entered his dark suite. The whole evening had been exhausting, and all his efforts of smiling and flirting led to the same glazed boredom in Favay's eyes.

He could not fail his country, but he hated the thought of a lifetime with that woman.

"Are you ready?"

Stiltsken stood on the balcony, the floor covered by a carpet carrying three skeins of gold thread next to several golden robes from the evening's spectacle.

Rompell smiled. Of course. Stiltsken had kept his word.

He hopped onto the carpet and waited for Stiltsken to do the spell. Stiltsken held his palms out and sang out in his deep voice. A rush of wind lifted the carpet. Rompell's stomach lurched as it carried them out the window. Stiltsken guided it with his voice and magic, more masterfully than the best court sorcerers Rompell had seen.

They kept to the shadows between spires before gliding into a room in a tower on the edge of the palace grounds.

All the exhaustion and frustration of the evening washed away as Hidaya stood from beside the pile of straw nearly three times her height. Her eyes were wide as the carpet landed on the stone floor.

Rompell leapt off the carpet and rushed to her side. He pressed his hands to her face and kissed her, drinking in her scent, so much sweeter than the gallon of oils and perfumes Favay wore. She leaned against him, returning the kiss before resting her head on his shoulder. He wrapped his arm around her, holding her tight. Staying like this could not last, but he would remain as long as he could.

Pressing his forehead against hers, Rompell said, "I am sorry for—"

"This is only because she saw us look at each other," Hidaya said. "I don't know what she wants from this, but she is testing you."

"We will win." Rompell kept hold of her hand and gestured to the pile of gold skeins. "Stiltsken, your father, and your troupe unraveled some of the robes tonight. If you and I can do a few more, it should be enough."

Hidaya squeezed his hand and they sat near the mound of robes as Stiltsken began his work.

He moved to the pile of straw and whispered a song. The straw smoldered and burned before lighting on fire. As the pile collapsed in on itself, the fire consuming the straw, Stiltsken arched his arms. The smoke traveled like a hypnotized snake drawn to the circular shape Stiltsken created with his hands. As more smoke pulled in, Stiltsken moved his hands closer together. The smoke compressed, forming a fine ash.

"Your servant has more secrets than I thought," Hidaya said as she picked up a robe.

Rompell cut part of the robe with his hunting knife, creating a place to begin unweaving the golden thread.

"He's a loyal friend," he said.

She raised an eyebrow as she pulled at the loose thread. With a hard tug, she began undoing the fine work of the Gathrayan weavers. Rompell picked up a different robe and joined the work.

Hours went by slowly and Hidaya sang quietly to pass the time. After a while, Rompell sat watching her, listening to her sweet voice, wishing his duty would let him stay with her.

Stiltsken sat across from Rompell and gave him a sharp look. Rompell returned the glare as he set to pulling thread. Stiltsken's eyes focused on the thread, his forehead creased and dotted with sweat. Stiltsken had often explained how exhausting it was to keep long-term concentration to manage larger spells. All of his work would leave him with a splitting headache in the morning.

Gray light peered in through the open windows. Pulling himself from Hidaya's side ripped at Rompell's heart. However, he pressed his lips to her cheek before joining Stiltsken on the carpet.

"I will keep you safe," he said. "No matter what."

Hidaya rose, a strength in her eyes. "You have done all you can." She looked down at the seven skeins of gold. "Do not hold yourself to promises you cannot keep."

Many words ran through Rompell's mind, but he had learned not to use empty words with Hidaya. He pressed his hand to his forehead and bowed to her. Stiltsken sang out a long, low note, and the carpet rushed out of the tower.

The warmth of the sun through the high windows of the Emperor's Court did not reach Hidaya as she knelt before Favay and her father. Stiltsken stood gray-faced and exhausted with other servants. Rompell sat on the steps leading up to the dais, his hand pressed to his breast as he pretended to look at Favay with devotion. Favay's eyes remained focused only on Hidaya, staring as if analyzing a peculiar specimen.

"Have Her Glorious Highness's wishes been fulfilled?" the spokeswoman said.

"As Her Highness has desired, so has it been done," Rompell said.

The guard carrying the seven golden skeins held them out. Favay's servants placed them on a velvet-lined tray and carried them to the princess. Favay gave them a quick glance and Hidaya wondered if a viper might be as warm as Favay as she whispered to her spokeswoman.

"Her Glorious Highness will not accept these," the spokeswoman said. "What can be made with so little? She expects twenty tonight."

Hidaya's head snapped up and her shoulders shook.

"I have done what was asked. I—"

A guard struck her across the jaw and Hidaya bit back the rest of her words. They had barely made seven spools. Twenty could not be done.

Rompell's face had an appearance of calm, but the twitching of his hand betrayed his agitation. Hidaya forced herself not to look at him. Giving into her feelings now would only give Favay more fuel for her game.

Too soon, the guards shoved her back into the tower. Flatbread and water came along with servants carrying in basket after basket filled with straw. Once completed, the pile covered a third of the room and almost reached the ceiling.

The servants and guards left and Hidaya sat alone as she sobbed. The tears were hot, the image of Favay sitting on her throne burning in her mind. Rompell was out there, pretending to adore her, as much a prisoner as she was. And, she was here, waiting for the inevitable execution.

That could be the only end of Favay's game. She would see how far she could push Rompell by toying with Hidaya. Then, she would break him with Hidaya's death.

Hidaya moved to a place on the floor where the sun rose. She curled onto her side and tried to sleep. A shadow blocked the sun's warmth and she opened her eyes.

Stiltsken stepped off his flying carpet and dropped several robes beside her. "Your father and your friends are working on pulling apart others."

"She will only ask for more tomorrow," Hidaya said as she sat up.

He looked down at her with his cool blue eyes. "You and I know that, but Rompell must believe you can be saved."

"So he is free to woo the princess," Hidaya said.

Stiltsken squatted beside her.

"He once had such clear ambition." He tilted his head. "But, then you came, infecting him with the same infatuation that has destroyed many great men."

He leaned closer to her and whispered, "I should have followed my instincts and made you disappear."

Hidaya held his gaze. His magic might have been unexpected, but she had been right about his intent to ride Rompell into power. She had tried to mention her suspicions once to Rompell, but he had laughed and said she misunderstood his friend. Tonight, it was clear she did not.

Rompell could still feel the warmth of Hidaya's kiss as he stood before Favay and the twenty skeins of gold were presented. His fingers were raw from the night's work. Hidaya's looked worse.

His whole body shuddered as Favay's spokeswoman pronounced, "Fifty skeins or her head."

He could do nothing but bow and say, "It will be done as you wish."

The guards led Hidaya out, the fire in her eyes dimming and her face bearing the weight of death. He spared a glance at Stiltsken. His servant nodded.

They would play the game again, giving Hidaya one more night to live.

Too soon, he was swept into the day's false splendor. The morning was spent riding elephants through the streets, leading to a grand feast at one of the minor palaces scattered throughout the capitol.

Drummers and dancers performed as Rompell's chin drooped and he dozed off. Stiltsken shoved his shoulder and Rompell snapped awake. Favay sat watching him, a hint of amusement in her eyes. He tried to give her a smile but could not force his cheeks into position. She was cruel and unworthy of this extravagance.

He and the other princes trailed after Favay as they went through the motions of a late afternoon round of archery. At the end, Favay beckoned Rompell with a flick of her hand. Once he was close, she said in a well-practiced, airy voice, "Will you escort me to the palace?"

His heart jolted. This either was in his favor or the first steps of his downfall. He bowed and said, "If that is your wish, Your Glorious Highness."

He glanced back at Stiltsken and was steadied by his servant's nod. Stiltsken would continue the work to help Hidaya. Rompell would concentrate on pleasing Favay.

Rompell took his place a step behind Favay and the rest of the courtiers stepped into line behind him. The princess led them through the ornate gardens and to the skiffs waiting to carry them downriver to the Emperor's palace. Rompell's pulse quickened as he joined Favay on her skiff, alone except for a guard and two servants.

Lanterns floated along the river, marking their path as the sun finished setting and the stars appeared. Rompell leaned back on a pile of cushions only an arms-length away from Favay as men rowed the boat in silence. It was the closest to alone he would ever be and he needed to use it to his advantage.

Her eyes wandered to the sky and the trees surrounding the river as he spoke empty words of flattery and adoration. A hole seemed to be growing within him, dragging him down with each second she ignored him.

The palace came into view as she said, "I have decided to show you my face."

Rompell sat up, not sure how to respond. Being granted a look at her face was one step below her offering her hand.

"I am unworthy of the honor," he said.

"No man is worthy."

She pulled aside the veil covering her face. Rompell's fingers curled as he forced his expression to remain calm. He had to appear adoring even as he gazed upon the woman who kept hold of Hidaya's fate.

She was not the beauty poets claimed her to be, with her eyebrows a little thick and her nose slightly hooked. In a room full of women, she would be wholly unremarkable.

Her dark eyes, however, bore into him, carrying the power of her rank.

"Tell me I am more beautiful than the girl you have been helping these past few nights."

A weight thudded into Rompell's chest. He thought to laugh and deny what they both knew was true. Losing her hand meant the suitor who won would punish his kingdom for his failure. It also meant Hidaya's death.

His calculations made, he pressed his hand to his chest and gave her a look of false-adoration. "There is no woman more beautiful than you."

As they reached the docks, Favay leaned close and whispered, "My hand is yours if you banish the girl. Otherwise, her death will be by your hand."

Hidaya laid the final skein on the mound where the straw had been. Stiltsken said her father and his troupe had spent the day unwinding the golden tapestry used in the performance.

Fifty skeins.

And tomorrow would bring a hundred.

"Hidaya."

She looked up. The carpet had been silent as it landed. Stiltsken stood at the rear, his arms folded behind his back, his face betraying nothing. Rompell held his hand out to her.

"Princess Favay has made her decision. You must come with me."

Hidaya placed her hand in Rompell's and he drew her close to him on the carpet. They sat and Stiltsken sang it into flight.

The carpet moved deftly around towers. Hidaya's stomach lurched as the carpet made a sudden drop. It rose again, dodging past guards standing watch.

She leaned into Rompell as he kept his arms around her, holding her tighter than usual. His plan was unclear. He might be trying to make her disappear or was disappearing with her. The rush of wind flying past was too loud to talk.

They landed at an outpost just beyond the city's edge, where a few shelters for travelers surrounded a well. The walls of Alqon and the palace spires rose in distance, illuminated by the starlight and lights of the buildings. Rompell clung to Hidaya's hand as he helped her off the carpet.

Looking in his eyes, she saw them running from the capitol, leaving behind the court and beginning their lives. A pain filled her breast as she pictured Gathray burning for his betrayal.

"Where do we go now?" Hidaya said.

Rompell turned his head away. "You've been banished from the capitol."

Hidaya glanced at the city. It was a small price for her life. However, a hollowness was threatening as she said, "And you?"

Unfallen tears were on the edge of his eyes as he looked at her. "I gain the title of husband, which has the same honor of being her dog."

Her chest felt as if struck by a full-force wind. A small part of her had believed this would end differently, that he would shed his title and they could simply be. It had been a foolish wish.

"If I could go with you and know Gathray would be safe, I—"

She hooked her arm around his neck and kissed him. Someday, this ache would leave and she might love another. It would not, however, be the same.

He pulled her tighter against him, his lips firm against hers. Though her whole body pulsed, telling her to stay, she pulled away.

"You are a better man than she deserves, Rompell of Gathray."

Tears broke and ran down Rompell's cheeks. Hidaya's own tears refused to come. She had to help him have the strength he needed. If he was to become the future emperor, he needed to learn to hide his true self better.

"There is much I wish could be and, if I were free, much I would say." He held her hand tightly.

"We should go," Stiltsken said.

She clutched his hand. Looking into his eyes, there were too many unspoken words and too many wished-for futures. A thickness filled her throat as he raised her hand and kissed her palm.

Her own tears broke free, but she turned away before he could see her face. He lingered, but Stiltksen said, "You must be ready when she summons you."

Rompell's hand tore away from hers and he ran to the carpet. The fabric flapped in the wind as it took off in the air. Hidaya dared look up, her eyes meeting Rompell's a final time before the carpet sped off into the horizon.

With him gone, she collapsed against one of the buildings, finally letting out the cry of sorrow she had been holding.

Tomorrow, he would be betrothed to the Emperor's daughter, and soon be crowned Prince and Heir to an empire. And she and her father's troupe would return to their lives as traveling performers. He would never see her again, but she would hear of him everywhere they went, never truly able to let him go.

Chapter 6

Adeline sat at the edge of her chair, leaning forward, rapt in Alvin Westengaard's spellbinding oration, fanning herself in the summer heat. Her hand clasped Serena's. Other women in the audience gasped as he read from his latest novel, describing the lovers wandering in a blizzard, seeking each other.

Lost in his words, she could almost forget the dread of waking tomorrow to face her sixteenth birthday. If only her birthdays could be like Serena's, full of celebrations and games. However, ever since turning twelve, her magic had turned her birthday into a day of pain.

At least she had these few precious hours to enjoy an evening out with her best friend.

"And as the cruel hands of winter crushed away their lives," Westengaard said, his handsome brow glistening from the fervor of his delivery, "they clung together, a statue to forever be preserved, an eternal monument to true love, embalmed in ice."

Adeline rose with the rest of the audience, joining the applause thundering through the small theater.

"I told you he was wonderful," Serena shouted to Adeline as she grinned, tears wetting her cheeks.

Westengaard bowed, his blonde hair swept back in a glorious wave. Here was a man who could match the tragic heroes of his stories. Several women had fainted as he read of the lovers dangling from a cliff, only to be saved by the rope their clever dog had tied. The women had been carried out, interrupting the rapt silence of the audience.

Serena linked arms with Adeline as they joined the growing line waiting to meet the author. Both young women shared a blush as he signed their books and granted them a polite smile.

As they left the line, a few ushers handed out signed photographs of Westengaard sitting at his desk, his pen poised and ready as his eyes looked out an unseen window.

"Now, that is how a man should look," Serena said as they tucked their books into their bags. They climbed into the carriage Serena's parents had loaned her and set out for Adeline's house. The horses shied as a new motorcar honked and sped past.

"So unrefined," Serena said as she leaned back in the carriage.

The ride home was too brief as Adeline and Serena giggled about Westengaard and the wonders of his story. Adeline was disappointed as the carriage soon stopped in front of her home.

"I do wish you could come with us on Uncle Mitchell's yacht tomorrow," Serena said. "I had wonderful plans for your birthday."

Adeline forced a smile and squeezed her friend's hand. Tomorrow was not a day she wanted to think about.

"Papa says he has many surprises in store. I will have to go another day."

"I like your father, but, sometimes, he is too strict."

Adeline held back a sigh. It was Mrs. Hunter who was strict, not Rompell. He followed each recommendation Mrs. Hunter made for Adeline's safety. Especially with magic. Especially on her birthday.

She squeezed Serena's hand again, wishing her life were as simple as the other girls' at school. If only she could tell Serena the truth of that night with the fire. Though, if Mrs. Hunter's commands kept something like that from happening again, Adeline would follow them.

Serena stepped down from the carriage and hugged Adeline. "Happy birthday."

They kissed each other's cheeks and Adeline entered her house. A soprano's voice wafted from the phonograph in the sitting room where Rompell tinkered with a small device to add to his magic tricks. He was hardly older than when he had brought her here seven years before, yet had transformed from the vagabond street magician to a respectable landlord.

Seeing her, he smiled and motioned for her to join him. "How was your evening?"

"It was wonderful, Papa." She flopped on the couch with a sigh.

"So, this 'Westengaard' is everything Serena said he is?"

"Oh, yes." She recounted Westengaard's baritone voice, crafting the light and shadows of the reading, filling the whole room with only his voice and presence. "And he signed my book!"

She pulled the hardback from her handbag and offered it to Rompell.

"*Of Crowns and Hearts* by Alvin Westengaard. Very dramatic." He opened the book and read the inscription out loud, "Adeline, may your heart be filled with the wonders of love." He rubbed his hand on his chin, trying to mask his chuckle.

"I think it's wonderful." Adeline snatched the book from him. "It's so romantic and tragic." She pressed the book to her chest. "They sacrifice everything to be together. Even their lives. I hope, one day, to have so great a romance."

Rompell crossed to the phonograph and turned it off. "We have both had enough tragedy in our lives. I would much rather your future romance end with, 'And they lived steadily, though happily, ever after.'"

Adeline leaned her head on the couch. "If Mrs. Hunter has her choice, I'll never find love. I'll be just as stuffed up and lonely as she is."

Rompell let out a tsk. "Mrs. Hunter is a kinder woman than you give her credit for. She cares for you greatly. And, I would think you would find her own romance tragic enough to respect."

"My father died a hero, but his death brought my mother to her final illness," Adeline said. "She couldn't keep living because she loved him so much. She tried to stay for me, but his draw was too great. But, Mrs. Hunter—she acts as if her husband never lived."

"It is her own pain that drives her to protect you." Rompell bent down and kissed Adeline's forehead.

"I just wish I didn't need her protection."

Her first two birthdays after Rompell adopted her had been full of games and laughter. Her eleventh birthday had been her and Serena's first visit to the dragon races, joining the crowd's cheering as she and Serena stared in wonder at the magnificent creatures racing in the sky.

Then, on her twelfth birthday, everything had gone wrong. Her head had throbbed throughout the morning and she was forced to lie in bed with cold, wet rags over her eyes. By afternoon, the furniture shook and glass cracked as her magic veered out of control. Rompell ran and got Mrs. Hunter, who had sat by her bed the rest of the day to hold back potential damage.

The following birthdays had only gotten worse.

Rompell sat beside her and squeezed her hand. "Do not be ashamed of who you are, Adeline. But, you must be careful."

Her shoulders slumped as she nodded.

"If all goes well, tomorrow will be a fine day. You have been practicing the exercises Mrs. Hunter gave you?"

Adeline nodded. She draped across her corner of the couch. He was right, but she was still burning to go on Serena's uncle's yacht. Having magic was incredibly unfair.

"I am proud of you, Adeline. And, after tomorrow, you are welcome to join Serena. However, I have promised to protect you. Help me keep that promise."

She glanced up at him and smiled sadly. "Serena had a full party for her birthday while I must be locked away."

"You will not be locked away."

"I suppose." She stood, her book in hand. "Goodnight, Papa."

"Goodnight, Little One."

She kissed his cheek and moved toward the stairs.

"You dropped this—"

She turned as Rompell's voice trailed off. He stared at Westengaard's photograph in his hand. His tanned face was now pale, his cheeks tight and drawn.

"What is it, Papa?"

She moved beside Rompell and looked at the signed portrait.

"This is Alvin Westengaard?" Rompell said, his voice nearly hoarse.

"Yes." She pressed a hand to his forehead. "Are you all right?"

Rompell brushed away her hand and marched to the fireplace. Before Adeline could stop him, he tossed the photograph into the flames.

"Papa!"

Rompell's fists dug into his hips as he looked down at the burning portrait.

Reaching his side, Adeline said, "Papa, that was mine."

"The man is not what he appears, Adeline. Do not go to one of his lectures again."

"But—"

Rompell turned, a hardness in his eyes. Adeline shrunk back, feeling as if she were a child again.

"The man is false and dangerous. Keep your distance." He reached out for her book, but she pulled away. "Get rid of anything connected to him."

"What makes him so dangerous?"

"I cannot explain this tonight. There is too much. Too much—" Rompell ran his gloved hand through his hair, his eyes feverishly scanning the floor. "He is supposed to be in the Culparr Mines. He cannot be here." He rubbed his eyes. "I hope I am only mad."

"Culparr Mines? Isn't that the prison in the Surris Mountains?" Her eyes widened as she clutched the book to her chest. "Mrs. Hunter said only the worst abusers of magic are taken there." She swallowed. "But, he is only a writer."

Rompell dropped onto the nearest chair, his hands pressed together in front of his face. He shut his eyes as if trying to clear his mind. His age weighed on him, his normally smooth features betrayed by crow's feet and lines across his brow.

"What has Mr. Westengaard done?" she said.

Rompell opened his eyes and glared into the fire. "His real name is Benjamin Stiltsken. He once pretended to be my friend. Then, he stole my wife and children."

A chill ran through Adeline, the air leaving her lungs. Rompell spoke so little of his past, but she had pieced together hints of the family he had lost. Something terrible had happened, but he never said what.

She crossed to the fire and tossed the book in. All of the excitement of the evening joined the ash flaking off the paper and wafting up the chimney.

Pressing her hand to her father's arm, she said, "What did he do?"

"Go to bed, Adeline." He stood and stirred the fire, quickening the demise of her book. "And shut your window tight."

"But, Papa—"

"Go to bed. Now."

She frowned and considered arguing. She was almost sixteen and deserved better than this. However, his hard glare sent a pain in her chest. One day, he would tell her more of his past and what evil Stiltsken had done. Tonight, she would learn no more from her father.

Climbing the stairs to her room, she imagined Rompell as a younger man, battling Westengaard over a beautiful young woman. The battle played through her mind as she went through her evening grooming and changed into her night clothes. Perhaps he and Westengaard had been in love with the same woman, playing in a constant tug-o-war over her heart. The woman had chosen Rompell, they had built a life together, and Westengaard must have lured her to her death to ease his jealousy.

Tears wet her pillow as Adeline laid on her bed and imagined what other tragedies had filled Rompell's youth.

Adeline jolted awake as Rompell knocked on her door. "Adeline, breakfast is waiting."

The rich smell of cinnamon and fresh bread mixed with the scent of bacon. Adeline pressed a hand to her stomach, trying to hide an undignified grumble. She removed her night clothes and pulled on her fresh brassiere.

Only a few years before, the embarrassed Rompell sent her to Mrs. Hunter to learn the ways of shaping and containing the female figure. Serena's mother and Mrs. Frizban, who cooked and cleaned for them a few times a week, had taught her a few other tricks and made some adjustments. It had been one of many moments Adeline wished her mother had survived her sorrow and could teach Adeline with more gentleness than Mrs. Hunter.

She pulled on a fresh dress and sat at her boudoir to sort the snags in her golden hair. The ornate curls of the night before were now a frizzed mess. It would be worse by days end. Still, she brushed out the snarls, leaving her hair spread out as if shocked by an electric storm. She stuffed everything into a snood, the knitted hairnet with rosettes along the edge hiding the disaster. She pinned it in place and turned her head in front of the mirror. It was not as fine as she typically liked, but it had enough dignity for her to hurry down to breakfast.

She took a breath as she reached the top of the stairs. Today, she was sixteen years old. In some circles, that made her a grown woman. It was best to enter with dignity.

Envisioning herself a grand princess entering a ballroom, Adeline held her skirt out with one hand, letting it flare. She swept down the stairs as Serena and she had often practiced.

Rompell stood at the head of the table. He smiled, but his eyes were pained and distant. Adeline returned the smile with as much warmth as she could give.

Fresh cinnamon rolls lay steaming at the center of the table, ringed with bacon, cut strawberries, whipped cream, and a small bowl of chocolates.

Rompell bowed to her before twirling his hand. "Your breakfast, milady."

"You do look a real lady," Mrs. Frizban said from the kitchen doorway. "So grown up."

Rompell pulled out the chair for Adeline as he said, "You are welcome to join us, Mrs. Frizban. You made this excellent feast."

"Please do," Adeline said. Mrs. Frizban's chatter often warmed the table on mornings when Rompell was quiet. Today, it would be greatly needed.

With her apron set aside, Mrs. Frizban joined them. With a few encouraging questions from Adeline, Mrs. Frizban filled the conversation.

"My youngest, Stewart, you know Stewart, don't you, Miss Adeline? He's home for the summer from Marksdale. Gone up to the university there, he has. I've always said he's my brightest. Even has a scholarship. I've tried to thank the committee, but the college says the donor gave strict orders of keeping it anonymous."

Rompell prodded his food as he avoided Adeline's glance. She suspected it was the same benefactor who subsidized the rent of widows and men broken by the factories, who provided many of his tenants' children with anonymous scholarships and had provided a home for a matchgirl he'd found in the snow seven years before.

"Stewart may stop by." Mrs. Frizban gave Adeline a pointed smile.

Adeline gave a false-smile back. Stewart was as squat and round as his mother, but without her warmth. Any man Adeline was going to be interested in had to be far more heroic than Stewart Frizban.

"Has he employment for the summer?" Rompell said.

"No. His brothers will run the construction business while Stewart readies his mind for greater things."

"John Havish, the tanner, is always looking for extra workers," Rompell said. "It may be good for Stewart to have some physical exercise to balance the workings of his mind."

Adeline hid a snort with a false-sneeze. Stewart's rotund frame could do with some physical exertion.

Mrs. Frizban's conversation wound to other things and the meal slowed as stomachs filled. A buzzing rose in Adeline's ears, blurring Mrs. Frizban's words. She rubbed her temple to ease the piercing pain growing through her forehead. Adeline shut her eyes, hoping she was wrong about the signs. This could just be a usual headache.

Then, her fork rattled on the table.

She opened her eyes and clamped her hand on the utensil. It tried to move on its own, but she held steady. Her spoon began to rise, the handle clanking against the plate

Rompell pulled his pocket watch out and made a show of looking at it. "I must apologize, Mrs. Frizban. Adeline and I have an appointment to keep."

He stood, his hand pressing down his own rattling silverware. "Adeline, why don't you finish getting ready for the day while Mrs. Frizban and I clear the table."

"Why, thank you, Mr. Rompell." Mrs. Frizban patted Adeline's hand. "You have a pleasant day, my dear."

Adeline forced another smile before hurrying up the stairs. As she shut the door to her room, the pins in her hair began shaking and pulling at her. She ripped them out and tossed them on the dresser. The small pool of bobby pins hovered over the table in a metallic cloud. Adeline barely dodged one of her bracelets zooming across the room. The other drawers of her jewelry box shook as if trying to break open.

Rather than wait for more objects to start flying, she moved down the hall and into Rompell's bedroom. The space was dark and austere, the bedspread folded tightly, no decorations on the walls. The top drawer of his dresser rattled but nothing broke free. Adeline dropped onto his stiff bed and pulled the thin pillow over her head. Far too soon, the same throbbing headache from her past four birthdays returned.

It was as if a spike were being driven between her ears, the pain pulsing. Tears quickly wet the pillow. She tried to hum the song Mrs. Hunter had taught her to counteract the headache, but the melody broke as she cringed and hissed.

Time became a blur of pain, broken only by Rompell entering, his boots echoing on the hardwood floor as he paced.

The door opened and shut, followed by Mrs. Hunter saying, "Drink this."

Adeline gagged on the thick syrup as it poured down her throat.

"Give her one of these chocolates every hour and keep a cool rag on her head." Mrs. Hunter unbuttoned the bodice of Adeline's dress and loosened the brassiere. Adeline gasped in breath. "It will help if you can read to her. Hearing your voice should sooth her and give her something to focus on."

Mrs. Hunter smoothed back Adeline's hair from her sweating forehead. "I endured similar spasms when I was a young woman. They will subside in a few years and she will come out with a deeper and richer power. However, it must be endured first. She will be fine by morning."

"Thank you," Rompell said.

"You were right to bring her to me all those years ago," Mrs. Hunter said. "She could have badly damaged herself and others without training." She moved to the door. "I left her gift in the sitting room." There was a sigh. "I do wish she could have a pleasant birthday."

The door shut and Rompell pulled the hard-backed chair to the bedside. He set a wet rag over her forehead and eyes. The coolness made the pain ebb a little. The chair creaked as Rompell leaned back. He began reading from *The Rosetown Journal*, nearly keeping skepticism from his voice as he repeated the tales of gossip and scandal Adeline had already giggled over with Serena.

She said nothing, letting herself relax to the richness of his deep voice. The words blurred together, but his voice remained a beacon she held onto as she took measured breaths.

As he read Lady Petunia Ophombauch's editorial on the overuse of calla lilies, Adeline's chest began to spasm. Her heart and lungs were pounding against her ribs, every muscle tense. Her whole body convulsed. She wheezed for breath as she thrashed, no control over anything. This part was often worse than the steady headache.

Sweat layered her skin as the convulsions stopped. Her cheeks bulged and her stomach's contents rushed up. She turned onto her side and hung her head over the edge of the bed. The bile rushed out and Rompell had a bucket in place just in time.

Once her stomach had emptied itself, Rompell wiped her face and helped her drink some water to clean her mouth. He kept his hand supporting her back as she lay down again. Once she began sucking on another of Mrs. Hunter's chocolates, the headache and throbbing subsided a little.

The day wore on in a cycle of Rompell reading, stopping as Adeline convulsed, and then wiping off her sweat before giving another chocolate. Each convulsion brought more aching, more soreness, and left her more exhausted than before. She dozed off a few times, but her sleep broke as another spasm or sharp pain shot through her.

The only signs night had come were the cool breeze wafting in through the window and the crickets echoing outside.

Each muscle was exhausted and her head throbbed with a dull ache, but it was far softer than the piercing pain from before. Slowly, Rompell's words came into focus.

"They joined hands, the prince and his lady, their lives intertwined forever."

Rompell snapped the book shut and muttered, "These youthful romances rarely consider future arguments over washing dishes and changing diapers."

"They're still wonderfully romantic," Adeline said, her words slurred.

His hand grasped hers, his grip sure and strong. "I see the sleeping princess is waking."

Adeline smiled. "What of your own romance, Papa? How did you fall in love?"

The silence was filled with the night breeze and ticking of the clock on the dresser. Rompell tapped his thumb against her hand before saying, "Such things are better forgotten."

"What of Stiltsken? And your wife?" Adeline began to sit up, but pain pulsed through her head. She dropped back down, the headache easing once she lay flat. "Did you love the same woman?"

Rompell's chuckle carried his tiredness. "Stiltsken's true love is himself. Women are only the ladder he uses to get what he wants."

"But your wife—"

"My wife and children are casualties in a long war." His voice grew quiet. "I thought I had won."

"What did he do to you?" She held her breath, hoping he might answer.

Instead, he rose and said, "I'll go get another book."

"What was her name?"

Adeline pressed her lips together. In a moment, he would brush aside her question as always, leaving his past in Sandar. It was as if he never existed until the night he lifted her from the snow.

Her heart leaped as Rompell sat in his chair and said, "Her name was Hidaya. She was the daughter of a traveling performer and I—I was a prince."

Adeline pushed back the rag covering her eyes, ignoring the dull ache of her headache as she looked up at him. His eyes were serious, a pain in them. She felt the truth of his words, despite the many times he mocked her and Serena's discussions of the latest gossip from *The Rosetown Journal*.

Tonight, though, he was not teasing her.

"You were a prince?" she whispered.

"I was." From a pocket hidden in his shirt, he removed a copy of the gold coin he had given her on the night they had met. He flipped it through his gloved fingers before holding out the side bearing his face. "And for three horrible months, I was Rothgan XII, Emperor of Sandar."

Her eyes widened. The pain and exhaustion washed away as he spoke, his words carrying her back through the years. She felt as if she were walking hand-in-hand with him through his memories, light finally illuminating the dark corners of his past.

The Third Tale of the Magician

Rompell held his arm out as his servants finished tying on the leather and gold arm guards along his forearms. Carved into the metal were blessings the gods had spoken when crowning the first emperor. He had worn these every day since the morning three months before, when Emperor Kaloman XV had been found on his bedroom floor, dead from poison. It had been a dark day and he still waited for these blessings of strength, wisdom, and power to come to him.

The tent flap opened and Stiltsken entered, dressed in deep blue robes embroidered with delicate yellow birds and leaves. For the first time in weeks of traveling, Rompell smiled. He waved off his servants and gripped his friend's arm in greeting.

"How is my sweet empress?"

Rompell waited for the sly raise of Stiltsken's eyebrow followed by a quip. Favay's warmth had remained as steady as ice over their year-and-a-half of marriage. He was grateful to leave Stiltsken behind with his watchful eyes on the palace while Favay sent Rompell to demand tribute from several northern kingdoms.

Stiltsken's blue eyes were grave as he gripped Rompell's shoulder and leaned close. "Didn't you receive my letter?"

"What letter?" Rompell frowned.

The clank of soldiers' feet approached and Stiltsken stepped away. "I wrote to warn you. They traced—"

Rompell's brows lowered as the tent flap flew open and General Baqir led a squad of soldiers in.

Raising a parchment bearing Favay's seal, Baqir said, "By order of

Her Glorious Majesty, Empress Favay of Sandar, you are arrested for the assassination of our beloved Emperor Kaloman XV."

Rompell's hand went to his ceremonial dagger. He looked to Stiltsken. If ever there was a time to set a carpet flying and use his magic to help, this was it. Stiltsken gave Rompell a small nod.

Rompell lunged forward, reaching for one of the soldier's pistols as he slashed with his dagger. Baqir grabbed his wrist and twisted it, forcing the dagger to fall. Several soldiers shoved Rompell to the ground, pushing his face against the rug. They ripped the armguards off his arms and stripped his robes from him, leaving him in his tunic and pantaloons. He was sure a few gave him extra kicks just for the pleasure of it.

Once chains were cuffed on his wrists and ankles, the soldiers yanked Rompell to his feet. Rompell looked to Stiltsken again, but his friend only stood watching, his arms folded behind his back.

He had to be waiting for a quiet moment, some time he could sneak Rompell away. Perhaps dirtying his hands now ruined his plans to clear Rompell's name. Whatever the truth, Stiltsken would pull through as he always did.

The soldiers dragged Rompell from his tent and threw him into a waiting prison wagon.

Today, he was supposed to be riding on an elephant, leading columns of imperial soldiers in their triumphant return from the northern kingdoms. Baqir would have been behind him, having led the destruction of several towns from kingdoms who refused to send their full burden of taxes to the Emperor's seat in Alqon. Rompell had stood as a figurehead as the soldiers flattened the towns, sending the citizens running from burning fields.

It had been a harsh campaign, but necessary. Whispers of the weak Gathrayan prince had haunted the palace halls. Favay had sent him to prove his might. He could not let so small a rebellion stand if he was to remain emperor.

And he would remain emperor.

Despite the rocks and rotten vegetables his subjects threw at him as the prison wagon drove through the streets of Alqon.

Despite standing in the Emperor's Court, hearing his own wife announce his execution in three days.

Despite being paraded through the palace as the nobility and courtiers lined the grand halls, spitting on him as he passed.

Despite the soldiers tossing him in a dungeon cell and beating him with rods before pulling off his chains and leaving him there.

Curled up on the stone floor in the darkness, his body aching and scrapes bleeding, he knew he would rise again. He was innocent of the crime and the truth would be found. He had done his duty and given up Hidaya to become this.

This would not be his end.

Morning was marked by soldiers dragging him to stockades facing the scaffold where he was to be beheaded. The sun beat down as a ring of soldiers kept shouting citizens from charging him. Their cries of, "Murder the traitor!" and other slurs pounded at him.

His legs shook and his back was arched as evening finally came and soldiers returned him to his cell. He sank onto the cold floor and gulped from a dipper of water. The bread was dry and hard, but he devoured it, taking in every crumb.

Too exhausted to think or feel, he leaned against the wall and drifted toward sleep. Vague nightmares shuddered through him as he dozed. In one, Hidaya stood before him, holding out her hand. He reached out to her, but a dark cloud swept around her, dragging her away.

"Rompell."

He started awake. A dim light emanated from a glowing orb floating in the air. Stiltsken knelt beside him, holding out a full canteen of water.

Rompell embraced his friend and slapped his shoulder before taking the canteen. He gulped down water before saying, "How close are you to clearing my name?"

Stiltsken sat back and rested his arms on his knees. He tilted his head, his eyes analyzing Rompell.

"I have done everything I can for you," he said.

Rompell lowered the canteen and raised his head. Pressing his hand to the wall, he tried to stand, but his aching legs could not hold him.

"I am innocent. Favay must know that. I wouldn't—"

"In the games of power, innocence is the greatest crime," Stiltsken said.

"I have done nothing but serve her and fulfill my duty. You must get her to come to me, to listen, to—"

"Emperor Rothgan XII is dead, my friend."

The words knocked into Rompell. He slumped against the wall, the dim fire of hope he had been holding onto now flickering into smoke.

Looking to Stiltsken, he whispered, "No. I am emperor. I gave up too much to—" His hands shook as he pressed them to his head. "What of our allies in the court? We can—"

"They abandoned you the moment you were accused," Stiltsken said. "No one will risk adding their necks to the executioner's list."

Rompell rubbed his forehead. Those men and women were cowards anyway, hiding behind their wealth and position.

Rompell raised his head. "We are escaping tonight, then." He held out his hand. "Help me stand."

Stiltsken glanced at the outreached hand before rising. "If you escape, you will be hunted."

"We will go to the kingdoms who hate Favay's rule. I will band them together and retake the throne."

"Including the northern kingdoms, whose towns you burned?"

Rompell winced. "There are other kingdoms. There is Gathray."

"A small kingdom who only survived this past year because you sent gold." Stiltsken shook his head. "There is no kingdom who can stand against the Sandarian Empire, and none will take in a fallen emperor."

Stiltsken folded his arms behind his back. Rompell rested his fists on his knees as he looked up to the man who had stood with him for over three years. He had always pulled through.

"You came with a plan, didn't you?"

"I have always had a plan," Stiltsken said.

Rompell started to smile but was too exhausted for it to fully form. "What must I do?"

"You have already done your part." Stiltsken squatted beside Rompell, a cool calmness in his eyes. "You saved me from my own prison, set your price, and I have one last payment."

He pulled a pouch from a pocket and poured out a dozen gold coins. "These are all that remain of the first and only coins honoring your reign."

He held one up, the dim light casting long shadows on the imprint of Rompell's face. Rompell stared at the lines on the coin. The presentation of the first coin was supposed to be a grand ceremony with dancing and spectacle. Instead, Stiltsken released the coin, letting it clatter to the ground.

"My debt is paid, Rompell of Gathray." He dusted off his arm and stood. "I am sorry to leave you here. I could not have become the Empress's trusted advisor without you."

Heat pumped through Rompell as his eyes widened. He fought against his own body and forced himself to stand. His hand gripped the wall to stay steady and he hunched over, but he stood.

"What—what do you—"

Rompell snapped his mouth shut. He knew exactly what Stiltsken meant, and it stung. Every laugh they shared, every moment he had confided in him, every time Stiltsken gave him an assuring nod, had driven to this end, with Stiltsken standing tall and Rompell fighting against collapse.

"I would rather not end things this way." Stiltsken pulled a metal vial from his pocket and tossed it to Rompell. "All I can offer is the same peaceful death Kaloman had."

All exhaustion burned away as rage rushed through Rompell. He shoved against the wall to gain momentum and launched himself toward Stiltsken. His former friend flicked his hand. The cell door swung out, slamming into Rompell's side. He stumbled back but charged again. Stiltsken stepped out and the iron door shut.

Rompell threw himself against it and pounded his fists. He cursed at Stiltsken, cried his innocence, and screamed his rage. His throat grew raw, his voice hoarse. He slumped to the ground, his jaw clenched and fists balled, plotting the many ways he would kill Stiltsken.

A second day in the stockade ended with Rompell lying on his cell floor, clutching the coins with his face on them, glaring at the vial. The jeers from today had been drowned out by his blood pulsing in his ears.

He should have seen the truth. From the moment he opened that blasted chest in the cavern, he should have been wiser. He shouldn't have trusted so much of his fate to one man.

A key clanked in the door and he sat up, waiting for his final meal. The door opened.

"You've only a few minutes," said the guard.

"Thank you," said Ferrab, his eldest brother, passing coins into the guard's hand.

Rompell's breath stilled as he stared at his brother. Ferrab either believed the lies or he had come to say goodbye. No matter the reason, it was good to see so familiar a face.

His heart jumped as Solvan followed Ferrab in, leading in their weeping mother. Her eyes were shut and she clung to Solvan's arm as he guided her. Rompell looked to her and his brothers, readying himself for their final goodbye.

Ferrab grabbed Rompell's elbow. "Can you stand?"

Rompell held onto his brother's shoulder as Ferrab pulled him up. "Stiltsken—He—"

"The rumor is he's secretly become Favay's consort in your absence," Ferrab said.

"I didn't see." Rompell clung to his brother's arm. "I should have—"

Solvan pulled the cloak off their mother. A jolt ran through Rompell as she transformed into a clay statue. Ferrab kept hold of him, stopping him from falling.

"We had Father's sorcerers make this as soon as we heard rumors you were accused of murdering Kaloman," Ferrab said. "With a drop of blood, it will be enchanted to look like you."

Rompell stared at his brothers. He had fulfilled his promises to Gathray, but he had barely spoken to his brothers since marrying Favay. Yet, here they stood, risking their lives for his.

"It will walk to the scaffolding and die in my place?" Rompell said.

Solvan nodded before pricking Rompell's finger with a needle. A drop of blood formed and Rompell touched the clay statue. The air rippled around it, as if weaves of light were untangling and then reforming. The clay changed from his mother's shape to his. Rompell stared as his own bruised and exhausted face came into full form.

"Mother, we must leave him," Ferrab said, loud enough for the guard to hear.

Solvan placed the cloak over Rompell's shoulders. The light shimmered and he felt energy wrap around him.

Pulling the hood over Rompell's head, Solvan said, "You need to weep. No guard is going to look twice at a grieving mother."

"Wait." Rompell let go of Ferrab and dropped to his knees. He gathered the coins and vial Stiltsken had left. The vial would prove useful once Rompell had the opportunity for revenge. The coins would remind him to never be so blindly trusting again.

With his dark souvenirs in his pocket, he held his hands out to his brothers. "I am ready."

They hefted him to his feet and helped him stumble out. It was not hard to bring tears as he pictured Stiltsken sitting close to Favay, whispering lies into her ear. He shook with anger but kept up the false-weeping as his brothers escorted him from the dungeon.

More gold in the palm of guards' hands and quiet statements of, "My mother thanks you," earned them a path to the servant's corridors.

Solvan grabbed a few baskets and handed one to Ferrab. To Rompell, he said, "Keep your head down and be silent."

It was an easy command to follow. Each step away from the dungeon seemed easier than the last. Ferrab and Solvan walked straight through the corridor as if on usual business. His own servants passed, hurrying to their next task. He hid behind his brothers, sure the servants would see through the disguise if they looked closer.

It was dusk as they exited near the stables. He tried not to stare at the palace grounds, thick with patrolling soldiers.

"There's our escape," Ferrab whispered.

He led them to an old nag hitched to a cart full of manure. Solvan scooped up a handful of dirt and poured water on it from his canteen. They each rubbed mud on our faces and arms. Ferrab passed the final bribe to the cart's driver, who walked away with a far heavier purse.

Ferrab climbed up to drive it while Solvan walked behind with a pitchfork.

The stink was terrible, but it kept the guards at a distance as they approached the gates. Rompell stared at the platform where the false version of himself would be executed in the morning. They needed to make it far by tonight.

"Traitor deserves it," a passing servant said. He touched his forehead and saluted the palace. "May the Empress live in peace."

Once past the palace's servant gates, Rompell let himself breathe. The foul stench of their cart, however, made him wish he had held his breath longer.

The cart seemed to crawl its way through Alqon. As full darkness came, they reached the outskirts where Rompell had left Hidaya. Tonight, however, the open space was filled with merchants and vendors set-up to make money off the execution.

They went past these tents and into the desert. At last, they came to a valley hidden between dunes where two men waited with five camels.

Ferrab helped Rompell from the cart and smacked the rear of the horse with a shout. It took a few more slaps before the horse went trotting off into the night, the cart wobbling behind it. Rompell stumbled before dropping onto the sand. He pulled off the cloak and rolled onto his back, staring up at the broad, open sky. A cool wind washed over him.

"We still have far to go." Solvan gripped Rompell's arm and helped him to his feet.

The two Gathrayan servants pushed Rompell onto a camel. With a whistle, Ferrab kicked his camel into a trot and led their small caravan deeper into the desert.

Rompell barely held his seat, even with the servants riding on either side of him, pushing him back into the center of the saddle. They stopped briefly for water at a well, far from prying eyes and then continued on the rest of the night.

The sun was high in the sky as they reached a small outpost. There were a few buildings, but most had collapsed. This outpost had been abandoned years before but had not been reclaimed by the desert yet.

They dismounted and the servants took the camels to the well for watering. Ferrab and Solvan helped Rompell into one of the abandoned buildings.

He lay on the ground and fell almost instantly asleep. The sun was high as he woke in the afternoon. Solvan led him to a washbasin and Rompell cleaned himself and dressed in the fresh clothes his brothers gave him.

As he stared into the water, Rompell could almost hear the drums announcing his execution. Alqon was too far away for him to truly hear, but the echo remained.

He was fortunate to be here and breathing. His brothers had risked much by saving him, but what came next? He was the rightful emperor and Stiltsken had to be punished.

Contemplating how to make this right, he stumbled back to his brothers. Ferrab handed him bread and dried meat. Rompell tore into the food and gulped from his canteen.

Once he finished eating, his brothers sat across from him, their faces grave.

"We are glad to keep you alive," Ferrab said, "but, we must consider your future."

"I've been thinking as well." Rompell leaned forward and drew a circle in the sand. "The King of Tarris has never liked Favay." He pointed to the right of the circle. "If we can gain him as an ally, then we can turn to—"

"There will be no allies." Ferrab took in a tired breath. "No revenge."

Rompell's fingers tightened into a fist as he stared at his brother. "We can't abandon the throne. If we stand together, we can show the truth to the other kingdoms. They will—"

"Even if the truth were known, no one would stand with you after what your armies did in the north." Solvan waved his hand. "Let them believe you are dead and go begin a new life."

Rompell kicked at the sand. "But, I am not dead. I am the Emperor. I should be—"

"You are dead." Solvan pointed at Rompell. "We saved you because you are our brother, and you kept your promises to Gathray. But, Rothgan XII has been defeated. Bury him, Rompell."

Rompell charged to his feet and Solvan did the same. Standing with his face near his brother's, he growled, "All we need are a few good allies."

"You burned any you could have had when your troops attacked the northern kingdoms."

Jabbing his finger into Solvan's chest, Rompell opened his mouth to retort. However, Ferrab rose and pushed them apart.

"Solvan and I have already agreed on your fate," Ferrab said. "I hope you will agree with it as well."

Rompell folded his arms and glared at his brothers. "You save me, and then what?"

Ferrab walked to their pile of belongings and picked up a satchel. Returning to Rompell, he opened it and handed it over.

Rompell's arms shook as he stared inside. There was a thin blanket, a hunting knife, a canteen, enough food for a day in the desert, and three bronze coins.

Tossing the satchel down, Rompell said, "These are the gifts of exile."

"Exile is more merciful than death," Ferrab said. "The emperor's seat is lost and there is no place for you in Gathray. Too many know your face. As a wanderer and exile, you have a chance to live."

"Wherever I go, they will know me."

Solvan picked up the satchel and held it out to Rompell. "No one will be looking for the face of a dead emperor in that of a beggar."

Rompell's chest heaved as he glared at the satchel. His brothers now sent him off alone, to be a vagrant in his own empire. There had to be a better path.

Looking into the eyes of his brothers, however, he could not see it.

Solvan set the satchel at Rompell's feet.

"We have given you your life but can do no more for you."

Ferrab stepped toward Rompell and pressed his hand to his shoulder. Rompell glared at him. Stiltsken had betrayed him. He was grateful to be breathing, but now his brothers abandoned him.

"I wish you could come home, but you cannot." Ferrab smiled sadly. "You must find a new life."

Rompell's gaze drifted from his brothers to the open dunes visible through the broken doorway. His mind returned to the night he had sent Hidaya into exile from the capitol. He had thought to go with her, to abandon everything he had worked toward, to betray Gathray.

But, he had done his duty, and here he stood.

She was out there, somewhere in the empire. By now, she was probably married and living on happily without him.

He had to find her, even if it took searching the whole of the empire. If he could find her and see her happy and at peace, then he would know he had made at least one right choice.

Bending down, he picked up the satchel. He looked to his brothers one last time. Ferrab embraced him and Solvan gave him a nod.

They stepped back and Rompell turned toward the desert.

Chapter 7

Adeline closed the gate behind her and looked up at the Bradford School, unchanged in the past eleven years. It had the same flowers in the windowsills and manicured rose bushes lining the walk leading to the angular main building, the newer wings spread out behind it. She liked the old building, despite the dim hallways and creaking pipes.

Her boots clacked on the scrubbed brickwork of the walkway leading to the front stairs. Rustling above was her only warning before Jack Kingston stepped around the corner of the roof. With a grin, he gave her a broad wave.

"Good morning, Miss Winkleston!"

She hurried her pace as he bounded down the ladder. She jumped as he popped up by her side, smelling of something acrid and rotting.

"It's a good, bright morning for Visiting Day, isn't it? I'd offer to carry your bag for you, but—" He held out his dirt-encrusted hands. "Been cleaning out the gutters. Found a dead squirrel stinking up one corner."

He wiped his hand on his dusty pants before trying to smooth his dark, unruly hair.

Adeline forced herself to keep from shaking her head. He was a pleasant enough young man, despite his constant layer of dirt and loose-fitting clothes. She even enjoyed their brief conversations when they ran into each other between evening classes at Primhurst Community College. However, their morning conversations at the

Bradford School always ran along the same inevitable pattern.

"A band from Willington is coming to play at McBriar's a week from Friday," he said as they walked up the front stairs. "There'll be good food and dancing. Might also be a brawl or two to keep things interesting. If you'd like to join me, I can come get you at eight."

He kept his grin stretched across his face, though his eyes dreaded her reply.

"Thank you, Mr. Kingston," she said. "But I'm quite busy for the next few weeks."

"That's all right." He shrugged. "How about breakfast sometime? There's a bakery down—"

Reaching the door, she said, "I really should be getting inside."

"Of course, miss." He opened the door for her. "Always a busy morning on Visiting Day."

Adeline escaped into the school and hung her jacket in her classroom. Since starting college the year before, she had gone out with a few men like Jack. Sitting across from them at old, scratched tables in a dance hall, she would look at their calloused hands and remember her mother's hands after a day of scrubbing other people's floors. It was a life Rompell had helped Adeline put behind her. These were nice young men, but she could never fall in love with a man who cleaned gutters for a living.

On the other hand, there were the men she met at lectures and galas with Serena. They were all named something like Hubert or Humphrey and had growing fortunes and fine motorcars. Most of them were bores without a spark of wit. There might be a hero among them, but her doubts were growing.

All she wanted was a man of charm and handsomeness to appear. He would sweep her heart away just as her father had her mother's. Such a wonderful romance was worth waiting for.

With her classroom already gleaming from yesterday's polishing, Adeline walked upstairs to the dorms. Stepping onto the third floor, she was grateful again to have been brought home by Rompell. Having her own room, and the freedom that came with it, was far better than this stuffy space.

Today, the hallway felt brighter as girls chatted and giggled, springing in and out of rooms as they put on their best uniforms and did their hair.

A hand pulled on her skirt. The eight-year-old Suzie Magdale grinned up at her and pointed at a gap in her mouth.

"Miss Winkleston," the girl said, each "s" whistling through her teeth. "Look! I get a wish, don't I?"

Adeline squatted down and furrowed her brow as she looked into the gap. "How remarkable! You must have been very brave when it came out."

Suzie held out her hand still holding the tooth. "I'm going to hide it so my fairy godmother can find my wish."

"Very good." Adeline smiled and squeezed Suzie's other hand. "Shouldn't you be dressed first, though?"

Suzie giggled as she pounded her way back to her room. Adeline rose and began shepherding girls to their rooms. Silence waved down the hall, the giggling snuffing out as Mrs. Hunter marched through the hallway. Adeline wished the girls really understood the headmistress. If they did, they would not be so afraid.

"Miss Winkleston, thank you for coming early." She paused to give a stern glance to a girl still in her underdress. The girl scurried back into her room. "I must check on the refreshments. Can you handle all of this?"

She twirled her hand, gesturing at the doors.

"They will be ready on time," Adeline said.

Stepping closer, Mrs. Hunter said, "Do check on Miss Appleton. I think the girls have swamped her again."

Adeline stifled a laugh and tried to match Mrs. Hunter's serious expression. Once Mrs. Hunter left the hall, Adeline walked along and rapped on the doors.

"Come along girls. Time to look your best."

A series of huffing and a girl's cry of pain led her to Miss Appleton.

"If you would only put your curlers in properly!"

Adeline stepped into the bedroom where Miss Appleton was trying to unsnarl a hair brush tangled in a girl's hair.

"I can take care of it, if you like," Adeline said.

Miss Appleton huffed and stepped back from the teary-eyed girl. "I don't know how some of our girls will grow up into ladies."

The ten-year-old broke into heavier tears. Adeline let Miss Appleton stomp out before gently shutting the door.

"What was your name, again?" Adeline said as she stood behind the girl.

"Lily Fairchild, Miss Winkleston," the girl said.

Leaning close, Adeline whispered, "Close your eyes, Lily, and your hair will fix itself."

The girl glanced at Adeline before shutting her eyes. Adeline gently stroked the girl's hair and hummed a song, sending wisps made of light along Lily's strands of hair. Other girls in Mrs. Hunter's magic class had taught Adeline this when she had gotten a hard candy stuck in her hair once.

The magic unraveled Lily's naturally tight curls and pulled them into perfect ringlets. Once the hair settled, Adeline pinned a portion with a barrette and tied a ribbon to pull back the rest.

"Look in the mirror," Adeline said.

Lily opened her eyes and gasped with delight. She hugged Adeline. "It's so beautiful."

Kneeling down, Adeline said, "You are a beautiful girl. Your hair can look almost like this every day, if you did your curlers as Miss Appleton asked."

"But she's an old grump."

Adeline laughed, but then pressed her lips together. "She can still teach you a few things."

"Is this how you keep your hair so pretty?"

Adeline smiled kindly. "It is, though I have a few other tricks."

Lily did show some promise with magic, but Mrs. Hunter said there needed to be a few more tests before adding her to the secret classes. If a girl did not have enough power to endanger herself, Mrs. Hunter felt it better not to intervene. She claimed it was better to not have the burden of knowing.

Adeline watched Lily join her friends down the hall. Part of her wished she could be so free and light, to forget her own power. There were a few handy tricks but keeping everything hidden was often tiring. Sometimes, she could feel her power building within her like water pressing against a dam. In those moments, she used the exercises Mrs. Hunter had shown her to slowly release the energy. Days were easier when she could just keep her magic restrained and tried to pretend it did not exist.

Soon the girls were assembled downstairs and the whirlwind of Visiting Day reached its full force. Adeline preferred her days as a girl, when Rompell excused her from most Visiting Days. They would go sailing, to the dragon races, a play, or anything other than the mad press of parents attempting to demonstrate the grandness of their own daughter.

For the boarding girls, however, these monthly visiting days were the only time they saw their parents. She would help them make the best of it.

Even though it was the end of her first year as an instructor, standing among her former teachers was strange. Still, she kept her polished smile and elegant posture under the endless barrage of parents' questions.

"Yes, I am a recent graduate."

"But what kind of certification do you have?"

"I spent the year after graduation studying at the local college. This year, I am taking evening classes while working as an assistant instructor."

When it came to her subjects, basic mathematics and science, some fathers would puff up their chests and say, "But doesn't that muddle with the girl's brain? I can hardly keep my own ones and zeroes straight."

"Part of being a Bradford Girl is understanding how the world works. Our girls are quite successful." Adeline did not mention that Mrs. Hunter believed understanding math and science of things made the girls with magic better able to handle their power.

"I hear you're assisting Mrs. Hunter's private class. Why isn't my daughter a student?"

Giving the answer Mrs. Hunter had drilled into her for the past few weeks, Adeline said, "The girls in the class have certain talents which need nurturing. Your daughter is a wonderful girl and has shown great promise in the choir."

The talent rotated depending on which girl was spoken of. Most parents would huff and then say, "She really is so talented, isn't she?"

At last, the recital began and the parents moved to creaking chairs in the assembly hall. They sat with proud smiles as the different age groups shared their plays, poems, and songs. Adeline stood in the rear doorway and took a moment to blow air in her cheeks and flex her jaw. She never expected smiling to cramp so many muscles in her face.

Mrs. Hunter held her skirt with one hand as she walked to Adeline. "Some of the board members asked me to a meeting this afternoon. Can you manage our class today?"

Adeline nodded. It was not her first time, but she always felt nervous as she guided the girls through basic spells.

Touching Adeline's shoulder, Mrs. Hunter said, "You've done well today. Few of my new instructors have mastered talking with parents so easily."

Adeline found herself smiling. Mrs. Hunter never gave

compliments unless she meant them.

"Thank you. Though, I much prefer the girls," Adeline said.

"Ah, yes, but the girls do not write the checks which keep our doors open."

The recital ended and Mrs. Hunter stepped in front of the assembly hall. She spoke of progress the whole school had made, of statistics and figures, and the occupations and marriages of Bradford School graduates.

At the closing reception, parents stood with refreshments in hand as they chatted with their girls. Adeline held her vigilant smile, even as a rotund widower said, "My daughter speaks highly of you, Miss Winkleston. Very highly."

He set his thumbs in his suspenders, displaying his gold watch chain and making sure to brush his gold cufflinks. Adeline could only stare at his mustache that would complement a terrier.

"I would be honored if you joined me for dinner tomorrow, to speak of how fine a girl Abigail is."

Adeline was grateful to say honestly, "Thank you, sir, but I am busy with classes."

He forced a chortle. "Well, one evening off may do you some good." He absently rubbed his hand along the girth of his stomach. "It's no good working too hard. Stress will get us all, if we're not careful."

"I really cannot spare the time," she said.

He walked away, but two other widowers made their approach. They seemed to think her role as an instructor made her more inclined toward men with wealth and children. Only one was respectable looking, but he was at least fifteen years older than her. She was relieved a little when a hefty-bosomed mother pinned her in the corner and gave a lecture on the fair treatment of her daughter as the star pupil. Adeline nodded and put on her concerned face, letting the woman carry on.

At last, the morning ended, the parents left, and classes resumed.

The afternoon went by swiftly, despite the girls being chattier than usual, and the day girls were sent home. As the boarders went outside for some exercise in the fresh air, Adeline tidied up her classroom and set aside her graded papers.

Pulling on her hat, she checked her reflection in the nearest window. As she adjusted the tilt of her hat, she tried to remember who she had promised to go on an evening with next. There had been so many invitations from men worthy of interest, especially with her college classes ending last week.

Opening her pocket calendar, her eyes widened. There was even one tonight.

Squinting, she tried to decipher the scribble. His name was either Daniel or Mitchell. The faces of a dozen young men rushed through her mind, but she couldn't remember which he was.

The classroom door slammed open, breaking her concentration. Two girls tumbled in, gasping in breath.

"Miss Winkleston, Bridget—she's on the roof," the taller girl said while the other sobbed.

The two nine-year-olds started to yammer through an explanation. Adeline's mouth clamped shut. Bridget was in Mrs. Hunter's magic class and Adeline had just tutored her on levitating teacups. Apparently, Bridget had decided to climb the school house with the help of her magic.

Forcing a smile, Adeline gave their shoulders a warm squeeze. "Everything's going to be all right."

She hurried into the hallway and turned toward Mrs. Hunter's office.

The headmistress was gone at meetings. Biting back her worry, she ran toward the back door leading to the grounds. Her feet slipped on the tiled floor as she stopped by the assembly hall.

Jack stood on his ladder, whistling as he lowered the banners from

Visiting Day.

"Mr. Kingston!" she said.

He jolted back, nearly falling from the ladder. Grabbing on with both arms, he looked at her.

"We need your help. A girl's on the roof."

Jack gave her a firm nod as he steadied his feet on the ladder. "I'll be right out."

Adeline ran out to the back porch. Miss Appleton stood on the other end of the lawn, shrieking at several girls somersaulting, ignorant of the crowd of girls standing in terror beside the school house. On the roof, Bridget clung to a chimney, her boots slipping against the shingles.

"Step away, girls." Adeline tried to summon all of Mrs. Hunter's commanding presence as she waved the girls back. Bridget's face was red and tears poured down her cheeks. Adeline's lips pursed and she began to raise her hand. If it were just her and the girl, a quick spell would help the girl float down to safety. However, in front of this crowd, Adeline could do nothing so visible.

Jack ran past her, carrying a long ladder and a rope on his shoulder. The girls moved back as he ratcheted up the ladder. The top ended just above the second story's rail gutter, almost a body length below Bridget.

Adeline was glad the girl hadn't decided to climb the three-story West Hall.

Jack's foot pressed to the bottom rung. Adeline touched his shoulder.

"I'll go up."

"It's dangerous, Miss." He gave her a false smile. "Besides, I've been looking for a chance to be a hero."

Adeline forced herself not to groan. "She doesn't know you and I can't catch her if she falls."

Jack glanced up before holding out a rope. "Toss the rope around the chimney and have her pull the loop under her shoulders. I'll hold onto the end and lower her down."

Adeline looped the rope around her shoulders and began to climb. Her heeled boots were unsteady on the rungs, but she pushed on. Each step set her heart beating faster. She kept her eyes on Bridget, forcing herself to focus.

"Stay still," she said. "I'm coming."

She climbed, keeping her voice calm as she talked to the girl. Once at the top, she tossed the rope and whistled. With the spark of magic, she looped the rope around the chimney.

"Just pull the loop under your arms and Mr. Kingston will lower you down," she said.

"I can't." Bridget panted, her fingers white as they clung to the brick. "I'll fall."

"Everything's going to be fine. I'm right here." Adeline stayed with the top rung of the ladder at her waist and stretched her arm up. Her hand was still several inches below Bridget's feet. "Put on the loop and slide down to me."

"I—I just wanted to see how high I could go." The girl hiccupped.

The ladder shook as Adeline pressed her hands to the roof and climbed till her feet were on the top rung.

"Miss Winkleston," Jack shouted. "I can't catch both of you."

Adeline ignored him as she stretched across the roof. She grunted just before placing her hand on Bridget's foot. Her heart battered at her ribcage. However, she had to calm the girl before they could get to safety.

"I'm right here," Adeline said. "Do you remember the spell you used to get up here?"

Bridget shook her head.

"I'll hum it with you to help you stay in place while you put the rope on."

Adeline coached Bridget through a few calming breaths. Bridget shouted as she slipped. Adeline sang out a note and stopped Bridget's fall.

She held out her hand, keeping the spell in place. "See? I've got you."

With a bit more coaching, Bridget pulled the loop on, one arm at a time.

"Mr. Kingston has hold of you. All you have to do is let go."

The girl shook her head.

"I'm right here. You're not going to fall. Let go on the count of three."

Adeline counted, taking a deep breath between each number. At "three", Bridget released her hold. She screamed as she slid down the roof. Adeline quietly sang a spell. She stopped as the rope went taut and Jack lowered Bridget safely to the ground.

Turning to scout her way back down the ladder, Adeline glanced below to check on Bridget. Her heart jolted at the long distance between her and the crowd of girls below. She forced herself to take some calming breaths.

The air caught in her throat as a man astride a white horse rode onto the grounds and stopped behind the girls. He was handsome, with dark, thick hair and the solid build of a classic hero. Adeline would have been quite happy to meet such a man when not clinging to the sloped roof of the Bradford School.

"Jack, how can I help?" The man guided his horse around the girls.

"Bronhart? What are you—?" Jack nodded toward the ladder. "Can you help Miss Winkleston?"

Bronhart dismounted his horse and ran to the ladder. Gripping the sides, he said, "I've got it steady, miss."

Adeline held back her questions of how this gentleman knew Jack as she scooted down the first few rungs, the ladder shaking with each step. Her waist was just below the top rung as her skirt went taut. Her cheeks went pink as she glanced at where her skirt was caught on a nail sticking out from the gutter.

She bit her lip. Her skirt must have snagged as she scooted back to the ladder. And now the handsome stranger had an unfortunately clear view of her undergarments.

Smoothing her petticoat, to hide what she could, she forced her face to be calm despite the rising warmth. She rubbed her fingers together as she considered a spell. She had already risked enough exposure with Bridget and certainly couldn't risk Bronhart noticing the magic. Just a tug or two would get her skirt loose.

She pulled with one hand, but the skirt stuck fast. Leaning against the ladder and rising on her toes, she stretched out her other hand to pull.

"Be careful, Miss Winkleston!" Jack called.

She tugged harder. As her skirt came loose, she jerked back. She tried to grab the ladder, but it was too late.

Her stomach lurched as she fell. She tried to remember any spell, but the thundering in her chest drowned out her thoughts. The girls screamed and Bronhart shouted, "Out of the way!"

She gasped as he caught her. The force of her landing knocked him over and they both tumbled to the ground. She lay, her whole body shaking. Panting, she flexed her fingers and toes. There were some aches, but she seemed intact.

The group of girls circled Bronhart and her, chatting in hushed whispers, their eyes wide. Several older girls stared at Bronhart as they covered their mouths to hide their giggles.

Adeline rolled onto her knees and stared at where her hat had fallen, the brim crushed. She was fortunate to not be so broken. Bronhart knelt beside her and offered his hand. Glancing into his brown eyes, the rest of her breath left her. She placed her palm on his and he helped her stand.

Keeping her hand in his, he smiled. "Nathaniel Bronhart, miss."

"Adeline Winkleston." She wasn't sure if the heat in her cheeks was from the excitement or the flutter in her chest. "Thank you."

"I'm happy to see you safe." He let go of her hand and motioned toward where Bridget clung to Jack's arm. "I'm sure the girl needs you."

She forced herself to step away from him. Bridget ran to her and Adeline put her arms around the girl. The child sobbed as she clung to Adeline.

"Ladies, you've had enough excitement for the afternoon." Mrs. Hunter's voice cut through the chatter as she marched across the lawn. "Inside."

The girls hurried into the boarding house. Mrs. Hunter snapped to Miss Appleton and said, "Tell the cook to prepare some tea."

Bridget clung tighter to Adeline as Mrs. Hunter approached. The headmistress squatted beside Bridget and gently pulled her from Adeline.

"I didn't mean to use—" she said with a sob.

"I hope you've learned some wisdom today." Mrs. Hunter dabbed Bridget's cheeks with a handkerchief. She cupped Bridget's chin. "A Bradford Girl faces challenges with courage and calm. Miss Winkleston demonstrated that quite well today." She lowered her hand. "Please make sure you don't give her another opportunity."

Standing, she said, "Inside, please."

Adeline glanced at Mrs. Hunter, surprised at the lack of a stern lecture. She had received enough of her own as a child.

Bridget seemed equally surprised as she backed away. Realizing she was free, she ran to follow the other girls. Her friends hugged her as they went into the school.

With the girl dismissed, Mrs. Hunter turned toward Mr. Bronhart.

Before she could speak, Jack stepped forward and pumped the man's hand. "Bronhart, I'm glad you stopped by. I didn't know what I'd do if Miss Winkleston fell."

"Mr. Kingston, how do you know this man?" Mrs. Hunter said.

"He works with my brother, Henry."

Adeline stared at Bronhart in his fine-tailored suit and riding boots. She tried to remember any mention of what Jack's brother did for a living. This man certainly wasn't a groundskeeper.

"And you happened to be riding by?" Mrs. Hunter appraised Bronhart with a quick glance.

"Henry's flu turned worse this afternoon. I tricked him into going to the doctor and he's been sent home." Bronhart held out a note to Jack. "There's the list of medicine. Doctor said he'd be all right with a day or two of rest."

"I'll have to tie him to the bed." Jack took the note and nodded to Bronhart. "Thank you."

He turned to Mrs. Hunter. She waved her hand. "Go take care of your brother. I'll expect you to be here early tomorrow to finish today's work."

"Yes ma'am. Thank you. I—" Jack turned to go and Bronhart held out the reins of his horse.

"Ride it back to the office stables. That'll take you closer to home," he said. "I can take the trolley."

Jack nodded his thanks as he lightly mounted the horse and took the reins. His riding posture and command of the horse were better than Adeline expected. With a few clicks of his tongue, he trotted off the grounds.

Adeline's gaze turned to the tall stranger who had rescued her and now helped Jack. Her lips pressed together, wanting to speak to him, but her words were lost. Especially with Mrs. Hunter standing so close.

"If you'll excuse me," Mrs. Hunter said, giving Adeline a quick glance, "I must check on the girls. Miss Winkleston, why don't you go home and get some rest?"

"I'm done for the day." Bronhart's words toppled over each other. He pulled his coat straight and said more calmly, "I can escort you home, miss, if you wish."

The hint of a smile flinched near the corner of Mrs. Hunter's mouth but was gone before Adeline could be sure. The headmistress turned and walked to the school as if she had heard nothing.

Adeline had to unpin her tongue from the roof of her mouth before saying, "I would be very grateful."

His smile broadened and she found herself giving her own smile. He waited at the front steps as she gathered her purse from the classroom. Once she returned, he offered his arm.

With her arm on his, they walked from the grounds and strolled down the street. She wasn't sure if his steps were slow to lengthen the walk or due to concern over the fall she had taken.

They took the electric trolley and chatted as they passed down streets. The conversation came easily as she grinned at him, taking in the warmth of his eyes and the strong line of his jaw beneath his dark, well-trimmed beard.

As they strolled down Nightingale Lane, slowly approaching her front door, he said, "Expanding the minds of youth must be rewarding work."

"I suppose. They are sweet girls."

"I am sure they learn such things from their teacher."

She stifled a giggle as she blushed. "And, what do you do?"

"Nothing so noble. I am an account manager for Mackabee and Sons, the accounting firm."

"Oh." She had expected a man of his physique to have a more adventurous occupation.

"It is good, steady work," he said, "but it is not my passion."

"And, what is that?"

He grinned. "A great secret."

She looked at him, wondering what secrets such a man could have. If he had magic, he would not mention it so casually, yet a part of her wished he did. It would make things much simpler.

He leaned closer to her and said, "If you are free Saturday morning around nine, I will show you."

"Yes," she said.

She wasn't free yet, but she would be once she sent a note to the fellow she was supposed to go out with.

"I recommend wearing riding clothes." He wrote the time on his calling card. "It is not for the faint of heart, mind you."

"I suppose I can be brave." She tucked the card into her purse.

He laughed. Her cheeks warmed as their eyes met and he leaned closer to her. A few men had stolen a kiss on her cheek, but none on her lips. This close to Bronhart, her lips pulsed. His eyes seemed to trace her face and her heartbeat thudded in her ears.

"Good afternoon," came Rompell's voice from behind them.

Adeline jumped, her head knocking against Bronhart's. Her cheeks had to be full crimson. Keeping her head down, she turned to face her father. Her cheeks burned even more as she realized Rompell stood at the waist-high picket fence that she and Bronhart had just walked past.

"Papa," she said, motioning toward her companion. "This is Nathaniel Bronhart. Mr. Bronhart, this is my father, Rompell. He—I—" Her tongue and brain seemed to disconnect.

Bronhart stepped forward and offered his hand. "Pleased to meet you, sir."

Her father bore a thin smile as he gave Bronhart's hand a firm shake. Adeline wished she could send her father inside so she could try to rekindle the lost moment.

"I will leave your daughter in your care, sir," Bronhart said. Adeline leaned against the fence, all brightness of the moment fading. "She is a remarkable young woman."

Turning to her, he grinned and said, "Good evening, Miss Winkleston. I will see you Saturday morning."

"Of course." Her own smile spread. She could hardly contain her sigh as his tall figure disappeared around the corner.

"Papa, you will not believe what has happened today." She pressed her hands to the fence and leaned toward Rompell.

Glancing down the street as he opened the gate, he said, "I do not know how it has happened, but I am sure of *what* has happened."

They walked into the house as she repeated the events from the afternoon, starting with the girls coming in her room. When she told of falling off the roof, she flopped onto the couch.

"He caught me, as if I weighed nothing."

She broke into giggles. Rompell stood with his hands resting on his hips, nearly holding a raised eyebrow in check. Sitting up, she said, "He is so handsome. And a gentleman and—"

"And you will see him Saturday morning," he said.

She dropped her hands into her lap. "I know I just met him, but—"

"You are a grown woman, Adeline, and can judge men for yourself. Just be careful to not let your infatuation run too hot too quickly. If he is a worthwhile man, it may be wise to take things slower than you wish."

She took his gloved hand as she smiled. "When I saw him, it was like how you spoke of first seeing Hidaya, where it is as if life has just begun."

Rompell sat down next to her. "What I first felt for Hidaya was nothing compared to what it became." He brushed back the hair from her brow. "Do not seek such love yet. Not until you truly know a man. Once it is right, you will know."

The doorbell rang, its brassy burr echoing around them.

Adeline shot up and ran to the door. She glanced through the peephole and gasped. Her evening's date was a half-hour early. She held a hand over her mouth as she stepped back. How could she go out with anyone after the afternoon with Bronhart?

Rompell looked through the peephole before pressing his gloved fingers to her chin and giving her a mock-frown. "You look quite ill, Little One."

Her shoulders drooping, Adeline said, "I feel fine, Papa."

Rompell touched the back of his gloved hand to her forehead. "It seems your walk with Mr. Bronhart has left you with a terrible fever."

She bit her lip to keep from giggling. "I do think I am ill. Thank you."

"Such poor news for this young man." He waved his hand. "Go on into the kitchen. I'll send him off."

She grinned as she kissed his cheek. "Thank you, Papa."

He squeezed her hand. "For you, Little One, I would do anything."

Chapter 8

Friday night, Adeline cancelled her evening out and, instead, spent hours with Serena guessing what Bronhart's surprise would be. Both were proved wrong Saturday morning as Bronhart grinned and led Adeline to the stables behind the dragon racing stadium.

Many times, she had sat among the bleachers watching the fierce creatures in flight, the dragon jockeys performing grand twirls and dives as they fought for the lead. Mrs. Hunter always warned her to be careful at the dragon races, for dragons were sensitive to magic and behaved erratically. Even when the stables were open for the public, she had never come.

Her heart quickened as Bronhart led her between the dim stalls, the air reeking of sulphuric manure.

"Pardon the smell," Bronhart said. "It will be worth it."

He greeted a few of the stable hands as he led her past the dragons resting in their stalls.

Adeline gripped his arm. Their diagonal pupils watched her as she passed, their heads following her movement. These were purebred razorback dragons, bred for speed. She had heard of dragons used for hunting and a few dragons used for pulling machines at factories. However, dragons were expensive and temperamental, making them challenging to manage for everyday use.

Up close, they were impressive, their scales sheening as their taut muscles moved. She just wished they would stop staring, their eyes following her and their nostrils sniffing. One made a clicking noise before snarling and ramming its head against the iron gate of its stall.

Adeline jumped back and Bronhart put his arm around her.

"They're gentler than they seem," Bronhart said. "This way."

He led her to a stony field behind the stables where several racing dragons lay lazily on their side, smoke curling up from their nostrils. Two of them raised their heads and watched her.

Bronhart whistled and the reddish-brown dragon rolled onto its feet with a deep grumble. A chill went down Adeline's spine as she stared at its horns and massive teeth. The creature walked over and sniffed the air, spitting out its long, black tongue.

Scratching under the dragon's chin, Bronhart said, "This is my boy, Timnoth."

She slowly smiled. She knew he had to be more than an account manager. "You're also a dragon jockey?"

"Only amateur. Won a few races in college, but nothing close to the professional leagues. As for Timnoth, he's a mixed breed and unsuited for the professional races. The razorback dragons are strong enough to fly a full half-hour, but he's only good for twenty minutes. Still, he provides a steady, smooth flight."

"Do you own him?"

Bronhart laughed. "No. My uncle's a trainer up in Willington. His friend owns him and lets me come ride now and then. Gives Timnoth some good exercise now that he's retired. He's getting a bit weak, poor old fellow."

Bronhart scratched behind Timnoth's horn, and the dragon flapped its foot as it stretched out one of its great wings. A grumbling purr rose from its throat.

"Would you like to ride him?"

Adeline's eyes widened as she stepped back. It would be exciting, but she had already fallen once this week. Yet, when would she have the chance again?

His smile faltered. "It's all right if you don't."

"I will do it." She gave a sharp nod, partially to bring up her own courage.

Bronhart's grin broadened and he motioned toward the warehouse. "Let's get the gear first."

Glad she had worn her riding pants, as he had suggested, she helped carry out the chain bridle. Bronhart hefted out the saddle and placed it on Timnoth. Standing up close, the dragon was massive, rising one-and-a-half times the size of a horse. The creature clawed the ground and tossed his head as he waited.

"Dragons are misunderstood beasts," Bronhart said as he climbed up the ladder and dropped the saddle on Timnoth's back. "As long as you treat them well, they'll do the same to you."

He talked her through the purpose of each piece of equipment as he pulled it onto the dragon, finishing with the bridle. With all steps complete, he helped Adeline into a helmet and a jacket with padding. The jacket nearly wrapped around her twice. She belted it as best she could, using her shadow to measure her profile.

A flutter ran through her as his hands touched her waist and he helped her onto the dragon. Once seated, she could feel the strength of the dragon's muscles. Bronhart climbed up after her. Her cheeks flushed as his arms reached on either side of her. Timnoth tossed his head and stretched his wings.

"And now we ride," Bronhart breathed into her ear.

She gasped as they darted into the air. The wind churned around them as the dragon flapped its mighty wings and they soared over Pippington. She held on tightly to the saddle as the air chilled her face. After a few broad swoops, she loosened, stretching her arms out as she laughed. Bronhart yanked back on the reins, keeping the dragon at a gentle pace. Adeline looked down at the city, watching the lines of familiar boulevards. It was a strange and beautiful sight.

Bronhart pulled them into a tight circle, Timnoth tilting sharply. Adeline slipped, her heart jolting with the drop. By instinct, she hummed a quick note and pushed her hand, sending a small wave of magic to center herself on the saddle.

Timnoth's head jerked up and he surged forward as if something had chomped at him. Adeline fell back against Bronhart. She grabbed the saddle and shut her eyes. Bronhart shouted and pulled hard on the reigns, kicking his heels into the dragon's sides. Timnoth's tail snapped and he bellowed out a roar. He swerved and dipped, his movement erratic, smoke rising out of his nostrils. His back arched as he bucked. Adeline shouted as her fingers dug in harder on the saddle. His flapping slowed and they dove toward the ground.

Adeline thought through spells. There were girls in the secret Bradford School classes who had talent with animals. She had little, but she had to try something.

Forcing her hand to unclench, she pressed it against Timnoth's rough scales. She hummed a low note, remembering the calming spell Mrs. Hunter had taught her. It worked on sobbing children. She doubted it would work on a dragon but had to try.

Timnoth's neck straightened out and his body soon followed, the beast returning to proper flight formation.

"There you are," Bronhart said, rubbing Timnoth's side. "Good boy."

He led the dragon in a few gentle circles as they returned to the open ground near the stables. Timnoth landed with the lightness of a sparrow. Adeline's jaw unclenched as Bronhart helped her onto the waiting stepladder. Her legs wobbled as she stepped onto the gravel and she bent over as she breathed. Timnoth twisted his long neck and pressed his face close to hers, his yellow eyes seeming to seek command.

"Back off now." Bronhart pushed Timnoth's head back. "You frightened the lady enough today."

Adeline pulled the oversized jacket tighter around herself as she glanced at the dragons chained to the side, waiting for their flights. All of them stared at her more intently than before.

"I need some air." The words barely wheezed out of her mouth.

Bronhart unclasped her helmet and pulled it off.

"I'm sorry. He's never done that—"

"I need to go." She unbuckled the belt and pulled off the jacket. Bronhart's pained eyes watched her and his lips moved as he tried to find words. "I'll wait outside."

She sprinted out through the stable. The dragons raised their heads as she passed, grunting and grumbling as they stretched toward her. She pushed herself faster, barely dodging around one of the stable hands.

Once outside, she gasped in breath and took in the less-sulphuric air. She leaned against the wall and dropped to the ground, pulling her knees to her chest. Resting her head on her arms, her throat clenched and tears came.

It had been a beautiful ride, but her magic had ruined it.

Now Bronhart would feel guilty and she could explain nothing. If only she could shed her powers and be free. Being able to easily fix her hair or do some tricks wasn't worth moments like this.

Bronhart pounded out of the stable. Panting, his hair messed from pulling off the helmet, he knelt beside her. She raised her head. The worry in his brown eyes warmed her but didn't break the knot pinching at her throat.

"If I had known he'd go wild, I never would have taken you up." He held out a handkerchief. "Are you—"

He offered his other hand. "If you can forgive me, perhaps we can go on a simple walk." His soft smile eased the tightness in her chest. "There's far less risk in falling."

She did her best to return his smile, to ease the guilt he should not have. It was a weak attempt, but his eyes relaxed. She took his hand and they rose. As he took her arm, his hand clasped around hers. A true smile broke through and she leaned close to him as they stepped out to the street.

Rompell strode past the bleachers where citizens of Pippington watched the Surris Rangers in their rodeo showcase. The riders swung their lassos and their horses went through barrel races and parading routines. Every year, they came and performed, allowing them to be seen in public. It was an excellent cover for their true work of tracking and capturing magic criminals.

When it came to Westengaard, it seemed they were better at the tracking than the capturing.

Entering the tin shed at the edge of the arena, Rompell wished they would capture the man already. Then he could forget about the past and focus on his quiet life with Adeline. There were no political maneuvers, no scheming and lying, no empty alliances. Everything was supporting his daughter, managing his properties full of widows and the less privileged, and enjoying the quiet community of his neighborhood.

It was a simple life and the Surris Rangers' incompetence could ruin it at any moment.

Seeing Rompell, Ed Callais tipped back his wide hat with an upturned brim and let out a huff. The air blew the whiskers on his large, white mustache.

Rompell dropped a newspaper on the desk between them. He stabbed his gloved finger at the photograph of Westengaard.

"It's been three years," he said, "and he's still here. Last year, you said the Culparr Mines were almost repaired."

Rising from his chair, Ed rested his thumbs in his decorated leather belt, the embellishments punctuated by a large belt buckle engraved with a flying dragon. "Mr. Rompell, most folks say hello before they start shouting."

Rompell glared. There was no need to waste time on politeness.

"You met us thirteen years ago at the port here in Barthan,"

Rompell said. "You escorted us to the Surris Mountains. You know who he is and what he is capable of." His gloved fist pounded against the table. "Why is he still free?"

"How many times do I have to tell you? He's a warlock. He's had a long time to twist magic around him. We've got to be careful. If we use a normal spell against him, he can pull in that power. That'll be no good."

"So, you keep doing nothing?" Rompell leaned forward. In every meeting, Ed used these excuses.

"We've still got eyes on him." Ed folded his arms. "And, I'll tell you this again: he's still got the magic shackles we put on him in the Culparr Mines. He's weak and we've got a few tricks of our own to keep him that way."

Rompell's cheek twitched as he glared. He couldn't believe he had to repeat, "He almost conquered an empire."

"I know plenty about what he's done." Ed pointed at Rompell. "You handed him over to us. You've got to trust us."

"And what will you do when he moves to conquer Barthan?"

"He'll be stopped." Ed gave Rompell a nod. "We've got eyes on him. Inspector McCay's squad is watching him, and you can bet Madame Blue's keeping a close watch herself."

"And you trust Madame Blue?" Rompell raised an eyebrow. Almost every trace of dark magic or magic used for deception or theft in Pippington could be traced to Madame Blue's network. Mrs. Hunter and others with magic worked hard to avoid her attention.

"No one's stupid enough to trust Madame Blue." Ed pointed at Rompell. "But, you can bet she'll not let him interrupt her business."

Rompell thought about asking how Ed could be sure but shook his head instead. He took a breath before saying, "And what of the young woman you say he kidnaped?"

This young woman was part of the excuse Ed and the Rangers always used. Once they trapped Westengaard, there was little chance of finding her. Rompell was sure she was locked away somewhere, transformed into a statue or something else. Transformations were usually temporary because things want to return to their original form. It didn't work for all spells, but it did for most. If Westengaard had the girl trapped, much of his power had to be tied to keeping the spell stable.

Ed lowered his head as he fidgeted with his belt loops. "We're still watching for her but haven't seen a hint for years." Raising his eyes to meet Rompell's, he said, "If it came down to her or Barthan, we'd save our nation, but we're still looking for her."

Rompell stood straight, his hands relaxing at his side. If it were a weaker magic user, he would seek the girl and help. Westengaard, however, could have no sign Rompell was here. The moment he knew of Adeline, she would be in danger. Rompell would not sacrifice her to help this unknown young woman.

"Tell me immediately if he breaks free of the remaining spells." Rompell rubbed his fingers together, feeling the thin leather hiding his curse. "I will do whatever is needed to help you stop him."

"We'll get him all locked up again soon enough." Ed nodded to Rompell. "I've given you my word and I aim to keep it."

Rompell kept Ed's gaze and returned the nod.

They were not friends, but he trusted the man to do what he could. It was not enough, but Rompell had to be careful. He had few other allies who knew of magic. Most were like Mrs. Hunter, working to protect those with magic and help them learn how to manage their powers. He couldn't call on school teachers and charity workers to fight Westengaard. Ed and the Surris Riders were the best he had in this ignorant nation.

Chapter 9

Adeline twirled the end of her scarf as the three advanced girls tried to use magic to raise water out of their glasses. They groaned each time the orb lost shape and splattered apart. She stood back, letting them fail as Mrs. Hunter had instructed her to.

Leaning her head against the wall, she thought of the night before, sitting close beside Bronhart as he told her of growing up in Willington, Barthan's capitol. The gray buildings and busy streets took on a warmth as Bronhart spoke of his childhood home. She could have listened to him all night if Rompell hadn't walked into the sitting room and said, "It's late."

Her face grew warm as she remembered standing on the porch, answering, "Yes," to his invitation for dinner on Wednesday. He turned to leave, but stopped, his brown eyes looking into hers. Her heart thudded as he leaned close and pressed his lips to hers.

Though his beard tickled her chin, she drank in the moment. A thrill she had never experienced before ran through her and she leaned into him. He pulled away and gave her a broad grin before stepping out to the street.

Adeline had leaned against the doorway, her hand pressed to her breast, her heart following him as he left.

Standing in the classroom now, Adeline touched her fingers to her lips to hold back a set of giggles. There was so much to tell Serena tonight.

"Miss Winkleston, can you—"

"She can't hear you. She's too busy dreaming of the gentleman who rescued her last week."

"I saw him." The second girl giggled. "He is handsome."

"Have you kissed him yet?" the first girl said.

"I would have," the sixteen-year old said.

A burst of laughter followed.

Standing, she now understood part of Mrs. Hunter's coolness. It kept girls from asking such prying questions. She glanced at the girls not much younger than her and smiled.

Adeline was not Mrs. Hunter.

"He took me riding on a dragon," she said. "But if you want to know more, we must finish our exercises."

She hummed a few notes and used magic to gather the spilled water. The droplets formed an orb. The girls' eyes went wide as the orb rotated in the air. With a twist of her fingers and a few sung notes, Adeline split the orb into four and sent the water back to the glasses.

"Again," she said.

The rest of the lesson went well, with Adeline rewarding each successful attempt with another tidbit from her time with Bronhart. She hid the trouble on the dragons and her kiss, but gave enough for the girls to lean forward, their eyes wide as they listened.

Hopefully, they knew better than to tell Mrs. Hunter.

The afternoon was less exciting as Adeline led her regular class of younger girls through their multiplication tables. Her day ended by taking them to the greenhouse to check on the flowers they had potted. She quizzed them on leaves and how osmosis pulls water through the flower's roots. At the end of her lesson, she dismissed the girls for their afternoon playtime. She made sure to give Bridget a warning glance as the girls ran outside. Bridget ducked her head but smiled as Adeline gave her a quick wink.

She leaned against the planter and let out a breath. The girls were fun to teach, but each day left her exhausted.

A hiccup followed by a sniffle led her to a corner of the greenhouse. Lily sat holding her potted flower, the leaves turning yellow, the bud drooping.

Adeline squatted beside the girl and smiled. Taking the plant, she said, "Let me see if I can help it. You run along."

Lily returned her smile and ran to play with the other girls. Adeline carried the pot back to the table. Humming, she envisioned the water in the soil rising up the flower's roots and veins. A warm green light rose through the stem as the water passed through it, the flower perking up.

Something behind her crashed to the ground and Adeline jumped. She pivoted on her heel and stared at Jack, his mouth hanging open, his eyes bulging.

A coldness shot through her and she fumbled with the pot. Half the soil dropped on the ground as she shoved it onto the table. It slid into a few other pots, sending them crashing onto the ground. Adeline pressed a hand to her head.

Spade in hand, Jack scurried over and began scooping up dirt.

"Didn't mean to startle you, Miss." He grabbed several empty pots from under the table and delicately placed the flowers inside.

"What did you see?" Adeline whispered.

"Nothing unusual." His voice was higher-pitched than usual. "Just a—a glowing flower."

She bit her lip as she glanced at the door. At least all the girls were gone. "Please, Mr. Kingston, you cannot tell anyone."

He set the rescued flowers and their pots on the counter. "Why would I? I've never said anything about seeing Mrs. Hunter light a fire with the flick of her hand." He glanced at the door. "Nor that girl who floated past the window a few weeks ago."

Her eyebrows raised and she held back a moan. He wasn't supposed to know anything. He was just the part-time groundskeeper.

"Mrs. Hunter said it's just some new tricks with electricity." Jack looked at her, a hint of pleading in his eyes. "It is electricity, isn't it?"

"Yes." She nodded more sharply than she meant to. "Electricity. We've been doing experiments."

"Right." Jack scratched his head. "I'll keep things quiet. Don't you worry."

She forced a smile. "Thank you, Mr. Kingston."

"I'm sure the girls are waiting for you." He motioned toward the soil still on the floor. "I'll manage the rest here."

Taking his gift of an exit, she gave him a final thank you and hurried through the door. She nearly ran to her classroom where her hat and handbag waited.

She needed to be more careful. Saturday's disaster on Timnoth had come too close. Today, Jack had seen too much and might start asking questions. Taking several steadying breaths, she forced herself to slow her step.

The simplest solution was to act as if her magic didn't exist. She would break the habit of using magic for common, everyday things, and only use her magic in lessons. Then, she could relax when near Bronhart and simply be herself.

Bronhart rushed down the steps of Mackabee and Sons, leaving behind the tight grid of desks where financial clerks calculated fortunes, and headed toward Adeline's house on Nightingale Lane.

His work was steady and his commissions were good, but each day felt as if trapped in a dark box, surrounded by the scratch of fountain pens across paper.

His conversations with his friend Henry Kingston helped ease the monotony. Henry was a quiet, serious man, but his honest opinions eased the blustering and gloating of Bronhart's clients and of Mr.

Mackabee himself.

The past two-weeks had gone even more quickly as thoughts of Adeline filled his days.

He had been to dinner with many women, including debutantes covered in diamonds and jewelry. They batted their eyes and laughed as they tapped his shoulder with their fan, but their only interest was themselves. He kept his smile polite, trying to ignore their reeking vanity, and was glad when the evening ended.

With Adeline, everything was fresh and new. Her laugh was genuine and her smile pure. When they talked, her blue eyes looked into his and he almost lost his words. She listened and replied with intelligence, never mocking him. Sitting beside her, with her golden-blonde hair framing her face and resting on the soft curve of her neck, all he wanted was to take her in his arms and hold her close.

He enjoyed the moment they had broken propriety and their lips touched. Holding her close, he drank in her sweetness before dragging himself away. Whenever they parted, every step felt as if he was being stretched apart, half of his heart still with her on the doorstep.

However, between him and taking Adeline's hand forever stood the tall shadow of her father.

In the few nights he had visited for dinner, Rompell sat watching Bronhart, his polite smile doing nothing to soften the hardness in his eyes. Adeline had told Bronhart of Rompell rescuing her from death as an orphan in the snow and raising her as his own. He was a man Bronhart could respect but would be impossible to impress.

This thought slowed his steps as he walked up to Adeline's door on Nightingale Lane. His shirt was wet with sweat and his stomach twisted, but there was only one path to the future he wanted.

He clenched and unclenched his fists as he silently repeated the speech he had been planning in their few weeks of courtship. Tonight was a rare chance, while Adeline was out with Serena.

Straightening his shoulders, he muttered, "It must be done," and knocked on the door.

His heart thudded but he forced his breath to remain calm. The echo of Rompell's footsteps seemed deliberately slow. Bronhart kept his gaze steady as Rompell opened the door and gave him a cool glance.

"Adeline is out tonight with Serena," Rompell said. "I thought she told you."

"She did, sir." Bronhart pressed his hand to his side to keep it from shaking. "I wanted to speak with you alone, sir."

Rompell stepped aside, his arm gracefully motioning for Bronhart to enter. He led Bronhart past the sitting room and into the study. There was a narrow desk with several neat stacks of paper, a line of books on a shelf, and a landscape of some rolling, green hills. It was remarkably ordinary, as if the normality were an art itself.

Sitting, Rompell waved toward the chair across from him. Once seated, Bronhart tapped his foot on the ground and bounced his hat off his knee.

"What is your business tonight, Mr. Bronhart?"

Rompell leaned back in his chair, resting his chin on his gloved hand as he waited.

Bronhart set aside his hat and swallowed. He had proposed accounts to some of the wealthiest men and women in the city. None of their raised chins or diffident stares were as intimidating as Rompell's bored look.

"I think it is clear I care much for your daughter, sir." He attempted a smile but was sure it only appeared a wince. "I have only known her a short time, but—you see—" He forced out the final words, "I wish to ask for your daughter's hand in marriage."

He wasn't sure if the ticking clock or the beating pulse in his ears were louder as Rompell's face remained still. Those dark eyes bore through him, seeming to penetrate to his deeper thoughts.

"You are sure?" Rompell said at last.

"I have never been so sure of anything."

"And you don't want anything else?" Rompell raised an eyebrow. "Her arm, perhaps?"

Bronhart's teeth ground against each other. "Sir, I am serious."

"How can you be? How long have you known her?"

This was the question Bronhart had prepared for. Leaning forward, he said, "Only three weeks, but—"

"And in three weeks, you know her well enough to marry her?"

"I do. The moment I saw her, I loved her, and these past few weeks have deepened my attachment. Adeline—she is pure, beautiful, full of joy. There is no woman like her, sir."

"Adeline is an easy girl to love, and you are welcome to love her." Rompell leaned back in his chair. "You are respectably employed and a gentleman, despite a stolen kiss."

Bronhart's cheeks were warm, but he held his head high.

"I can imagine a future with you and Adeline happily married," Rompell said. "And can see myself approving of the match. However, at this moment, I cannot."

Rompell's final words pierced Bronhart. Gripping his armrest, he said, "What must I do to earn your approval?"

Rompell held up his index finger. "First, wait at least two months before asking me again. If you truly love her now, you can wait."

Bronhart started to smile. "I can do so, sir. I would wait seven years if I had to."

"Only a fool would wait seven years," Rompell said. The next finger rose. "Second, you must tell me which of Adeline's qualities makes her most unique."

"She has a beauty that—"

Rompell dropped his hand on the table. "Beauty is a common trait and can change."

"But, the kindness of her heart—"

"Kindness can be broken by bitterness."

Tapping his fingers on the armrest, Bronhart forced himself not to throw up his arm. This man was playing games with him. He had made an honest offer and deserved better. His love for Adeline and his ability to provide for her should be enough.

Still, he kept his voice level and said, "What quality are you looking for, sir?"

"Talk with Adeline. She will know what I mean."

"Whatever quality it is, it will not change my love for her."

"It had better not." Rompell tumbled a coin through his fingers, the piece of silver disappearing and reappearing. "We will meet here in two months, Mr. Bronhart."

The finality of Rompell's words sent Bronhart rising from his chair. He half-bowed to Rompell before striding toward the front door.

He was halfway across the sitting room when the door opened.

"I think I left my glove on the front—"

Adeline stopped as she saw Bronhart, her blue eyes wide.

He met her eyes and all the tenseness from talking with Rompell faded. Stepping closer, he said, "Good evening, Adeline. Your father and I were discussing your best qualities." He raised her hand and kissed it. She bit back a giggle as she blushed. "And which is your most unique one."

Watching her, he hoped she would let the secret slip. Her face, however, paled and her smile disappeared as she drew her hand away.

"And he told you?"

"Not yet. He said to ask you." He touched her arm. "Are you all right?"

"Just tired. It's been a long day. I—" She pulled at her one glove as she glanced at Serena. "I'm sorry, but I'm not feeling well."

"Perhaps I can—" Bronhart began.

"You did say you were tired, didn't you?" Serena said as she gave Bronhart a pointed glance. "We can always go out another night."

Adeline smiled and turned to Bronhart. "Could you help Serena to the car?"

He gave her a puzzled glance before nodding. Though he longed to stay, he suspected she knew why he was there and wanted to speak to her father alone. He kissed her cheek before offering his arm to Serena.

As he walked Serena to her parents' motorcar, he said, "What do you think makes Adeline most unique?"

Serena grinned. "She's a wonderful friend. And, quite clever."

Bronhart forced a smile. These were far from the qualities Rompell probably meant. It was a trick question, one he might never answer unless he could read Rompell's mind. If answering this question was all that stood between him and marrying Adeline, he would find the truth.

Clamping her hand on the glove that had drawn her home, Adeline glared at her father. The evening had been nearly perfect. She and Serena had sat close at dinner, Serena's eyes wide as she listened to the latest details of Adeline's romance with Bronhart. Though she hid her magic from Serena, she told her everything else.

Then, she had come home, and there stood Bronhart.

If Rompell were reasonable, he would have seen how true her and Bronhart's love was. In three weeks, it felt as if they had known each other for whole lifetimes. She was nineteen and a grown woman. She should be able to choose her future.

"Why was Nathaniel here?"

"No matter how old the daughter," Rompell said, "it is difficult for a father to give her hand to another."

An ache spread through Adeline's chest. "You told him no. Why, Papa?"

"I told him to wait," he said. "Two months is nothing in a whole lifetime."

She shook her head, a tightness filling her throat. "I love him, Papa." The first tear fell. "Two months will not change our hearts."

Rompell's eyes narrowed. "In a few weeks, you cannot know a man well enough to marry him. Marriage is about a lifetime. It should not be leapt into without careful consideration."

"I've thought it through."

Every day in the past week, when she should have been grading papers, she pictured her future as Mrs. Adeline Bronhart. It was a wonderful future, with a fine townhouse, evenings full of galas and dinner parties, and him always by her side. They would build a life together, him growing in his business while she built their society connections. All that was stopping her was Rompell's stubbornness.

"If you love him, I will not stand between you," Rompell said. "But, first, he must truly know you."

"He does know me. Better than anyone besides you and Serena."

"I gave him a second condition." Rompell moved toward her. "To learn your most unique quality."

Adeline shook her head. "He will never know."

Touching her chin, Rompell said, "If he will be your husband, you must trust him with this secret."

Adeline stepped back, brushing his hand away. "He doesn't need to know anything. I only use magic while teaching at the Bradford School. I've given it up."

"Magic is not something you can 'give up'." He raised his gloved hand. She stared at the thin layer of cloth keeping the world safe from his curse. "If it were, I would have been free long ago."

"Even if I told him, he wouldn't understand," she said. "It is better to keep it a secret."

"Secrets are part of why Stiltsken so easily turned Favay against me."

Adeline raised her chin. "But, if you had stopped Stiltsken, you wouldn't have found Hidaya again."

Rompell flexed his gloved fingers. "Hidaya may have had a better fate had I not found her."

He ran a hand over his face before forcing himself to look at her. "Magic is a part of who you are, Adeline. His affection is genuine, but he does not truly know you. You must tell him the truth. If he is meant to be your husband, he will stand with you."

"What do I even have magic for?" She sang out a note and pushed her palm forward, sending a plume of flame up the chimney. "To do parlor tricks and everyday chores? All I want, Papa, is a normal life with Nathaniel."

"You will never have a normal life."

Adeline flinched as she stepped back. There had been fights before, but Rompell's voice had never snapped so hard at her.

"I knew that when I found you in the snow, and especially after you nearly burned down the school." He held his palms out. "You and I have powers we must live with. You at least have others, like Mrs. Hunter, who can help you carry your burden. Let Nathaniel carry it too."

"Once he knows I have magic, that will be all he can see." Adeline gathered her skirt and stormed past Rompell to the stairs. "Goodnight, Papa."

She felt his eyes follow her as she marched up the stairs. With her door slammed, she dropped onto her bed and let the tears fall. She clutched her pillow to her chest and rubbed her finger where Bronhart's ring should be. To appease her father, she could wait two months. As for her magic, it would be a burden on her relationship with Bronhart. There was no reason he would ever need to know it existed.

No. She would marry Bronhart and carry on a normal, happy life.

The Fourth Tale of the Magician

"He's watching you again," Shera said, her grin deepening the wrinkles in her weathered face.

Hidaya glanced up from sewing beads on her costume. As usual, the worker turned away, his head hanging and shoulders hunched as if it were a crime to look at her.

This was an exhausting game. The man had been hired yesterday by Skandon, the troupe's foreman, to help raise the tents. Ever since, she could feel his gaze following her whenever she walked past.

She could handle men smiling at her and giving a friendly wink. They were common, especially when performing, and easy to ignore. This was different. The worker's stare was intense and she could feel his focus even without seeing him.

Every time she glanced over, his back was suddenly to her, and all she could see was his shaggy, neck-length hair, his lean build enveloped by his too-loose clothes. The man had travelled a hard road, but it didn't excuse his staring.

Hidaya turned her attention back to sewing coins and beads on her skirt.

"He'd be handsome if he trimmed his beard," Shera said as she sewed ribbons on her vest. "You should see his eyes when he looks at you. Sadder than a lost dog."

Hidaya tossed down her skirt and stood. This had to end.

The worker slammed his mallet against a tent spike as the other men worked to secure the anchors for the center tent pole. His back faced her and his rhythm held steady as she marched toward him.

The nearby troupe members looked up from preparing for the opening show in two days. Hidaya was sure rumors of his stares had spread and most watched for their own amusement.

She just might give them a good show.

Standing behind him, she balled her fists on her hips. "Why do you keep watching me?"

His aim slipped, his mallet swinging loose and almost hitting his leg.

"I am sorry." His voice was barely above a whisper. "I have not earned the right to speak with you."

"You'll have the right if you tell me your name."

He shifted his grip on the mallet's handle before hitting the stake. "It might be better if I do not."

She frowned. There was something familiar in his voice, but she could not place it in her memory. Keeping her stance firm, she said, "Whoever you are doesn't matter."

"I think it does."

She leaned toward him. "At least look me in the eye."

Taking in a deep breath, he stood straight and stretched his shoulders. She folded her arms and tapped her fingers. Each step seemed weighted by stones as he turned and raised his head.

She gasped as her heartbeat quickened, heat rushing into her face as she met his brown eyes. She wanted to doubt her instinct, for this was impossible, but the warmth and sorrow in his eyes confirmed the truth.

Her palm flashed out and smacked his jaw.

"You are supposed to be dead."

He blinked, his eyes wide.

She spun away and hurried toward her father's tent. A sob pressed its way through her chest and burst out of her. Tears came and she broke into a sprint. He called her name and ran after her.

Every emotion she had tucked away in the corners of her mind shoved their way back, tumbling over each other. She had done so well these past few weeks and all of it was broken in a single glance. Anger and sorrow mixed with the one hopeful thought she had forced back again and again: He was alive.

"What's wrong?" Terrivan asked as she passed. He reached for her, but she dodged past him and dove into their tent.

She dropped onto her cushions and pulled her blanket to her chest and rocked. This might be true, or this could be another repeat of her dreams ever since parting. The visions of having him walk into her tent and embracing her, the barriers between them gone, always ended with her waking, her pillow wet with tears.

She had wept the day he married Favay and for three days after hearing of his execution. Too many hours had been spent struggling to forget him, focusing on trying to return smiles of other men, to seek a life beyond him.

Now, a year after his execution, she had nearly done it.

And then he appeared, tall and handsome underneath the dirt and untrimmed hair, wholly alive and real.

She yelled into her blanket. She had been ready to move on, to carry on with her life. Now that he was here, she didn't know him. It had been three years since they had stood before each other. Those emotions were rushing back, but three years and the fall from the emperor's seat would change a man.

"Hidaya."

Her father opened the tent flap and stepped inside. He knelt beside her and pressed her hand to her back as she wept. Once her sobs slowed, he whispered, "I barely believe this myself. When you are ready, Rompell will tell us how he is here."

Rompell's name seemed so strange coming from her father's mouth.

She gulped in air as she sat up and faced her father, his eyes full of concern. Gripping his arm, she said, "We must do this now."

"Give yourself time." Terrivan brushed back the hair from her cheek. "I have told him to stay on." He smiled wryly. "A dead emperor has few friends."

She shook her head. "I have to know."

He squeezed her hand before walking to the tent's opening and beckoning with his arm. Rompell's back was rigid, though his head hung and he kept his eyes turned away. Terrivan led him to a set of cushions across the tent and Hidaya remained in the corner, the blanket pressed to her chest, protecting her.

She watched as Terrivan asked questions and Rompell told them of his brothers saving his life and sending him into exile. Her heart ached for his pain as he spoke of wandering in a stupor, becoming a beggar in the street. Then, he had awoken and worked for farms, caravans, and river barges, seeking news of Terrivan's troupe wherever he went. Whenever he heard a hint of where they might be, he found a way there, but was always a few weeks behind.

Hidaya's eyes drifted to his sandaled feet, calluses along the edge. His hands were lined with dirt, nicks and scrapes along his knuckles. He had traveled across much of the empire he had lost, suffering nights in the cold without food, always pressing on, seeking her.

He did not speak the words, but she could feel it in the few times his eyes drifted toward her, bearing his longing and pain.

As he came to the day Skandon hired him, Rompell raised his gaze and looked to Hidaya. Her heartbeat skipped a beat and her cheeks warmed as their eyes met. The sureness of the prince he had once been returned as he said, "You have a good life here, and I am glad."

He held his hand out to Terrivan. "Thank you for offering me a place here, but I should move on."

Hidaya set aside her blanket and rolled onto her knees.

He could not leave so quickly.

She needed to search through her emotions, to find what was truth and what were lingering remnants of what they had lost. Watching him leave and not knowing where he went seemed far worse than the certainty of knowing death had taken him.

"Where will you go?" she said.

"I don't know." Rompell lowered his head. "I might take a ship to Barthan. They don't use magic there."

Hidaya's tongue felt as if made of stone. She wanted to tell him not to go but could not say the words.

Terrivan scratched his thick beard as he glanced at her. "I remember the boy prince who married the Emperor's daughter. I worried for him then, and I mourned him after his execution." He gripped Rompell's shoulder. "The man sitting here is free of that prince. If you're willing to work and live as a better man, you are welcome here."

Rompell looked to Hidaya. She shied away from his eyes and stared at the ground. She had to speak but couldn't. He began to rise. Her heartbeat pounded at her ears.

Raising her head, she said, "Stay. At least until the carnival is done."

Rompell nodded. "Then I'll stay."

The rest of the day and the next passed too swiftly. Hidaya found herself pausing from helping set-up booths to watch Rompell as he worked. He stood as an equal among the men, quieter than most, but digging into the work as hard as the rest. This was not the prince, looking on and overseeing those beneath him. That part of him, the part that had frustrated her so often, seemed to have been shed, leaving only the man.

Late in the afternoon on the second day, Shera stopped beside her, her eyebrow raised.

"Things'll move along much faster if you two would do something about that staring."

Hidaya's cheeks reddened as she went back to her work.

Later, after eating a dinner of curried chicken and rice with her father, she took a quiet walk through the familiar tents. She smiled and talked with old friends, telling herself she was only enjoying the cool evening. Yet, her feet drew her to the outer edges of their camp, to the tents where the workers stayed.

Several pipes played alongside a sitar and set of drums. People whooped and clapped in between happy chatter. Hidaya smiled as she came to the open space where many of the workers and performers danced together. She waved off a few of her friends as they called for her to join, her eyes instead focused on Rompell as he danced with Skandon's eight-year-old daughter.

He clapped and spun with the child, both laughing. Tonight, he had a freeness she had never seen, the burdens of position loosened from his shoulders.

Several other children joined Rompell's dance as they jumped and sang with the music. One of the boys leapt into a spin and Rompell clapped before saying, "Well done, but can you do this?"

He stretched out his arms, clearing the area around him. He bent his knees and launched himself into a backflip. Hidaya's eyes widened. He didn't have enough momentum.

Rompell landed, his face planting in the dirt. The children went silent, but the rest of the dancers didn't seem to see.

A laugh burst out of Rompell and he pushed himself to his feet. He held out his arms as if he had triumphed, despite the dirt covering his tunic and face.

Skandon's daughter broke into giggles and the other children followed suit. Hidaya found herself grinning. He had played like this a few times back in Gathray, only to receive a glare from one of his father's advisors.

Her heart jumped as she realized he was looking at her. Her grin fell, but he gave her a tentative smile as he crouched next to several of the boys and whispered to them.

The children came to her and said, "Come and dance."

She let them lead her to the crowd. Jumping and swaying with the music, she joined the dance, singing out with the rest of the troupe as she celebrated the night before their show. Laughter and lightness filled the air. A few times, she and Rompell danced together, their hands touching briefly before the crowd separated them.

As the music quieted down and the troupe went to their tents, Rompell came to Hidaya's side. Her heart pounded with each step as he walked with her to Terrivan's tent, his arms folded behind him. Her fingers curled, wishing to seek his, but she kept her own arms at her side. The walk was far too short as he asked about different people in the troupe and she answered.

They reached her tent, but she lingered, finding something else to say to keep him there. A silence came as their eyes met. Her lips tingled, wishing for the return of his against hers. Yet, she forced herself to only smile and say, "Goodnight."

She had to be sure before she gave in to the growing longing in her breast. Once she did, she could never lose him again.

Two nights of performances passed. Hidaya stole what moments she could with Rompell, laughing and talking with him with an ease they had only had in stolen moments in Gathray. On the third night, the show neared its climax and Hidaya stood on the catwalk where Rompell assisted with the rigging.

Rompell hooked a rope to her harness. His hands lingered at her waist, but he drew back. Hidaya looked away from the elephants dancing below as the band played. She should be counting the beats leading to Terrivan's final trick to close the show, but her eyes turned to Rompell's and the music below seemed to fade.

Without thinking, her hand clamped around his. Putting his trembling arm around her, he pulled her close and rested his forehead against hers.

"Will you walk with me?" he whispered. "As my wife?"

His lips were close to hers and she filled the final distance. He pulled her tight against him as their lips pressed together. She wrapped her fingers in his hair. Lightness and joy filled her breast as so many years of sorrow faded away, drowned out by a fullness coursing through her.

They were each other's at last, free of his rank, free of everything.

The drums grew louder, building the suspense leading to her father's final magic trick. Hidaya forced herself to part her lips from his. He snuck a quick kiss before she pushed herself from the railing. She tried to force a serious expression for the trick but couldn't help beaming as she floated to the floor below, knowing that Rompell of Gathray was free to be hers.

Chapter 10

Bronhart leaned back in his office chair, flipping open and closed the lid of a ring box. He glanced at the clock. There was work he should do, but his eyes kept going back to the calendar.

Only one month more.

He would be sure the wedding was soon after. Each day of parting with Adeline was getting harder. Their conversations were full of their future homes and children, of their evenings freely enjoying each other's companionship. If he could just propose and know she would soon be his wife, then he could concentrate.

However, he could not go against the man who had rescued and raised her. No. Bronhart had to find the patience to endure another month.

He glanced up as Henry Kingston stepped into the office. "Do you have a moment?"

Bronhart motioned for Henry to enter. As Henry shut the door, Bronhart said, "How are things with Miss Havish?"

"Steady, it appears," Henry said. "However, I have not come for advice today."

Bronhart grinned. Waiting for Rompell's approval had been made a bit easier by coaching Henry in his own courtship.

Henry set a folder on the desk. "I was going through some accounts, when I came across the name of Miss Winkleston's father."

Bronhart sat up. "Where?"

"It was in another account." Henry opened the folder to a bill of sale for an apartment building. "That's an extremely large cash payment."

Bronhart squinted at the enormous sum of macs.

"And here's another."

Bronhart moved to the edge of his seat and stared. "With these assets, he could own two mansions on North Lane."

"But he doesn't. I looked into a few more accounts. It seems he has at least a half-dozen apartment buildings, all paid for in cash." Flipping to another page in the folder, Henry said, "It took some digging, but I kept an eye out for Mr. Rompell's name for the past week or so." He slid the page over to Bronhart. "This is a deposit at our bank almost ten years ago."

Bronhart's eyes widened. "Who has that much gold?"

"Who has so many apartments but charges such low rent?" Henry set an advertisement for one of the apartment buildings in front of Bronhart. "I have never seen so much gold gained through honest means and such low rent means he is making little, if not losing money, on his investments."

Bronhart thumbed through the folder. These were enormous sums, but the rents were low enough to take almost a century to earn a return on the investment. His frown deepened as he thought through what Adeline had said of Rompell. Perhaps the funds were from his days in Sandar. If they had been gained illegally, it helped explain why he was now hiding in a quiet city like Pippington.

Yet, there was no hard proof here.

"I had wished his accounts were above reproach," Henry said. "And I hope his business is honest. I just thought you should know."

"Thank you," Bronhart said as he shut the folder.

Henry nodded and leaned on his cane as he left the room.

Reclining back in his chair, Bronhart eyed the folder. This did not change how he felt about Adeline, but it did mean he needed to watch Rompell closely. For now, he would stay silent on the matter.

Adeline hugged the three girls a few seconds longer before standing. "Your parents are waiting."

The girls skipped out of the classroom and off toward their summer holiday. Adeline hummed to herself as she locked the classroom and strolled down the empty hallway.

As the last mother and father arrived and embraced their daughter, Adeline pictured herself and Bronhart in their place. Bronhart would twirl the girl around with his strong arms and the girl would chatter away, telling them of her day and the wonders she had learned.

It would be wonderful, but there was so much to do until then. She had been saving up for new shoes but had held back buying from Mr. Talbot's shop. She would rather have a pair from Cordwainers, but those elegant shoes cost almost a year's salary. Talbot's shoes were reliable and reasonably priced, but far less fine.

Rompell, she knew, could give her any wedding she wished, but she wanted to do as much as she could on her own. He would provide the dress, of course, but there could be no magic involved. And, the more she did on her own, the more he would see she was an independent young woman ready to be a wife.

She hid a smile as she stopped across from Mrs. Hunter. The headmistress stood firm, her eyes betraying her wearing patience as a mother complained over the color of her daughter's hair ribbon.

"We will take it into consideration, Mrs. Thornton," Mrs. Hunter said.

"You see to it." The mother kept hold of her girl's shoulder and escorted her out the door.

Seeing Adeline, Mrs. Hunter waved for her to come inside her study. Entering, Adeline looked at the dark wood and red interior. The chairs and desk had seemed so much larger as a girl.

"I have been meaning to speak to you," Mrs. Hunter said.

"Especially with your twentieth birthday coming next month."

"Papa and I have already made plans." She pushed away the dread rising at the mention of her birthday. When she was with Bronhart, it was so easy to forget the inevitable day of misery. "I will stay in bed all day, eat the chocolates you sent over, rest, and try to avoid breaking the house." She shrugged. "The same as every year."

"I have warned you, Miss Winkleston. Of everyone I have helped through such birthdays, the twentieth is one of the final, but worst, events."

Adeline's hand clamped on the back of the chair as she dug her toe in the carpet. "But, it will pass."

"It will, but you risk much by staying here on your birthday." Mrs. Hunter walked toward her, concern in her dark eyes. "You are already quite powerful. The only ones who surpass you are in the Surris Mountains."

"What does it matter?" Adeline said as she leaned against a chair. "No one can know about my power, except some school girls."

"I have told you many times: the key is to use it quietly, in secret. Use it to cool a fever, calm the wind around you, grow a dying fire, all subtle, quiet ways your magic can improve your life. It can be a useful tool." She crossed the room and sat in her chair behind the desk, motioning for Adeline to sit across from her.

"I am concerned. Your power jumps with each birthday. Combined with how you have grown this past year, you will soon surpass what I can teach you."

"I know how to manage my powers," Adeline said. "I don't see what else there is to learn."

"There is always more to learn." Mrs. Hunter tapped her fingers on the desk. "And you must be careful. If you are not watched by someone with greater power than I have, you could burn down your house, make it rise off the foundation, or split the roof apart."

Adeline sighed. "I've never gone that far."

"You have never been so powerful." Mrs. Hunter folded her hands in her lap. "However, your focus on Mr. Bronhart has distracted you, and your father says it is quite a serious romance. To be frank, do you think you will marry this man?"

Adeline raised her head. She was too grown up to be intimidated by Mrs. Hunter. "I know I will, but Papa won't give his permission."

"Mr. Rompell told me he is willing to, after a bit of time."

"He also said I have to tell Nathaniel about my magic."

Mrs. Hunter raised an eyebrow. "Now, that may be unwise."

"That is what I told Papa."

"I never told my late husband about my magic and we were quite content. Those without magic do not understand these things." She waved her hand. "I will speak with Mr. Rompell on the matter. However, I am still concerned about your growth in power.

"There is little more I can teach you. I have been invited to the Surris Mountains by some of the Rangers and will be leaving in a few weeks. I would like you to come with me."

Adeline frowned. The Surris Mountains were rugged, distant, and dirty. Though her mother had been born there, she had no connection to the place. She had gone to the rodeos put on by the Surris Rangers, sometimes wondering if any of them knew her mother. However, remembering how quiet and distant her mother grew whenever she asked about Surris, Adeline never spoke to them. It seemed disrespectful to her mother's memory.

"What would I learn there?" she said.

"What they see fit to teach you. Your talent is clearly more in material magic than persuasive magic. I am sure they would help you improve your finesse and control."

Adeline's fingers curled closed. It would be better if they just drained her magic, freeing her from worrying about it.

Hiding her thoughts, she said, "How long would we be gone?"

"It takes almost a week by train and then a day or two by wagon each way, plus about a month to do anything worthwhile. We would be back about a week before the next school year."

Adeline's fingers clasped together. "No. I cannot be so far from Nathaniel for so long."

"If you really are meant to marry him, a month or so will be nothing."

Adeline forced herself not to roll her eyes. How could Rompell and Mrs. Hunter have forgotten what love was like?

"It will be forever."

Mrs. Hunter's eyebrow moved even higher, but instead she said, "After the wedding, will you continue working here?"

"I don't know. I will be a married woman and will need to manage the household."

Mrs. Hunter's brow furrowed. "You have very interesting ideas of married life. I am glad I continued my education and teaching after Geoffrey and I married. If I had not, I would have been in a very poor state when he died and wouldn't have been able to provide for our daughters and son."

Standing, she said, "My offer for going to the Surris Mountains stands until I leave on the train a week from Friday. As for your position here, I will presume you will be returning to your post until we are sure of what your future is."

Adeline said her goodbye and gave a polite smile, but, in her heart, she knew her answer and her future. None of it would be near the Surris Mountains.

Chapter 11

The summer air was warm and light as Adeline sat on the patio of the Gourmand, Bronhart across the table from her, his hand cupped around hers. She looked out over the lake, enjoying the reflection of the sky on the still surface.

If only this moment could stretch and blot out tomorrow. Each minute closer to her birthday was more dangerous, but she would enjoy this evening with Bronhart.

It took her a few seconds to realize that Bronhart had asked her, "And what do you want most for your birthday?"

"Oh, I—" She looked down at the lace gloves covering her hands. If she could, she would be free of her magic and never have her birthday come. Instead, she said, "I think you know quite well."

Bronhart raised her hand and kissed it. "Only two more weeks, as long as your father keeps his word." He raised a finger. "However, I'm still not sure what unique quality he is looking for. I could go on for hours, if I needed to, but I don't know the answer he is looking for."

Adeline glanced at the other people in the restaurant. Their silverware clicked on their plates and their voices churned into a low rumble. The evening had been so wonderfully ordinary, yet Rompell's question lingered.

Looking again at Bronhart, she said, "I don't know that you'll ever have the answer he seeks."

Bronhart squeezed her hand. "Then, we will be patient."

The dinner wore on in pleasant conversation and laughter. She ate a little of her chicken and linguini, but each time she picked up the fork it seemed heavier. At last, she went to cut a piece, but her hands shook too much to hold her knife still. Setting it down, she flattened her palms on the table.

Bronhart frowned while snapping to the waiter. He quickly settled the bill and held his arm around her shoulders. She felt safe with his arm there, yet her body trembled more and her forehead grew hotter.

Once outside, Bronhart hailed a cab. As they rode in the back seat, he held her tightly to his chest, his lips brushing her forehead. Adeline shut her eyes, her head beginning to throb. If only they could be married already.

As Bronhart helped her out of the cab, her stomach clenched. She held onto him to stop from falling. A second later, everything she had eaten from dinner came pouring out of her mouth and onto his suit.

She held a hand to her mouth as she stepped back. "I—I'm so sorry."

Her legs shaking, she hurried toward the door. She grabbed onto the bush and pulled herself forward. There was no wind, but the windows began to rattle. As she reached the front porch, a crack split a second-story window. She reached for the door handle. Rompell threw open the door and grabbed her before she fell.

As Rompell lifted her, Bronhart said from close behind, "I will carry her."

"Not with vomit all over you. Take off your shoes and go to the kitchen."

Adeline whined as a dagger of pain pierced her skull. This was hours earlier than usual. Rompell moved swiftly up the stairs. He carried her to his room and a stripped-down bed he had prepared. He wiped her face and gave her some water before pressing the piece of chocolate into her mouth.

"I hope we have enough," he whispered.

In minutes, he helped her out of her fine dress, leaving her in her chemise and bloomers. He assisted her into a cotton nightgown, two more ready just in case. She moaned as her muscles clenched and her teeth froze together. The bed thumped on the ground as it hopped. Rompell placed his knee on it while shoving her down and laying leather straps across her, pinning her arms down.

He set a wet rag across her forehead and kissed her cheek. "Everything will be fine, Little One."

She lay alone in darkness, her muscles clenching as the inevitable began.

Bronhart kicked off his shoes as he tried not to smell his shirt and waistcoat. He cringed as he carried his shoes into the kitchen. At least Rompell could afford indoor plumbing. He turned on the faucet. The water came in spurts, globs splashing up at him. His face and shirt were soaked by the time his shoes were clean enough to wear.

The kitchen door creaked open. Rompell dropped a stack of clothes on the counter.

"These should fit well enough," he said. "Leave your clothes by the sink. I'll have them washed."

Pulling off his coat, Bronhart said, "I can go get a doctor."

Rompell waved his hand. "She will sleep it off. Just a bit of stomach flu. Happens now and then."

There was another set of loud thumping, followed by Adeline's scream. It ripped at Bronhart's core, calling for him to save her from an unknown torture. Several of the cupboards slammed open, one whacking Bronhart in the back of the head.

Calmly, Rompell shut and latched them. "I've been meaning to fix the hinges."

"Are you sure?" Bronhart said as he pulled off his shirt and replaced it with Rompell's. The sleeves were a touch long, but otherwise, it was a good fit.

"You did well to bring her home so quickly," Rompell said. "That is enough."

Shrugging on the jacket, Bronhart said, "I know we are only courting, but may I sit by her tonight? I can't walk away knowing she's in so much pain."

Another scream filled the air. Rompell glanced up at the ceiling with a cringe. "No. It is better for you to go."

"But—"

"Has she told you her most unique quality yet?"

"No, but I love her. Isn't that enough?"

Rompell prodded Bronhart's discarded shirt with his foot. "I think your love has been quite proven." He slapped his hand on Bronhart's arm and began guiding him to the front door. "As for marriage, I believe your proposal would be a fine gift for Adeline's birthday. Just wait for the day after tomorrow."

Despite her moaning upstairs, Bronhart smiled and said, "Really?"

"You have been patient and are admirable." Rompell stepped back. Bronhart blinked as he realized he was outside the house. "Good night and thank you."

The door slammed shut. Bronhart looked up at the cracked window, Adeline's moans and groans echoing in the street. He wanted to stay and help but could do nothing. She was in her father's care. If Rompell was going to trust him, he should trust Rompell, no matter what secrets the man hid.

Chapter 12

A knock pounded on the door downstairs. Rompell snorted as he woke fully. He stretched as he stood, the forgotten book in his hand still open. Adeline moaned and he pressed his gloved hand to her rag-covered forehead.

At least she had fallen asleep. It wasn't restful, but it was relief. He wished Mrs. Hunter had been wrong about her twentieth birthday.

Panes of his bedroom window were broken, glass on the floor. The curtain rod was bent, hanging from one hinge. His dresser was toppled over.

The knock came harder.

With deep bags under his eyes, his hair disheveled, and his legs a bit numb, he stumbled into the hallway. The small table outside the bathroom lay with two broken legs, a vase lay shattered across the floor. He tossed a piece of the banister out of his way as he walked downstairs. The couch was overturned, his favorite chair ripped down the middle.

The knock came a third time followed by a voice calling, "Good morning."

It was louder and less muffled than it should be. He looked up. The front door hung on a single hinge like a tooth about to fall out. A woman in a tweed coat and brimmed man's hat peeked in through the gap.

"Are you Mr. Rompell?" she said.

Rompell smoothed back his hair. "I am." He grabbed the door

and jerked it off the sliver of metal left on the hinge. "What can I do for you?"

"Inspector Gertrude McCay." The slim woman held out her hand.

Rompell checked to make sure his glove was intact before taking her firm grip and giving a brief shake. He would have to tread carefully with the inspector. Countless newspaper articles expounded on her brilliance as she solved one impossible case after another. As he looked at the impossibilities, he wondered what magic her stories hid.

He kept his face neutral despite the chaos around him. An inspector of her fame wouldn't be here for a common house call.

McCay gestured toward the yard of upturned bushes, the flower garden a mound of scattered dirt, a few window shutters sticking out of the ground.

"Seems you had some vandalism last night," she said. "Would you like to make a report?"

He shook his head. "Thank you, but I will take care of the matter myself."

McCay leaned against the door jamb and tilted back her hat. "Margaret Hunter of the Bradford School asked me to look in on an—" She frowned as she read off her notepad. "Adeline Winkleston and her guardian. She hoped I could help explain things."

Rompell glanced at the chaos outside. If Mrs. Hunter had truly sent McCay, he wished Mrs. Hunter had told him. However, it was a confirmation of McCay's knowledge of magic.

"There'll be trouble if your neighbors are left to their gossiping imaginations," McCay said. "If I make a police report and leak it to the newspaper, your neighbors will read it and believe that's the truth. Makes their questions much easier."

"Mrs. Hunter didn't tell me you were coming," Rompell said.

"She said to let things be if there wasn't anything too noticeable." She glanced out at the yard. "There are a few things that seem noticeable."

Rompell scanned the street. Across the way, Mrs. Plimpnell was peeking through the curtains again. Sometimes, he had Bronhart and Adeline sit on the porch just to give her something to gossip about.

This, however, would be blown into a much larger controversy if he left Mrs. Plimpnell to her own devices.

Stepping aside, he motioned for McCay to enter. "It was about two this morning. At least three thieves, just teenage boys. One had a knife. I had to fight them off."

McCay's pencil ran swiftly over the paper. "Excellent. What should they look like? Generic is always best."

"What about handkerchiefs over their chins, and it being dark?"

"One or two more details will help quiet curiosity. The fewer unanswered questions, the bet—"

"Mr. Rompell!" Mrs. Frizban ran through the doorway. "What a mess! Are you all right?"

"As best I can be, thank you." Rompell tried to smile at her, but his cheeks were stiff. "I thought you were taking the day off."

"Doesn't mean I can't drop off a nice cake after your sweet girl's birthday. Shameful after spending her whole birthday day inside." She cried out and nearly dropped the cake. "Inspector McCay! What a pleasure to meet you. My daughter Mabel has a scrapbook of all the articles about you. She's a clever one, she is. Might be a detective someday too."

Mrs. Frizban handed Rompell the cake before fishing around in the bag on her arm. "If I could just have something for you to sign. She would be so delighted, just delighted."

McCay reached in her suit pocket and pulled a small photograph and a pen. "Mabel was her name? And how is that spelled?"

As Mrs. Frizban spelled out her daughter's name, Rompell set the cake on the table. When the table began to totter, he moved it to the kitchen counter. He winced. There might be enough damage to cost using his curse to raise some funds.

"There you are." McCay handed over the photograph.

"Lovely. Just lovely. I—" She looked at the room. "Mr. Rompell, what happened here?"

"That's what I came to investigate." McCay snapped open her notepad. "Appears there were a few hooligans about, hoping for quick money and to cause trouble. Mr. Rompell, however, is a formidable fighter and tossed them out. Doubt they'll be back."

"Now, don't you worry, Mr. Rompell," Mrs. Frizban said. "The police have sent their best. She'll arrest those hooligans in no time." She let out a gasp. "Is Miss Adeline all right? She must have been frightened."

"She was quite brave," McCay said. "Got a good slug or two in."

"Adeline!"

Rompell groaned as Bronhart ran into the house. Before he could stop him, the young man was sprinting up the stairs shouting Adeline's name.

"Pardon me, ladies. Mrs. Frizban, could you help the inspector take an account of the damage?"

"I'd be quite honored."

Rompell sprinted after the young man, his long legs skipping a few stairs with each step. Bronhart's face was pale as he stood in the hall, pivoting between doors. He threw open the door to Adeline's room as he shouted, "Adeline! Are you all right?"

Hoping his own love as a young man had not made him such a fool, Rompell said, "She is in my room, asleep."

Bronhart looked between the three other doors on the floor. "Which one is it?"

"Aren't you supposed to be at work?"

"I had a meeting cancelled a few blocks away." Bronhart lifted an enormous bouquet that was barely bound by the crook of his arm. "I thought I'd drop these off for Adeline. It might help her feel better."

Rompell took the flowers from Bronhart. "It is a kind thought. I will give these to her when she wakes."

"Papa?" Adeline moaned.

Bronhart moved to run toward the door, but Rompell grabbed his arm.

"She doesn't want you to see her like this."

Bronhart jerked away his arm and ran. Rompell dropped the bouquet sprinted after him but was not quick enough to stop Bronhart from throwing open the door. Adeline lay in her chemise and nightgown, the leather straps holding her down, her arms bruised where her body had jerked against them. Rompell rubbed his forehead, praying the young man could keep a cool head and ask questions.

"Nathaniel?" Adeline said. She winced and let out a hiss of pain.

"What has he done to you?" Bronhart bent down and began to unbuckle a strap.

"A word, Mr. Bronhart," Rompell said from the door.

"A word?" he spat. "You claim to help her, when you lock her up like she's mad! I am taking her to a doctor."

"A doctor cannot help her."

All of this would be so much easier if Adeline had told Bronhart the truth.

Bronhart sprang to his feet and charged at Rompell, his fist connecting against Rompell's jaw. Ignoring the sting of Bronhart's blow, Rompell pivoted into the hallway. He kept his hands loose at his side, leaning on the balls of his feet, ready to dodge the next attack.

"I've trusted you," Bronhart said, "ignoring signs you've got a dishonest business, because Adeline loves you. And then, this—"

Bronhart's fist lashed out again. Rompell blocked it with his arm and twisted it aside.

"Nathaniel!" Adeline said.

Bronhart threw another punch. Rompell backed down the hall, dodging easily. Adeline had mentioned Bronhart had done some boxing during college, and the training served him well. However, fighting in the ring was not the same as facing a warrior on the battlefield.

"What sort of dishonest business do I run?" Rompell said as he swiveled, letting Bronhart's fist crack against the wall. There was another dent he would have to add to the repairs.

"Your businesses are built on stolen gold."

Rompell caught Bronhart's next punch with his palm. Though the movement jarred up his arm, he wrapped his fingers around Bronhart's fist, forcing the man to hold still a moment.

"Where did I steal the gold?" He kept his voice low and cool. Bronhart could not have learned his secret, but this was too close.

"From the Sandarian Empire."

Rompell laughed, not able to stop himself. Bronhart swung again and Rompell stepped back. Bronhart twisted with the unused inertia, falling toward the stairs. Rompell reached for Bronhart's arm, trying to stop him, but the young man tumbled down to the first floor.

Bronhart panted as he lay at the bottom. He was a bit out of breath but seemed whole.

Inspector McCay leaned against the far wall, tapping her pen on her chin as she watched. Mrs. Frizban stood at the kitchen door, wringing her hands.

"If you are quite finished insulting me, Mr. Bronhart," Rompell said as he walked down the stairs. "I would appreciate if you joined me for a brief drink in my study. I think we could both use it."

Bronhart stumbled to his feet. "I'm not leaving without Adeline." He crouched into a fighter's stance and swung once Rompell reached the main floor. McCay let out a tsk. Rompell sighed as he grabbed Bronhart's arm with both hands and threw him over his shoulder.

Bronhart lay sprawled on the floor but began to rise again. Rompell pressed his foot on Bronhart's wrist.

"I served in the army during the Sandarian revolution, Mr. Bronhart," Rompell said. "After we won, I had nothing left, so the

Consul gave me a few gifts to help me begin my life here."

He moved his foot and held out his hand. "A drink, Mr. Bronhart?"

"Former soldier?" McCay said scribbling on her notepad. "Very good."

Bronhart's eyes remained skeptical, but he took Rompell's hand and stood.

"What happened here?" he said.

"Mr. Rompell fought off ten thieves last night," McCay said.

Bronhart's eyes widened.

"It was only three," Rompell muttered as he motioned toward the study. To Mrs. Frizban, he said, "Would you help Inspector McCay, and see if someone can fix the door?"

"Of course."

Rompell led Bronhart to the study and forced himself to not slam the door as they entered. Books were scattered across the room, some split in half. Rompell was glad nothing precious was here.

"It must have been quite a struggle," Bronhart said.

"It was." Rompell scanned the books still on the shelves before picking up a few on the floor. Bronhart began to help stack books on the desk, the only piece of furniture still standing.

"What happened to Adeline?"

Rompell was glad Mrs. Hunter had given him a false explanation to share after Adeline's twelfth birthday. However, it would be easier with the book.

"She has Septorum Disease," Rompell said. "It is a rare disorder and she is embarrassed by it."

"She should have told me."

Rompell found the book and tossed it to Bronhart. "Whether she should have, or not, it is what she has done. See page one hundred twenty-three."

Rompell set up the overturned chairs and Bronhart sat down as he flipped the pages. Letting Bronhart have a few minutes to read the scientific lies of Doctor Matticus, Rompell opened his drink cupboard set in the wall. Most of the glasses were broken, but three remained and the bottle of Sandarian mead was intact.

Bronhart frowned in concentration while Rompell set out the glasses. He sat across from his daughter's suitor and sipped from the drink. He would see about the matter of being called a thief in a moment.

"She endures this every year?" Bronhart said.

"Yes."

"No wonder she dreads her birthday."

"Yes."

Bronhart set down the book as he stood. "May I speak with her?"

"First, sir, I want to know why you think I am a thief."

"My friend Henry, an auditor at my firm, was investigating some real estate transactions and your name came up. He traced the initial capital to large sums of gold being traded for cash."

Rompell swirled his drink. He had hoped time had covered his tracks better. What he had done wasn't illegal, but it would be hard to explain. "And by these coincidences, you assume I am a master thief?"

"Most men who hide their accounts have gained their wealth by dishonest means." Bronhart shifted in his chair. "And, the rents you charge for your apartments. They are quite low, sir. There is no way you can be profiting from them."

"I have no need to make a profit." Rompell set down his glass. "My apartments are full of those who would be on the street if the rent cost more. I make enough to pay for my living expenses and that is all." He took a drink before saying, "Choices I made as a young man caused enough suffering. I came here in hopes of doing better."

"I am sorry, sir." Bronhart's foot tapped as he looked down. "As I said, things appeared suspicious."

"I prefer my life to be private," Rompell said. "And I don't like announcing who I am helping."

He flicked a coin through his fingers, more from habit. Despite the soreness in his jaw, he respected Bronhart. The young man adored Adeline, just as she deserved. Bronhart's imagination worked as hard as hers, which might lead them to a few patches of trouble, but they would learn. In time, Adeline would reveal her magic to Bronhart. It would be a difficult time, but, if they truly loved each other, they would stand together and build a strong, happy marriage.

Rising, he held out his hand to Bronhart. "If you can promise to trust me, and not assault me in my own home, I am willing to welcome you as Adeline's future husband."

Bronhart pushed to his feet. "When you offered permission last night, I thought you were just getting rid of me."

"I was." Rompell couldn't stop a smile from forming. "But I also meant it."

"What changed your mind?"

Rompell gestured at Bronhart's shirt. "Any man who loves a woman after she's vomited on him is quite admirable."

A smile broke Bronhart's weary face. He grabbed Rompell's outstretched hand and shook it. "Of course, sir. Thank you. May I go see her?"

Rompell waved his hand. "I will be close behind."

Bronhart leaped from the room and sprinted upstairs. Rompell took his time finishing his drink before strolling into the sitting room. The house was quieter with Inspector McCay gone and Mrs. Frizban sweeping the floor. He would pay the housekeeper a double-wage this month.

Once upstairs and at his room, Rompell leaned against the doorframe, invisible to the young couple. Bronhart knelt by Adeline's side and kissed her hand. She clasped his as they spoke in whispers. Adeline gasped and Bronhart's worried expression broke into a grin. He kissed her before placing a ring on her finger.

Rompell rubbed his chest, trying to push away the rising ache. It had been so long since he had felt the pure joy Bronhart and Adeline held. Before them was an imagined future of happiness, the worries and weight of life forgotten.

He wished he could go back to the day he stood before Hidaya, his hands shaking just as Bronhart's did. How he missed the smell of her hair as she leaned against him, the brightness of her laugh, the brush of her hand. Each day, he felt the hole of her absence.

Taking Adeline as his daughter had eased his loneliness. The years had been brighter than he had hoped when he lost Hidaya and their sons. But, soon she would be gone.

She and Bronhart would visit, of course, and Rompell would play with their children. However, it was Bronhart who would hold her close on days of sorrow, Bronhart who would spend his days at her side.

This was the way it was for all fathers. It did not make the ache any softer as her bright eyes turned to him, her smile wide as she raised her hand to show the ring.

With this promise made to Bronhart, he had to let his sweet Adeline go.

The Fifth Tale of the Magician

Rompell laughed as he grabbed his three-year-old son, Amal, and tossed him over his shoulder. He caught his six-year-old-son, Jabir, around the waist. As he spun, the boys giggled and Jabir shouted, "Faster!"

If he could keep going, he would. There had been too many tragedies in the past year and every moment of brightness needed to be enjoyed. However, his own dizziness was threatening to take over. Rompell slowed to a stop and lowered the boys to the ground. Amal raised his arms for another ride.

Picking up his skins full of water, Rompell said, "Back to the tent. Time to sleep."

Jabir groaned, but followed as they wound through the tents. Rompell nodded to the few who remained with their troupe as he walked. Where their caravan once had dozens of tents packed together, only ten remained. Too many good men and women had been lost to the Tirrus plague. Many more left when Terrivan passed on, leaving care of the troupe in Hidaya and Rompell's hands.

Rompell would be true to promises made to his father-in-law. He would protect the troupe members and build the caravan again.

Tomorrow would be their new beginning.

He was still shocked by the letter bearing the King of Periv's seal, requesting his troupe perform for the prince-heir's wedding. Rompell preferred being on the performance side of the wedding, being paid well for good work instead of entering a loveless and dangerous marriage. The acceptance was sent and all they needed now was to perform and receive payment.

Jabir and Amal broke into a run as Hidaya stepped out of their tent, rocking their infant daughter Tamina on her shoulder.

"We were attacked by dragons, but Papa and I fought them off." Jabir slashed through the air with a stick.

Hidaya held a hand over her mouth to keep from laughing as he danced around. His arms flailed as he reenacted the battle he and Rompell had played out while walking to the well. Rompell pressed his lips together, holding in a chuckle. Jabir took their mock-battles very seriously.

"You must be tired after so brave an evening," Hidaya said, nudging him inside. He began his usual protests, but one twitch of Hidaya's eyebrow sent him marching into the tent, Amal close behind.

Hidaya broke into giggles and Rompell returned her smile as he set the water skins beside the tent flap.

"Jabir was very courageous," he said. "Especially the fifth time he told me to pretend I'd fallen. But, as I lay, wounded in battle, I saw this."

He held out his fist and waved his other hand over it. Pulling his hand away, a wildflower appeared and he held it out to her.

Hidaya raised an eyebrow. She had taught him sleight-of-hand tricks and was never impressed. Rompell still tried, making it a game between them.

Placing his hand over his breast in mock earnestness, he said, "For the mistress of my heart."

"Does this mistress know you are married?" Hidaya took the flower.

With his arm around her waist, Rompell said, "I told her my wife is only the best of women."

"Those are wise words."

Rompell laughed before kissing her, pulling her closer while keeping enough room for her to hold Tamina. Hidaya returned the kiss and looped her free arm around his shoulders.

It had been a good eight years of marriage. The past year, watching the plague ravage their troupe and the empire, seeing her father die, and rationing what little food they had during the last few weeks, had been made bearable by having her to lean on. They were together and would find a way through.

Jabir made a loud gagging sound as he stuck his head out of the tent. Rompell kissed his wife a bit longer before pulling away and raising an eyebrow at their son.

The boy scurried back inside.

"I'll get them to bed," Hidaya said, slipping out of Rompell's embrace and handing him Tamina. A warmth spread through him as he held his daughter, smiling as he looked into her small face and round brown eyes. With a kiss to her forehead, he stepped inside the tent to help Hidaya with the warzone that was bedtime.

The next half-hour was filled with several rounds of stopping Amal from jumping and shushing Jabir so Rompell could rock Tamina to sleep. At last, Rompell and Hidaya were victorious, and the boys were cuddled in their blankets, their mouths open as they snored lightly.

Rompell set Tamina in her basket and laid beside Hidaya. She put her arm across his chest and curled along his side. He stared up at the roof of the tent, the moonlight shining through the canvas. Hidaya's stomach grumbled and Rompell glanced at her.

"How much did you give the boys tonight?"

"A third," she said. "And how much of your ration did you move into my bowl?"

He grunted a laugh. "Enough."

Shutting his eyes, he leaned his head against hers. Tomorrow, they would reach Periv, perform for the prince's wedding, and be paid. The troupe would celebrate with a grand feast and Rompell would use the rest to rebuild what the plague had taken.

Rompell rode his horse alongside the lead wagon, the side still bearing a painting of Terrivan's face as he blew fire. The road had been quieter than most leading into capital cities. Carts going to Periv should have passed them, full of merchants seeking to take advantage of a royal wedding.

However, even the huts and houses they passed were empty except for a few chickens in the yards. They crested the hill leading to Periv and Rompell felt as if a bull had rammed into his chest. Where the city had been lay a few mud houses along the shore of a bright and gleaming lake.

The troupe's chatter stopped and Hidaya kept her arms around her sons as she looked to Rompell. He rode a few steps ahead, glaring at the palace spires rising from the lake.

Magic was palpable in the air. His arms trembled and he wanted to smash something.

Checking the pistol and hunting knife he kept in his belt, Rompell said, "I'll see if there's anything to scavenge."

"We should leave," Hidaya said.

Rompell ignored her and he rode the switchbacks down to the valley floor. He could feel the deadness as he passed through a row of buildings still above water. A few stone statues stood in yards, posed as if doing daily tasks. Glancing again, Rompell suspected these were not statues.

The magic needed to do this was enormous, greater than a single sorcerer could do.

He rode to the shore and looked into the depths of dark blue. Fish swam in and out of buildings as if they had always been there.

"A strange thing happened a few months ago."

Rompell turned his horse around and faced Stiltsken. He stood only a few horse lengths away, layers of gold hanging around his neck, his silk robes rich with embroidery, his hands covered in jewels. Life as Favay's close advisor had done well for him. Far too well for a traitor.

Rompell's hands were steady as he raised his pistol. With a kick of his heels, he sent his horse charging forward and fired off three shots.

Stiltsken dodged to the side, flicking his hand with a whistle. A sphere of fire erupted in front of Rompell. His horse reared. Rompell leaned forward in his saddle but the horse bucked, sending him flying. He rolled across the ground, his pistol clattering from his hand, the gravel stinging as it scraped his cheek and arms.

Leisurely, Stiltsken walked over and stood above Rompell. He held out a coin bearing Rompell's younger face and smiled.

Rompell bit out a curse.

He had asked the troupe's magician, Shera, to put a tracking spell on the coins and then given the coin to Jabir, telling him, "Keep this with you."

The child must have used it to buy sweets. That act somehow had led it back to the hand of Rompell's enemy.

"Imagine my surprise when I found this coin," Stiltsken said. "It took my spies many months, to find the fallen emperor. And then, there you were, married to the young woman you claimed to have given up. What a miracle, to see my old friend alive."

Rompell tossed gravel at Stiltsken and rolled to his feet. Gripping his hunting knife, he said, "You already murdered me. What else do you want?"

Stiltsken tilted his head, letting the light wind fill the silence before he said, "It pained me to send you to your death, but it is what had to be. Your sacrifice strengthened Favay's rule, making her sympathetic to her people."

He stepped toward the lake. "There have been a few uprisings, but Favay's sorcerers and I have taken care of them." He gestured toward the sunken palace. "I have come far since freeing myself from your shadow."

Rompell grit his teeth. How had he fallen for this trap? He had been suspicious of the King of Periv's sudden interest in his troupe but needed a better life for his people.

Ignoring his aching shoulder, Rompell scooped up a rock the size of his fist. He threw it at Stiltsken. With a flick of his hand, Stiltsken sent out a wave of magic, shattering the rock. The powder hovered in the air.

"Your only crime was to stand in my way." Stiltsken held out a closed fist. "I brought you here to show you the power your fall gave me." He opened his palm, revealing a vial full of a glittering, gold-sheening liquid. "But, as a man and friend, you deserved better. Let me make things right."

Rompell laughed. Gesturing with his knife, he said, "I'll be glad for the day Favay sees you for the traitor you are."

He kept his knife pointed at Stiltsken as he backed away, moving toward the wagons.

"Your sons need bread." Stiltsken followed him. "And your wife, so worn since her father's death. Drink a few drops and your fortune will turn."

Rompell turned his back to Stiltsken and hurried his step. He would make his own fortune, working by the sweat of his brow and his own wits.

"You were a good friend, Rompell. You do not deserve where fate has led you." Stiltsken reached Rompell's side. "Set yourself free of poverty and starvation. Let me help you one last time."

Stiltsken grabbed Rompell's shoulder forcing him to stop. Shoving

Stiltsken's hand away, Rompell spun around.

"What more can you do?" he shouted. "You already took my life."

Holding the vial out, Stiltsken said, "I am giving you the power to change your fate."

Rompell grabbed the vial and raised it to smash it on the ground. His arm stopped as a vision rose.

He saw their troupe leaving them, their horses collapsed and ribs pressing against skin stretched by starvation. He saw his sons hollow-cheeked, their eyes bulging as they stared at food they could not have. He saw Hidaya wrapping their daughter in black cloth and laying her on a funeral byre.

The vision faded as his arm lowered and his fingers clamped around the vial.

"Take it and save your children," Stiltsken said.

Rompell breathed in. He should throw it in the lake. However, he tucked it in his pocket.

Stiltsken reached to touch his hand to his forehead in salutation. Rompell took the opportunity to smash his fist against Stiltsken's jaw before marching to where his horse had stopped to eat some grass. Once he mounted, he did not look back as he rode to where his family and troupe waited.

The road to the nearest town was longer than Rompell remembered. They trudged on, their food running out on the second day, their water on the third. A wagon axle broke and the troupe packed what they could in the remaining wagons.

On the fourth day, they arrived at the edge of a small city. After filling their water skins and canteens, they moved to an open area to set-up camp. As others raised tents, Rompell counted out their dwindling money.

It was pitiful.

He went into the town and haggled with a merchant. It took much of his remaining strength to carry back the baskets of rice and lentils. As he and Hidaya gave half their food to their sons, he rubbed his thumb along the vial hidden in his pocket.

He could not trust Stiltsken, but he could not watch his children suffer.

Hidaya helped their sons and daughter to sleep as Rompell walked with several of the other men, assessing the repairs they had to make on the wagons and tents, the few remaining costumes and instruments, and the rest of their sad lot.

Returning to the tent, he sat beside where Hidaya lay.

Sitting up, she leaned against him. "We will find a way out. Papa always said mercy and miracles happen when you are at your lowest." She ran her fingers in his hair and smiled. "How else would you and I have found each other again?"

Rompell kissed her and leaned his forehead against hers.

They laid down together, holding each other close. He watched her as she faded into sleep.

She was his wife, mother to his children.

He had to keep her safe.

After an hour of trying to sleep, he got up and took a walk among their small caravan. Their elephants were gone, sold to feed them during the plague. They had a few of their tricks left, but they couldn't afford hiring enough men to raise the main tent. They could rebuild the troupe, but it would take investing in new costumes, new animals, and more performers.

He reached in his pocket and pulled out Stiltsken's vial. In eight years, he had kept no secrets from Hidaya. Yet, he could not bring himself to reveal this vial to her.

He flipped it through his fingers as he made another lap around the camp. In each of the tents were men and women who had chosen to follow him after Terrivan died. They were his friends and had become family over the years. Their children were being sent to bed as hungry as his own.

Reaching his tent, he sat inside, leaving the flap open as the sky lightened and the sun prepared to rise. He pressed his head to his knees as he prayed.

There were ways to survive, but most meant breaking up the troupe and letting each take what little they had.

He held up the vial, the first sunbeams gleamed through the liquid. A vision rose of Hidaya in bright clothes, laughing as she sat with their children. The troupe was in their former glory, the main tent raised, and a crowd pushing in to be the first to see the show.

His hands shook as he opened the vial and poured the liquid onto his tongue. It was acrid, metallic, and disgusting. He forced himself to swallow. A solid coldness poured through his veins and he bent over, hissing in pain.

He grabbed one of the inside poles to pull himself up. His eyes widened as metallic gold spread along the wood. He jumped back with a shout. Tilting his head, he prodded it. The pole was cool, solid gold.

With a laugh, he clapped his hands. He picked up one of Hidaya's hairpins. The pewter turned to gold.

"Papa?"

Jabir and Amal peeked from behind the curtain separating their area of the tent. Rompell motioned for them to come.

Their eyes grew wide as Rompell picked up one of Jabir's wooden toys, turning it to gold. Kneeling beside them, he handed it to Jabir. The boy turned it over, smiling at the gleaming toy.

Rompell grinned and placed his hands on Jabir and Amal's shoulders. "Things will be better. We will—"

Gold ran down their arms, spreading like paint pouring down a wall. Amal's eyes watered as he gasped for air and reached for his father's hand. Rompell caught his son's fingers, feeling the warmth just before they became hard and metallic.

"Just hold on," Rompell said. There had to be a way to stop this. "I'll—"

"Papa?" was Jabir's last word before gold spread across his face and he stood a statue.

Rompell touched their cheeks. His chest ached, his heart raced. He rose, pressing his hands to his shirt. The cotton remained cloth.

This was a nightmare. That was all. He would wake in a moment and all would be well.

"Rompell?" Hidaya said as she touched his shoulder.

A shiver ran through Rompell as he jumped back, holding his hands away from him.

"What's wrong?" she said with a yawn. "I—"

She gasped and then snapped her mouth shut as she saw her sons. Her warm hand gripped his.

"Hidaya! No!"

Coolness spread up her hand. Rompell turned to her. Tears welled in her eyes as she gasped as if drowning. Rompell tightened his hold on her hand. If he held hard enough, he could stop the gold from spreading up her arm and to her shoulders.

Her other hand reached out to him. Rompell panted as he stared at her face, now solid gold. Remembering the many legends he had heard, he pressed his hands to her cheeks and kissed her lips.

She remained gold.

A sob wracked through him, an ache cracking against his ribs as he fell to the ground. Panting, he pressed his hands to his head. He shut his eyes and held his breath. This could not be true.

Yet, he opened his eyes, and there stood his sons and Hidaya, fully gold.

"I'm so sorry," he breathed. "I shouldn't have—"

Tamina broke into a wail, her cry shattering through Rompell.

He ran to their trunk of clothing, letting it turn to gold as he opened it. From the top, he grabbed a pair of gloves. They stayed leather.

He pulled them on and then touched everything near him. Nothing changed.

It would still be better to be careful.

He grabbed a blanket and wrapped it around his wailing daughter before lifting her into his arms. She snuggled against his shoulder and calmed.

Tears streamed as he held her tightly. His teeth clamped together as he turned to face the statues of his wife and sons.

He yelled, releasing the anger building within.

He had been a fool and should have known better.

He would find a way to restore them. And along the way, he would destroy Stiltsken.

Chapter 13

Adeline held out her hand, raising her ring finger just slightly, the diamond gleaming in the morning light. Where most women had oohed and gasped, Mrs. Hunter let out a quiet, "Hmm."

"It is wonderful, isn't it?" Adeline loved watching it glitter on her finger, reminding her of the promises she and Bronhart had made to each other.

"He must have sacrificed much to get it for you." Mrs. Hunter took a sip out of her teacup as she glanced at the sitting room. "Your father's letter made the damage seem far worse."

Adeline waved her hand. "Papa hired a few workers to help clean up. Just one or two windows to replace now. Nothing much." She sighed as she looked down at her ring. "All is well."

"I wish you had come with me to the Surris Mountains." Mrs. Hunter set down her cup and whistled, sending her spoon stirring on its own. "You would have gained much by going there."

"It would have mattered little." Adeline pulled Mrs. Hunter's spoon from the cup and set it to the side. "I have decided to give up magic."

Mrs. Hunter's eyebrow arched up. "Magic is a part of who we are. It is not some poor habit you can merely give up."

"I have passed my twentieth birthday and Nathaniel believes the Septorum Disease excuse. I see no reason to use magic, except to assist your classes next year."

Mrs. Hunter took a long sip of her tea. "So, you plan to continue as a teacher at the Bradford School?"

"Only another year. Nathaniel and I have decided to marry next spring."

"Spring is many months away. Are you sure you wish your engagement to be so long?"

Adeline smiled. Bronhart had argued with her, pushing for a date in the fall or winter. However, he had agreed once she had explained why neither would do.

"We are fully dedicated to each other and fall is much too soon to plan a fine enough wedding. As for winter—"

Adeline glanced at the empty fireplace and shuddered. She remembered lying beside her mother, watching her final breaths puff out as mist in the air. Then came the night she laid in the snow, preparing for the freezing cold to take her. It would have won if Rompell hadn't rescued her.

Her voice soft, she said, "I wish there to be flowers and sunshine on my wedding day."

Mrs. Hunter watched her as if analyzing a puzzle.

"You have grown up well, Miss Winkleston," she said, "and will always be welcome at the Bradford School."

Adeline smiled. It would be strange to leave the Bradford School behind after she and Bronhart were married.

"I came today because I have a gift."

Mrs. Hunter pulled a letter from her handbag and placed it on the table between them. Adeline's name was written in elegant cursive across the envelope. Something drew Adeline to it and she reached out her hand. Closing her fist, she placed her hand on the armrest.

"In my visits to the Surris Mountains every few years," Mrs. Hunter said, "I have asked to speak with the Dumond family."

Adeline's heart jumped at the mention of her mother's maiden name.

"My requests were turned down many times, but I happened to meet your mother's sister during this visit."

Adeline dug her fingers into her armrests. She always wondered about her mother's family, but it was easier to not think of people she was sure to never find. Especially if they were anything like her grandfather on her father's side, sitting in his mansion and pretending she did not exist.

If her mother's family knew about her and cared, they would have sought her. With magic, they should have found her quickly. They should have been the ones who lifted her from the snow. Instead, Rompell had saved her.

Her teeth clamped together as she bit back the dark swell of emotions. These were feelings she shouldn't have a few weeks after her engagement. Life was simpler if she thought of her mother's family as strangers completely unconnected to her. She did not need them nor their magic.

Mrs. Hunter pulled a scroll from her bag and rolled it across the small table. A long list of names connected with lines spread on the aged paper.

"Like most families in the Surris Mountains," Mrs. Hunter said, "the Dumonds trace their heritage back to the nobility who escaped Barthan during the revolution centuries ago. They even claim royal heritage, but I do not see what that matters in this modern age."

She placed a finger toward the bottom where "Mariana Dumond Winkleston" was written. Adeline's throat clenched at her father's name beside her mother's and a line flowing down to her own name.

There they were, mother, father, and daughter, together.

It was only a few words, yet a tear fell down her cheek. "When did they add my name?"

"Apparently, your grandmother refused to add it for years. But, your mother's elder sister, Arastella, added it while I was there." Mrs. Hunter touched the letter. "This is from her. She believed you had died soon after your mother."

Adeline stared at the list of names, wondering why her aunt had given up on her.

"Your aunt wants to meet you, to introduce you to your mother's family." A rare softness entered Mrs. Hunter's eyes. "I have worked with many orphans at the Bradford School. Few have such a chance to connect with their past."

"It is a kind invitation," Adeline said, keeping her voice soft to hide the emotions pulsing through her. She did not know how she felt. Anger mixed with the warmth of connection. She wished Rompell was here, to hold her hand and give her strength.

Staring at the letter, she pictured arriving in the Surris Mountains and meeting her aunt. Her heart would crack apart as she met a woman who surely looked much like her mother.

Yet, it would take at least a week to reach the mountains and another week or two to return. Besides, Arastella was only a name. What good would come from facing a past which had been closed off long ago?

"I must stay here and plan my wedding to Nathaniel," Adeline said

Mrs. Hunter laid her hand on the scroll, her eyes bearing a firmness.

"This is your heritage, Miss Winkleston. Before you marry Mr. Bronhart and 'give up' your magic, I suggest reading your aunt's letter and looking at the names listed here. These men and women are your family, even if you do not know them. You gained your magic ability from them. That is a great inheritance which cannot be ignored.

"I have already interfered more in your personal affairs than I wish, but I think you should consider your aunt's invitation. Perhaps your honeymoon can be a chance to meet your mother's family."

Adeline shook her head.

"My papa is my family." Except for her parents, the names on the scroll were merely words. "And, once we are married, Nathaniel and I will begin our own."

She rolled up the scroll. A pressure eased within her, seeing the traces of magic in her lineage hidden once more. She held the scroll out to Mrs. Hunter. "I am glad to see where my mother is from, but I have no need to know them."

Mrs. Hunter's dark eyes watched Adeline, a calculation clearly forming.

"It is a gift," she said as she rose. "Congratulations on your engagement. Mr. Bronhart seems an admirable man."

Adeline escorted Mrs. Hunter to the door. Once the headmistress was gone, she let out her pent-up breath.

Mrs. Hunter would never understand her need to be free of the magic weighing on her. And now, the letter and scroll loomed on the table, their presence taunting her with a past better left forgotten.

Taking the letter and scroll from the table, Adeline carried them to her bedroom and stuffed them in a drawer full of ribbons and other odds and ends. The tightness in her chest eased as she slid the drawer closed, separating herself from memories her mother had left in Surris.

Chapter 14

The cool breeze of fall stirred the leaves outside as Adeline twirled in front of the set of mirrors, the white dress spreading around her.

"I love it," Serena said as she held the notepad in her lap.

Adeline looked down at the laced sleeves and bodice, beads along the edge of the skirt. It was beautiful and everything she had pictured for the past few months. Each day held another wonder as she planned her future with Bronhart. This would be the perfect dress for beginning their life together.

"How much?" Rompell said as he looked at Mrs. Chancey.

"Oh, not much more than the others."

"How much?"

Adeline's face paled as the curved woman named a price several hundred more than the budget Rompell had given her. She glanced at her father. He could afford it. She didn't want him to use his curse, but he could, if he had to.

Rompell snapped open his pocket watch and glanced at it. Standing, he said, "That is not in the range I gave you."

"But look at her radiance." Mrs. Chancey placed a veil on Adeline's head. Adeline gave her sweetest smile and batted her eyes. Seeing her so beautiful and happy would soften him.

Rompell tucked his pocket watch away as his face remained unmoved. "We will make one more appointment. If the dresses shown are not in the agreed range, we will find another dressmaker."

Fluttering the skirt, Mrs. Chancey said, "I am sure we could negotiate."

"I have given you a range, madam. I have been a customer for a long time and I expect my wishes to be respected."

Once changed back into her regular dress, Adeline walked out arm-in-arm with Serena, Rompell behind them.

"It's a beautiful dress," Serena whispered. "I am sure you'll change your father's mind."

Adeline laughed and squeezed her hand. "I am sure too."

As Rompell drove away in his motorcar, Adeline and Serena sat close together in the back seat, speaking of colors and types of flowers, and all the wonders that would come in April's wedding. She chatted with Serena all the way to her friend's home and walked her to the door.

Rompell remained silent, even after Serena was delivered to her house and Adeline moved to the front seat.

"Papa," Adeline said. "A few hundred macs is a small sacrifice. It is a beautiful dress."

"Mrs. Chancey will come down at least two hundred on our next appointment," he said. "And then make the cost up in tailoring. I just want you to think about it a few days before deciding."

She smiled and kissed his cheek. "It is the perfect dress. I shall not find better."

The hard line of his jaw eased and he squeezed her arm.

As they drove back to their home on Nightingale Lane, Adeline spoke of her future with Bronhart. Rompell listened with a warm glint in his eye. She leaned against his arm, glad to see him so happy for her even as she prepared to leave his home.

However, she and Bronhart would always be close by. Rompell would come for dinner and games on Sunday. She glanced at him, picturing the softness in his eyes as he held her and Bronhart's first child in his arms.

There was so much future joy she would give him in return for all he had done for her.

As they turned onto Nightingale Lane, a gleam flickered, leading her gaze to a polished motorcar sitting in front of their home. Gold decorated the white motor cover and edged the windshield. It was a fine vehicle, far better than anyone in their neighborhood could afford.

Rompell's frown was deep as he drove up their narrow driveway. Turning off the engine, he said, "Stay here."

He stepped out and approached the motorcar. Adeline waited a breath before exiting. She hated it when he forgot she was a grown woman who could manage protecting herself.

Pulling off her lace gloves, she walked toward the house entrance. Her heart leapt toward her throat as a middle-aged woman stepped out from their covered porch.

"Good afternoon!" The woman and her white chiffon silk dress floated down the porch steps. Her brunette hair highlighted with gray streaks formed a wreath framing her round face. It was complemented by her hat covered in white feathers.

Wearing a warm smile on her painted face, the woman said, "You look too much like your father to not be Adeline Winkleston."

Adeline twisted her glove in her hand, trying to push down an ill feeling. This woman did not mean Rompell, but Adeline said, "I am adopted."

The stranger's brown eyes twinkled and she laughed. "Yes, I know you are. And, given what a fine young woman you've become, Mr. Rompell has done excellent work raising you."

Almost as if his name summoned him, Rompell stepped between Adeline and the stranger.

"I told you not to speak to her directly, Mrs. Dolan," he said.

"She is a grown woman now," Mrs. Dolan said. "You may have raised her, but you are no longer her legal guardian."

"She is still under my protection."

"She needs no protection from her only living family."

A shiver ran through Adeline as she glanced at the motorcar. Part of her wished this woman was from her mother's side, that the Dumonds cared enough to come to her. However, the gilding on the motorcar and Mrs. Dolan's polished appearance brought her back to standing in front of a wrought iron fence along North Lane, staring up at a mansion she could never enter, her father pointing at the grounds and saying, "And that's where I first saw your mother."

She stepped closer to Rompell, his tall form blocking her from this stranger.

"Spencer Winkleston has no right to contact her," he said.

Mrs. Dolan's smile remained but a graveness entered her eyes. "He is her grandfather and she is all he has left."

Adeline's teeth clamped together. Five years ago, she had read of one of her father's brothers dying in a boating accident. Two years ago, the other brother died from influenza. Both had merely been names in the paper. Giving them anymore thought reminded her of them standing in her grandfather's shadow at her father's funeral, neither giving her even a glance. Spencer Winkleston, however, kept his eyes on her and her mother, his cold glare speaking his hatred.

"Mr. Winkleston has already sent three letters inviting her to his mansion but has heard nothing."

"I burned the letters," Rompell said. "They broke our contract."

Adeline looked up at her foster father. "What contract?"

Keeping his hard eyes on Mrs. Dolan, Rompell said to Adeline, "When he signed your guardianship over to me, he promised never to contact you." He glanced at her. "He already caused you enough pain. I wanted you to be free of him."

Adeline touched her father's arm, wishing he had told her. He meant to protect her, yet protecting her didn't mean keeping such secrets from her. Even from a grandfather who brought shivers of anger whenever she pictured her dying mother. Still, she turned to Mrs. Dolan and said, "What does he want?"

Meeting Adeline's eyes, Mrs. Dolan said, "He is dying."

"Dying?" The word felt strange. In her mind, Spencer Winkleston remained the tall, strong figure he had been over a decade before.

After her father's funeral, he had left her and her mother with nothing. If he or her uncles had helped them even a little, her mother may have lived. Without Rompell, Adeline herself would have died as a child.

She began to open her lips to decline, but stopped as she looked to her foster father, standing strong beside her as he glared at Mrs. Dolan.

Her memories drew her to the evening a few years before, when he had taken her to his warehouse and shown her the statues of his wife and sons, hidden safe inside a large wooden crate. She held his hand, sitting close beside him as he wept, telling her how he had lost them and given his daughter to his brother to raise.

She turned her gaze to Mrs. Dolan, who held out her hand, her eyes pleading.

Her grandfather had lost all three of his sons. If his pain was anywhere near the sorrow Rompell had shown that night, perhaps he had changed.

"He wishes to see you before he is gone." Mrs. Dolan said. "The doctors say time is growing short. Will you come, Miss Winkleston?"

"He abandoned her," Rompell said, "and left her to die. He has no right to—"

"I will go." The words burned in Adeline's throat, but she forced them out.

Spencer Winkleston may have abandoned her, but she would spare a few hours to see him. Any dying man deserved a single chance.

"Thank you. He will be so grateful."

Adeline doubted her grandfather was capable of gratitude, but she would go all the same.

"We will follow you." Rompell marched to his motorcar and yanked the passenger door open. Adeline gave Mrs. Dolan a polite smile before joining Rompell.

The warmth of the earlier drive was gone and they rode in silence across Pippington to North Town. She and Serena had ridden in a carriage along these avenues, admiring the mansions and expanses of gardens from afar. Even Serena's parents appeared paupers when beside these homes.

They followed Mrs. Dolan's white motorcar up the driveway to the sprawling Winkleston Manor. Adeline gripped Rompell's arm as they came closer to the entryway lined with marble pillars.

As the car stopped, Rompell's gloved hand wrapped around hers and he looked her in the eye.

"The letters said nothing about his health. They were only requests to meet you." He glanced down. "All I want for you, Adeline, is happiness. You've found that with Bronhart. I didn't want the memories of your grandfather ruining anything."

Her throat tightened as a tear threatened to come. However, she would not show tears in front of Spencer Winkleston.

"He may be my grandfather," she said, "but you are my papa."

She kissed his cheek as a valet opened the door for her.

"Thank you again for coming," Mrs. Dolan said as she led them through the wide double doors. Adeline gaped up at the entry way's chandelier, the light reflecting on mirrors lining the top part of the walls, all of it highlighting the delicate artwork on the ceiling.

"Mr. Rompell, will you please wait here?" Mrs. Dolan gestured to a set of velvet-lined couches around a crystalline table. "Mr. Winkleston wishes to speak to her alone."

Adeline looked to Rompell. She wanted him to go with her but did not dare say anything. He gave her a small nod and stepped into the lobby area.

Leading Adeline down a long hall, Mrs. Dolan spoke cheerily of the labyrinthine rooms and halls making up the mansion. Adeline's eyes traced the lush carpet lining the marble hallway, wondering if it were the same her father had run on as a child. Though, with black cloths covering much of the furniture and hanging over paintings, the building felt as if the life had drained from it.

Servants stood at attention at nearly every doorway. Once she and Mrs. Dolan passed, whispers echoed behind them. Adeline could feel gazes following her.

A crowd of men and women in dark mourning clothes packed a sitting room. The women's eyes were reddened as they dabbed with their handkerchiefs. The room hushed as Mrs. Dolan led Adeline in. Adeline gave a polite smile but could feel the cheapness of her silk shirt and cotton skirt.

"I'll speak to Mr. Winkleston," Mrs. Dolan said.

Adeline stood to the side, listening to the massive grandfather clock tick away. The men and women whispered to each other as they glanced at her, suspicion in their eyes. She could feel them scrutinizing every detail about her. Some of the girls at the Bradford School had done the same as she had grown up, but their stares did not feel so cold.

A man in his early forties entered with a brisk step, his hair slicked but his suit coat wrinkled as if he had slept in it. Under his arm, he carried a thick stack of folders, some papers looking as if about to fall. He glanced around the room before marching toward her.

Holding out his empty hand, he smiled. "Miles Taggart, Mr. Winkleston's attorney."

Giving his hand a polite shake, she said quietly, "Adeline Wink—"

His eyes widened. "Don't say another word, miss." Stepping closer, he whispered, "So, you're the girl." He nodded toward the crowd. "Don't let the vultures know who you are."

Her forehead wrinkled, but she didn't have time to contemplate as Mrs. Dolan opened the mahogany doors and waved for her to enter. Mr. Taggart stayed close to Adeline, acting as a wall between her and the crowd.

The room beyond was dim, with just a sliver of sunlight illuminating it. A lamp lit the expansive bed where Spencer Winkleston lay.

Wishing she had Rompell or Bronhart to lean on, Adeline walked toward her grandfather. Her hands shook and each step faltered. She felt like a small girl again, scared and lost as she tried to understand her father's death.

Back then, Spencer Winkleston had stood tall, his white hair thick, his body firm and strong. Standing over him today, his skin was gray and hung on his gaunt frame. His glazed eyes focused on her and he raised his bony hand toward her.

His reddish lips flexed before he said, "You came."

She could feel the sorrow in his eyes, yet she could not feel sorrow for him. If he hadn't rejected her mother, Mariana Winkleston might be alive and have her arm wrapped around Adeline. His cruelty had taken so much from her. She wanted to run back through the mansion and to Rompell but could not move her feet.

"Mrs. Dolan says you are a teacher at the Bradford School."

Adeline could only stare.

"Respectable institution." He smacked his lips together and wheezed in a breath. "That Sandarian barbarian has raised you quite well."

Her eyes widened and her jaw clenched. She was better than saying harsh words to a dying man. Instead, she turned toward the door. She had come and done her duty and could leave in peace.

As she took her first step, however, her eyes drew to the portrait on the wall.

There stood a painting of her father, his blue eyes so much like hers, so bright with youth. He stood in a noble pose bearing a dashing smile. Adeline turned her head away as her throat tightened and tears came.

Rompell had been good to her and she loved him, but it was not the same as with her parents. Her chest ached as a longing she had often pushed away pulsed within her. If only, just once, she could bring Bronhart to meet her parents, to have them smile proudly and have her mother giggle with her as they discussed her romance.

But they had been stolen from her.

"I did wrong by my boy," Spencer Winkleston said, "and by you. Let me make it right."

She turned and stared at his outstretched hand.

Rompell was the one who had made things right.

"I want nothing," she said, her voice soft.

"You are my granddaughter," he said, "and are worth far more."

His hand shook as he motioned for her to take the chair beside him. Adeline remained standing, her hands folded in front of her.

"I have lost my boys," he said. "You are all the future I have. I—" He wheezed out a cough. "Tell me—tell me about your life, tell me what I missed."

Adeline's chest ached as she stared into his pleading eyes. Somewhere in their aged haze, she saw a glint of her father. She wanted to turn and go but could not abandon this worn man. She could not forgive him, but she could give him a glimpse of the life he could have shared with her.

The afternoon wore on into night. Adeline broke her story only for brief meals of soup and for a doctor to check on him. Mr. Taggart and Mrs. Dolan stepped in and out of the room. Mrs. Dolan was clearly the true master of Spencer Winkleston's affairs and deftly managed the waiting crowd.

As the clock outside rang a late hour, her grandfather faded into sleep. Despite being in a stiff chair in a strange room, Adeline tilted her head and drifted to sleep herself.

Her head snapped up and she jumped from the chair as she woke. The morning sun peeked through the narrow opening in the curtain. The sliver of light illuminated the white cloth the doctor had lain over her grandfather.

The room felt colder and her breath became short.

"Come with me." Mrs. Dolan wrapped a shawl around Adeline's shoulders and pulled her through a side-door leading to a balcony overlooking the garden. Adeline gasped in the fresh air and dropped into one of the iron chairs.

She huddled in the chair, shutting her eyes, trying to push away the memory of waking at her mother's side, only to see her gone. Now, her grandfather was gone as well.

She half-heard conversation as tea was brought with breakfast. Still, she kept her eyes shut, trying to center herself.

An arm wrapped around her shoulder and a forehead pressed against hers.

"All is well, Little One."

She burst into tears and threw her arms around Rompell's shoulders. He hugged her tightly, much as he had when she was a child. Opening her eyes, she pulled away. The tenseness in her chest eased further as Bronhart entered the patio.

"I sent for him once Mrs. Dolan told me Mr. Winkleston had passed." Rompell stepped to the side as Bronhart came closer.

Adeline rose from the chair and threw her arms around him, her lips swiftly meeting his. He pulled her tightly against him. She smiled at his tossing aside of propriety, even in front of her papa.

Pulling away, he brushed back the hair from her face. "Is everything all right?"

"I did what I had to, but I want to go home."

"Not yet," Rompell said. "Mr. Taggart wishes to speak with you, when you're ready."

"Can it be done quickly?" She looked up at the cold walls of the mansion. "I don't want to be here any longer than I must."

Bronhart and Rompell sat on either side of her as they joined her breakfast. Though polite conversation was made, each second grinded by slower than the last.

Finally, Mr. Taggart joined them at the breakfast table, his suit even more crumpled than before.

"Thank you for waiting," he said. "I had to help Mrs. Dolan get the jackals out of the mansion."

He set down a stack of folders and slid the top one to Adeline. "Usually, we wait a bit longer before sitting down with the family to read the will, but—" He glanced at the glass doors leading to the balcony, watching for any listeners. "Mrs. Dolan and I suspect rumors are already spreading."

"I need nothing from him." Adeline slid the folder back to Mr. Taggart.

"I recommend waiting till you know what you're rejecting."

Bronhart squeezed Adeline's hand and Rompell gave her a steadying nod. To Taggart, she said, "Go ahead."

Taggart pulled on a pair of spectacles before reading, "The final will and testament of Spencer Theodore Winkleston. With the passing of my three sons before their time, I have determined to place sole heirship on the progeny of my third son, Conrad William Winkleston: his daughter, Miss Adeline Winkleston."

"Sole heirship?" Bronhart said. "Of what? Are there any assets attached, or only the Winkleston name?"

"We're getting to that." Taggart adjusted his glasses before reading on, "Per consultation with my account managers, I have determined a few itemized donations and gifts for charities and extended families. The sum of the remaining assets, inclusive of my businesses, estates, properties, and investments are to be bequeathed to Miss Adeline Winkleston as full and complete heir."

Adeline's eyes grew wide as she stared at the paper in Taggart's hand.

This mansion was hers.

As was so much more.

The words on that paper felt like a bribe, seeking her forgiveness. She had thought he would give her nothing or a token piece of jewelry. This, however, she could not comprehend.

Taggart set down the paper and looked her in the eye. "He made this a week ago, when his doctor made it clear the end was coming too quickly. He was sorry for tossing out your father and wanted to right the greatest wrong of his life."

Rompell's gloved hand rested on hers. "How much?"

Taggart tapped the folders on the table. "Everything should be here." He flipped to the top paper and slid it across the table to her. "It is itemized in here. There should be three mansions and estates, a whole city's worth of property, and a portfolio of factories and other businesses."

Adeline stared at the words and numbers, but they were only a blur.

Bronhart leaned over the paper and frowned. "There are very few cash assets. Most of this is investments and property." His breath caught in his throat and his eyes widened. "But, together, everything is worth more than six million macs."

Her eyes flicked between Rompell, Bronhart, and the numbers lined up on the paper.

She pressed her hands to her head as the dreams for her future tumbled together. All of her worries of paying for the wedding, saving up for a pair of Cordwainer shoes, and the challenges of having enough to build the life she wanted with Bronhart melted away.

Turning toward her fiancé, a broad smile crossed her face. His bewildered expression faded and he kissed her.

"What a life we will have together," he whispered. "What a life."

Chapter 15

Adeline leaned back in her chair, taking in the fading colors of fall throughout the garden. Beside her, Serena read Petunia Ophombauch's words from *The Rosetown Journal*:

> *Miss Winkleston wore a gown of white and summer peach, the gossamer as light and airy as her laugh. She is a bright young woman, with manners and grace to match the finest of ladies. Sitting to brunch in the exquisite garden of her new estate, we spoke in close and candid words.*

Serena turned the page. "Oh, Adeline. You do look beautiful in these pictures."

Adeline sat up as Serena held open *The Rosetown Journal*. The first portrait was of her standing with a parasol beside one of the manor's fountains. Her smile in the picture was meant for Bronhart, who stood behind the photographer. He had been beside her every moment he could since becoming the wealthiest heiress in Pippington. Even after a week since her grandfather's passing, it was strange to look out at her newly inherited grounds, knowing all of this and so much more was hers.

Flipping to the next page, Serena gasped. "Your father looks so handsome."

"What?" Adeline grabbed the paper from Serena. There lay a black and white picture of Rompell standing in his fine suit, leaning against a fence as his grave face looked out over the garden. The caption read,

Rompell, the sentinel of Miss Winkleston's life.

"Oh no," Adeline whispered.

"What's wrong? It's very well done."

"Papa asked them not to take his picture." Adeline wrung her hands.

It had been wonderful meeting Petunia Ophombauch after reading her column for so long. She had all the smiles and warmth Adeline had imagined, yet some of her questions had been too prying. She didn't mind telling her own story, but Rompell's was one which needed to remain hidden.

Serena smiled as she squeezed Adeline's arm. "Your father will just have to get used to the attention. He deserves to be commended." She gave Adeline a wink. "Though, all the widows in town will be coming to visit."

Adeline moaned as she pressed a hand to her head. There was no simple way to explain his wife had been transformed into a golden statue.

Leaning on her elbow, Serena looked up at the heights of the mansion. "Are you sure you still want to stay at Rompell's?"

"It is home." Adeline's eyes traced the pillars decorating the outer walls. The chill she felt while inside was fading, but she still glanced over her shoulder as she walked the halls, waiting to be tossed out as a fraud. In time, she would be used to the place, but she was not ready yet. "At least until Nathaniel and I marry. Moving here will be better with him beside me."

"I could not be happier for you." Serena let out a contented sigh. "It is so wonderful."

"We will find you a man with a few million of his own," Adeline said with a laugh, "and he will buy a nearby mansion and you and I will see each other every day."

"I would be content to find a man who's interested in more than himself."

They giggled together and Adeline's smile broadened. She had so much to fill her life now. Yet, there was an unease pressing in at the edge that she couldn't shake away. It could simply be the lack of her parents, but it was just as likely something else. However, once she and Bronhart were married and she got used to this new life, the unease would fade.

The first few months were filled with nights of her arm resting on Bronhart's as she attended balls and galas. Her gowns were finer than even the dress she had hoped to wear to her wedding. She was grateful to Mrs. Dolan for guiding her to the best designers and seamstresses in Pippington. Everyone in her new life welcomed her warmly, complimenting her and guiding her as she took on the role of heiress.

It was strange to leave this ethereal world of jewels and witty conversation to return to Nightingale Lane. Whenever she came home, the house seemed even smaller. Yet, it eased her to sit with Rompell each night, telling him the wonders of the evening. During her tutoring sessions, she told the Bradford Girls of the latest splendor, even after Mrs. Hunter gave her a stern glance.

The first snows of winter came with an invitation to the dinner table of Mrs. Petunia Ophombauch herself. As Adeline sat in the gilded room, the crystalline chandelier glittering above, she grinned.

"Get yourself a pair of Talbot's shoes," the round hostess said as she cut into her pheasant. "They are beautiful and like walking on air. Save your young feet, my dear."

"I grew up wearing Talbot's shoes," Adeline said, tucking her feet adorned in a new pair of Cordwainers under her chair, ignoring the sharp pinch around her toes.

"Oh, really?" Mrs. Ophombauch sat up, the carefully curled

ringlets framing her face bouncing with the movement. "Your feet must be well-formed."

Adeline took a moment to cut through the asparagus which had been splayed like a peacock's tail. Peter Talbot's new shoes were quite beautiful, but she couldn't bring herself to buy a pair. His shoes were a part of the past she needed to leave behind as she took on her new role.

"How about you, Bronhart," Mr. Ophombauch said. "Have you met the fine Mr. Talbot?"

Bronhart looked up from prodding his plate as if unsure what was food or decoration. His smile was as charming as ever, though Adeline could see the disinterest in his eyes. He had worn the same expression at their last four dinners. She had marked the first to tiredness, but it was beginning to worry her.

"I don't believe so," he said. "I mainly wear factory boots."

"You must order a pair of Talbot's shoes." Mr. Ophombauch pounded his fist on the table. "Those factory rags are unworthy of your feet. Believe me, you will be glad."

The front doorbell rang and the butler hurried out of the room.

"I do hope it is our special guest." Mrs. Ophombauch looked to her daughter, Amelia. The plain young woman, bedecked in sheening fabric, blushed and fluttered her eyes.

Adeline tried not to raise an eyebrow. There were many girls like her among high society, whose greatest attraction was their father's wealth. Some were pleasant enough, but Amelia lacked the wit to overcome her plainness.

The butler entered. "Mr. Alvin Westengaard."

Adeline's knife clattered onto her plate. Her legs begged for her to leap from her chair. He had been at some of the larger events she had attended, but she had been able to avoid him among the crowd. Tonight, with such a small dinner party, there was no escaping him.

"A bit slippery, eh?" Mr. Ophombauch said as he snapped to one of the servants. "We can get you a different knife."

"It's all right." Adeline looked across the table at Bronhart. He sat up with a frown.

"You look quite pale, Miss Winkleston," Mrs. Ophombauch said. "Is that the new Whitcomb powder at work?"

"No. I—"

Her breath caught in her throat as Alvin Westengaard entered. His sapphire-blue eyes met hers and her heart skipped a beat.

If she did not know his past as Benjamin Stiltsken, she might have swooned under such a glance, her fiancé forgotten so close to her. However, she dug her fingers against the edge of the table. Goosebumps spread across her arm and a chill shuddered through her.

"Pardon my tardiness," Westengaard said, his voice smooth. He kissed Mrs. Ophombauch's hand before kissing Amelia's and giving her a teasing wink. She tittered out a laugh, her face turning pink. He stopped beside Adeline's chair.

"This must be the famous Adeline Winkleston."

He held out his hand. She kept her palms clamped to her armrests. All eyes at the table watched her, waiting for the polite gesture.

He bent down and whispered in her ear. "I think I am just as nervous to meet you."

Her breathing eased as he left her side and took his seat beside Bronhart and across from Amelia.

"And where were you, dear Westengaard?" Amelia tapped his arm with her fan.

Westengaard drew his fingers through the air in a sharp line. "I was crossing the street, when a thief attacked me. It took my greatest skill to fend him off." He brushed his fingers on his coat as he grinned. "I had to return to my townhouse and make sure I was dressed fine enough to be in your presence."

The Ophombauch women laughed while Bronhart stabbed his pheasant with a fork.

Westengaard turned in his chair as a servant set his plate. "Now, Mr. Bronhart was it? What is your line of business?"

"He's my account manager," Mr. Ophombauch said. "Best I've had at Mackabee and Sons. When I learned he was engaged to Miss Winkleston, I said to myself, 'Now, there's a young man who knows where to make investments.'"

His chortle was joined by the two ladies and Westengaard. Adeline attempted to smile while her eyes met Bronhart's. His jaw was set firm as he maintained a polite smile. She fumbled with her knife before finally having a large enough piece of pheasant to eat. She set the meat in her mouth and chewed on it but could not bring herself to swallow.

"We met long before she knew of her inheritance," Bronhart said.

"Ah, but you had to be aware of the Winkleston fortune," Mr. Ophombauch said.

"I thought the name a mere coincidence."

Westengaard laughed. "Let the man be, my friends. Mrs. Ophombauch, you wrote the story of their meeting yourself. A hero riding in on his steed to assist a maiden? It is the same romantic beginning I would dream for one of my novels."

"I heard Miss Fairhaven wasn't so happy about it," Amelia said nearly under her breath.

Bronhart's knife slipped and scraped on the plate.

"Your knife must be slippery too." Mr. Ophombauch snapped to another servant. "Must not have been washed properly."

"I was on an errand to help a friend," Bronhart said, "and happened to be fortunate enough to assist Miss Winkleston."

Westengaard smiled at Adeline. "When such miraculous things happen in common life, I always hold onto the article." He took a bite of his pheasant before saying, "It is too bad your father could not join us tonight. I asked Mr. Ophombauch to invite him. You see—" He smiled at Mrs. Ophombauch. "I believe Rompell and I are old friends."

Adeline nearly choked on her food. She grabbed her glass of water and forced down a swallow. Bronhart began to rise to assist her, but she waved for him to stay.

"Oh, really?" Mrs. Ophombauch leaned on her elbow.

"I was a young man, a bit impetuous," Westengaard said. "I travelled to Sandar and served in the army to overthrow the false government. Rompell was my commander. He might not remember me. I was only one of a few hundred Barthanians serving under him."

"Is that how you are able to write such adventures?" Amelia said, her eyelids fluttering rapidly.

Adeline had seen such flirting before, but this fluttering seemed more than was healthy.

"I learned many things during that time," he said. "Which have helped me build my tales of fiction." He grinned at Adeline, his eyes bearing a false innocence. "I am sure you can imagine."

The words seemed to crawl on Adeline's skin. Setting down her glass, her eyes on Bronhart, she said, "I think I am falling ill."

Nearly leaping from his chair, Bronhart said, "Would you like me to take you home?"

She nodded. His stride was quick as he came around the table and pulled out her chair. Standing, she said, "Please forgive me. Thank you for the invitation. I shall return it as soon as I can."

Westengaard and Mr. Ophombauch stood and bowed as Bronhart held tightly to Adeline's arm and escorted her out. Even before the door shut, Adeline could hear Mrs. Ophombauch and Amelia speculating the cause of Adeline leaving.

Once alone in Adeline's motorcar, Bronhart said, "If you were ill, you should have told me."

"I was not ill. I just—" She pressed her lips together. "They were being so foul to you."

Bronhart lifted her hand and kissed it. "You should hear the rumors in the office, but it doesn't matter. Not as long as you and I know the truth."

She smiled and leaned her head on his shoulder as he drove her back to her childhood home. The comforting walls were a relief as she kissed Bronhart good night and went inside.

As usual, she found Rompell in his study, tinkering with some old contraption. He raised his head and glanced at the mantle clock. "You're home early."

She swallowed, unable to break the knot in her throat. "Westengaard was there."

Rompell dropped the tool in his hand as his own face paled.

"He said he served under your command when you were a soldier fighting in the civil war of Sandar."

"Blaggard."

"It was in the Ophombauch's home." She sat in the chair beside his desk. "The rumor will be spread through all of North Town by morning. What are we to do?"

"He is playing dangerously close to the truth," Rompell said. "However, the truth is worse for him than for me. He is a war criminal and cannot announce I am a dead emperor."

"I—I couldn't speak once he entered. I felt—Oh, Papa, he will be at other parties and balls. What am I to do? I cannot stand to be around him, but I must make appearances."

"What good are these balls and dinners, Adeline?" He tossed a book toward the wall. "You dress in expensive clothes and have empty conversation. There are better ways to spend your wealth and time."

"It is what is expected of my new station."

"What is expected is not what is best." He dropped into the chair across from her. "I did what was expected as emperor and got sentenced to death. You must find your own path, Adeline."

He grunted. "If only the Surris Rangers would do their job, but they keep making excuses and saying he's not dangerous." Rubbing his forehead, he said, "Maybe you and I should go abroad a month or two and let all the rumors calm themselves."

"I cannot leave Bronhart."

Rompell had been in love. He had to understand at least that, even if he didn't understand her role now that she was an heiress.

"Then marry him. I will arrange everything for tomorrow. It only needs to be you, Bronhart, Serena, and myself, doesn't it? We can have a reception later for friends."

"And Bronhart's family."

Rompell threw up his hand. "Yes, of course.

Shaking her head, Adeline said, "I will not be married in winter."

"Then use your magic to wake up some flowers." He grunted. "Whatever needs to be done."

"I won't use magic," she said. He was so angry at Westengaard he wasn't listening to her. "And, if I disappear, there will be rumors of a scandal."

"Let there be a scandal, as long as you are safe."

"I cannot," she said. "I have built a life here, and I shouldn't have to give it up because of him."

Rompell tapped his foot as he glared at the wall. Adeline waited, watching his cheek flex as he thought. At last, he turned to her. A weight hung on her as his tired eyes looked into hers.

"I already lost my family once to him." His lips pressed together before he said, "I cannot risk losing to Westengaard again."

Reaching across the table and taking his gloved hand, Adeline said, "Then I will avoid him and warn Bronhart that he is your enemy. That should be enough."

"Let us pray it is."

Chapter 16

Bronhart leaned against the small window in his office, looking out at the light-gray sky. Soon, the slush remaining from winter would melt, spring would finish coming, and Adeline would finally be his.

Once they were married, she would ease off the constant social gatherings and they could simply be husband and wife. He wished she had taken up his joking suggestion a few weeks before of just eloping. Her eyes had gone wide and jaw dropped.

"There will be talk," she said. "Everyone is waiting for this wedding."

"As am I," he replied.

However, he had let the notion go. Each time the wedding came up, it seemed to be more of a spectacle than a day to celebrate their marriage.

He hated the mansion, the massive grounds he had gotten lost in twice, and how people groveled to Adeline. He hated even more how she could not see it. Each day that passed, he was sure she was wearing another layer of make-up or a few more jewels.

Yet, in quiet moments as they sat in her father's parlor simply talking, he could see the girl he had met so many months ago. He had seen his sister and a few family friends prepare for weddings and it seemed to make the women lose their common sense. All he had to do was wait a few more weeks, marry her, and he would have his Adeline again.

His thoughts broke off as a clerk entered and dropped an envelope embossed with gold on his desk.

"Mr. Mackabee sends his congratulations."

Bronhart frowned as he picked up the envelope. Opening it, he grinned. Giving someone else good news was a fine relief.

He strode to Henry's small office and opened the door. Henry's brow furrowed as he looked up from his calculations. Bronhart tossed the envelope onto his friend's desk.

"Three months of work and we did it."

Henry raised an eyebrow before opening the envelope. His eyes widened and he snapped the envelope shut.

"Two tickets for Saturday's gala and dance at the Morveaux." Bronhart slapped Henry's shoulder. "All those late nights helping me have paid off. Miss Havish will be in for quite an evening."

Smoothing his hair, Henry said, "These are finer than I expected."

"You've no need to worry." Bronhart leaned against the table. "You've been planning this for weeks, and, as I've told you, Adeline and I will be there. If anything goes wrong, I'll do all I can to help you."

Given Henry's pale face as he stared at the envelope, Bronhart doubted any more encouragement would help.

Standing, he said, "Trust yourself, Henry. You're a solid fellow and Miss Havish is fortunate to have you."

Returning to his office, Bronhart let himself grin, despite the stares of clerks as he passed. If all went as planned, Henry would charm Miss Havish and Bronhart could break away from a vapid conversation to talk to Henry. He would make it through this week and a few more before marrying Adeline.

Adeline listened to the birds announcing the coming spring as she walked the garden of her mansion with Mrs. Dolan.

"And here is where the band will play and over there will be the dancing," Mrs. Dolan said as they entered one of the four courtyard areas. "A white tent will be over here with drinks and cakes, and we'll decorate this wall with garlands."

"It sounds beautiful," Adeline said as she half-listened.

She had invited Bronhart to come, but he had been occupied with work. Once they were married, she would speak to him about leaving his employment. They had no need of the money and there was so much to manage here.

"Flowers should be in bloom right on time," Mrs. Dolan said as she led Adeline to the front gate, "and everything you requested should be arranged. Is there anything else I can do?"

Adeline glanced up at the mansion. The chill she felt inside had eased as she had ordered new furniture and changed out some of the paintings on the walls. It was still not home, but Rompell's house was becoming so quaint.

"I might be moving here sooner than originally planned," she said.

"That will be excellent," Mrs. Dolan said. "Everyone is eager to welcome you. I will make sure everything is ready for whenever you choose to come."

Mrs. Dolan walked back to the mansion while Adeline stepped out of the gate and onto the wide sidewalk lining North Lane. She looked down the line of hedges leading up to the mansion's broad doors and elegant entryway. Only a few more weeks and the grandest of weddings would be here, celebrating her and Bronhart's new life together.

She smiled and let out a sigh. Her smile dropped as bicycle tires screeched and a familiar voice behind her said, "Good morning, Miss Winkleston!"

Turning, she faced Jack Kingston sitting on his bicycle and grinning at her.

She had seen him in passing only a few times over the past few months, but most of his work at the Bradford School was in the morning while hers was in the afternoon. Their few conversations had been brief greetings, with a few words of him congratulating her.

It was easier than discussing the flicker of magic he had seen last year.

"What an estate." He hopped off his bike and wheeled it over. "I knew you inherited quite a bit, but—" He whistled. "This is fine indeed."

She blinked at him, trying to understand his sudden appearance. "Thank you, Mr. Kingston."

"You're welcome. You know, I've been pretty lucky myself." He jabbed a thumb at his chest. "Just got accepted to the Officer Academy for the Pippington Police. Can you believe it?" He laughed. "Me? An officer?"

She couldn't quite believe it, but gave a quiet, "Congratulations," instead.

"Here we are, you an heiress, and me a soon-to-be officer. Wouldn't have thought that in our morning chats at the Bradford School."

"Certainly not."

"Well, I'm sure you're quite busy, especially with the wedding coming up." He nodded toward the street. "Should be off myself. Got hired to wash some windows down the lane." He tapped his hands on the bicycle. "I suppose you've got plenty of servants, but if your steward needs to hire any extra hands, let me know. Always can use more work."

He passed her his business card and mounted his bicycle. "Congratulations again, and best of luck to you."

Adeline watched him ride off on his bicycle, whistling brightly as he sped down the lane. His life was so simple compared with hers. Part of her envied him until she glanced at the finger smear of dirt on the card he had passed her.

He was part of a chapter of her life she had to close behind her. She would be polite to people like him and Mrs. Frizban, but her wealth carried her into higher spheres now. She had a role to uphold and a reputation to build. There was no time for her former position to weigh her down.

Chapter 17

Lights ornamented the entryway of the Morveaux with several spotlights shining on the cherubims and carved clouds weaving along the archway. Adeline nodded to other couples as Bronhart escorted her to their reserved box seats. In the box, they joined her friend, Helena Velis. The fellow heiress' hair was laced with ribbons and pearls, her dress complemented by the handsome young man adorning her arm.

Adeline kissed Helena's cheeks in greeting and then half-listened to Bronhart discussing something about business with Helena's date. Her eyes flitted across the crowd as she ran her finger over the waxed tips of her ringlets, holding everything in proper place. It was an elegant crowd as usual, but her chiffon dress embroidered with beads and glittering crystals remained the usual step above.

The curtain rose and the lights dimmed, cutting off her survey of the rest of the boxes lining the theater. Her eyes drifted as the tenor sang his aria of love for the soprano. She frowned as she placed her hand on Bronhart's wrist.

"Where are the cufflinks I sent yesterday?" she said.

"I left them in my office," Bronhart said as he ran his thumb over the dull gold. The diamond tipped cufflinks matched her dress much better. Hopefully, few would notice.

The music wore on, the voices beautiful but unremarkable. The orchestra was satisfactory but did not have the same wonder as her first night at the Morveaux. As the recital wore on, she yawned into her hand and tapped her fan against her leg.

She sat up as intermission came and the house lights rose.

"Now, there is a rare sight," Helena said as she looked through her opera glasses. Adeline raised hers and followed the gazes of every man in the theater.

Sitting at the center-left of the boxes was a woman with hair more golden than Adeline's, dressed resplendently in an emerald satin gown, a gold scarf fanned around her waist. Adeline leaned forward to get a better view of the dress. The woman flicked her wrist before placing her hand on her escort's shoulder. A pang throbbed in Adeline's forehead and she moaned as she dropped her opera glasses.

Bronhart touched her arm. "What's wrong?"

Adeline rubbed her temple. The headache was a dull shadow of those warning of her birthday. However, it was not her birthday. She shut her eyes. A dull buzzing was around her and it centered from the woman in the box. The stranger had powerful magic that felt skewed and wrong.

Picking up her opera glasses, Adeline wished she had a spectroscope. Whatever spell this woman was using was drawing the eyes of most men in the room. Though, a woman of her beauty hardly needed a spell to help her.

"Those seats are reserved by the Astrellar fortune," Helena said. "I've only heard of business partners being given seats as gifts."

"Astrellar?" Bronhart sat up and took Adeline's opera glasses. The delicate gold leafing looked odd beside his masculine face. His jaw tightened as he handed the glasses back to her. "What is she doing to him?"

"To who?" she said.

"The woman is Cassandra Astrellar." Bronhart glanced at Adeline. "Her fortune makes yours look like nothing."

"And the man with her? The skinny one with spectacles?"

"My friend Henry Kingston, her account manager at Mackabee and Sons." He shook his head. "Mackabee must have threatened his job. Henry won tickets for seats on the main floor tonight. He is supposed to be down there with the woman he's been courting."

Adeline raised her opera glasses and looked at Henry. Cassandra smiled as she spoke to him, but his face remained stern and pale as he stared straight forward.

"Perhaps his spectacles prevent him from seeing what a beauty she is," Helena said with a laugh.

Adeline forced her own laugh even as she tried to keep her jaw from clenching. Regardless of what magic she was using, her presence would draw attention from Adeline. There were so few weeks before the wedding. Even a few papers in Willington wished to cover the event. This Cassandra couldn't be allowed to swoop in and steal her attention.

"He can see her beauty as well as any other man," Bronhart said.

"Rupert, what do you think of her?" Helena said to her date. When he said nothing, she whapped his leg with her fan. "Rupert!"

He broke from his dazed stare focused on Cassandra. "Oh. I hadn't noticed her."

The lights dimmed once more. Through the next set of songs, Adeline and Helena leaned close to Bronhart and lobbed questions at him. He spoke of what he could about her wealth, her position, and so on, but, as the third song ended, he said, "Ladies, pardon me, but I would like to enjoy the concert."

Adeline folded and unfolded her fan as the last few songs were performed. She was sure the singers were quite good but could not listen. Instead, she glared at this Cassandra Astrellar, wondering what spell she used to create such an allure.

As the final song was halfway through, Bronhart reached over and clamped his hand on Adeline's fan, keeping it closed.

"Please," he said. "Just a few moments more."

The soprano's final note ran on, seeming never to end as it faded. Adeline joined the standing ovation but kept her eyes on Cassandra. Her head throbbed, but she would discover this woman's secret.

"Ladies and Gentlemen," came the booming voice of the announcer. "Please, join us on the dance floor for the rest of the evening's festivities."

The red curtains drew back and a set of gilded white stairs rose from the stage. The evening's singers lined the stage and sang as the guests began walking up the steps to the ballroom above the theater. Sparks and lights made quite a show, but it was not as much of a spectacle as the men jostling each other to move closer to Cassandra as Henry escorted her to the theater floor.

Adeline remained in the box, letting the jostling crowd pass into the ballroom. She was not going to subject herself to such foolishness.

The floor cleared and Bronhart led her down the stairs. She gripped his arm as Westengaard passed, arm-in-arm with some middle-aged woman. Adeline stepped back, bumping into Helena.

"Is everything all right?" Helena said. "You do seem distracted tonight."

"Everything is fine," Adeline said. She hesitated, letting a few more couples separate her from her father's enemy.

She and Bronhart followed the crowd and entered the ballroom.

The ceiling was meant to look like a sky of stars, with sheer, glittering fabric and twinkling lights. Acrobats and aerialists spun from ropes, light reflecting on their costumes. There was a fine display of food and champagne, but Adeline still let out a, "Hmmph."

"What is it?" Bronhart said.

"Mrs. Hampnell had similar decorations for her gala last month."

Leading her to the dance floor, Bronhart said, "It is still beautiful."

She took his offered hand as they joined the first waltz. "I suppose. But, let's cancel the aerialists for the wedding. These are becoming overdone. I will find something more original."

Guiding her deftly across the floor, Bronhart said, "Actually, I was hoping we might simplify a few things for the wedding. All we need is a quiet affair."

"Everyone is anticipating our wedding," Adeline said as they swept across the floor in elegant circles.

"I am not." Bronhart nodded toward the men breathing plumes of fire near the entrance. "We don't need spectacle and drama to prove we love each other."

"Our wedding is about more than us, Nathaniel. Everyone is watching us. My wedding must be what all other weddings this year are compared to."

"What is all this for? If you are in favor with society, they will compliment you. If you are out of favor, even the best wedding will be insulted." He shook his head. "Even if just dressed in a nightgown, you would look beautiful."

She scoffed. "And have our names scandalized? I think not."

"It was only a joke."

She sighed. He should know better than to even joke about such things. Anyone could be listening.

His eyes drifted, avoiding hers. She kept her head high and smile strong as she let him guide her through the rest of the waltz. A frown came to his face as he stared at one corner of the room. She followed his gaze to a young woman in a nice, but common gown standing beside a rugged but handsome man in an ill-fitted suit. The woman was vaguely familiar, but Adeline could not place her.

"Who let the common folk in?" she said with a laugh.

Bronhart grunted as he released her and marched out of the circle of dancers. Adeline hurried her step but tried to keep her gait as elegant as she could.

"Nathaniel!" she whispered loudly. He paused to hold out his arm.

"Let's go outside," he said.

Adeline glanced at the crowd of men forming around the circle of dancers, salivating at Cassandra. A few moments outside and away from this disgusting show would be a relief.

Bronhart escorted her to the open garden surrounding the Morveaux and led her away from the main view of the doors. Once alone, he pulled his arm away and turned to her, his brow furrowed. She stepped back at the frustration in his eyes.

"The young woman you just called common is Evelyn Havish," he said. "She's who my friend Henry was supposed to bring here tonight."

Adeline blinked as she frowned. "But he is with someone else. Why is she here?"

Bronhart ran a hand through his hair. "I don't know. Henry must have given her the tickets he won. I guess her escort's some family friend or the like."

Adeline leaned to look through the windows but could see little beyond the sheer curtains. "Perhaps your friend has gone on to wealthier prospects."

"Not Henry." Bronhart tapped his hand against his leg. "From what he's told me, Miss Havish is kind, intelligent, and comes from a good family."

"What does her family do?"

"Her father owns the largest tannery in Pippington."

Adeline wrinkled her nose. "That's a disgusting business."

"It's a necessary business." Bronhart pointed at Adeline's shoes. "The leather for those Cordwainers you always moan about probably came through his shop."

Adeline scoffed. She rarely mentioned how much her feet ached after a night out, but the pain was worth the beauty.

"Those are probably the best clothes she has," Bronhart said, "and she has as much right to be here as you do."

"Her right may be the same, but the appropriateness is not." Adeline stretched out her arm, admiring her glove. "She would be happier at some bar like McBriar's."

Bronhart threw up a hand. "I might be happier at McBriar's tonight."

"Why would you want to go to such a stuffy hole?"

"I think the Morveaux's just as stuffy." He shook his head before looking at her, his shoulders hanging with tiredness. "Don't you hear yourself? A few months ago, you weren't caught up in all this fashion and falseness."

Adeline raised her chin, showing the profile of her neck. She had always cared about fashion, but never could afford what she desired.

"I lead fashion now, Nathaniel," she said.

"Money is a disease." He took her hand between his and looked her in the eyes. "Where's my Adeline? The woman I proposed to is disappearing and I don't know how to save her. I'm trying to be patient, but I don't know if I can marry this—this brat in front of me."

"A brat?" She snapped open her fan. "I was an orphan and came from nothing. How can I be a brat?"

"You weren't one a few months ago."

Her eyes widened and she jerked her hand away. "I have become a lady of high standing and must hold my place."

"You're slipping away, Adeline, and I won't fall with you." He held out his hand. "I still love you, but you need some time away from all this nonsense. I haven't been an account manager long, but I've already seen too many fall under the spell of their own wealth.

"Let's leave Pippington for a week or more. We can go somewhere quiet and maybe I can find my Adeline again."

She placed a hand to her breast. "This is who I am, a lady of high society, respected and admired by all of Pippington." Her throat choked around the final words, but she forced them out. "If you are to be my husband, you must accept that."

Bronhart shook his head and waved his arm. "It's been a long night already. I'm going to get some champagne for us and I'll be back.

Maybe a few minutes alone will clear our heads."

With his shoulders hunched forward, he marched back into the ballroom.

Adeline twisted her fan in her hands as she watched him leave. Part of her ached as he walked away, yet he didn't understand her. He wanted things to be simple, but nothing was simple anymore. Not since she was handed her grandfather's fortune. There were expectations he couldn't understand.

Taking a few deep breaths, she nodded to herself.

Bronhart would have a drink and calm himself. He would return, they would talk, and all would be well. She would not give up on the man she loved. All he had to do was see she was right.

"How blind even the best of men can be."

She jolted back as she turned to face Westengaard.

He leaned against the railing, his jewel-tone blue eyes focused on her.

"We all play our games of fashion." He jiggled the gold chain on his waistband before touching a hand to his chest. "But, it is the heart which bears the true measure of us all."

Her head began to throb. She moved quickly toward the patio leading into the ballroom.

Striding beside her, he said, "Why do you always run when I enter the room?"

He touched her shoulder. She fought to keep walking but found herself stopping. "At every event, I hope to speak with the most beautiful of the beauties, but she runs like I am some plague come for her."

"I must go," she said as she forced herself to step forward. Her feet felt like they were encased in bricks.

Westengaard ran his fingers along her arm. A sick feeling ran up from her stomach despite the nervous warmth on her arm.

Bronhart would return soon and she would be safe.

Westengaard touched his fingers to her chin and turned her face toward him. Her breath slowed as she glared at his chiseled features.

She bit out, "I know who you are, Benjamin Stiltsken."

Westengaard pulled his hand away and laughed. "So, your father has told you about me?" He arched his hands up in mimicry of a magician casting a spell. "Are you afraid of the man who betrayed your father?"

She held her breath and forced herself one more step away.

Leaning close, he said, "I owe Rompell all that I am. Even, my very life. What he believes was betrayal was only my attempt to save him."

"Those are lies."

"Rompell is full of misunderstandings. He never gave me a chance to explain myself. Every time I tried, he ran off or tried to murder me."

Adeline moved another step forward and found her limbs moving freely. She tried to run but tripped on her pair of Cordwainers. Westengaard caught her shoulders and helped her stand. She jerked back, her heart racing.

"Has he told you the full truth?" he said, his voice hushed. "That he was an emperor? He could have been great, but there were conspiracies and assassins around. I had to fake his death to protect him."

"What about his curse?" She edged away from him, but he kept his approach.

"You mean his golden touch?" Westengaard raised his hand and stroked her cheek. She shivered. "I thought the spell only effected inanimate things, not the living."

Adeline's back hit a brick wall. Westengaard stepped closer, placing his arms on either side of her. Panic rose in her breast as she stared into his eyes, unable to look away.

"I would not wish such a fate on his darling Hidaya. She was a wonderful woman. When I tried to explain, he was blinded by the lies of the Surris Rangers. They fear magic and hope to rid the rest of the world of it. Why do you think he has hidden you?"

"What are you talking about?"

He raised her hand and pressed his palm to hers. "You must sense my magic as strongly as I sense yours."

If he knew, then there was no point hiding her magic. She hummed and flicked her fingers at one of the gas lamps lighting the patio. A flame arched out and she pulled it toward Westengaard.

"Nice little trick." He snapped and the flame disappeared.

She raised her palm toward his chest and hummed, trying to bring a spark. He grabbed her wrist, his fingers digging into her skin. She pulled at his grip, trying to jerk away, but couldn't break free.

"I have fallen in love with you, brave girl," he whispered, his face approaching hers. "And my love is one no one escapes."

His mouth covered hers in a semblance of a kiss. Disgust erupted within her as she pushed against his shoulders. Her repulsion faded as he wrapped his arm around her and pulled her tighter against him. Her senses became filled only with the musk of his cologne. She clutched his shoulder as a warmth swelled up through her, her lips pulsing with the sensation of his lingering kiss.

As his lips pulled from his, her eyes looked into his.

A giddiness rushed through her, washing away the fear of a moment ago. All of his words were truth. Rompell had been blind to Westengaard's loyalty and brotherhood. There was no better man than him, nothing worth living for except his acceptance. He was the completion of her soul and heart, the piece she never knew was missing.

A glass shattered on the ground. She gasped in breath as Westengaard looked away. Peeking around his shoulder, she saw Bronhart standing pale-faced and ill, a broken glass of champagne at his feet.

Bronhart balled his fists, his arms shaking as he tried to understand the scene before him: Adeline pressed into Westengaard, an innocent bliss on her face as their lips locked together. Her eyes turned to Bronhart and she giggled as if sharing a secret with Westengaard. The author turned his head, glancing at Bronhart. His blue eyes bore the coldness of a victor who knew his enemy was defeated before the battle began.

As Bronhart struggled for words, his heartbeat pounded.

Adeline had gripped his arm so tight when Westengaard had passed him earlier in the evening. He had dismissed it as the usual fear she showed whenever Westengaard appeared. At parties, Adeline always avoided him by taking Bronhart's arm and crossing to the opposite side of the room. Bronhart knew there was some history between Westengaard and Rompell, but it didn't seem enough to justify her shaking.

But at this moment, as Westengaard faced him, a protective hand on Adeline, the truth was far too clear.

"How long?" Bronhart could barely push the words out.

"I've spent weeks trying to hold back the truth in my heart," Westengaard said, "but tonight, coming here and seeing her tears, I could not restrain myself any longer."

Pulling his elbow back, Bronhart charged forward. Adeline jumped in front of Westengaard and grabbed Bronhart's arm, stopping his momentum.

"I didn't know—" Adeline said, her eyes pleading with him. "I didn't realize how wrong we are for each other, Nathaniel. But, Westengaard, he—"

Bronhart jerked his arm away and glared at her. Part of him still loved her and wanted to deny what he saw. Yet, things were too clear for him to lie to himself. Any further words from either of them would only drive his anger.

His fingers dug into his palm and his fists shook as he marched into the ballroom. He was a fool. He should have seen the signs. He should have broken off the engagement when she had inherited an entire nation's worth of wealth. The girl he had proposed to was gone forever.

Henry bobbed around the dance floor, looking as miserable as Bronhart felt. Cassandra was beautiful, but Bronhart could sense her vanity from where he stood. Adeline and Westengaard soon joined the couples on the floor.

Bronhart wandered to the buffet table but took only a glass of champagne. He rolled the liquid in the glass and considered drinking. Losing himself in the blindness of alcohol might improve the night for a moment, but he was liable to do something foolish. He should leave and abandon the evening but could not bring himself to go. If he lingered, maybe he would find both he and Adeline were in some horrible dream. They would awaken and find the past few months were a lie.

Yet, as the evening wore on and Adeline laughed in Westengaard's arms, reality was becoming disturbingly clear.

It was time to leave. However, his friend Henry walked alone for the moment. He would see if Henry needed assistance before abandoning this pit of sparkles and lies.

He quickened his step as Miss Havish's drunk escort marched toward Henry with the marked intent to leave him in pain.

"You're not even going to fight for her?" the ruffian said, his speech slurred.

"I do not see the need," Henry said.

The ruffian jabbed his finger into Henry's chest. "Too afraid to fight for her? You're just a scrawny little dog yapping. I'll show you what a man should be."

His elbow cranked back. Bronhart sprinted the last few feet and grabbed the ruffian's fist before he could punch Henry. Bronhart had already had a bad enough night. He might be able to save Henry's.

"Sir," he said as he let go of the man's arm. "Your choice is to leave now peaceably or be escorted out by security."

The ruffian snarled and lurched forward. Bronhart moved to block him, but the man's fist connected with Henry's face. Bronhart winced as Henry's flew off his feet and fell onto his back. Without hesitating, Bronhart bowled his shoulder into the ruffian's chin and followed with a right hook to the gut. The ruffian snarled and swung for his face. Bronhart dodged and brought his left fist into the ruffian's nose. A crunch was followed by a trickle of blood.

Bronhart only wished that nose belonged to Westengaard.

Security officers scrambled across the floor and dragged the fuming ruffian out the door. Rolling back his shoulders, Bronhart waited for them to take him as well. However, a few nearby women said, "He's quite a hero, gentlemen. He was only protecting his friend."

As the security officers walked away, Bronhart helped Henry to his feet.

Purple bruising was forming around Henry's eye and his spectacles were bent and crooked.

Brushing off Henry's shoulder, Bronhart said, "You should have taken boxing in college. I thought coming from a farm would have made you handier in a fight."

"I'm usually better at dodging." Henry tried to adjust his bent spectacles.

"How can you let a man like that bring your girl?" Bronhart said.

Henry squinted out of the one good lens. "It's been a complicated week."

"Right." Bronhart grunted and thumped Henry's shoulder. "Be careful of Madame Astrellar. She may be wealthy, but I don't trust her." He paused as he glanced at the doors leading to the garden. "Though, I don't trust my own date tonight."

Henry rubbed the forming bruise. "I thought you were here with your fiancée."

"I thought I was too." Bronhart's chest ached as he gestured toward the dance floor, where Westengaard and Adeline glided through the crowd.

How many lies had she told him? How much had she hidden?

"She seems to have forgotten that and is off with some author fellow."

"That's Alvin Westengaard, isn't it?" Henry said.

"I believe he is." He folded his arms. "And that he'll be escorting her home."

Anger burred deeper into Bronhart's chest as Adeline and Westengaard broke off from the crowd of dancers and disappeared through the doors leading to the gardens. His brooding cut off as Henry gripped his arm.

"Tell Madame Astrellar I had to leave on urgent business."

"Is she so difficult, Henry? You never lie."

Henry stumbled to the nearest flower arrangement and dove behind it. The wave of men flocking to the patio door marked Cassandra's entrance to the room.

Even if he couldn't help himself, he would save Henry.

He ran across the room, pushing his way through the crowd till he reached Cassandra's side. Pulling on his practiced charm, he smiled at her and offered his arm. Her gaze set a chill through him, but he kept his smile firm.

"Mr. Kingston sends his apologies." He gestured toward the main entrance leading to the street. "An emergency came up—with his brother. He had to leave immediately. I have offered to escort you home."

She tapped his arm with her fan. "Thank you, but I will find my own escort. Good night, Mr. Bronhart."

Bronhart let his face drop into a scowl as she strode toward the door. Her hips swayed with the confidence of beauty. This woman knew exactly what she was doing to these men and used it to her advantage. Apparently, Adeline was just as manipulative.

Walking toward the main doors alone, he took one last glance at the dance floor.

Adeline and Westengaard had disappeared. His jaw tightened as he forced himself to shove away images of her in Westengaard's arms.

Stepping onto the street, he took in a deep breath of the cool air and began the march to his apartment. A long walk in open air might help him to clear his mind and begin forgetting his fiancée. It was time to let go of Adeline Winkleston, for it was clear she had let go of him.

The Sixth Tale of the Magician

The palace walls shook and cannon fire echoed. Rompell dodged into a doorway as plaster cracked and fell from the ceiling. Servants ran past, shouting while seeking safety as the rebel army filled the city.

Hidaya's face, turning from flesh to gold, hovered in his mind as he kept his rifle level with his eye. It had been nearly two years since losing her, but she still haunted every step.

He had disbanded the troupe, paying his friends handsome sums to abandon him, and gone to Gathray. By the time he traveled across the empire and bribed his way into a private meeting with his brothers and father, word of Stiltsken and his magicians turning the citizens of Periv's capital into stone had spread.

His father and brothers embraced him and Solvan's wife took Tamina in her arms, her eyes warm as she looked at his daughter.

By the end of the week, they had decided to take their fate in their own hands.

Ferrab remained in Gathray to protect their homeland while Rompell rode as an officer and advisor in Solvan's army. Their rebellion began like a ripple and turned into a crashing wave as more kingdoms gathered under Solvan's banner. They charged forward, defeating the imperial sorcerers one-by-one, cutting the capital off from the rest of the empire.

Even with their victories, support began to fade as Stiltsken and his sorcerers fought back, sending a sleeping curse to stop armies, turning more to stone.

As each innocent turned to stone, the Gathrayan sorcerer repeated, "Objects want to return to what they are. He and his sorcerers must continue using magic to keep each person transformed. No one can maintain so much magic at once."

Then, a month ago, came Favay's assassination, her death brought by the same poison that had murdered her father.

General Baqir had taken the throne, but Stiltsken remained the hidden ruler.

Rompell would make sure that rule ended today.

He glanced at the remaining five soldiers who infiltrated the palace with him. These were men he trusted, who he had gone to battle with. He was proud to approach the end with them.

A fierce battering from the cannons shook the walls again. He and his soldiers ducked back as more guards sprinted to reinforce the fortress walls surrounding the palace.

Solvan's army fired cannons, heaved battering rams at the gates, and raised ladders to scale palace walls. Such an attack would take days, if not weeks, to break into the palace. Fortunately, the frontal attack was not the one that mattered.

With the hall cleared, Rompell motioned for his squad to advance. There had been a few skirmishes in the halls, but their winding path through the secret corridors meant to protect the emperor had proven safe.

A bitter smile crossed Rompell's face. At least some good had come from his brief time in power.

His squad took position at the foot of a command tower overlooking the city. Three watched the entrances while two scouted the narrow staircase. Halfway up, they whistled for the rest of the squad to follow.

Climbing the stairs, Rompell prayed their spies were correct about where Stiltsken would be, and that his former friend hadn't abandoned the city.

At the top floor, Rompell crouched as he peeked around the corner and into the hallway. Three guards stood by the door of the command room, scimitars and pistols in their hands. He waved to Harun. The marksman raised his small crossbow armed with darts dipped in sleeping potions.

With two quick shots, a pair of guards fell against each other, slumping immediately. The third guard turned, raising his rifle. Harun's third dart hit him in the neck and the guard thumped to the floor.

Rompell gave his officer a slim smile and nod before leading them into the hallway. He waved for them to stay behind him as he opened the door.

Stiltsken stood at the balcony, the tendons in his neck taut, sweat rolling down his brow as he held his palms out. He sang in hushed tones as he faced the battle, balls of light and fire rolling from his hands and joining the cannon fire. Buildings in the city exploded as spheres of magic hit.

Rompell knelt as he reached in the pouch at his belt and raised his spectroscope. Flaring threads of light surrounded Stiltsken, the strings stretched as if about to snap apart. Wherever the magic was weakest, the bullet had the best chance of shooting through.

He raised the rifle.

Harun had better aim, but Rompell had earned this shot.

Taking a steadying breath, he rested his finger on the trigger.

"Captain!"

Rifles fired behind Rompell. He turned, only to have his face meet the heel of a guard's boot. Knocking against the wall, his rifle fired, the bullet ricocheting across the stone walls. Harun threw himself against Rompell's attacker.

Rompell kept hold of his gun as he rolled into the room. He kicked the thick door shut as he ripped the glove from his left hand. His fingers brushed the door and gold spread across the wood. That should seal the door for long enough.

His soldiers would fight their way to safety while he kept Stiltsken trapped.

A sphere of blue flame rammed into the floor beside Rompell, singeing his shirt. He scrambled to his feet and jumped behind a knocked-over table, slapping his left hand against it as he fell. The part remaining wood exploded as Stiltsken fired another barrage of magic. The energy rebounded off the gold. Stiltsken cried out as it flashed back at him, blinding him briefly.

Rompell took his chance as he rolled to his knees. The barrel turned to gold as he raised the rifle and fired. Stiltsken fell as the bullet hit him in the thigh. Rompell cocked the rifle, but the trigger stuck, the gold fusing the mechanisms in place.

He muttered a curse as he charged toward Stiltsken. With a whistle, Stiltsken flicked his hand. The carpet rippled under Rompell's feet. He jumped onto solid stone as Stiltsken crawled toward a smaller carpet near the balcony.

Leaping the rest of the way, Rompell swung the butt of his rifle into Stiltsken's chest. There was a loud crack and Stiltsken wheezed. He panted as he raised his hand. Sparks came from his fingers, but his breathing was uneven as he tried to whisper out music. Rompell pushed Stiltsken's arm away and knelt on the man's chest.

His own breast heaved as he pictured his sons and his wife, as he remembered being huddled in the palace dungeon waiting to die. He swallowed as he gripped Stiltsken's neck with his bare hand, waiting for gold to spread across the traitor's skin.

A slow smile crept on Stiltsken's face and he panted out a laugh. "I can't be hurt by a spell I helped create."

He slapped his palm on Rompell's chest and sent a shower of sparks. Rompell's whole body jolted as he fell back. Stiltsken rolled onto his stomach and crawled on the ground.

Rompell grit his teeth. If he could not have his first choice in revenge, he would take his second.

From another pouch at his belt, he used his gloved right hand to grab a pair of cuffs made by his brother's sorcerers. Stiltsken lay on top of the smaller carpet and pressed his hand against it. He wheezed out the song to make it rise. The carpet shot up a few inches before flopping against the ground. Stiltsken tried again, his own jaw tight as he fought to center his magic.

Rompell marched steadily forward. Stiltsken held his hand out. A pitiful sphere of magic sputtered and puffed away. Rompell slapped the cuffs on his enemy's wrists.

Stiltsken yelled as the sparks stopped shooting from his hands. Shouts erupted throughout the city. Rompell could feel the magic in the room fall away, almost like a curtain dropping and revealing the sun.

With a snarl, Stiltsken pushed himself toward Rompell. Catching Stiltsken's arm with one hand, Rompell swung his bare fist into Stiltsken's face. His knuckles stung, but the bruise spreading across Stiltsken's cheek was satisfying.

Shoving him to the ground and kneeling on his back, Rompell bent down and growled in Stiltsken's ear, "Take what you have earned."

The door collapsed inward and Rompell's squad stumbled in carrying a makeshift battering ram. Rompell stepped back, his adrenaline falling. The burns on his chest where Stiltsken's magic had hit him started to sting. As his soldiers bound the traitor, Rompell grabbed his glove from the floor and looked out at the city.

The imperial soldiers didn't know it yet, but Solvan's army had won.

Rompell's squad cheered as they shoved Stiltsken from the room. Rompell avoided his enemy's blue eyes as he looked across the palace to the tower where Hidaya had been imprisoned.

The emptiness he had been shoving away for the past two years crashed over him, threatening to drown him. It had been easy to ignore as he fought battle after battle, focusing instead on his hopes of destroying Stiltsken.

There was still work to be done to imprison Stiltsken in some dark hole and forget him, but the main revenge was over.

A sob broke out as Rompell leaned against the wall. He tried to push back the image of his sons and wife turning to gold. He had won, but he had no reason to celebrate victory.

Leaving the window, he forced himself to march after his men. All he had left to do was make sure Stiltsken never harmed anyone again.

Chapter 18

Rompell woke from his doze on the couch as the clock on the mantle chimed three in the morning. Adeline would be home soon and chatter about the evening. Much of the conversation lately had been wrapped up in judging other women's dresses. In the next day or two, he would take her with him as he checked on several of the widows living in his apartments, some with six children in two small rooms. Hopefully, it would remind her where she had come from. He wouldn't let the allure of her new wealth steal her heart away.

The clock struck four. Perhaps she had returned while he slept. However, her room was empty, the bed still perfectly made.

He shut his eyes as he stretched out on the couch and tried to sleep. Bronhart would have her home safely, but he would feel better once she walked in the door.

Five-o-clock rang and he paced the floor.

She had never been out this late before. Sitting and waiting would do no good.

He pulled on his coat and shoes before driving to Bronhart's apartment. Bounding up the stairs, he thought through every reason she hadn't returned, but nothing felt right.

He pounded his fist on the door and Bronhart opened it. Bags hung under the younger man's reddened eyes and he still wore his dress shirt.

"Where is my daughter?"

Bronhart leaned against the doorway and let out a snort. "I don't know. She left with that author, Alvin Westengaard."

Rage ignited like a fuse through Rompell. He grabbed Bronhart by the collar and growled, "What do you mean she left with Westengaard?"

"Exactly what I said." Bronhart pulled at Rompell's arm.

Rompell shoved Bronhart's shoulders, pushing him into the room. Slamming the door behind him, he said, "I left her in your protection!"

"From what, sir?" Bronhart stepped back and jerked his shirt straight. "I left her alone for a moment and returned to her in Westengaard's embrace. It's clear this wasn't their first meeting."

Rompell's fists tightened, but Bronhart wasn't the man who deserved his anger. "Things are not what they appear."

"Appearances are clear: I've been made a fool of." Bronhart strode to the door and opened it. "I have no business with your daughter anymore. I just wished I had listened to you and waited longer before proposing. Then, I might have seen the truth."

"I wish you could see the truth," Rompell muttered.

If only Adeline had told Bronhart about her magic at the beginning. Then, there would be a chance of explaining what was happening and why Westengaard was dangerous. As things were, Bronhart was right to be angry.

Jabbing his finger against Bronhart's chest, Rompell said, "There is more going on here than I can tell you. What you saw last night—I know it appears true, but it's not. Do not give up on Adeline just yet. If I—" His throat tightened. "If I am right, she will need you."

Bronhart grunted. "Find another man. I am done."

Rompell bit his lip as he glared at Bronhart. This wasn't worth his time. He had to find Adeline.

"I am sorry for what has happened," Rompell said. "I will do all I can to make things right."

Bronhart raised an eyebrow but said nothing as he waited for Rompell to leave.

Returning to his motorcar, Rompell thought through where Adeline would be. As he climbed in the driver's seat, the answer was far too clear. He slammed his boot on the gas pedal and swerved around the old carts pulling wares into town. Once at the carriage loop outside of Adeline's mansion, he swerved to a stop.

He ran to the door and jerked on it. The blasted thing was locked. He pounded his fist on the pane till a bleary-eyed servant opened the door. Shoving past the man without any greeting, Rompell sprinted into the mansion, trying to remember where in this labyrinth Adeline's bedroom lay.

He ran down several hallways and up two flights of stairs before skidding to a stop in front of Adeline's room, his coat flaring around him. Panting, he threw open the door.

In the midst of an ocean of ruffles, Adeline lay on the canopy bed, her arms stretched in peaceful rest.

"Adeline!" Rompell shook her shoulders.

She snorted as her eyes fluttered open. His stomach knotted as she looked up and gave him an enchanted smile.

"Oh, Papa, I had the most wonderful night."

She stretched with a yawn before letting out a drunken giggle. Rompell leaned close and smelled her breath. The foulness of morning was on it, but not the stench of alcohol.

"What happened last night?" He kept his fists clenched and forced his voice to stay level. If he was right, no amount of shouting would help.

Another giggle pattered out. "I'm engaged, Papa, but not to Bronhart."

His whole chest panged as if his heart were being ripped out by sharp claws, but he said nothing.

"You see, Papa, you were wrong about darling Westengaard." She sat up, her eyes wide and glittering. He had seen such a look in the eyes of many maidservants in Sandar, and, toward the end, in Favay's eyes.

It had taken him too long to realize what it meant.

"Everything you accused him of, all those crimes—he only wanted to help you."

"Including framing me for murder, leading to my execution?"

"There were assassins! He had to keep you safe. See, Papa, he loves you as much as I do. You must forgive him." She held up her hand. A gargantuan emerald had taken the place of Bronhart's ring. With another giggle, she said, "We are going to be married."

Rompell grabbed the tasseled cording on the bed canopy and ripped it away. "I'll turn you to gold before I let that beast marry you."

"Papa! He is my true love."

"This is far from true love."

He twisted the cording in his hand. He did not want to do this to his own daughter, but she had to be protected.

Grabbing her by the shoulders, he dragged her onto her stomach. She cried out, but he shoved her head against the pillow while he bound her hands together.

"Papa! What are you doing!"

She kicked at him, but he dodged away. From the nightstand, he grabbed a handkerchief and shoved it in her mouth. Her shouts became muffled and he stepped back.

"Your mind and heart have been poisoned," he said. He had failed her, but still had a chance to end this. "When your head clears, you'll understand."

He shut the door behind him, trying not to hear Adeline's muffled protests. To the first servant he passed, he said, "Adeline is ill. I fear it is contagious. No one should enter her room. I am off to get a doctor."

Returning to his car, he flexed his gloved hands before gripping the steering wheel.

Where were the Surris Rangers? Their excuses were even emptier now that Adeline was Westengaard's target.

He had trusted them too much.

Plans formed as he drove back to his house and ran to his study. He opened the top left drawer and pulled on the hidden lever, opening the side panel leading to a space the length of the desk. From there, he removed his saber and revolver. He had carried these while riding into battle alongside his brothers. If Westengaard's magic was as weak as the Surris Rangers claimed, there was a chance these would do their work.

He rolled the saber in a blanket and tied a ribbon. If anyone asked, it was a gift for Adeline. He tucked the revolver into one of the large hidden pockets in his coat. Today, there would be no tricks for children.

Running a hand over his hair, he took one last look around his study, seeking anything else to use as a weapon.

He jumped as the front door bell rang.

Forcing himself to take a deep breath, he marched to the entryway. The burning in his chest eased as he glanced through the small window. Beyond stood a very perplexed Mrs. Hunter.

At least something might go well today.

He opened the door. "Inside. Now."

She frowned as she entered. Handing him a note, she said, "I received this from your daughter an hour ago."

Rompell opened it and stared at Adeline's florid handwriting.

"It is a letter of immediate resignation, due to her engagement to Alvin Westengaard. The message is strange enough, but—" She ran her finger along the edge. "It is dripping with magic I don't recognize. Where is she?"

Rompell handed the note back to her. "At her mansion, under Westengaard's enchantment."

Mrs. Hunter's frown deepened. "He is not in the mage registry."

Rompell raised an eyebrow. "There's a mage registry?"

"Of course. One must be organized to keep magic hidden."

Rompell shook his head. "Anyone who's a real danger wouldn't register."

"What sort of enchantment is she under?" Mrs. Hunter pulled a spectroscope from her handbag and looked at the note. "There are traces of a love potion, but I'd have to see Adeline herself to make any antidotes." Lowering her spectroscope, she looked to Rompell. "And what of Mr. Bronhart? If he truly loves her, there might be some power in his kiss."

"I doubt he loves anything right now."

Mrs. Hunter set the spectroscope and note back in her bag. "Westengaard cannot be too strong of a mage, if Inspector McCay hasn't mentioned him."

Rompell swallowed as he looked at the crafted normalcy of his sitting room. Everything had been hidden so well for so long. Yet, if he was to save Adeline, he needed Mrs. Hunter's help. She had to know the danger they faced.

"Westengaard's real name is Benjamin Stiltsken," he said. "Our war with each other is what led to my exile here in Barthan." His jaw tightened as all the bitterness of the years stung. "He is a warlock and this is the third time he has used his power to ruin my life."

"Are you sure he's a warlock?" Mrs. Hunter's eyebrows raised. "The Surris Rangers claim the few remaining ones are locked in the Culparr Mines."

"He escaped." Rompell rubbed the back of his neck as he paced the room. "I told them he was here, but the Rangers said his magic is mostly blocked. They won't move on him because he has a hostage."

"Blocks on his magic wouldn't be enough," she said. "Warlocks can drain magic from others, even if just temporarily." Her eyes widened. "And, Miss Winkleston is quite powerful."

Rompell found himself letting out a pent-up breath. At least she understood what was at stake.

Opening the door, he said, "Please, go to her and see what you can do."

Mrs. Hunter nodded. "Of course. And where are you going?"

"To see if I can fix an old mistake."

Tears streamed down Adeline's face as she rocked herself back and forth, pulling against Rompell's knots. If only she could get him to understand.

She called out to Westengaard in her mind. Her love would carry her cries to his soul and he would come. Once they stood together, Rompell would accept the truth. He would see their love and forgive Westengaard.

With a loud thump, she fell to the floor. Her arm ached, but she ignored the pain as she tried to roll onto her knees. Her ruffled nightgown tangled around her legs, locking her there.

"She is in here," a servant said as heavy footsteps approached.

Adeline lay on her side, praying it was Westengaard here for a dashing rescue.

The door opened and there stood Mrs. Hunter, her dress and hat as sensible as ever. The servant beside her cried out and moved to run to Adeline.

Pressing a hand to the woman's arm, Mrs. Hunter said, "It is part of the treatment. A touch unorthodox, but necessary."

The servant frowned, but Mrs. Hunter shooed her away. With the door shut, Mrs. Hunter knelt beside Adeline and pulled out the handkerchief.

"You must tell Papa he is wrong about Westengaard. Papa—he hates him so much, but he doesn't understand. Westengaard is everything now. He is the sky to cradle the cloud of my heart, the bosom of the ocean to lay my ship in."

Pulling out her spectroscope, Mrs. Hunter said, "This is why I had you teach math and science instead of poetry."

She whistled a quick note and the cording around Adeline's wrists unknotted and slid away.

With her hands free, Adeline pulled herself to her feet. "Please help me dress. I must see my Westengaard."

Mrs. Hunter tapped a chair. "Take a seat. You've had a stressful morning and we must make sure you are in your best health before you see Mr. Westengaard."

"Even if I am ill, he will be by my side and nurse me. He will—"

"Sit down."

Adeline immediately followed the command.

"Just a few tests after all this stress and then you'll be free to see Westengaard all you want."

Adeline smiled at her mentor. At least Mrs. Hunter understood her love for Westengaard. With her help, Rompell would be persuaded and her wedding with Westengaard would be the happiest moment of her life.

Rompell watched Mrs. Hunter drive her motorcar away. Hoping the address he had followed Westengaard to once was still correct, he drove through the streets and parked a few blocks away.

He walked past one of the squares where he sometimes did tricks. A few children ran toward him. He forced a smile and flicked a smoke snap in their direction. Blue smoke curled up and he turned down an alleyway, giving the appearance of disappearing.

He wound his way to the alley behind Westengaard's townhouse. The windowsills were flounced and gilded, but matched the other townhomes trying to mesh with North Town's mansions and fine shops.

Walking with purpose, he opened the back gate of the townhouse and approached the rear door. It was locked. He fiddled in his pocket before finding a few pins and prodding the keyhole with them. Something clicked and he opened the door.

Slipping inside, he shut the door quietly and crept down the hallway.

Westengaard's voice echoed from upstairs, light and full of humor. Another man's nasal voice replied. Rompell dropped the blanket and pulled out the saber and revolver. If his curse would have done any good against Westengaard, he would have pulled off a glove. However, he wasn't going to make that mistake again.

Careful to step on the carpeted section, he walked up the stairs.

"Well, back to work, then," the nasal voiced man said.

A door shut. Rompell jumped up the last few steps, reaching the second floor just as Westengaard turned to face him.

Rompell raised the revolver and fired. Westengaard dropped out of the way and whistled. The bullet skewed to the side, landing in the wall. From behind the door, the nasal-voiced man screamed.

Rompell fired off the rest of the five bullets in quick succession. Westengaard flicked his hand, and a mirror ripped off the wall. It shattered as the bullets went through it, one nicking Westengaard's arm.

At least the man could bleed.

Running toward his enemy, Rompell tossed away the gun and raised his saber.

"Good morning, Rompell." Westengaard grabbed a metal candlestick from a nearby shelf. "I'm surprised you took so long to come."

Rompell swung his saber, but Westengaard blocked his blow with the candlestick. With a grunt, Rompell swung for Westengaard's neck. The warlock spun out of the way and leaped down the stairs. Rompell ran after him.

As Rompell reached the middle step, Westengaard swung up his hand and hummed a few notes. The carpet ripped from beneath Rompell's feet. He thumped down the stairs, the saber clattering out of his hand. His back ached as he came to a stop at the bottom, sliding against the wall.

Westengaard strode down the stairs. Rompell grit his teeth as he rolled to his feet. Ignoring the aches along his back, he charged forward. Westengaard moved to dodge, but Rompell guessed the maneuver and rammed his elbow into Westengaard's chin. With a huff of air, Westengaard's back knocked against a table. Rompell rammed his knee into Westengaard's groin. Westengaard let out a wheeze of pain before planting his hand on Rompell's chest.

With a single note, Westengaard used his magic to push Rompell crashing through the wall behind him.

As dust and plaster fell, Westengaard marched toward him.

"Are you finished, or shall we play a little longer?"

Grunting, Rompell rolled to his feet. Westengaard could use more of his magic than expected. Still, Rompell had a few tricks.

He grabbed a stack of books and tossed them at Westengaard. The warlock snapped, sending them aside. Rompell used the distraction to leap to the saber. As he reached for it, Westengaard whistled. An armchair slammed into Rompell, shoving him away from the saber.

Westengaard smoothed his hair. "I assume you have already seen Adeline this morning. Lovely girl."

Though his back ached and his side was bruised, Rompell glared. "Your war is with me. Let her go."

Rompell pushed himself off the wall and ran toward Westengaard. With a twist of the warlock's hand, the saber rose, the point toward Rompell's chest. Rompell stopped only a finger's breadth away.

Wrapping his hand around the hilt, Westengaard said, "I think our conversation will be much more interesting in there."

He gestured with his free hand. Rompell stared down the length of his own blade. There was no helping Adeline if he died.

The room he entered was dark, shadows of odd shapes filling a corner. Westengaard flipped a switch, flooding the room with light.

Rompell's heart dropped as if tied to an anchor. There stood the golden forms of his wife and two sons.

They should have been safe, locked away in his warehouse where he had hidden them for over ten years. He had revealed them only to Adeline. Now, his moment of trusting his daughter betrayed him.

"All I had to say was I might be able to help and Adeline took me to your darling family." Westengaard gripped Rompell's shoulder, but Rompell shook him off. "She truly loves her 'dear papa' and would do anything for you. What a wonderful girl."

Rompell eyed the saber still in Westengaard's hand. Why hadn't the Surris Rangers listened to him?

"What do you want?" he said.

"Only your blessing to marry Adeline." Westengaard placed his hand on his breast. "She does love me so dearly."

"Just slay me and be done." Rompell spat on the ground. "Take your revenge and let her go."

"Oh, Rompell, I thought you would understand. Murder is a poor revenge. Your enemy is dead, but what then? They have missed out on the years of misery they gave you. Revenge is about fairness. You placed me in a prison and now I will build one around you."

"You already took my wife and children from me."

"And you took my empire and power. We are hardly even."

Westengaard crossed to Hidaya's side, her eyes locked in panic and confusion.

Raising his hand, he lit a blue flame on his palm. He held the flame to Hidaya's hair and a few drops of gold melted away. Rompell balled his fist, wanting to jump forward. But, he hesitated. Westengaard was toying with him and he couldn't take the bait.

"Such a delicate state to be in," Westengaard said. "One accident, and they could melt down, disappearing, unable to be saved." He walked to a hidden cupboard on the wall and pulled out a vial. "The gold potion I gave you was an ancient one I found with a bit of my magic mixed in. I thought it was gone forever, but then I discovered this." He held out the vial in his palm. "There is enough in here to cure just one statue."

Opening the wood cork, he dipped his finger in. He dabbed his finger on the scarf around Hidaya's shoulders. Rompell's heart quickened as a small patch of fabric restored from the gold. He stepped forward without thinking, his arms aching to wrap around her, to press her close, to smell her sweet scent and hear her heartbeat.

Westengaard closed the vial and tucked it into his coat pocket. Touching his fingers to Hidaya's chin, he said, "Don't you want to hear her voice again? To kiss her soft lips?" He walked to the two boys and set his hands on their heads. "Or to see one of your sons grow to be a man?

"All I ask is your blessing to marry your daughter and bend her will to mine."

Rompell glared at the vial. Here was a glimmer of hope, but it could not cost Adeline.

"I will do nothing to help you ruin my daughter," he said.

Westengaard raised the golden ball formed from Hidaya's hair before tapping Hidaya's cheek. "So much wealth standing here." He held out his palm and the blue flame rose again. "Just a little melting and I'd want for nothing."

Raising the vial in his other hand, Westengaard said, "Or, you can wait till my wedding day with Adeline. Then, you can choose which one to save."

"I will find a way to murder you," Rompell said. He glared down at his gloved hands, wishing they could transform Westengaard.

"At the cost of your wife and children?" Westengaard shook his head. "I don't think you will. And, I wouldn't go to anyone for help.

One word to another and I'll melt them bit by bit."

He slid the vial into his pocket and walked toward Rompell, his arms opened wide. "Aren't you going to welcome me as your soon-to-be son-in-law, my dear Papa? Give me Adeline and I give you a piece of your family."

Rompell wished only for a blade in his hand to cut his enemy down. He should have fought harder with the Surris Rangers and sought another prison for Westengaard. There had to have been more he could have done.

Yet, here he stood, the choice clear but foul.

The words burned like coals in his mouth as he said, "You have my blessing."

Westengaard grinned and slapped Rompell's shoulder. "We must go tell Adeline immediately. You have made me the happiest of men." Walking to the door and throwing it open, he said, "Come, Rompell. I know she waits anxiously."

Rompell followed, his feet feeling as if wrapped in concrete. Once at the door, he turned to look back at his wife and children, but Westengaard shut the door.

"Not until after the wedding."

"Let me see her first," Rompell said as he and Westengaard entered the main entry of Adeline's mansion. Rompell had never expected such a large room to feel so suffocating. "To make sure she is dressed."

"Of course," Westengaard said as he waved his hand. "We want no impropriety. Once we are married, her honor and mine will be one."

Rompell swallowed to hold back the rising bile in his throat. Each step hurt as he approached Adeline's door. Several maids stood outside, their faces worried. He pushed past the servants and entered.

Mrs. Hunter looked through a spectroscope at several vials lying on the sitting table, some of them giving off steam. Adeline giggled in a plush armchair, rambling on about Westengaard. Each happy chitter stabbed deeper into Rompell.

Seeing him, Mrs. Hunter said, "This is the strongest love spell I have ever seen."

"I told you," Adeline said, her head bobbing as if all her intelligence was gone and it was left as light as a balloon. "It is true love."

"Westengaard is here," Rompell said, the words bitter in his mouth. "He cannot know you are here."

"Of course he knows I am here," Adeline said. "Our hearts are one."

"Do you think he can track her?" Mrs. Hunter said.

"Yes." Rompell slowly crossed the room.

"Even so, I think it best if we take her to the Surris Mountains, or—"

"She will stay here," Rompell said, "And the wedding will proceed."

Adeline leapt from her chair and spun. "Oh, Papa!" She skipped to him and threw her arms around his neck. Kissing his cheek, she said, "You have forgiven him, then? I knew you would, once you knew how he loves me."

Tears broke from Rompell's eyes as he put his arms around her and held her tight to his breast. His tears wet her hair as he kissed her forehead. He had adopted her to protect her, to give her a home. He could not sacrifice her to Westengaard, but, for now, he did not know what else to do.

Mrs. Hunter's voice was low as she said, "What is wrong? What happened?"

"Adeline, get dressed. Mrs. Hunter, we will speak later. Thank you for making sure Adeline didn't fall ill from last night."

"But she—"

He glared at her and gave a sharp shake of his head.

Mrs. Hunter's eyes narrowed as she placed her vials back in her briefcase. She clipped it shut and walked outside.

He hoped she could sense something was wrong and would seek help. For now, he had to remain silent.

Forcing a smile, Rompell turned to Adeline. She pouted as she picked up her handkerchief and dabbed his cheeks. "Papa, you're crying."

"Only for you." The words were like stones lodging in his throat.

"He is far better than Nathaniel, isn't he?"

"He is far greater," Rompell whispered. He touched her chin. Perhaps he should turn her to gold. Then, he could steal the vial from Westengaard. No. Westengaard would just melt her and the rest down into slag. Then, there would be no hope. "Get dressed. He is waiting."

Rompell stepped out of his daughter's room, letting the maids in to assist her. He leaned against the wall and held a hand to his chest, wishing the feeling of a dagger piercing him would leave. However, as he escorted Adeline down the stairs and passed her into Westengaard's waiting arms, the dagger only dug in deeper.

He would save her. He didn't know how, but he had promised to protect her and he would keep his word.

Chapter 19

Bronhart trimmed his beard for the first time in weeks. Just over a month had passed since Adeline had left with Westengaard from the Morveaux. The following week, he had been fired for asking about suspicious numbers in several high-value accounts. He had stolen the files, had Henry help him find the truth, and anonymously left them with the police. Henry, a man to keep his integrity, had quit the next day.

He had done a few day jobs, doing grunt work or helping at the dragon stables so he could pay rent, while applying to any accounting jobs within Pippington. However, as he and Henry quickly learned, Mackabee had spread rumors about them. Few respectable businesses were willing to even speak with him.

If the job he interviewed for today didn't work, he would go back to his parents in Willington. Hopefully, there, he wouldn't open the daily paper to see the latest details of Adeline and Westengaard's romance.

"Tonight, Miss Winkleston was radiant as Mr. Westengaard escorted her to the annual charity banquet for retired farm animals."

He always threw the paper down and grunted in disgust. Yet, he could not keep himself from picking up *The Rosetown Journal* and staring at her face. Something had changed in her so suddenly and her eyes seemed those of a stranger. He knew he should let her go, but something nagged at him.

These thoughts had dragged a week or so before he attended Henry's wedding to Evelyn Havish. It had been a simple affair in a chapel brimming with more people than he could count. He had joined a crowd of men squeezed along the sides. As Henry looked into the eyes of the woman he loved, Bronhart had to look away. His throat became tight and he forced his way out of the room.

He stayed only briefly at the reception afterward, despite several older women catching his arm and telling him of the graces of their daughters or nieces. His breath had returned to him as he entered his apartment and sat alone in the quiet. He wanted to let Adeline go, to forget her and meet other women and enjoy their company. But he could not.

Hopefully, his interview today would help him build a new life.

Fully groomed and wearing one of his better suits, he arrived at the new *Talbot's Boots* in North Town. Stepping inside, it appeared as common a shop as any other, except for the bustling line of people waiting to be consulted by the shoemakers.

The shop girl grinned at him, batting her eyes. He returned her smile only from politeness and said, "I have an appointment with Mr. Talbot."

Soon, he was led into a modest office where Peter Talbot sat at a desk drowning in paper.

For being a young man with so much sudden good fortune, Bronhart had expected him to be taller and have thicker hair. Yet, looking him in the eyes as they shook hands, Bronhart felt a steady warmth. There was no pretension, no false-friendliness. This was a simple man who was no more than he appeared to be.

"Glad you answered the announcement." Peter waved his hand over the papers covering the desk. "I'm grateful business is going well, but I can hardly manage keeping accounts straight anymore. Need someone with a good eye for numbers."

As Peter led the conversation, Bronhart found his face loosening into a smile as he answered. Peter bumbled through a few questions. He was clearly more of a craftsman than a businessman. Bronhart could do a lot of good here.

The interview wound down and Peter raised his eyes from the list of questions. "By the way, how was your wedding to Adeline Winkleston?"

Much of the room's warmth faded and Bronhart's jaw went tight. Yet, looking into Peter's eyes, Bronhart couldn't see any lies. This was a genuine question. It almost made him want to laugh.

"You must not read *The Rosetown Journal,*" he said. "It turns out her late father was a disinherited son of wealth, and she is the sole heir of his fortune. It appears I was no longer worthy enough and the lady is now engaged to some man-about-town named Alvin Westengaard."

"The author?" Peter fumbled with his papers. "Forgive me. I did not know."

Bronhart let himself smile. Now that Peter's shoes had made him a public figure, his own failed romance had been mentioned in the papers. "From what I have heard, you know something of broken engagements."

Peter blinked a moment before returning the smile. "I suppose I do."

Rising, Peter said, "I've a good feeling about you, Mr. Bronhart. And, well, I—" He held out his hand. "I've a few other applicants, but I think you're the one for the job."

Bronhart took Peter's hand and gave a firm shake. Working for this simple man would be far better than Mr. Mackabee. He would begin his work and build his life without Adeline.

Adeline lay across the sitting couch, reading the article in *The Rosetown Journal* once more.

> *Alvin Westengaard is the polish that brings out the shine in Miss Adeline Winkleston. He adorns her arm magnificently and raises her to higher social spheres. With Miss Winkleston's wealth and Mr. Westengaard's finesse, this soon-to-be-wed couple will be the pinnacle of Pippington Society.*

Adeline sighed as she raised the emerald ring on her finger, letting the light glimmer in the stone. Even after over a month of being engaged, it was still a wonder. Such a grand ring was worthy of her new station. With Westengaard at her side, all of society recognized her merits. Even with the ring, she had dozens of men watch her with eagerness. She let them stare while she stroked Westengaard's arm, reminding them her heart was taken.

The room seemed to brighten as Westengaard entered, his smile warm and his eyes focused only on her. He knelt beside her and raised her hand to his lips. A thrill ran through Adeline and she sighed.

Clutching her hand in his, he said, "I always dreamed of having the sort of romance I have written about." He pressed his lips to her cheek and whispered, "The reality is better by far than the dream."

Adeline tittered out a giggle.

"Where have you been all day?" she said. "It is nearly two o'clock. Serena came to brunch, but it was not enough to ease my loneliness."

Sitting beside her, he said, "I am a writer, my love, and must place words to the page."

"Then we shall make a place for you to write here." She waved her hand toward the large windows overlooking the garden.

"A writer needs his mind as well and I can hardly hold onto a thought when so near you." He raised her hand and stroked her fingers. "I can smell your magic like a fresh spring rose just about to blossom. It is as nearly intoxicating as your beauty."

Her cheeks were warm as she pulled her hand away. "I'd rather not have my magic. It has only ever been a burden."

He stroked her chin. She found her eyes drawn to him, unable to look away. This happened so often when they were close, but she didn't mind.

"Do not deny who you are." He breathed on her hand and a soft light spread across her fingers. "It is a part of you and it is marvelous."

She closed her hand, shutting off the spark of magic. This was always what he said when they discussed her powers. He didn't understand how little she needed it and how much better her life would be if she were to let it go. Even so, he loved her, and would accept in time.

"Magic is useless," she said. "Anything we can do with magic has been solved by inventors and new machines. The world is much simpler without it."

"That is because you haven't seen a world with it." Standing, he kept her hand in his. "Let me show you."

She found herself rising before she had decided to and walked with him into the study.

He shut the door, the air feeling still despite the light coming through the gauzy curtains. From his jacket pocket he pulled a leather case. Inside was a pair of goggles, the leather band thick, the metal around the glass engraved with strange letters and runes, flecks of gold decorations remaining as signs of a more glorious design.

"These are antique spectroscopes," he said, "from when our ancestors ruled this nation in their proper place." He held the lenses to the light. A prism of color stretched across the floor, the colors forming smoky shapes.

"How do they differ from the spectroscope I already have?" She stroked the leather, feeling the power emanating from them, calling to her.

"These are far more than your toys. These allow you to see deeper into magic's threads. Magic fills the air around us. We breath it and it runs in our veins, but we cannot see into its depths." He held out the goggles. "Try them."

Adeline frowned before placing them on her face. Color flooded her eyes, making them water. As her vision cleared, swirls of blue, red, green, and yellow mixed together, richer in substance than she had ever seen. The colors were as light as clouds yet glowed as if pulsing with life. The longer she stared, the more individual threads became clear, bound together like the fibers of a plant stem.

"It's beautiful," she said, her mouth open in wonder. "Mrs. Hunter would love these."

"These must be another of our secrets," Westengaard said. He reached out a hand and plucked a thread of yellow light and then a thread of red with his other hand. He hummed and the threads vibrated before wrapping around each other, binding into an orange light. Westengaard released it, and the thread shaped into a bird made of light flittering about the room.

"The deeper magics, the ones which can change this world, need such sight and understanding," Westengaard said. "With practice, you will begin to see the threads of magic without needing any tools." He touched her chin and guided her head. "Now, look at me."

She gasped.

A dark haze surrounded him, like a pocket of night in the middle of a bright day. A few threads of color bled out in thin tendrils, but it was weak. Around his wrists and forearms were bands made of silver, looking almost like shackles. The longer she stared, the more a thousand colors blasted at her eyes, bright and tangled into complicated knots and twists.

A pulsing formed in her forehead and quickly spread to a throb, similar to the headaches warning of the magic attacks on her birthday.

Shutting her eyes, she looked away.

"My body escaped from the Culparr Mines, but my magic is still locked away," he said. "Enough of my power bleeds through to attach to yours. I have tried to undo these shackles, but I need your help, my love."

He turned her shoulders and said, "Open your eyes, Adeline, and see the truth."

Though she tried to keep them closed, she could not stop her eyes from opening.

Her breath stilled as she stared at the mirror. Colors swirled, surging and waving around her like a wild mane. A white light framed her, the brightness stinging her eyes.

Westengaard's cheek pressed close to hers, his darkness even blacker beside her brightness. "Your physical beauty, Adeline, is already great, but here is your true magnificence."

Adeline's body froze as if she were locked inside. All she could see was the glowing light. The touch of Westengaard's arm around her waist as he pressed close to her side felt as if it were far away.

"Our ancestors once ruled Barthan," he whispered. "The people, in their hearts, know their proper role and are waiting for us to take our rightful place." His fingers laced with hers. "We will marry and restore our kingdom."

A sharp pang shot through Adeline's head. She ripped off the goggles and tossed them on the table. The colors disappeared around her. She pressed her hands to the table. Her head felt dull, as if half of her senses had been cut off.

Resting his hand on her back, Westengaard leaned close. "You must see it now." He touched her chin again. The pang in her head worsened as she found herself standing and looking him in the eye. "You, my sweet Adeline, will be the mother of a dynasty."

She blinked, wishing the throbbing in her head would go away and she could think clearly. Her frown softened into a smile as she finally understood his words.

With a laugh, she teasingly slapped his arm. "Is that the plot of your next book? With me as the heroine?"

Westengaard's soft expression dropped into a scowl and his eyes narrowed. "That is exactly what I meant." He held out his arm to her. "But, to tell better stories, I need your help to set myself free."

"Of course, I will help you." She winced, trying to push back the throbbing in her head. "But, we will have all our lives to set you free." She squeezed his hand. "You will see, once we are married."

"Yes. Once we are married." His smile returned and Adeline found a lightness filling her breast. Yet, as he leaned in to kiss her, the sharp pang in her head turned into a stab.

She cried out and stepped back, clamping her hands to her head.

"Is everything all right?" he said.

"Oh, I'm—" She didn't know what was wrong, but the pain wouldn't leave. "I just need to rest. Why don't you come back tonight, just before dinner?"

He kissed her hand and she clamped her teeth together, trying to hold back a whimper. The pain lessened a bit as he reached the doorway and said, "Till tonight, my love."

With him gone, she sat at the table and leaned her head against her arms. Tears streamed down her cheeks and a tightness filled her chest.

Was it because she missed him or was it because of the pain?

So much was suddenly unclear. Looking again at the emerald ring, she took deep breaths. She just needed to calm herself and focus on her future with Westengaard. Once they were married, things would be simpler and their days would be full of joy.

Serena wanted to be happy for Adeline. Her friend's face was radiant as she leaned close to Westengaard, nuzzling her nose against his as she giggled. The crowd of finely dressed men and women around her laughed. Helena Velis was her own dazzling planet orbited by a group of young men. Everything was grander than Adeline and Serena had ever dreamed of in all their hours of lying on each other's beds, pouring over every detail of *The Rosetown Journal.*

Yet, the pricking of goosebumps along the back of her neck had persisted ever since reading of Adeline's engagement to Westengaard.

She had excused Adeline not giving the news herself because the papers had declared it the morning after Adeline broke from Bronhart. Adeline had filled her in on details of Westengaard's dashing proposal over brunch the next day.

But, when Serena said, "But what of Mr. Bronhart?", Adeline's eyes went blank. Her face creased with a frown and she said, "What of Mr. Bronhart? Why would I keep a glass stone when I could have a diamond?"

The words still grated at Serena. Bronhart was a good man who deserved better. But she kept up her smiles and support. She was still the maid of honor and Adeline's closest friend since childhood. Her role was to be loyal to Adeline, no matter which man's hand she accepted at the altar.

She attended all the dress fittings, tastings, and discussions of flower arrangements. It would be a beautiful wedding, and she was excited for the extravagance. All the beauty did nothing, however, to remove her unease when near Westengaard. There was something about his smiles and devoted looks which troubled her.

She couldn't place what bothered her, so she sat in the corner at another evening party in Adeline and Westengaard's honor, mostly forgotten as she busied herself with playing cards. Rompell sat across from her, his dark eyes grave as he tracked Adeline and Westengaard through the crowd. He was like a sentinel on edge, waiting to strike if needed. He smiled politely when necessary, but Serena hadn't seen a genuine smile or laugh in far too long. Adeline's father had always been a serious man, but he usually had a warmth about him. Today, that warmth was gone.

Setting down the card marking the end of her turn, she whispered, "I still don't understand how she forgot Mr. Bronhart so quickly."

Rompell busied himself with shuffling his cards. This wasn't the first time she mentioned this, but each time he pretended he didn't hear her or changed the topic.

"I am glad she is happy, but her engagement to Mr. Westengaard is so sudden. She said nothing of ending things with Bronhart. I know it's been weeks, but I still am confused."

"What does it matter who Adeline marries as long as she is happy?" Rompell flexed his gloved fingers before selecting his next card. "As her father, my duty is to support her, no matter her choices."

Serena pressed her lips together before saying, "But, Adeline told me you hated Westengaard."

Rompell waved his hand. "Westengaard and I have discussed our past disagreements and have come to an understanding."

"She is my best friend. The closest I have to a sister. I will support her, but—something is wrong, and I don't know what."

Rompell lowered his cards and looked at her, his eyes seeming to waken from a deadened stupor. He placed his gloved hand on top of hers.

"No matter what happens, remember you love her." Pulling his hand away, he said, "If everything goes as I expect, she will soon need you more than she ever has."

He glanced across the room and returned a false smile to one of the women. The smile was gone once the woman looked away. Leaning close, he whispered to Serena, "You must not ask these questions aloud again. You must pretend to be happy for Adeline."

Serena frowned, searching for the answer in his eyes. "What do you think will happen?"

Rompell flicked a card through his fingers, making it disappear. "Be true to her, Serena. That is all I can say."

It took a moment for Serena to hear Adeline calling her name. She felt as if walking in a haze as she came to Adeline's side, the voices and faces a blur. She smiled as Adeline introduced her to yet another young man who seemed only interested in Serena so he could be close to Adeline. Her eyes drew back to Rompell in the corner, his presence a dark cloud in the airy gathering.

Taking the gentleman's hand as she followed Westengaard and Adeline for a walk, she could only stare at Westengaard's broad shoulders.

Whatever was going on, she would help Adeline. She only wished she had a better idea than Rompell's vague words and the prickling on the back of her neck.

Chapter 20

Sand spread across the polished table. Sweat dripped down Adeline's back and dotted her forehead as she stared at the tiny grains. Her head already ached, and she had only been doing the exercise for a half-hour. Yesterday, Westengaard had led her through exercises for nearly eight hours, barely stopping to eat. Today, he stood on the other side of the table, his arms folded as he watched her struggle in silence.

They should be off having a luncheon, or going for a drive, or a stroll to show off their love for each other. For the past few weeks, he had seemed less interested in going outside and more focused on helping her deepen her connection to her magic. She hated it, yet, every time she looked at him, the wave of warmth filled her breast, spreading and tingling through the fibers of her soul. She wanted to please him, to see his smile and know he approved.

For him, she would keep trying.

"Concentrate on each one," he said. "Just one at a time."

Adeline's head throbbed as she hummed, forming a pocket of air beneath a group of sand, raising it up. Westengaard batted his hand through the air and the grains scattered.

"One at a time." He punched his fist against the table. "If you had been taught properly, you would have mastered this as a child."

"I'm doing my best." Her lips trembling, Adeline dropped into the nearest armchair. His disapproval stung. Forcing her head to remain high, she said, "We haven't been out lately. Perhaps we might go look at the china we selected from the caterer again. There is nearly a month left till the wedding, and everything must be just right."

"That is your servants' duty."

He stood beside her and touched her shoulder. Her sorrow faded, though her headache remained, and she found herself smiling up at him.

Kneeling beside her, he cupped her hand. "Learn to do this and we will go anywhere you want." He smiled and tapped her nose. "We will remind everyone of our love."

"I will try again," she said. "But, couldn't we do this outside? It is a beautiful day."

"And risk others learning our secrets? No. That is far too dangerous."

He helped her stand and guided her back the table. Keeping his arm around her waist, he said, "Once more, my love."

Adeline glanced at her father, still reading the paper, snapping the page each time he turned it. Concentrating was easier when she focused on him, pushing aside the giddy feelings she had around Westengaard. He was a steady presence and she was glad he seemed to tolerate Westengaard better.

Turning her attention to the pile of sand, she tried not to grimace as she focused on a single grain. Measuring her breath as Westengaard had shown her, she focused her energy and power. Other grains of sand floated and swirled together, making it difficult to concentrate on the grain. She set the grains down and took another breath.

This time, she focused on the sand around the single grain, repelling them away from the center. With the single grain secluded, she began to lift it. A yellow light formed around it and she gasped. The floating sand dropped and she stepped back.

Westengaard grinned. "You saw it, didn't you?"

She nodded, her eyes still wide. "It was magic, but—I could see it."

He waved his hand over the table. She could feel her magic drawing into him as the sand rose to form a sphere. In it, she could see filaments of orange and sparks of green, faint lines of magic forming together. He lowered his hand and the sand gently fell back onto the table.

"You are uncovering your true power." He tapped his forearm. "With just a little more practice, you will set me free."

She smiled, but something ached within her, pushing against her joy. Still, she kept her face joyful. He did not need to know about the bits of unease that struck her now and then. Her heart was his and that was all that mattered.

"But, I must keep my promise to you. Where would you like to promenade today, my sweet Adeline?"

"Let me change and then we can visit Mr. Gossamer's shop to check on our gloves. I'm quite excited about the lace on—"

A knock rapped on the door. Adeline used the already damp hand towel to pat her forehead dry as Rompell opened it.

"An officer of the law wishes to speak with Miss Winkleston," said the servant.

"Send them away," Westengaard said. "My fiancé and I are much too busy today."

Adeline began to nod but stopped. Whatever the police officer had come for must be important.

"Send the officer in."

Once the servant was gone, Westengaard said, "You need to trust my judgement."

"The officer will only come bother us later." She touched his arm and smiled. "I'd rather focus on you this afternoon."

Westengaard gave her a half-smile in return, but it was almost a sneer. He folded his arms as the door opened and a young man entered, his wavy hair barely contained by his hair polish. There was something familiar about him, yet she couldn't place him. It was as if there were a hole in her mind where he should be.

The young officer's grin faltered under Rompell and Westengaard's glares.

Sitting in one of the armchairs, Adeline motioned for him to take the chair across from her. "What can I do for you, sir?"

The man wiped his palms on his patrolman's uniform as he sat.

"It's good to see you again, Miss Winkleston. A lot's happened these past few months, but it's turned out well. Here you are, a fine lady." He tapped the brass badge on his chest. "And, just as I told you, I'm a newly minted officer of the law."

She flexed her cheeks, attempting a smile in return. Yet her mind grasped for his place in her memory.

"It is good to see you too," she said.

"I am Miss Winkleston's fiancé, Alvin Westengaard." He stood beside Adeline, a protective hand on her shoulder. "What is your business here?"

The officer rose and held out his hand. "Sorry. Should have introduced myself." Pumping Westengaard's hand, he said, "Officer Jack Kingston, Patrolman of the Pippington Police."

Letting go of Westengaard's hand, he said, "Sorry again. Inspector McCay says the first thing any officer should do is give a good handshake and let folks know who you are." He waved his hand at Adeline. "But, seeing as Miss Winkleston and I worked together at the Bradford School, I thought introductions weren't needed." He turned to Rompell. "And you must be her father, Mr. Rompell?"

Rompell kept his dark eyes on Jack as he gave a firm handshake.

Adeline rubbed her forehead. Her days at the Bradford School were a distant dream, her hours of teaching girls and sitting with Mrs. Hunter a haze. She hadn't thought about the memories often, and figured the haze was merely from her excitement over marrying Westengaard.

Yet, as she sat across from someone who clearly knew her, who had spoken to her, other blanks spots rose in her memory. Biting her lip, she tried to remember Bronhart's face. She hadn't thought of him in weeks, and now all she could conjure was a vague image.

She had loved him, though she loved Westengaard more.

Bronhart was not a man she should forget.

"You are on Inspector McCay's team?" Westengaard said. His fingers dug into her shoulder as he glared at Jack.

"I'm still earning my way there. But, due to some unexpected circumstances involving a few frogs and some missing men, she's taken a personal interest in mentoring me."

A coolness settled on Adeline's skin and she raised her head.

To the common public, Inspector McCay was a brilliant detective who solved impossible crimes. To those who knew of magic, McCay was a master of storytelling. McCay worked with Mrs. Hunter now and then and had even come to give special lessons to her secret class at the Bradford School.

If he worked with McCay, and had worked at the Bradford School, he had to know of magic.

There was another memory with McCay. Something with fire and Serena. Adeline's eyes drifted to her father. It was an important memory involving him as well, but the details were vague.

"I know I'm interrupting your afternoon," Jack said, "but I'm helping with a case and was hoping to ask Miss Winkleston some questions privately."

"Regarding?" Westengaard stepped toward Jack. Westengaard was slightly taller and broader, but Jack kept his place.

"It's best if I speak with Miss Winkleston alone, sir."

"You may ask Miss Winkleston anything you wish, but I will remain."

"That's really up to the lady, sir." Jack gestured with his officer's hat. "It'll take no more than ten minutes. You gentlemen can spare ten minutes, can't you?"

Westengaard opened his mouth to speak for her again, but Adeline waved her hand. "Oh, let him see me. I'm sure it is nothing."

Keeping his glare on Jack, Westengaard kissed Adeline's cheek before exiting. Rompell watched Jack a moment, seeming almost about to say something, but then followed Westengaard into the hall.

As the door closed, Adeline said, "Pardon me, but what was your role at the Bradford School again?"

Jack frowned as he sat across from her. "I was a gardener."

Smiling with the pretense of remembering, Adeline said, "Oh, yes. Of course."

Leaning toward her, Jack's frowned deepened. "Are you sure you're all right, miss? Your eyes—"

"I've a headache," she said. "What do you need, sir?"

"Right." His words didn't hide the skepticism wrinkling his brow. He sat back and pulled an envelope from his pocket. "I came because I'm afraid you've been given a poor shake."

He handed the envelope to her. She opened it, revealing a check she had written for an orphanage Rompell had mentioned a few weeks before.

"Turns out that orphanage is a front for smuggling," Jack said. "I did some prodding after McCay shut the place down and found your name among the donors."

She frowned at the numbers written in her own hand. "What happened to the funds?"

"That's what we're trying to track. I was hoping you might have noted anything suspicious."

She shook her head, seeking to remember the conversation. Rompell had mentioned the orphanage and Westengaard leaned over her as she wrote the check, whispering the good she was doing. Neither would have led her wrong.

"There is one thing," Jack shifted, scratching his head before saying. "Your father's name is on the deed."

Her spine straightened as she sat up. "He isn't involved in anything illegal."

"I don't think he is," Jack said, giving her an apologetic look, "but, I've got to follow the leads I have."

He pulled a notepad from his pocket and flipped it open. "A consultant McCay brought in traced some transactions and found deposits to Mr. Rompell's accounts that match other donations you've made. It matches up a little too nicely, and—"

He leaned toward her, dropping his voice to a whisper. "The signatures—Common officers would think they're real. But, I've looked at them with a spectroscope." His lips pressed together. "There's magic involved."

"What are you talking about?" She pushed herself up from her chair as her heart jolted. This man may be on McCay's team, but that didn't mean she would reveal her magic. "That's preposterous."

"It's like that day in the greenhouse, where you—"

Her cheeks reddened as she looked at him. What had happened in that greenhouse with this young man?

"I know what your father's done for you," he said. "If someone's framing him, I want to help."

"Who would frame my father?" she said, marching to the door.

Jack slid his notebook in his pocket. "I don't know. I came because I hoped you might know of an enemy he might have."

"He has no enemies," she said. Months ago, she would have been foolish enough to think this was Westengaard's doing. Now that she knew his heart, she knew he would be as worried for her father as she was.

Arriving at the door, Jack held a card out to her. "If you think of anything, leave a note for me at the police station. I'm often there late, if you need to talk in person."

She glared at the card. "You come here to call my father a thief and then make ridiculous claims about magic?" Snatching the card from his hand, she threw open the door. "I will speak to your superiors."

Jack's eyes pleaded with her. "I'm just—"

"You've been dismissed, sir," Westengaard said as he stepped into the doorway.

Putting on his officer's hat, Jack said, "Thank you for your time, miss."

He nodded to Westengaard and marched down the hall. Adeline watched Jack go, her skin cold. He knew far more about her than he should, but she remembered nothing of him. With his closeness to McCay, this was dangerous.

Touching Westengaard's arm, she said, "Make sure he leaves."

"Of course, love." Westengaard strode down the hall, creating an intimidating shadow behind Jack.

Facing her father, who stood silently in the hallway, she said, "Papa, a word."

Rompell followed her inside. As she shut the door, he said, "What's wrong?"

She held onto the door handle to keep herself steady. Her head pulsed with pain, but she had to complete this.

"Papa," she said, "it can't be true, but Officer Kingston claims the orphanage you suggested I donate to was a front for you to embezzle from."

Rompell's brow furrowed and he tilted his head. "Is that exactly what he said?"

"It's what he implied."

"Westengaard asked me to mention the orphanage to you," Rompell said, his words measured. "I had no other business with it. Perhaps you should ask Westengaard."

A pang ran across the left side of her forehead and her glass of water on the table began to shake. Pressing a hand to her head, she glared at Rompell.

"He wouldn't knowingly lead me to thieves."

Rompell stepped closer to her and lowered his voice to a whisper. "He has done far worse, even turned whole cities into stone. Draining your wealth from you would be nothing." He touched her cheek, pain in his eyes. "You must remember who the man you are to marry is."

Adeline cried out as it felt as if a taut rope in her head had snapped, the two ends lashing out and leaving a pulsing migraine. The glass of water exploded and her legs faltered. Rompell caught her, holding her tight to his breast.

"Keep fighting, Adeline, until you find yourself."

He helped her onto the fainting couch as Westengaard's heavy footsteps approached from the hallway. Rompell kissed her cheek and whispered, "I am sorry, Adeline. I wish I could protect you better."

Her eyes widened as she stared up at him, trying to understand what he meant.

Westengaard pushed Rompell out of the way and knelt beside her. "What did he say to you?"

Adeline looked up at him, waiting for the comforting wave of warmth she felt whenever their eyes met. Instead, her headache only grew worse.

Trying to blink back tears of pain, she said, "I need some time alone." She patted his hand. "Take some time to see to your writing. I just need to rest."

The throb increased as Westengaard bent down and kissed her. It felt like hot poison touching her lips.

Rising, Westengaard said, "Rest, my sweet Adeline. I will return in a few hours and we shall go out for the evening."

Adeline forced herself to smile. "I'll look forward to it."

Westengaard walked to the door and snapped to Rompell. Her father glanced at her before following Westengaard from the room.

With them gone, the air seemed to clear. She lay on the sitting couch and forced herself to breathe.

Her mind shot between the blank spaces in her memories and the strange revulsion she had felt a moment ago. Maybe someone was poisoning her, trying to keep her from marrying Westengaard. It could be one of the thousand jealous women among high society. Or, Rompell could be manipulating her love for Westengaard, letting his hatred cloud his judgement.

Whatever the truth was, she wished her pain would leave her. This should be a time of joy and celebration, preparing to marry the man she loved. Magic and all its complications had no place here.

Chapter 21

There were only two weeks left before the wedding as Adeline stood behind a curtain, waiting to be announced as one of Leticia Hampnell's Eight Wonders of the City. Tonight, she was a centerpiece of the banquet benefiting orphans. Her eyes drew to the curtain dividing her and Westengaard. She ran her lace-gloved finger over the fabric.

Being apart from him was growing harder, even with her headaches a dull but steady throb. He had shortened her lessons, which had made things better, but her attempts to tug at the magic wrapped around his arms left her exhausted. Sometimes, she lay collapsed on the floor for hours before she was ready to make their social appearances.

Evenings like this were a relief, especially when she was about to be the center of an event she had read of for so long.

She prepared her pose as Mrs. Hampnell's voice called, "I present you a miracle-worker of shoes, the owner of *Talbot's Boots and Other Footwear*, Mr. Peter Talbot."

Adeline still didn't understand how a shoemaker of such common origins could become so popular. She stuck with Cordwainer's shoes, despite the constant pinch in her toes.

The crowds' thunderous applause subsided and Mrs. Hampnell said, "Our next guest is an orphan herself. By some miracle, she was restored to title and wealth. Her tale, as many of you already know, is filled with sorrow and hardship. I present Miss Adeline Winkleston."

Adeline batted her fan and smiled broadly, waving with a lace handkerchief as she stood before the crowd. It gave her all the thrill she had dreamed of when reading of this event in *The Rosetown Journal*.

She took her seat beside Peter Talbot. The holes in her memory faded enough for her to remember the many times he had sized her feet during childhood. His attempted smile and the sweat on his brow marked his nervousness.

Giving him a kind smile, she squeezed his arm and whispered, "It is good to have a friendly face here, Mr. Talbot."

He seemed to relax a little and she turned her batting eyes on the crowd. The ring of their applause was sweet and bright.

Her heart leapt as Mrs. Hampnell said, "Now, a man who has taken this city by storm, a man of mystery and letters, whose book of philosophy has challenged our greatest minds, whose most recent novel has captured our imagination and hearts, a man whose speeches and lectures ignite the soul and enliven the spirit. I present to you, Mr. Alvin Westengaard."

The curtain drew back and Westengaard strode in, swinging a fine cane. Several women fainted as he passed. Adeline rose, beaming with the knowledge that he was hers.

Reaching her side, he kissed her hand and gave her a dashing smile.

"And now they will meet our secret," he whispered.

Adeline's excitement grew as she looked down at the curtained-off stage.

Just over a week ago, she and Westengaard had entered Mr. Gossamer's shop to check on her gloves for the wedding. Instead of gloves, they had walked out with a wonder she had never expected.

"Mr. Westengaard introduced me to our eighth wonder just a week ago," Mrs. Hampnell said. "I was overwhelmed and impressed by her beauty and grace. Given Mr. Westengaard's marvelous way with words, I will let him finish the introduction."

He kissed Adeline's hand and walked to the podium. His deep voice echoed through the hall.

"Good evening, ladies and gentlemen," Westengaard said. "I was shopping for gloves in Mr. Gossamer's boutique, when I came across something far more precious and delicate."

Peter's hands clamped on his armrests. Adeline nearly frowned, but remembered the crowd was watching her.

"I immediately went to Madame Plesatti to inform her of the next great prima dancer," Westengaard said. "Though a mere girl, she bears such natural grace she could be a goddess of dance. And this speaks nothing of her beauty, which puts the stars, moon, and even sun to shame.

"Tonight, we will be graced with the lady dancing to Pavia's *Dance of the Dying Lover*. Not only was it choreographed by Madame Plesatti herself, but it is the lady's debut performance. Next weekend, she will premiere at the Morveaux, taking the lead role in Shara's *La Talentio*. And the following weekend, she will dance to honor my own wedding to the luminescent Adeline Winkleston."

Adeline couldn't help but giggle, fanning herself to hide her reddened cheeks as the crowd burst into cheers of congratulations.

There were so many people happy for her and finding such a wonderful dancer to grace their wedding was yet another treat.

"Without further ado," Westengaard said. "Mrs. Hampnell's eighth and final wonder of the evening. A beauty beyond nature, a grace beyond anything the world has yet seen. I present to you, in benefit of this city's orphans, the debut performance of Miss Flora Primrose."

Adeline's smile broadened as the stage curtain rose. To think, this wonderful girl had been tossed out by Mr. Gossamer, blamed for the commotion of men seeking her attention. Seeing her innocent face and wide-eyes, Adeline had felt drawn to her, a connection as if they had long been friends.

Mr. Gossamer's cruelty turned out to be worse as Adeline realized the girl was mute.

She had immediately taken her to the mansion and, that very day, Westengaard introduced Flora to Madame Plesatti, the greatest mistress of dance in Pippington. It felt a moment that was meant to be. She just wished Flora would stop trembling so much when Westengaard was near. Most women batted their eyes and gathered around him, but Westengaard's presence left Flora petrified.

Such a sweet young woman. She deserved this chance to shine, to receive the adulation of all of Pippington.

As the curtain rose, revealing the glass-enclosed stage, Peter pressed a hand to his chest, his eyes full of longing. Adeline smiled. Flora seemed to have a similar effect on many men. She might have been envious if she didn't have the love of Alvin Westengaard.

The dance began with Flora crouched on the floor, holding her legs to her chest. Her auburn hair hung loose around her, except where pinned behind one ear. On her feet were shoes made of blue griffin skin, the details fine and delicate.

A violin began a tragic tune, the music seeming to pull Flora to her feet. Each movement was elegant as her white dress floated around her. Sorrow creased her face, and her arms drooped like a wilting flower. The music rose in a single sweet line. She spun and pirouetted, leaping and moving with the melody. The rest of the orchestra joined. Her movements and steps became more wild and desperate. She leaped and bounded to the edges of the stage, as if she wished to break free, but then fell back elegantly from the barrier.

Adeline found herself pressing her hand to her chest, the beautiful sadness of the dance pulling at her. She felt as if flying across the stage with Flora, pounding at an invisible barrier, part of her shouting to be free, only to stumble back, exhausted.

Trying to pull herself from the sadness welling up in her, Adeline whispered to Peter, "She is marvelous, isn't she?"

He seemed not to hear as he leaned forward, his eyes following Flora across the stage. Her gaze turned to Westengaard, his face shaded by the dim lights. He leaned his chin on his hand, a slight smirk on his lips, his eyes those of a hunter about to defeat his prey. The look sent a shudder through Adeline and she scooted back in her chair.

Despite the silent crowd, she felt suddenly alone in the room, the young woman on the stage the only one who understood the sadness deep in her soul.

The constant throb in her head subsided as a drowning panic rose.

She breathed in as her heart thundered in her chest and she clamped her hands on the armrests.

Her eyes drew to Westengaard and all his layers of handsomeness peeled away. A shudder ran through her as each of his kisses flashed in her mind and her soul cried out against the lie she had been living.

A single tragic note held out, marking the end of the song. Flora crumpled to the ground as if dying. Adeline gasped as the sorrow which had overcome her rushed away and her throbbing headache returned.

She joined the crowd's applause and forced a smile, even as she tried to understand what she had just felt. Her confusion evaporated as Westengaard turned his grin on her and wrapped his hand around hers. She found herself returning his smile and going through the motions of conversation and laughter during the rest of the evening.

She wanted only to enjoy the night, to donate to the orphans and allow herself to be celebrated. However, the dark weight would not leave her chest and everything felt tight around her.

It was a relief to kiss Westengaard goodnight as her motorcar returned to her mansion.

He opened the door to walk her inside, but she squeezed his hand and said, "It is late. Go on home. I will see you tomorrow, my love."

The weight only grew heavier as the chauffeur drove Westengaard away. Her maids asked questions about the night as they undressed her and she tried to laugh and tell them of the evening. However, there was no joy left in her words.

At last, she lay alone on her bed, watching the moonlight glistening in the emerald.

Staring at it usually brought her peace, but, tonight, it only churned the knots of panic fighting with her happiness.

Chapter 22

Adeline gasped awake, feeling as if she were trapped in a box full of rising water, about to drown. Running her hands over her face, she tried to wipe away her dreams. She kept waking in the middle of the night, breaking from the recurring nightmare of being engaged to Westengaard. Night after night, the terror of her dreams was feeling more real.

She curled onto her side, rubbing her thumb across the ring on her finger. Tiredness pulled at her eyelids as she pictured herself beside Bronhart on their wedding day. She pushed against the lull of sleep, trying to remember how many more days she had to wait.

Strands of memories formed.

She stood at the Morveaux, watching Bronhart storm away. Then, she sat at Lady Hampnell's gala, her heart pounding as Flora Primrose danced. Her panic rose as Westengaard took her hand in his and kissed the emerald weighing on her finger.

With a shudder, she sat up, holding her hands to her face as she took calming breaths. As she lowered her hands, moonlight peered in from the curtains, glinting in the emerald on her finger.

She switched on the light and fell against the bed. Her hand clamped over her mouth, she held back a scream.

Grimacing, she pulled at the ring, tugging it off her finger before tossing it across the room. As it clinked onto the tile floor, she stared at the cavernous bedroom.

This was still the nightmare.

She was in her childhood home, asleep in the same bed she had slept in for years. Soon she would wake and join her father for their usual breakfast.

Yet, the fog was clearing from her mind, uncovering the horrific truth.

Pressing her fingers to her lips, she tried to shove away the longing for Westengaard's kiss. She pushed herself from the bed and walked to the balcony. Throwing open the door, she gasped in the night air.

The evening at the Morveaux flashed through her mind again. She cringed at the memory of Bronhart's face as she leaned against Westengaard.

It was real.

All of it was far too real.

She and Bronhart had fought, but that would be nothing in time. They would have found a way to make peace, if she hadn't fallen to Westengaard's spell.

How had she not resisted? How could her mind have been so dull? And, she had been under the spell for months now.

Bronhart was right to be angry. He had no knowledge of magic, no way of knowing her devotion to Westengaard was a lie.

And Rompell.

How much agony must he be in, watching her?

But he had stood there, letting Westengaard stand close, holding her against his side, his hand around hers, his lips on hers.

Why hadn't Rompell done something? Mrs. Hunter had come, but he had sent her away. Why had they left her in Westengaard's grasp for so long?

This wasn't like either of them. There had to be a game she couldn't see. Something she was blind to.

And she had woken before.

The moments had only been brief and in the middle of the night. Yet, each time felt like lifting her head out of water and gulping in fresh air. She tried to stay awake, but consciousness lasted no more than ten minutes. When morning came, Westengaard's spell enveloped her and her mind was no longer her own.

Her eyes drew to her wrists. She could almost see the tendrils of light where her magic was tied to Westengaard's. Though he was across North Town, she could feel his pull on her power.

Her hands shook as she pressed them together. She could not sleep. It was too dangerous. She had to stay awake and find a permanent escape.

But, she could not do that alone.

Entering her closet the size of her childhood bedroom, she stared at the mass of clothes she had acquired over the past few months.

These were what she had dreamed of for so long, but now all the ruffles, beads, and sequins were suffocating. Now, they only brought a wave of revulsion as she pictured herself on one of her many nights out with Westengaard.

Digging through, she found a simpler dress from her days still tutoring at the Bradford School. From her wall of shoes, she pulled the remaining pair of Talbot's boots. She sighed as she pushed her feet inside, her toes finally having room to breathe.

She stared at the boot as she rubbed the leather. There was something between Peter Talbot and Flora. The way he had looked at her was more than mere infatuation. However, she could do nothing for them if she could not free herself tonight.

With a few whistles, she tried to wrap her hair in a tight braid. Sparks of magic sputtered around her fingers, but her hair remained still. Holding back a groan, she pulled her unbrushed hair into a snood and pinned it.

She might be running off in the middle of the night, but she needed to look presentable.

Fully dressed, she hurried out of her room and down to the garage. A few times, she ducked into doorways, holding her breath as servants walked past, securing the halls. This may be her own mansion, but any of the servants could be Westengaard's spy.

Once at the garage, she pulled open the door and chose the motorcar closest to the front. The puttering seemed far too loud as she sped down the carriageway. Her foot pressed hard on the gas pedal and the motorcar lurched forward, bumping on the old cobblestone.

She passed the businesses close to the Bradford School. Mrs. Hunter would find a way to help, but Adeline could not risk the girls.

Instead, she turned down familiar streets and stopped on Nightingale Lane. She sprinted from the car and grabbed the doorknob of her childhood home. She pressed her hand to the keyhole and hummed a brief tune. Her power poured out like a sputtering faucet, the tumblers shifting in short bursts. She shut her eyes and concentrated on the waves of magic. Her panic had to be hurting her connection to her power.

The tumblers shifted and she threw open the door. Running up the stairs, she called, "Papa!"

Rompell stumbled into the hallway, turning on the lights. Standing in his nightshirt and trousers, he blinked at her.

Paleness crept into his face as he pressed his hands to her shoulders. "You are awake."

The hint of tears hung heavy in his eyes as he pulled her into an embrace. Once her head leaned against his chest, her tears broke and sobs wracked through her. He pressed his hand to the back of her head and held her as he had so many times before.

"I am sorry, Little One." He rubbed her back before leading her into her room and helping her sit on the bed. He sat beside her and wiped her cheeks with his sleeve.

"What has he done to me?"

"The same he has done to many others." Rompell's hand weighed on her shoulder. "I wish I had words of comfort, but you may succumb again at any moment."

She clung to his arm and shook her head. "We will escape tonight. And, if I wake under his spell, you will stop me from going to him."

"I wish I could." His head hung tiredly.

"We can escape. Mrs. Hunter will know a way to save me. We can go to Surris and work with the Rangers to break the curse."

Rompell's hand dropped from her shoulder. "If I had my way, I would have stolen you away already." He gripped her hand. "I would tell you how I hope to save you, but if you remember anything, you will tell him tomorrow."

"I will not." She swallowed back tears and pushed herself to her feet. "Come with me to the mountains Surris. I'm sure we can get help."

Rompell stood. "You must go forward with the wedding."

Her eyes widened, unsure she had heard him correctly. His face, however, was firm and serious.

"No. We must escape and find a way to stop him." She touched his arm. "You stopped him before."

Rompell grunted. "It took two years and nearly ripped apart an empire."

"His magic has weakened. There must be a way."

"I can do nothing!" Rompell's shout echoed in the room.

Adeline stepped back.

Turning his head away, he said, "You, under your enchantment, led him to Hidaya and my sons."

A hollowness ached in Adeline. Brief flecks of memory returned to her, of approaching the warehouse, of opening the containers and giggling with Westengaard. She sank onto the bed, her body cold.

"If he finds me doing anything to save you, he will destroy them." Rompell's voice was weak, as if he could not fill his lungs. He held his hands out to her. "When I adopted you, I made a promise to protect you. There are only two weeks before the wedding. I will find a way to save you, Hidaya, and my sons."

He sat beside her and touched her arm. "We must play his game a little longer, Adeline. Go back to the mansion and trust me. I will do all I can to save you."

She pulled her hand away as she rose. Her head pulsed and the threat of tiredness was nipping at her.

"And what if you must choose between us?" she whispered.

Rompell stood. "I will make sure I do not have to make that choice."

"But what if you do?"

His silence hung in the air between them, his eyes pleading with her. Yet, time was escaping her.

"I cannot go back," she said.

Though each step pulled at her heart, she marched out the bedroom door.

"There is a way to win." He followed her down the stairs. "But, Westengaard cannot know you have woken."

She reached the front door and turned to him, the strong man who had lifted her from the snow and carried her to a better life. Without him, she would have died long ago. There was little chance he could ever return Hidaya and the two boys to life but having them destroyed would break him. The sorrow in his eyes tore at her, but she could not give in. Not when she had a chance to fight.

"I love you, Papa," she said, "but I must find a way out."

Tears ran down his cheeks as he grabbed her hand. He seemed to fight for words before whispering, "Be careful."

She forced herself to let go of his gloved hand and hurried to her motorcar. Once inside, she leaned her head on the steering wheel and prayed. Her chest ached for her papa and as she thought through who was left to turn to.

Biting her lip, she set the motorcar in motion. This venture was likely to fail, but she had to try.

Arriving at Bronhart's apartment building, each step up the stairs to his door felt heavy. She took several steadying breaths before knocking.

Bleary eyed, Bronhart opened the door and stared at her as if she were a specter.

Her lips trembled as she forced back tears. She wanted only to fall into his arms and have him hold her as he once had, to look at her as tenderly as the day he had proposed.

However, Westengaard had broken any hope of that.

Instead, she barely kept her voice calm as she said, "I need your help."

"You can have no business with me, Miss Winkleston. Good night."

He started to close the door, but she moved her shoulder in the way.

"Everything with Westengaard is a lie," she said. "What you saw that night at the Morveaux—"

"You chose Westengaard's lies. Good night."

Adeline looked in his brown eyes, so full of bitterness and hurt. He had to have a sliver of love for her still, a part of him which would believe her. She did not know what he could do to help, but love had to have power. If she could just prove to him the truth, he would forgive her and all would be well.

"I did not choose him. He cursed me. He's a powerful warlock and—I don't have much time before I fall under his spell again. Nathaniel, please let me speak."

Bronhart let go of the door and folded his arms. "It is nearly two in the morning. If you really are in trouble, then come speak to me at a decent hour when you're sober."

Her eyes flared wide. "I am not drunk." She kept her hands from balling into fists. "Papa asked you what is most unique about me when you asked for his permission to marry me." She raised her palm. "I didn't tell you because I was afraid, because there is so much to explain, but I need you to listen."

She whistled and her magic sputtered again. Bronhart raised an eyebrow as a brief spark snapped from her wrist and across her palm.

"You want me to believe this?" He leaned against the door. "And try to prove it with one of your father's parlor tricks?"

She hummed as she pushed her other hand forward, hoping to gather enough air to shove Bronhart back a step. There was a puff of air, but too small for him to feel.

"Next you'll tell me Talbot's boots are made by magic."

"He's drained my power," Adeline whispered, staring at her hands. It had to be from the pull she felt.

Bronhart tapped his fingers on the door. He grunted before saying, "Let me call your father and have him take you home. Then you—"

Adeline shook her head as she backed away. There had to be some other story she could have told him, but she could only win his trust with the truth. But, she couldn't prove the truth.

"Goodnight." She hurried out of the building and to her motorcar.

Coming here had been foolish. She only had Serena to turn to, but how could the girl help? She would be too shocked to understand and sneaking in to speak with Serena would be challenging. Every time she had been at Serena's overnight, Serena's mother had caught them whenever they tried to sneak around.

Adeline drove through the empty streets, each minute ticking by, warning her she was alone and about to lose herself. Her yawns were coming more rapid, but she couldn't succumb.

Reaching a stop sign, she stared down the crossroads.

If she kept driving, she might reach the other side of Craggsville before falling asleep. Once she woke, all of this would be forgotten and she would run to Westengaard. He would ask too many questions, which might risk Rompell's wife and sons.

The Bradford School was within reach. But, again, she could not risk the children.

There was only one answer left.

Hope sputtered inside Adeline as she drove toward the police station.

Inspector McCay wouldn't be in, but if she could just leave a message, the Inspector might have a secret cure Rompell didn't know about.

She parked in the alleyway beside the station and approached a side door. Gritting her teeth, she used her faltering magic to unlock it. Dodging through a few hallways, avoiding the lone janitor, she reached the double doors with Inspector McCay's name on the plaque as commanding officer.

She stepped into the open office area full of messy desks stacked with papers and folders. The room was empty now, but she could still feel the flurry of the day's business. She approached an office enclosed in glass with curtains hanging down for privacy. Her hand reached for the doorknob. A loud snore reverberated from a desk behind her.

Spinning around, she looked for a place to hide. Her breath eased as she saw the snoring officer.

Nearly hidden by a stack of folders, Jack Kingston sat in his police uniform, the buttons on the jacket undone, his head on the blotter as he slept peacefully.

How, of all of McCay's officers, was Jack here tonight?

She wasn't sure if she was glad or worried.

Moving as quietly as she could, she tried to turn the knob to McCay's office. It was locked. She whistled, hoping her magic might work for one more door.

Just as the first tumbler moved, a bell above the door clanged. Adeline crouched behind a nearby desk. Jack jerked up with a snort before falling backwards in his chair. Taking the spare seconds, Adeline sprinted toward the double doors. She rammed her shoulder against the door, but it was stuck shut.

"Raise your hands and turn around," Jack shouted over the alarm.

Adeline cursed silently as she followed his command and faced him. With a frown, he lowered his pistol.

"Miss Winkleston?"

He holstered his gun and attempted to button his uniform jacket as he walked toward her. He missed one hole, leaving it askew. "What are you doing here?"

Staring at him, her exhaustion waved over her and tears of frustration threatened to replace tears of sorrow and fear.

Out of everyone she could turn to, this was who she was left with? A man whose hair was now sticking up on one side and flat on the other and with ink blotched on his cheek. He had shown competence when he had come to her mansion to tell her about the embezzling, yet he was only Jack.

"You look tired." He gestured toward the chair by his desk. "Take a seat. I'll turn off the alarm."

He pulled a set of keys from his desk as she sat in a chair. With a few clunks, the bell turned off, leaving a ringing in Adeline's ears.

Jack stepped into the hallway and came back with a tall glass of water. As he set it on the desk, a rotund officer burst into the room, his pistol raised.

"I set it off on accident, Griggs," Jack said. "Sorry about that."

Griggs huffed as he holstered his gun. "Who's she?"

"A witness."

"Civilians are supposed to register at the front desk."

"Not that kind of witness." Jack grinned and winked at Griggs.

Adeline glanced over her shoulder as Griggs returned the grin with a knowing nod.

"Wouldn't mind so pretty a 'witness' myself." He followed his words with a whistle. "I'll leave you to it, then."

Adeline's eyes widened and her cheeks reddened. She glanced at

Jack once Griggs left. Jack ran his hand over his head and let out a groan.

"Sorry about that." He sat in his chair and looked her in the eyes, seeming to analyze her. Leaning forward, he said, "How'd you do it?"

"What?"

"Break free of Westengaard's enchantment. McCay says it's the worst she's seen."

She sat up. "McCay knows I'm under a spell?"

Jack raised an eyebrow. "I reported it to her, after talking to you a few weeks ago." He laughed. "Any girl who can't recognize a man she's turned down so often has got to be under a spell." With a shrug, he added, "She already knew. Said Mrs. Hunter reported it."

Adeline sagged in her chair, the pressure in her chest easing. She was not alone.

"What is being done to stop him?"

Jack winced and scratched the light stubble on his cheek. "From what I've seen, we're behind where we should be."

"Is that why you're here so late?"

Jack's chair creaked as he leaned back. "I wish I could say yes, but McCay's the one who's managing your case." He pointed to his uniform. "McCay's letting me assist with some detective work, but I've still got to walk my regular beat. That, with a few evening classes, leaves me here late most nights." He held up a folder. "I was working on a case of hats turning into hedgehogs."

Despite her sorrow, Adeline laughed. With that spark of humor, something broke in her. She laughed harder, the laughs becoming sobs as tears dripped down her face. Each breath she took ached, every moment of closeness to Westengaard burning in her mind.

Jack frowned while opening his desk drawer and pulling out a handkerchief.

She took in deep breaths before drinking some water.

"I'd ask if you're all right, but I'm pretty sure of the answer." He held out the handkerchief. "I don't know everything about Westengaard, but I know he's dangerous. I'm not sure what he's done to you, but it's not right. How can I help?"

Looking in his brown eyes, she felt the earnestness of his question. Here, she might have the one answer and one chance to save Rompell's wife and sons, and, if she was fortunate, herself.

Chapter 23

Rompell set music on the phonograph before stretching his arms as he entered his study for another long night of planning. Only a week remained to stop Westengaard and save his family. Just over a week before, when Adeline had come to him, he had almost hoped Adeline would break from Westengaard's spell permanently. The next morning, her eyes were clouded once more.

Seeing his daughter lost in Westengaard's spell was unbearable enough. The hours of burning inside while Westengaard pushed Adeline to free him were harder. Most evenings, when they went off to parade in front of high society, Rompell escaped to the street corners of his past, doing tricks for children between talking with those who might be paid to do Westengaard's dirty work. Several times, his investigations led him to the latest abandoned building where Westengaard may have moved Hidaya and their two sons. Once Rompell arrived, however, there were no statues.

Tonight, after an evening of performing parlor tricks on street corners, he returned to his empty house. He wished for a few minutes of peace, pretending Westengaard didn't control Adeline and that Inspector McCay didn't have an officer in a patrol car hidden down the street. However, peace remained far from him.

He reached for his notebook full of scratched-out plans and ideas but stopped. Instead, he opened a drawer and removed the latest annual letter from his brother, Solvan. He unfolded it, reading again of the prior year of Tamina's life. She was nearly sixteen and stepping into her role as princess, believing Solvan and Briya were her parents. He rubbed his thumb over her photograph, where she posed in a dress covered in fine beads, her eyes showing her strength.

She was safer in Sandar, ignorant of him. He often wished he could go on the two-month ocean journey to Sandar and see her just once. However, in Sandar, he was supposed to be dead. Returning was too much of a risk.

Setting her photograph beside his notebook, he opened to his latest scribbled plan. Every day brought him closer to a solution, but the key piece kept evading him. He had to find a way to save Tamina's mother and brothers, as well as Adeline, but time was disappearing far too quickly.

A knock on the front door broke his thoughts. He set Tamina's photograph in the desk drawer and reached for his hidden revolver but stopped. The visitor was unlikely to be a threat. Even if it were a spy for Westengaard, a revolver would be too noticeable.

Looking through the front door's peephole, a bemused smile crossed his face. Peter Talbot stood on the other side, nervously shuffling his feet as he nodded to himself. Whatever business the shoemaker came on was unclear, but it would be a welcome relief from the knot of saving Adeline.

Rompell opened the door. "Mr. Talbot. Good evening. How may I help you?"

Peter's smile faded before it could fully form. His eyes focused on Rompell's shoulder as his hands fidgeted.

"Well, I went out for a stroll and I was—I was just in the neighborhood, and, um, I thought I'd say hello and thanks for sticking with my shop, even with all the scandals and rumors blowing around."

Rompell narrowed his eyes. It was an odd reason for a visit, and Peter was too kind and too simple a man to have a scandal. He had heard a rumor of Peter's broken engagement, but that had been over a month before.

"You must have been walking a while." Rompell motioned for Peter to enter. "Why don't you come inside and have a drink?"

"That'd be great. Just great."

Rompell poured some Sandarian ale and tried to make conversation, but Peter stood and flapped his jacket, trying to cool the sweat dotting his forehead. To give Peter a moment to collect himself, Rompell took Peter's jacket to the entryway closet.

The young man was far too nervous for a casual visit, so Rompell took a quick glance through Peter's pockets. Everything was ordinary. And, Peter was too honest a man to be Westengaard's spy. Still, Rompell had to be wary.

As he returned to the sitting room, Peter's voice pitched up awkwardly as he said, "How goes the wedding?"

Picking up his glass, Rompell said, "If you have read *The Rosetown Journal*, you know all I do."

"Letting your girl take full reins of the event?"

Rompell's teeth grit together, but he forced his face to remain pleasant and calm. "My choices and opinions hold no sway over Adeline anymore."

Peter seemed to nod to himself as he rolled his glass between his hands. "I—er—I hope it's not prying too much, but it seems you don't approve of Mr. Westengaard."

Rompell tried to keep his calm expression, but he could feel his true feelings shadowing his features. "As I said, my opinions do not matter."

"Right, well—" Peter's pitch turned even higher. "I heard the strangest rumor the other day." He coughed and took a drink to clear his throat. After swallowing, his pitch returned closer to normal. "My friend said Westengaard's actually a—He's a—"

Rompell kept his pose, but his gloved fingers pressed on the glass. He could almost sense the words even before Peter blurted, "A warlock."

Peter's glass thunked on the table as his hands shook. Forcing his own breath to be calm, Rompell swirled his drink and took a long, slow sip.

This shoemaker knew far too much but couldn't be Westengaard's spy. The nervousness was too genuine, and a spy would keep his mouth shut about magic.

"Where did you hear such a rumor?" Rompell said.

Peter dropped into an armchair as if his legs had failed him. Tapping his foot, he said, "Maybe I'm just mad, Mr. Rompell. This past year—You'll not believe me, unless—unless what I've heard is true."

Rompell sat across from him, keeping his voice steady and calm. "What have you heard?"

Peter seemed to fight to raise his head and meet Rompell's eyes. "That you're a sorcerer."

"I see. My secret has been revealed." He rolled his fingers and a spout of flame appeared before fading. That trick should distract him.

Peter jumped. "Then, it is true."

Forcing a laugh, Rompell rolled back his sleeve, revealing a lighter hidden on his wrist, the igniter attached to a string on his thumb. Holding his palm flat, he flicked his thumb. A flame rose from the lighter.

"I didn't know the street tricks I do for children were sorcery." He slapped Peter's shoulder. "I think all of your success is fraying your nerves."

"I'm doing all right."

"Financially, perhaps." Rompell swallowed the rest of his drink before standing. Too many questions were landing too close to the truth. The sooner he left Peter confused on his doorstep, the better.

"Come on, Talbot. I'll drive you home."

The motorcar ride passed in near-silence, despite Peter fidgeting in his seat. Rompell glanced in the side-mirror. Inspector McCay's officer was fulfilling their duty and following along. Fortunately, Peter noticed nothing as he gave Rompell directions to his apartment in North Town.

A few blocks from their destination, Peter said, "You remember the flower I had in my old shop?"

Rompell's jaw flexed as he tried to remember. There had been a flower with a hint of magic some months ago, but it had been nothing.

"Ah, yes. A pretty thing," he said.

Peter swallowed. "Turns out, it was a girl."

Rompell laughed. Part of the laugh was genuine, not expecting such an answer. The other part covered up the jolt in his chest as this puzzle piece tumbled together with others in his mind. There was something this was connected to, but he couldn't place it.

However, Peter needed to be sent home.

"Rest, Mr. Talbot," he said, "is the best remedy for madness."

"She's Miss Flora Primrose now."

Rompell's hands tightened on the steering wheel. Flora Primrose was the girl Adeline had been chattering about, who Westengaard had placed in the care of Madame Plesatti.

"I'm sure you've seen her in the shop, and then dancing at the Morveaux. She sent me a—a letter this morning." Peter took a breath. "She said she saw you in Misonwood, out in the Surris Mountains about ten years ago, escorting Westengaard as a prisoner."

Curse words silently rushed through Rompell's mind.

Peter should have known nothing of that past, nor of Rompell leading the prison wagon carrying Westengaard to the Culparr Mines. Only those in the Surris Mountains should have remembered, but none of them would have talked to Peter.

Thinking quickly, Rompell said, "She would have only been a girl. She probably confused another Sandarian for me."

"It wasn't a letter, actually—it was a little song she wrote. I sang it and all of a sudden I was there, alongside her memory. I know it sounds like madness, but—"

Rompell spun the driving wheel and rammed his heel into the brake pedal. The tires screeched and Peter's head smacked against the dashboard.

The engine still rumbled as Rompell turned and faced Peter. The shoemaker shrunk back in his seat.

"These are things you cannot understand, Mr. Talbot. They are not to be trifled with, especially Alvin Westengaard." He spat out the name. "I know the danger my daughter is in, and I have everything in place to protect her.

"Keep your distance, maintain your shop, and live your life. If things work as planned, Miss Primrose will be given her fair reward."

"She didn't mean to help him escape. She was under a spell—the same spell he's got Miss Winkleston under."

Rompell slammed his hand on the seat. Peter jumped.

Good. The man was scared.

He had better be. He was caught up in something much larger than his simple life. Rompell couldn't be distracted by trying to protect Peter along with Adeline.

"I have said more than I should," Rompell said. "Here in Pippington, magic must pretend not to exist. It is best you remember that. Keep to your shop and trust me."

Peter began to sit up but looked away. "Just, if you could tell me—what is the difference between a warlock and sorcerer?"

"Warlocks steal power. Sorcerers use only their own. If Westengaard were a warlock, you would be wise not to cross him."

"I see—" Peter dared look at Rompell once more. "If I can help, let me know."

Rompell laughed, trying to imagine the small shoemaker facing Westengaard. If Rompell could not fight him, there was even less Peter could do.

Waving his hand toward the exit. "Good night, Mr. Talbot."

As Peter opened the door, he muttered, "Thank you, Mr. Rompell."

The door barely closed before Rompell jammed down the gas pedal. He ignored the bumping on the cobblestone as he sped across the city.

Everything he knew coalesced like drops of water gathering in a dish. The final image left him cold.

For years, Ed Callais spoke of the girl Westengaard held hostage, keeping the Surris Rangers at bay. Every time, this girl was the excuse.

Flora Primrose must be the girl.

And she had been in flower form, sitting on a shelf in Peter's shop.

His hands shook with rage as he drove, hardly paying attention to where he went. Stopping at an intersection, his blood churned and his shoulders heaved. He stared at nothing, grasping at the shreds of what he knew.

The Surris Rangers couldn't have known where she was for all these years. He had to tell them but contacting them directly would give Westengaard reason to melt part of his sons or Hidaya.

He glanced in his side mirror at McCay's officer sitting in his patrol car, pulled over as he waited for Rompell's next move. Staring at the reflections of light in the mirror, he knew he needed to see this girl himself, to stand in front of her and look her in the eye.

Jerking on the steering wheel, he sped toward the Morveaux. McCay's officer followed a block behind. Once across the street from the massive theater, Rompell parked in a dim alleyway. He strode out to the street, pretending not to see the officer drive by.

Tonight, it was Jack Kingston, the young officer who had come to Adeline's mansion. He seemed an easy enough man to fool.

Approaching the Morveaux, he skirted around the group of men holding flowers and crowded around the side-entrance, hoping for a glimpse of Flora Primrose. Given their hungered expressions, traces of Westengaard's allurement spell were tied to Flora, leading these men to worship the girl. Such false attention might be nearly as bad as being turned into a flower.

If she had returned from flower to human, though, it meant Westengaard's ties to her magic were weakening. Either he was too busy drawing Adeline's magic to bother with Flora or his hold weakened over time.

From his pocket, he pulled a handful of smoke snaps and tossed them into the crowd of men. Shouts broke out as plumes of yellow, red, and orange smoke filled the alleyway. He dodged around the chaos. Security guards stepped forward, holding off the panicked crowd. Rompell slipped behind them and entered through the stage door.

He kept to the shadows but walked with confidence. Appearing to belong was often the key to being ignored. He went down the metal staircase and navigated his way to the dancers' dressing rooms. A group of stagehands passed before he slipped into the room marked with Flora's name.

It was a small, cramped space, half-full of bouquets with notes declaring love to the poor young woman.

Applause echoed outside and he moved himself behind the curtain covering the window. Flora soon ran in, shutting the door quickly and curling up on the chair as she shook, tears streaming down her face.

She was so young, barely a woman, her willowy frame trembling as she pulled her knees to her chest and rocked. Though no longer a flower, Rompell could feel her hidden prison. This girl was as trapped by Westengaard as he was.

"Miss Primrose," he whispered.

She sat upright, her head raised like a deer about to take flight. Rompell pushed aside the curtain. Leaping from the chair, she backed against the door.

"Peter Talbot came to me tonight," he said.

Her eyes widened.

"He said you told him of seeing me escorting Westengaard to the Culparr Mines."

She gave him a slight nod.

"How? You would have been only a child."

She shook her head and went to her dressing table. Despite her trembling hand, she picked up a notepad and wrote in crooked writing, *I was flower.*

"I know. Peter told me."

Shaking her head again, she wrote, *Many years.*

A pain ached in Rompell as he leaned against the desk, picturing her alone as a flower, trapped and unable to escape Westengaard's curse. It reminded him of the same loneliness that had swallowed him before he had adopted Adeline, when he would open the crates holding his wife and sons and stare at their metallic faces.

His voice soft, he said, "How long?"

A tear fell down her cheek as she shrugged.

"But, you are from the Surris Mountains?"

She nodded.

Rompell placed his gloved hand on her arm. She raised her head and looked at him, her eyes seeming unsure whether to trust or flee.

This was another man's daughter, a child lost to Westengaard's cruelty. How much pain had the years given to her parents, praying to find her safe? But, here she was, alive and whole. She was still in danger, but, if Westengaard could be stopped, she could return home.

However, no matter if Westengaard was stopped or not, Hidaya, Amal, and Jabir would remain gold. Westengaard claimed to have a potion, but it could not be trusted.

He could not bear to see the statues melted, to have no chance they might be restored one day.

Yet, it had been fifteen years.

A knot formed in his throat, but he forced himself to meet her blue eyes.

There were probably more victims of Westengaard like Flora sprinkled throughout Pippington and the surrounding towns. He pictured his daughter Tamina. She was safe in Sandar for now, but Westengaard would come for her in time. He pictured Adeline and her eyes full of fear the night she had come to him.

Were they worth preserving a set of statues?

A weight hung on his shoulders as the answer came, the silent bell of mourning for his wife and sons beating in his chest. If they could be preserved, he would, but no one else would fall victim to Westengaard.

Lowering his hand, he said, "The Rangers have been looking for you. Westengaard told them you are his hostage."

Her eyes grew even wider. He squeezed her hand with his gloved fingers.

"You, Adeline, and I are his prisoners, but we will break free."

He let go and stood to leave. Her hand brushed his arm and he glanced at her. On her notepad, she wrote, *How is Peter?*

"Ready to do something foolish to help you," he said. "Obey Westengaard and play along with his game. I will make sure he loses."

He touched her shoulder, wishing he could free her now. However, to do as he hoped was dangerous enough without adding Flora as someone to protect.

Leaving her room, he kept to the shadows and moved to a flight of stairs leading to an alternate exit. With each step, his plan came into better focus.

However, he could not defeat Westengaard alone.

Stepping into an alleyway, he glanced down the boulevard.

His best path to allies lay in the young police officer leaning against a building across the street, pretending to read a newspaper in the dim light of a street lamp.

Rompell skirted around the Morveaux using a labyrinth of alleyways he had walked in his days of playing beggar. Coming out a building or two away, he crossed the street and approached Jack from behind. The young man seemed not to notice as he glanced at the crowd of men waiting for Flora.

Leaning against the wall a pace away, Rompell said, "Tell McCay I need to speak with her. Immediately."

Jack casually turned the page of his paper and snapped his gum. Rompell swallowed, preparing to speak louder.

"Most men get angry when the police keep following them." Jack gave him a pointed look. "Some might even throw a punch."

Rompell frowned. It wasn't a plan he would make, but it might be enough. With his paper folded under his arm, Jack whistled and began crossing the street.

Pushing off from the wall, Rompell strode toward the officer and said loudly, "Why do you keep following me?"

Jack ignored his quick approach and kept walking.

"I haven't done anything you've accused me of." Rompell grabbed Jack's shoulder forcing him to face him.

Holding up his hands, Jack said, "Look, sir, I'm just following orders. If you want to complain—"

Rompell rammed his fist into Jack's stomach. Jack oofed and bent forward. A few men across the street were watching. Rompell tried not to wince before he swung his fist toward Jack's face. He couldn't fake the blow but was sorry to hurt the young officer.

Jack dodged to the side and hit Rompell's chin with his elbow, knocking him back a step.

For such a wiry young man, he left a sharp ringing in Rompell's head.

Rompell spun around for another attack but stopped as he faced the barrel of Jack's pistol.

Raising a pair of cuffs, Jack said, "In the name of Pippington, you are under arrest for assaulting an officer."

Rompell forced himself to glare as he held out his wrists. Jack nearly held back a smile as he snapped the cuffs on.

"It'll help if you make some trouble on the way to the motorcar."

With Jack pushing him along, Rompell shouted and pretended to struggle.

His heart pounded as Jack slammed the motorcar door shut and drove them to the station. With each glint of golden light on the window, he pictured Hidaya, Amal, and Jabir's faces. A few times, he considered telling Jack to stop the car and let him out.

Then, he closed his eyes and pictured Flora's innocent blue eyes looking up at him.

He could not sacrifice the poor girl.

The pressure in his chest grew as Jack took him to an interrogation room and left him alone. Each minute stretched on, but he stared at his gloved hands and tried to clear his mind.

Nearly an hour later, McCay entered and sat across from him, her steel eyes meeting his.

"Rumor is," she said, "you've got the same warlock problem I do."

Chapter 24

Westengaard hurled a manuscript at Arthur Burtson. The portly man cowered, sweat forming on his balding head.

"I am supposed to be a man in love," Westengaard said. "These words must ignite passion in the hearts of women."

"But, the last draft—you said it was too sentimental." Burtson melted against his chair.

Gripping Burtson's collar with one hand, Westengaard raised the sack-like man. Burtson's feet dangled over the floor and his face paled with fear. Westengaard smirked. After the endless hours of pretending to dote over Adeline, it was a relief to look in the eyes of a man who revered Westengaard as he should.

"It is my wedding speech," he said, "and will bond my bride to me."

He tossed Burtson back into the chair.

"Write it again."

Burtson hunkered over the typewriter, his hands shaking as he fumbled with the paper. With a grunt, Westengaard marched from the room and slammed the door behind him. Flicking his wrist, he sent magic through the locks, sliding them shut.

Without Westengaard, Burtson would still be a sad man, alone in his rented room, writing romantic drivel no one would ever read. Over the past decade, Westengaard had elevated the man's craft and sold it to the public, using Burtson's words as vessels to carry his magic. The invisible shackles along his arms held his powers at bay, but the words allowed him to stretch further, pulling strength from others.

Adeline had come close twice now to unlocking the shackles. Both times had ended with her collapsed on the floor, clutching her head as she shivered. The hours waiting for her to recover and try again took too long, wearing on his patience as he played his part of devoted fiancé in public. He had hoped she would release his full power by now and he could be rid of her.

However, she was still necessary, despite the moments she slipped from his control. These were coming more often, even with the enchanted jewelry he gave her. The jewelry helped, but he needed something stronger.

The wedding, fortunately, provided an opportunity to weave his spell tighter around her. Her mind's escape would be far harder and there would be fewer questions when he tucked her away from society, using her only to pull at his shackles and refuel his power.

He had felt such resistance toward the end with Favay. If necessary, he would provide Adeline a similar fate.

Whistling to himself, he pictured the moment his powers would break free. He would sit Adeline and Rompell beside each other and melt Hidaya and the children. Then, the few years in darkness in the Culparr Mines and the loss of his empire would sting a little less.

For now, he would keep his grip on Adeline and continue his close watch on Rompell. According to Westengaard's spies, Rompell was growing bolder, having secret meetings with Inspector McCay and the headmistress of the Bradford School. Their plans were unclear, but Westengaard would let Rompell have the illusion of hope.

Entering his bedroom, Westengaard's whistle cut off.

Floating over his dressing table was a midnight blue notecard with gold etched along the edges and gleaming letters reading, *Madame Blue requires your presence.*

He glared at the note.

Sometimes, this was a worse leash than the shackles along his arms.

The words shifted and formed into, *Immediately.*

He cricked his neck before touching the notecard. Once his finger pressed to the paper, he felt himself transported across the city, speeding at a dizzying pace through alleyways and past street lights blurring together. He knew, in truth, he lay collapsed on his bedroom floor. This knowledge did nothing to ease the sickening sensation.

His journey ended with a jolt as he appeared in a dimly lit space. It was nearly a room, the walls almost formed and the silhouette of furniture marking this as a parlor. White fire flickered silently in what had taken the shape of a fireplace and a single armchair rested before it, the back tall and wide like a throne.

Madame Blue herself sat there, her form a veiled silhouette, only her lace glove visible as she held out her hand.

Though this was a place only held within her mind and projected to him, he could feel her suffocating magic. He had only once truly been in the same room as her. She was among the crowd and he had felt her magic, its sense overpowering. He had sought her, thinking he nearly spied her in the corner of his eye. Yet, when he turned, there was only a crowd of women he had met before.

All of his work to ferret out this woman who had such a hold over the hidden magic in Pippington had been for nothing.

Once Adeline unlocked his power, Madame Blue would have her reckoning.

For now, he bowed and kissed her lace glove.

"I met your fiancée today," she said, her voice soft, as if whispering in his ear. "A beautiful child so ripe with power. I see why you are drawn to her."

Standing with his arms folded behind him, he said, "I am fortunate."

"Her wealth is not so poor an asset either," she said. "Rumors are you've lightened her purse."

"It is unwise to waste an opportunity." He gave her a tight smile.

Madame Blue's face remained hidden as she leaned her chin on her hand. "Rumors also say her mother is from the Dumond line. It explains her untapped potential."

Westengaard kept his face still even as his fist clenched. Few things could be hidden from Madame Blue for long, but he had hoped to hold onto that secret. The mix of noble lines leading to Adeline's magic made for a deep richness. Pulling on her power these past few months had helped him feel closer to his full self.

"It also explains why you are losing hold," she said.

His fingernails dug into his palm and his fist shook. She was prodding for a weakness, but he would not give it to her.

He said, "Our bond will be strengthened by the wedding."

"Which will only delay her awakening." Madame Blue folded her hands in her lap. "However, I see a better use for the girl."

Westengaard forced himself not to flinch. He had been surprised Madame Blue had left his affair with Adeline alone for so long. He should have known this was coming.

"Given the right persuasion," she said, "the girl would make a wonderful lieutenant."

"She has no interest in power." He grunted a laugh. "All she cares for are baubles and pearls."

"Which is why she must be molded and taught properly."

He shook his head. "She is better tucked away, kept as an asset to—"

"I wish you to break her," she said, "and I will gather her pieces and rebuild."

Jabbing his finger at his chest, he said, "She is mine. I have spent months building the spell holding her and—"

She rolled her fingers and the air cut off from Westengaard's lungs. He tried to breathe, but nothing would come. The vision of the room wavered and he could feel himself shaking on his bedroom floor, clutching his throat.

With a flick of her wrist, she released him. As he took in air, the room returned to focus.

"Your debt remains unpaid," she said. "Unless you wish my spy to return you to the Culparr Mines or for me to stop distracting the Surris Rangers."

He glared at her but nodded.

"Excellent. I expect it to be a memorable wedding."

The false room puffed away and he soared through the streets before jolting back to himself. With a gasp, his eyes opened.

Rising, he dusted off his coat, went to the window, and glared at the street.

He would find a way for Adeline to loosen his power before the wedding. If he could not, at least he had recovered Flora after transforming her into a flower in a meadow. Her powers were far less than Adeline's but draining her strength would carry him through a while longer.

A grim smile formed as threads of plans wove together in his mind.

Westengaard would continue letting Rompell and McCay play their games as he watched their moves. He had placed a few extra pieces on the board, holding them back. It was time to set them in motion.

He hated giving Madame Blue so powerful an asset like Adeline but breaking her would be a satisfying victory over Rompell. Once Adeline was disposed of, Rompell would become a hollow shadow.

It would be an excellent end to their game.

Chapter 25

Rompell adjusted his red scarf and tried not to scowl as Adeline's "intimate party" wore on at the Doreur Hotel. The fifty or so guests packed in the ballroom mingled and competed for who could give a wittier comment. He sipped slowly on his drink, watching the clock on the wall as Westengaard stayed close to Adeline's side, ever playing the attentive fiancé.

As long as Westengaard was here and doting over Adeline, he wasn't watching the white tents on Adeline's grounds. Rompell's heart thudded as he pictured McCay and her team sneaking across the lawn, setting tomorrow's trap.

It had to work.

He forced himself not to grimace as Petunia Ophombauch patted his arm and prepared for her gossip column for after the wedding.

"Miss Winkleston will be the most radiant bride. The rumor is the archway will be covered in daisies, but I think hydrangeas would be far better suited to Miss Winkleston's softness. Or, perhaps a desert flower, to celebrate your homeland?"

Rompell gave his nods and grunts of listening as he scanned the crowd. In the small interrogation room with McCay, Mrs. Hunter, and Jack, the plan had been clear. There were a thousand chances of failure, but he had to hope. Westengaard could not see a fraction of worry in Rompell beyond knowing his enemy was about to marry his daughter.

Unable to bear the conversation any more, Rompell said, "May I refresh your drink?"

Mrs. Ophombauch's round face carved into what was meant to be a charming smile. He took her glass and moved toward the refreshments.

Serena stepped to his side and whispered, "I wish there were no wedding tomorrow."

He squeezed her arm and gave her a steady look. "Stand with her. No matter how strange things become."

Serena gave him a confused glance but was called away by a guest before she could ask questions.

Rompell strode toward the champagne fountain, keeping a polite but brisk pace to avoid conversation.

"A toast!" Westengaard's voice boomed through the room. He raised his glass and smiled at Rompell. "To my former commander who, tomorrow, will be my own papa. To the man who saved Adeline so she could be my own."

A waiter handed Rompell a glass and he raised it in return. The crowd clapped and several women sighed.

Walking toward Rompell, Westengaard said, "What all of you may not know is this man once had a family of his own: A wife, two sons, and a daughter."

Rompell's gloved fist tightened around the glass, trying to hide his shaking. Every muscle in his face ached as he held his forced smile.

"A sickness spread through his family, and he lost each of them. One by one."

Rompell wanted to smack the empty sympathy out of the guests.

Stopping only an arm's length from Rompell, Westengaard opened his arms toward the crowd. "But, here in Pippington, he built a new life and a new family, with my darling Adeline.

"Both of them have lost so much, and tomorrow morning, I will unite with their small family. I only hope I can provide for Adeline as well as her dear papa has."

The guests clapped, a few women dabbing tears with their handkerchiefs. Adeline stood, her face beaming and proud tears on her cheeks.

Rompell's jaw clenched as he forced himself to nod and acknowledge Westengaard's speech. Westengaard gave him a false smile and placed his arm around Rompell's shoulders.

Leaning close, he whispered, "What sad game are you playing tonight?"

"I have kept my word," Rompell said.

"I know you, Rompell. You have not been sitting obediently, accepting defeat." Westengaard's arm tightened like a python around Rompell's shoulders. "What do I take first? Hidaya's hand? A son's ear?"

"You have Adeline. There is nothing more you need."

Westengaard eyed Rompell before stepping back and saying loudly, "You are right. We do have much to discuss."

He motioned for Rompell to follow him. Rompell took a steadying breath as he marched forward. Westengaard touched Adeline's arm and whispered in her ear. She giggled and looked up adoringly at him. He smiled and offered his arm.

"We will return in a moment," Westengaard said. He gave the crowd a grin. "Family business."

Rompell forced himself not to glare at Westengaard's back, wishing he had a dagger.

They reached a dimly lit boardroom down the hall from the ballroom. Once inside, Adeline said, "What's your surprise?"

Taking her hands in his, Westengaard said, "You know how dearly I love you."

Her pattering giggles stung Rompell. "Of course."

"Tomorrow should be a joyful day." Westengaard gave her a sorrowful expression. "But, as a man who adores you, I must ensure you are safe."

Her brow furrowed, but she held her smile. "You and Papa will protect me."

"Rompell, tell her what you have done."

Gritting his teeth, Rompell said, "Perhaps it is better coming from you."

Westengaard glanced at him, the glint of a smirk in his eyes. "You know your Papa and I once hated each other but set aside our feud for the love of you."

Adeline nodded, confusion entering her eyes.

"Rompell, your own father—" Westengaard pressed a hand to her shoulder. "I cannot bear this—" Facing Rompell, he said, "He has tricked you into funding false charities, taking the money, and telling the police I stole the funds."

Adeline's eyes widened and she faced Rompell. "Papa—is it true?"

Rompell glared at Westengaard. "And where are the officers to arrest me?"

"Is it true, Papa?"

"Is the plan to have them storm the ballroom, or take me away in secret to avoid questions?"

"Westengaard, he wouldn't—"

Her fiancé held up his hand. She pressed her trembling lips together as her innocent blue eyes stared at Rompell.

"I had hoped to wait till afterward," Westengaard said, "but they are ready now."

Rompell held out his wrists. "How can I fight the man who holds my daughter, my wife, and my sons hostage?"

Adeline frowned and held a hand to her head. Westengaard smacked Rompell across his jaw.

"How dare you make up these lies!"

He placed his arm around Adeline's shoulders. She moved to pull away, but he stroked the silver bracelet at her wrist and a blankness filled her eyes. That blankness stung more than the following sorrowful gaze as she pressed against Westengaard. Rompell wished he could shake her out of Westengaard's spell. However, he had to be patient.

"I wish only to bring Adeline the future she has earned," Westengaard said, "and to protect her from your deception."

"This is how the game ends?" Rompell said. "With a batch of petty lies and the police storming in?" He raised an eyebrow. "I expected more."

Westengaard charged forward, leaving Adeline behind him. He grabbed Rompell's shirt and jerked him closer. With a growl, he said, "My spies say McCay is already at Adeline's mansion. There will be little to see tomorrow, when my wedding goes as planned."

Rompell held Westengaard's glare. If McCay had been seen, it was likely she wanted to be. Part of him wished he knew more of her plans, to be sure all was right. However, this could be a feint to push Rompell to reveal his plans.

Letting go, Westengaard shouted, "Inspector Clemens."

Adeline gasped, tears breaking down her cheeks as a squad of officers marched into the boardroom. Rompell kept his head high as the inspector slapped cuffs on his wrists and pushed him toward the door.

Adeline's sob tore at him, pulling with the weight of promises he made when taking her in as his daughter. He had failed her for so long but staying here would do nothing. Instead, he marched forward, preparing himself for a long night waiting, trusting his few allies and praying one of their plans would work.

The Seventh Tale of the Magician

With a flourish of his hands, Rompell tossed a ball into the air, followed by a plume of fire from the hidden lighters at his wrists. The crowd around him clapped and opened their mouths in awe. He caught the ball and bowed, tipping his hat out to catch the cash and coins they wished to share.

Once most of his hat was full, he twirled it in his hand and dropped a smoke snap. A plume of green smoke flared up and Rompell dodged around the corner.

He dropped the macs and skoons into his gloved hand. It was a generous bounty. Turning around the next corner, he walked toward a woman huddled in a doorway, holding her two children close as they shuddered in the cold. He slipped a few more bills into the stack, along with the business card of the property manager for one of several apartment buildings he had bought over the past year. The money would cover the rent for three months. That should be enough time for the mother to find a job and build a better life for her children.

Striding past, he stopped just long enough to drop the money beside the mother. She stared up at him, but he avoided her eyes.

He would use the curse of his hands for good, but he could not bear when a starving mother looked at him. All he could see was Hidaya's eyes on the dark nights when they had given most of their dinner to their children.

The snowfall grew heavier and he turned up the collar of his coat, protecting his cheeks from the wind. The night would be bitter cold, the kind that made him miss the heat of Sandar.

In an hour or so, he would return to the small warehouse he had made home, where the golden statues of his wife and sons remained safely hidden in wood crates. For now, he wandered through alleyways, watching for a huddled pile of worn blankets or coats marking someone trying to survive the freezing night. He would give the stranger enough to bribe their way into a warm hotel bed for the night and then walk on, seeking the next who needed help.

His steps slowed as a child's singing set a tingle along his skin. He rubbed his arm.

It had been a long time since he felt so strong a spark of magic.

For a moment, he was brought back to the day he stood in the Culparr Mines in the Surris Mountains. He had traveled thousands of miles over several months, across two continents and an ocean, but had little satisfaction as he and the Surris Rangers tossed Stiltsken into a prison cell deep in the ground.

He shook his head, pushing aside this memory and the other dark events it dredged up.

Pulling his red scarf tighter around his neck and lower jaw, he moved to walk again.

The child's soft voice pulled at him, the sweetness thawing the hardness he tried to lock his emotions behind. He rubbed his chest and turned to follow the voice.

The song became fainter as he came around a corner. A small girl lay curled on her side, shivering in the falling snow, a match lit beside her. He could feel the magic in her voice even before the flame curled and spread out, creating a warm display.

The match puffed away and her eyes slowly closed, her lips already losing color.

Rompell walked toward her, remembering his last meeting with Tamina, his daughter, before he left for exile. In the two years of fighting to defeat Stiltsken, Briya, Solvan's wife, had become Tamina's mother. Watching the girl laugh and play with her cousins, Rompell knew he could not take his daughter from her new family and bring her to an unknown land.

As he said his goodbye, the small girl bearing Hidaya's round brown eyes threw her arms around him. He held her tight to his breast and kissed her cheek, using all his strength not to weep. Then, he set her on the ground and sent her back to Briya.

Someone, somewhere, had to be longing for this child lying in the snow as much as he longed for his daughter.

The girl was falling into a dangerous sleep as he knelt beside her. He wrapped her threadbare shawl around her and rubbed her hands between his. She was still so cold. He grabbed a match from her crate and struck it against the wall.

Her soft blue eyes opened. Relief filled him.

She was alive but needed warmth immediately.

"Little One," he said. "What are you doing here alone?"

He pulled off his overcoat. The layer of jackets and scarves beneath would keep him warm. Lifting the crate of matches from her, he wrapped his coat around her and pulled her slender body into his arms.

Chapter 26

Pivoting, Adeline checked each angle in the mirror. The cascade of lace on her dress billowed around her, complementing her soft veil. Despite the unfortunate events of last night mixing with the constant throbbing in her temples, she grinned. Looking at the emerald ring on her finger, a warmth filled her. Today, she would stand in front of Westengaard, placing her hands in his as they declared their love for each other.

She wished Rompell could be there. Watching him march out in shackles had sent a pang through her. However, once Westengaard took her hand and kissed her, the pain softened. There were still tears when she lay in bed, but the sadness eased while looking at Westengaard's silver bracelet wrapped around her wrist.

She had always wished Rompell would walk her down the aisle, but, as Westengaard had said, if he were so false, she was better off walking alone.

Seeing Serena's concerned expression, Adeline gave her a broad smile.

"Today shall be the best of days," Adeline said.

The other bridesmaids smiled and chittered out their congratulations. Serena gave her a weak smile and said, "I wish Rompell weren't ill."

"You are here," Adeline said, "and Westengaard stands at the end of everything." She kissed Serena's cheek. "All will be wonderful."

Serena nodded, the ruffles on her mauve satin dress bouncing with the movement. "I hope so."

Rompell was sure grooves had formed in the small cell from his constant pacing past the drunks lining the bench.

"Sit down," one grunted. "You're making me dizzy."

Speeding his pace, Rompell continued his laps.

He knew McCay and Mrs. Hunter were doing their part of the plan, but the endless hours of waiting, now capped with the gray of dawn forming in the window, was rubbing on his patience.

"Sandarian," a guard said as he unlocked the prison. "This way."

Without shackling Rompell's wrists, the guard led him down a hallway to a back door. The guard knocked once before sauntering away. Rompell frowned, his muscles tensing as he waited for the trap. However, Inspector McCay opened the door and nodded to a motorcar sitting in the alleyway, Jack in the driver's seat.

"Inspector Clemens tried to hide your arrest from me," she said. "Listed you as an anonymous drunk. Had to go to three stations to find you." She grunted. "And then, there's the paperwork."

She and Rompell climbed inside the motorcar. She nodded to Jack and the young officer set the motorcar in motion.

"Westengaard's spies have been dogging my heels all night." She handed Rompell a paper-wrapped pastry. "I've kept them on a good chase, but I don't think Westengaard's going to have time to act on anything else."

"Is she safe?" Rompell whispered.

McCay glanced at him, her eyes cool. "I guarantee no one's safety."

The morning sped on as the final touches of beauty were added to Adeline's ensemble. At last, a beaming Mrs. Dolan clapped her hands and announced, "It is time."

Adeline's heart fluttered. Several servants gathered her skirts and assisted her through the mansion and to the entry hall. Each step in her white Cordwainers sent a jolt of pain through her feet, but she kept her smile firm.

At the main doors, her eyes drew to the portrait of her birth father hanging above her. He and her mother would be proud of her today, tears falling down their cheeks. There was so little left to remind her of them, and now she had lost the man she had called Papa for so long. Glancing up at her father, she looked into his eyes. She might not have the man who raised her, but at least her birth father was here in some way, watching over her.

She and her bridesmaids walked through a white tent leading to the main pavilion raised a few days before. The music announced the wedding procession and the impact was as grand as she hoped.

Entering behind her bridesmaids, she grinned at the standing crowd. So many of the highest of society were here. Petunia Ophombauch and Mrs. Hampnell sat in places of honor in the front row. Mrs. Hunter stood near the rear, stiff as a soldier. Peter Talbot looked out of place behind Madame Plessati and Flora Primrose, but it was good to have such a notable tradesman among her guests.

And there, standing at the altar, was Westengaard.

She walked up the stairs to the dais and arrived at his side. He took her hand. Her heartbeat pulsed with each step as they walked toward the priest. Looking into Westengaard's eyes, the buzzing in her head grew. She tried to push it back, to enjoy the moment, but the pain worsened.

The room became silent and sparked with anticipation. She looked to the priest as he opened *The Book of Dalthon*. Before he could speak, a clear, sweet woman's voice came from the audience, breaking through the silence in a sad melody:

> *Hey nonny nonny hey, flowers and bows decorate the maid*
> *Ho nonny nonny ho, but I warn you to be staid.*
> *Hey nonny nonny hey, turn from the lady by your side,*
> *Ho nonny nonny ho for I am the True Bride.*

Adeline forced herself not to cringe as the buzzing in her head rose in pitch. The priest frowned and adjusted his spectacles before saying, "We are gathered—"

The voice sang again, carrying the same words. It was a soft voice, but each word sent a stabbing pain in Adeline's head.

Everyone shifted in their chairs, turning as one. Adeline blinked back the tears of pain before looking over her shoulder. A strange fear shocked through her as Flora Primrose walked down the aisle. Flora's eyes were dazed and empty, her steps stiff as if in a trance.

Holding her forced smile, Adeline rubbed her temple, hoping to push away the pulsing pain.

This had to be Westengaard's surprise, to add excitement to their wedding.

"My love, what is this?" she said.

Shock filled Westengaard's face. He raised his arms into an arc and his eyes widened as if he were enchanted. Flora opened her mouth and sang the song again. Adeline frowned. How had Flora gained a voice?

The thought flitted away as Westengaard walked down the steps and toward Flora. Adeline grabbed Westengaard's elbow and pulled, but it did nothing to slow him.

"Is everything all right?"

He ripped his arm away and spun around to face her. She stepped back, the hatred and fear in his eyes striking her.

"Witch!"

"What?" She shrank back.

This was all so strange. She had to be dreaming. Soon, she would wake, the headache gone, and Westengaard would be waiting for her.

"Oh, you play your innocence well." Westengaard tossed back his head and faced the guests. His arms wide, he said, "Now it is all clear, Adeline. Your deceit. Your betrayal. Your cruelty."

Adeline clutched her bouquet to her chest. "Westengaard, I don't understand—"

"You filled me with a poison that passed through my veins and burned the fire of desire in my breast." He pounded his hand against his chest as he stood over her. "I saw the signs, but I didn't believe magic was real. I was as ignorant and blind as everyone else. But now I see clearly: magic is quite real, and your spells blinded all of us. Your wealth is false, a lie you enchanted men into believing. Your father was no heir. He was a fire brigadesman, no greater than any other. Oh, to use your spells to gain wealth and then steal my heart. But, its rightful owner is here, Miss Adeline. Your reign is over and I am at last free."

Adeline's knees began to buckle under the weight of Westengaard's accusation. Serena darted forward and grabbed her, helping her stand. Another sharp pain twinged through her skull and Adeline moaned. Her bouquet fell and she pressed her hands to her head.

"It is finished, Adeline," Westengaard said.

Adeline's legs failed. Serena kept hold of her shoulders even as she trembled. All warmth drained from Adeline's face as Westengaard strode toward Flora.

"My heart knew my true bride when she first danced," Westengaard said. "She had such sorrow for the prison I could not see. I was bewitched by this woman—" He glared back at Adeline. "This witch who has lived among you, feigning purity and innocence. But, I tell you, her core is rotten."

He held his arms out to Flora. "But now, I am free of the curse, and we are at last reunited."

Adeline barely heard the gasps rushing through the crowd. As she faltered, Serena helped her sit on the stairs.

Adeline stared as Peter Talbot stumbled into the aisle, ran to Flora, and grabbed her shoulders, stopping her. He said something to her, but the words were lost in the whispers of the crowd and the constant buzzing in her head. Adeline winced as she felt the snap of strings of magic breaking apart.

A sob broke out of Flora and she threw her arms around Peter. They kissed, but Adeline could just stare. This felt like something distant, far from herself, something that was not the reality before her.

Rompell crouched in his hiding place behind white curtains at a corner of the large tent, Peeking through a small hole, he cringed as Peter Talbot stood in front of Flora as if to protect her from Westengaard. Though Peter had broken Westengaard's spell on Flora, freeing her mind and voice, they were far from safe.

He had warned Peter days ago, and again this morning as the shoemaker walked among the crowd. Rompell needed to keep hidden but had to try to stop Peter from putting himself in danger.

His gaze drifted to the set of curtains hanging beside him, separating Westengaard's "surprise" for the wedding. Rompell touched the cloth with his gloved fingers. To the guests, those curtains were only part of the decor. For Westengaard, they were part of his plan to ruin Adeline and Rompell. For Rompell, what lay beyond was priceless. All he could hope now was that McCay and her team would finish their part of the plan.

He glanced over at McCay as she knelt, glaring through the curtain at Peter. Her sniper was hidden on the grounds, a magic sedative in his rifle. The other traps had failed and the one remaining back-up plan was in motion. They had hoped to do this less publicly, but time was running short. McCay would manage the fallout later. For now, all they needed was a clear shot for the sniper. That wasn't going to happen with Peter and Flora standing in the aisle.

Rompell's heart pumped as he thought through ways to get Peter out. However, he couldn't reveal himself yet. Not until the statues of Hidaya and his sons were safe.

"If you'll excuse us, we should be going," Peter said.

He put his arm around Flora's shoulder and they turned toward the main exit.

Westengaard, however, strode past them and blocked their path. McCay flashed a light toward the sniper. Rompell held his breath, waiting for the shot.

He and the Inspector glanced at each other as nothing came. Her hand slipped to the pistol at her side. Pulling her hand away, she whispered, "Too loud. I'll check on the sniper."

Peter raised his voice. "She told me the truth. You—you're a fugitive."

McCay used the cover of gasps and murmurs to crawl out through one of the hidden exits she and her officers had made the night before. Rompell held his place, hidden between tent walls, peering through a slim gap.

His eyes scanned the crowd, seeking potential places he might use one of his parlor tricks to stir them up and get them out. Thinking through the possibilities helped him ignore Westengaard's long-winded speech and Adeline crumpled on the ground, tears smearing the makeup caked on her face.

"You do not believe the truth about Miss Winkleston?" Westengaard said. "All of you will see the lies she and her foster father have been hiding all these years, appearing friendly and kind while participating in the darkest evils."

Rompell ducked back as the wall of curtains beside him dropped. His curtain remained and he peeked through a gap.

The pressure in his chest eased as there stood the statues of Hidaya, Jabir, and Amal, but the crowd's whispers turned to confusion, staring at what appeared empty pedestals. McCay had said they were there, but it was a greater relief to see them. Westengaard's eyes were full of fury as he glared at the red scarf Rompell had worn the night before, lying on a pedestal.

Rompell let a small smile form. At least one of today's gambits had worked.

He hadn't been sure it would as he had drawn diagrams and explained to Mrs. Hunter and Inspector McCay how to set-up mirrors so the crowd would see only empty pedestals.

The trick should be enough to set Westengaard off-balance.

Peter pulled Flora with him as he moved to pass Westengaard.

Remaining in their path, Westengaard said, "Tell them the truth. Confirm what I say."

"I think that's enough, sir," a white-haired gentleman said, stepping from the crowd. "I've known Adeline Winkleston since she was a girl at the Bradford School. She even taught my little Nancy. She's a fine lady, and I'm not sure of this madness you're claiming is "magic". What sort of gentleman are you, making such a scene?"

Rompell glanced at the far wall of the tent.

McCay should have reached her sniper by now. The shot needed to be taken while Westengaard was distracted by the crowd rising to Adeline's defense.

"Peter! No!"

Flora's voice drew Rompell's eyes back to the pavilion.

She pushed Peter out of the way as thunder snapped and Westengaard sent an arc of lightning from his hand.

Rompell cursed.

Westengaard had more magic than expected.

Peter tossed something and purple smoke curled up. Rompell pressed a hand to his forehead.

He had given Peter those smoke snaps a few weeks ago as parlor tricks to show his nephews. They weren't made for fighting a warlock. And they certainly wouldn't help McCay's sniper as the smoke blocked his view.

The tent was full of chaos as guests rushed toward the exits. Serena's eyes rolled back and she fainted. A pair of men caught her and carried her out.

Peter and Flora crawled along an abandoned row of chairs. Green smoke curled up. As it cleared, Westengaard yelled and formed a ball of green light. He moved to launch it, but Peter threw another smoke snap. Yellow smoke formed around them, sparks flying happily through the air.

Westengaard's sphere of energy smashed into the chairs behind them, sending out a shockwave.

Rompell dove forward, keeping low as he ran toward Adeline. The whine of Westengaard's next spell stung his ears. Glancing back, he saw flames wrapped around Westengaard's arm. He hurried his step.

Peter tossed another smoke snap and Westengaard laughed.

"What do you think this child's magic will do?"

Rompell hesitated as Peter crept toward Westengaard from behind, partially hidden by the blue of his smoke snap and the smoke pouring from flames Westengaard sent toward Flora.

Adeline needed to be saved but Peter was being a fool.

Flora sang a soft melody, a blue light forming around her, holding back the flame. Westengaard pushed his fist forward, surrounding Flora with a pillar of fire.

Rompell's heart jumped as Peter swung his hammer against Westengaard's skull. The warlock stumbled forward, the pillar of flame dropping. He began to turn, but Flora threw a clay pot of flowers at him.

Westengaard shouted and the fire rose.

Rompell scrambled over fallen chairs, running toward Adeline as the tent's white ceiling lit into flames. He heard Peter's hammer slam against Westengaard's skull. Glancing over his shoulder, he watched as Westengaard's tall form dropped to the ground, unconscious.

He stared at Peter, the small man standing over the fallen warlock.

Apparently, Rompell had been wrong about the shoemaker.

The fire spread quickly across the tent, smoke billowing.

Rompell reached the stairs where Adeline lay, petrified by fear and shock. Peter and Flora joined him, seeming ready to help the girl.

"Go." He pulled his daughter and her massive dress into his arms. "Thank you."

Peter and Flora glanced at him, hesitating as if to help. Rompell nodded toward the exit and they sprinted out.

Though Adeline was a full-grown woman, Rompell cradled her in his arms, carrying her out of the smoke and fire devouring the tent.

Outside, madness roiled the grounds. Fire wagons clanged. The flames from the tent flared out, lighting the mansion wall. The crowd shouted and pointed. McCay, Jack, and a dozen other officers sprinted toward the tent where Westengaard lay unconscious.

All of the smoke and noise felt distant as he carried Adeline toward the garden. He set her on a bench and kissed her forehead.

"You are safe, Little One," he whispered, his throat choking on the words.

Her wide eyes stared at him and he reached to take her hand. As his gloved fingers touched hers, a shockwave of energy blasted out from her, sending him tumbling across the brick courtyard. Stunned, he tried to push himself up, but his arms could barely move.

The world around Adeline felt slow, as if something far apart from herself. Turning her head, she saw Rompell rolling across the ground and then lying still.

She pushed to her feet, her legs shaking. Her head didn't throb but was still clouded as her magic pulsed through her, bristling as if about to burst from her.

She raised her hand, filaments of energy crackling through her fingers. It stung as the energy arched across the emerald ring and silver bracelet. She ripped them off and tossed them away. Smoke rose as they smoldered on the grass.

From the corner of her eye, she saw the tent engulfed in flames. Her heart pounded as she tried to make sense of the noise and smoke. Vague images rushed through her mind, full of Westengaard towering over her, of Peter Talbot hitting him with a hammer, and of the rising fire.

She loved Westengaard, didn't she? Or was that the lie she had been trying to free herself of?

A boom drew her eyes to the mansion as flame punched out a broken window.

It matched the echo of her nightmares in the months after her father had died, saving a family from a similar fire. Hollowness began to flood through her as her eyes drew to the flames licking the entryway, where her father's portrait lay.

Nothing today made sense except the image of her father looking down on her, protecting her.

She could not let him burn. She could not lose him again.

She attempted to run, but her heels sank into the grass. Westengaard's lessons on controlling her power rushed through her head. Clenching her fists, she whistled, focusing her magic just enough to send air ripping through the laces of her shoes.

Kicking off the Cordwainers and gathering the endless ruffles of her skirt, she sprinted toward the mansion. Voices shouted and feet pounded after her. With barely a thought, she sent a shockwave of magic rippling in the air, pushing her attempted rescuers from her.

There was so little of her parents left. She could not lose her father's portrait.

She ran up the marble stairs and into the flaming doorway. The heat stung and the edges of her dress smoldered. Spinning, she sought the portrait.

It stood on the wall, the edges of the canvas blackening, but the painting intact.

With a shout, she pushed her hand forward. The portrait ripped from the wall and clattered to the floor. Another wave of her hand sent it skidding out of the mansion, flying over the grounds, and landing near the gaping crowd hundreds of yards away.

Her legs faltered and she fell to her knees. Smoke billowed around her and she coughed, wheezing for air. She pushed herself to her feet and stumbled toward the entryway, the walls creaking around her.

One of the massive doors crashed, blocking the opening and sending up embers and sparks. Covering her face, she drew back.

Fire arched along the arm of her dress. She screamed as it burned through.

The heat was overwhelming and her concentration was waning.

The ruffles of her dress ignited and she sent a rush of air, pushing the flame back. It shrunk for a second before growing with a roar.

There was a spell Mrs. Hunter had used, that night long ago in the Bradford School. Something with pulling flame into a box. Adeline tried to remember, but the room was so hot and the burns on her arm stung.

"Adeline!" A woman's voice called.

Peering through the smoke, Adeline pictured her mother standing before her, her hand outstretched. She reached out her hand, but the hovering image of her mother burst into an explosion.

She covered her face as wood and sparks splintered around her.

"Foolish girl," Mrs. Hunter said as she marched through the mansion's entrance. The flames curled back from her and she put her arm around Adeline.

Keeping hold of Mrs. Hunter's shoulder, despite the stinging pang along her arm, Adeline let the headmistress lead her through the smoke and out of the mansion. They ran together, moving swiftly across the grounds.

Once at the edge, away from the fire, Adeline collapsed. Her body cramped and she curled onto her side.

Rompell ran toward her, stumbling as he dropped to his knees beside her. He reached out to her, but Mrs. Hunter grabbed his arm.

"Watch for the burns," she said.

His eyes matched the sorrow Adeline felt deep within. Looking up at him, at Mrs. Hunter, and then the burning mansion, the wall in her mind fell.

She shook as the truth of what Westengaard had done to her rushed over her. Exhaustion overcame her and she fell into a blank numbness.

Chapter 27

Three days of lying on the bed in her hotel suite, curled on her side, layers of tears leaving tracks down her face had not broken Adeline's numbness. Staring at her father's portrait, the edges charred, helped her tolerate the stinging burns along her arm.

The pain beneath the bandages kept her awake through much of the night, which was a relief. Every time she drifted to sleep, Westengaard appeared in her dreams, smiling as he dragged her toward flames. She often woke with a scream, shivering and huddled on the bed. Serena would rush in from the adjoining room and sit beside her, holding Adeline's hand and whispering, "Everything's all right."

For all the hours Serena spent at her bedside, Adeline could not escape feeling alone.

Others had come through the suite. Mrs. Dolan led servants in and out and Inspector McCay had come once, reporting, "The world thinks you were hypnotized and we've got a steady lock on Mr. Westengaard."

Another time, she overheard Mrs. Hunter and Mrs. Dolan in the sitting room, but Mrs. Dolan had refused to let Mrs. Hunter past the bedroom door.

Then, Rompell had come.

He sat on the edge of an armchair, his head hanging and guilt weighing on his face. Tears broke as she turned away, unable to face him.

He was her Papa and his duty was to protect her.

But, for months, he had let Westengaard have her.

She understood why, with Hidaya and his sons at risk. And Inspector McCay had told her of Rompell coming for help, working with Mrs. Hunter, McCay, and Jack to set a trap at the wedding.

He had protected her, but it wasn't till the end. If he had really wanted to, he could have saved her earlier.

His single visit ended with him rising and leaving without a word.

She had cried, shuddering as she felt the phantom press of Westengaard's hand on her arm, the touch of his lips to hers. Too many months, she had been his prisoner as he drained her magic and used it to control her.

Her magic was as strong as when it had rushed back to her. The power and her emptiness were exhausting. The only relief came as she screamed into her pillow or let herself sob.

She glanced up as Serena returned to the room, pushing a tray on wheels with a silver dome hiding food. She began to pull aside the curtains, but Adeline said, "Keep them shut."

"It's a beautiful day." Serena sat on the edge of Adeline's bed and gave her a soft smile. It did not mask the worry in her eyes. She squeezed Adeline's uninjured hand. "The sun might do you good."

"I cannot—"

Adeline broke off as another bout of tears came. She hid her face against the pillow. Serena rubbed her back, whispering, "I brought a lovely broth."

Fighting her stiff muscles, Adeline pushed herself up. Serena pulled the tray closer and removed the silver dome, revealing a simple chicken soup. Adeline's hand shook as she took the spoon. Several times, she tried to ladle food into her mouth, but the broth fell as her hand trembled.

"Mrs. Frizban sent over some bread." Serena pulled a loaf wrapped in an old towel from a basket beneath the tray. "The officers watching your door helped me smuggle it past Mrs. Dolan."

Adeline frowned. "What officers?"

"Inspector McCay is keeping a pair of officers at the door, just in case," Serena said.

Adeline rubbed her thumb along the rough cloth covering the bread and glanced at Serena. There was so much she hadn't told her friend, including the night she had woken. It was still strange to picture Jack, ink on his face and his hair a mess, listening to her with a steady gaze, taking every word seriously.

If he hadn't been there, would McCay have known to help Rompell?

She swallowed before saying, "Is one of them Officer Kingston?"

Serena frowned in thought. "I haven't learned all their names yet." She pressed her finger to her chin before pointing vaguely. "There's a young officer who said he shared some classes with you. Is that him?"

"He also was the gardener at the Bradford School," Adeline whispered.

"The one who kept flirting with you?" Serena's eyes widened. "He's on duty right now. I'll send him away. There's no need for you to be bothered."

"No. He—" Adeline's forehead furrowed as she sought the right words. "He's a friend and—he helped Inspector McCay figure out I was hypnotized."

Adeline winced. She knew of McCay's skill at crafting believable stories for magic, but it was strange to repeat the lie to her friend.

"I'm glad he did. I knew something was wrong," Serena said. "You were so unlike yourself from the moment—"

Adeline's fingers clenched as she pictured Bronhart's glare the night at the Morveaux, just before Westengaard had cursed her. She had been so busy looking at the trappings of her wealth she had forgotten to look at him.

How he must hate her.

Serena's eyes lowered and she took a breath. "I never liked

Westengaard, but I knew I had to stand by you, no matter what."

"That is better than I deserve," Adeline whispered.

Serena touched Adeline's hand. "You would do the same for me. We are sisters, aren't we?"

Tears streamed down Adeline's face as she wrapped her uninjured arm around Serena. The warmth of Serena's embrace sent a rare spark of peace in Adeline's breast.

They released each other and Serena's smile broadened. The corner of Adeline's mouth turned up a little, but her cheeks were stiff and incapable of letting a smile form.

Patting the tray, Serena said, "Eat, before your dinner goes cold."

Adeline dipped the bread in the broth, listening to Serena speak on the weather and her parents. The broth and bread had no flavor, but they were filling.

Cleaning up the tray, Serena said, "Would you like a bath?"

Adeline stared at Serena. She didn't remember her last bath. It almost felt like some foreign activity she had only heard of. She nodded.

As Adeline sat in the bath frothing with bubbles, careful to keep her bandaged arm dry, Serena sat on a stool, telling about a play her mother had gone to the week before. Adeline's head leaned to the side and her eyes drifted closed. All was quiet and she let herself relax into sleep.

"My love," Westengaard's voice whispered, the sensation of his breath on her ear. "They have lied to you."

She floated in a blank void as she felt his hand wrapping around hers, drawing her power into his.

A shock jolted in her chest and her eyes opened. Gripping the sides of the bathtub, she stared at the wrist of her uninjured hand. Tendrils of magic stretched out, threaded with Westengaard's magic. The attachment was more tenuous than the night she had woken, but she had thought all ties were broken.

Adeline pushed herself from the bathtub, breathing hard in the steamy air as she tried to calm her heartbeat.

"Are you all right?" Serena helped Adeline into her nightgown. "Was it another nightmare?"

It was worse than a nightmare, but Adeline only gave a quick, "Yes," as she pulled on her dressing gown.

Serena followed close-behind as Adeline hurried into the sitting room. Her wet hair hanging over her shoulder, Adeline wound through the jungle of bows, ribbons, and bouquets. She didn't want to know how many empty words lay in the notecards. Mrs. Dolan rose from a chair, her eyes surprised but a forced smile on her face.

"I'm so glad to see you up, Miss Winkleston. Would you—"

Adeline passed her and approached the door. Mrs. Dolan hurried to her side and touched her uninjured shoulder.

"You may wish to be better dressed before stepping out. I have the best maids on call. If you'll—"

Adeline glanced at Mrs. Dolan, wishing the woman knew more. However, she could not help with protecting her mind from Westengaard. With a tug, Adeline opened the door.

Stepping out, her eyes met Jack's as he stood against the opposite wall beside another uniformed officer.

He frowned. "What's wrong?"

Adeline bit her lip as she tried to think of how to explain in front of Mrs. Dolan. Taking a step forward, she grabbed his arm and whispered, "Westengaard, he—"

A light flashed, blinding Adeline for a second.

"Oh, Miss Winkleston, it's wonderful to see you up," came Petunia Ophombauch's voice.

Adeline's hand clamped tighter on Jack's arm as she turned to face Mrs. Ophombauch. Lined along the hallway were several other society writers, each with their own photographer.

One of them held a newspaper with a headline reading, *Winkleston*

Wedding of Woe. Another newspaper read, *Debutante in Despair.*

Several more flashes went off, mixing with a barrage of questions.

"How do you feel, Miss Winkleston?"

"When did you know Westengaard had hypnotized you?"

"Have you made amends with your former fiancé?"

The thought of Bronhart sent an ache through Adeline, but she pushed that away as her eyes turned to Jack.

His grimaced as he whispered, "Miss Winkleston, will you let go of my arm?"

Her eyes widened at the small line of smoke forming where the magic in her hand was burning his uniform. Pulling her fingers away, she said, "Sorry—I—"

Another flash of light broke her train of thought. Fortunately, Mrs. Dolan stepped out and formed a barrier between the journalists and Adeline.

"Miss Winkleston still needs a few hours before she is ready for interviews. As I've told you, each will have their turn."

The writers began to shout over one other as they ignored Mrs. Dolan. Adeline stepped into her suite and motioned for Jack to follow. Once he was inside, she shut the door and whispered, "Westengaard still has a hold on me. I don't know how he is doing it. I thought—" She swallowed against the tightness in her throat, holding back tears. "I thought I was free."

"I'll go tell McCay," he said. "Anything else you need?"

Her eyes searched the floor until the answer became clear. Only one person could truly help her.

"Send for Mrs. Hunter, please."

Jack nodded and turned to leave.

She grabbed his arm once more, stopping him. As he glanced at her, the words lodged in her throat. Taking in a breath, she forced out, "And Nathaniel—if you see him—"

Staring blankly, she was unsure what she wanted to say. She had to make things right with Bronhart, but she wasn't sure how to begin.

"I might see him," Jack said, his eyes sympathetic, "but he's better friends with my brother, Henry."

"Still, if you do see him—try—try to explain—" She rubbed her cheek as she sought the right words.

"I'll tell him as much of the truth as I can." Jack gave her another nod. "No need to worry. I'll talk to McCay and Mrs. Hunter and you take care of yourself." He motioned toward Serena, who stood across the room, wearing a worried face. "I'm sure Miss Quinn'll keep on by your side."

Once Jack exited, Adeline let out a pent-up breath and leaned against the door. Serena hurried to her and put her arm around Adeline's shoulders.

"Did you dream of Westengaard again?" Serena said as she helped Adeline into a chair. Adeline's body shook as she leaned against the soft cushions.

"Yes," Adeline said. "I'm sure he's in his prison, but—"

"You'd feel more at peace if someone checked he was there."

Adeline nodded, wishing she could explain her real fears. Knowing Westengaard, he was plotting his way out. He may already have a plan and just be waiting. She shuddered and Serena squeezed her hand.

"If anyone can stop him," Serena said, "I'm sure Inspector McCay—"

Mrs. Dolan entered, slamming the door behind her. Adeline's heartbeat rose again as she looked up at her assistant.

"I think I've convinced most of them not to run the photograph." Mrs. Dolan waved her hand. "But I'm sure the rumors will fly and be added to the scandal. I can just see the headlines now: *The Heiress and the Officer.*"

Adeline closed the dressing gown over her revealed legs. Days ago, she would have been mortified by the photograph and barrage of questions, sure her place in society was gone. Today, she had no energy to care. The opinions of society were empty in comparison to the threat of Westengaard's spell consuming her once more, or of Rompell's family being melted down.

"Did you send them away?" Adeline said.

Mrs. Dolan patted Adeline's uninjured arm as she moved to the chair beside her.

"Of course not," she said. "We need them if you are to rise in triumph. I've taken the liberty of scheduling some of your servants to come and pamper you within the hour. Once you are looking your best, I think you'll be ready to face society."

"I really think she needs more rest." Serena stood behind Adeline's chair, keeping her hand on her friend's shoulder.

"We all wish to help Miss Winkleston." Mrs. Dolan gave her a condescending smile before looking to Adeline. "Yours is not the first broken heart I've been tasked with mending."

Adeline's heart was more than broken. Her soul had ripped in half and her mind had been stolen from her.

Gesturing at the towers of flowers filling the room, Mrs. Dolan said with a laugh, "There are plenty of young men eager to see your pretty face. I dare say all of Pippington is on your side, waiting with baited breath to hear from you."

Mrs. Dolan pointed toward a table covered by a mound of letters. "I've already sent acceptances to the more important events a few weeks from now but am sure you will wish to make a triumphant return sometime sooner. Since you own this hotel, I'm sure we can arrange a luncheon or some other gathering of a select few. We cannot let the world think you have been defeated."

"But I have been defeated," Adeline whispered.

"And now is your chance to rise."

"For what?" Adeline felt as if all the gifts and bouquets might fall on her, suffocating her. "Why does any of this matter?"

"Before he died, your grandfather charged me with guiding you through society," Mrs. Dolan said. "You have done well, but this scandal with Mr. Westengaard brings many questions to people's minds. How we manage this affair will determine how you are seen in society."

Adeline shook her head. "I don't care what they think."

Mrs. Dolan frowned. "You care very much, Miss Winkleston, as you should." She leaned toward her. "How society sees you matters to more than just you. The businesses you have inherited are impacted by how admired you are by the public.

"Heads of your companies are watching you. They already do not trust a young girl and they will be concerned if you cannot be composed in the face of simple heartbreak."

"It was not heartbreak." Adeline glared at Mrs. Dolan. "I was attacked and forced to think I loved a man—" She took in a breath as a sob broke through. "You do not know what it is like to be controlled, to not even own your own thoughts."

Mrs. Dolan sat with her hands folded in her lap. "Regardless of what you have faced, there are expectations to be met. As I said, servants are coming to ready you to face society. I have scheduled an interview with Mrs. Ophombauch at two. Once you have her on your side, we will—"

"No." The word was freeing as it broke from Adeline's lips.

"This failed wedding is your opportunity to grow your reputation. You are the victim and Mrs. Ophombauch can—"

"No interviews," Adeline said. "And cancel all appointments."

Mrs. Dolan patted Adeline's hand and gave her a look full of false-sympathy. "I know things appear hard, but just let me manage these things. You'll be dressed within an hour, speak with Mrs. Ophombauch at two, and end the evening at a fine dinner party at *The Gourmand*. Once all that is finished, you'll feel much better."

Adeline's brow furrowed as she stared at the woman she had trusted in so much. She had left financial matters in Mrs. Dolan's care even before Westengaard. Once Westengaard had consumed her mind, she let go more control, letting Mrs. Dolan manage her social calendar, plan the wedding, and manage meetings with the heads of her businesses.

The woman did not trust her. Instead, she saw Adeline as something to be managed and nothing more. Adeline's stomach knotted as she looked into Mrs. Dolan's eyes. The words were hard, but they had to be said.

"You are dismissed."

Surprise flashed in Mrs. Dolan's eyes, but her face remained calm. "I have your best interest at heart, Miss Winkleston. There is so much—"

Adeline raised her head. "I am the one who employs you, Mrs. Dolan. I have asked you to leave."

"You must consider your reputation, Miss Winkleston, I—"

Adeline pushed herself from her chair and walked to the door. Exhaustion was washing over her and she held onto the door handle to steady herself. However, she forced her back to remain straight and her head high as she faced Mrs. Dolan and opened the door.

"Thank you for your service," she said.

Mrs. Dolan's cheeks were taut as she rose, but she said nothing as she swept from the room. Once she was gone, Adeline shut the door and fell against the wall.

Grabbing Adeline's arm, Serena said, "You were so brave. I can't believe—"

"Help me dress," Adeline panted as she stumbled to the bedroom. "Please."

Serena helped Adeline into one of her simpler dresses. Falling into a chair, Adeline covered her face with her hands as she forced herself to breathe.

Kneeling beside Adeline, Serena said, "What do you need me to do?"

"Get rid of everything out there," Adeline said. "And—"

She wanted to ask for her father to come and help her sort out what to do. But, then she saw his hurt face as she had turned away from him. She was not ready to see him yet. Even with the threat of Westengaard breaking free.

"Let me know when Mrs. Hunter comes."

Chapter 28

A blast of afternoon sunlight woke Adeline from her doze as she lay on her bed. The past few hours had brought a brief respite of peaceful rest, broken only once by Westengaard tugging on her magic. The sensation had cut off quickly and she had fallen into deeper sleep.

Her grogginess cleared as a second curtain opened. She blinked and looked up at the figure by the window.

"You came," Adeline said.

"Isn't that what you requested?" Mrs. Hunter stood, clothed in a simple dark gray dress, her hands folded neatly in front of her. "Now that I am here, what do you need?"

Adeline stared up at her, a heaviness pressing in. Her voice cracked as she held out her hand. "Westengaard—he—"

"Officer Kingston and Inspector McCay informed me of the matter," Mrs. Hunter said. "Inspector McCay has tightened the spells around his cell." She gestured at the bed. "Based on Miss Quinn's report, it has improved your sleep."

Adeline nodded. "Yes, but, how—" She clenched her fist. "His magic is still tied to mine."

"Breaking his hold might be beyond my skill." Mrs. Hunter's eyes softened. "But I will do what I can. What else do you need?"

Adeline's lips trembled and she pressed a hand to her eyes, trying to push back her tears. "I don't know. I just—I just want to hide here, but I know I can't. I—"

"Let's begin with you sitting up," Mrs. Hunter said, "and then you can eat, and you can move step-by-step, even when your only desire is to hide in your bed and let the world carry on without you."

"I just—" Adeline whispered, "Everything's empty and—"

"It will feel that way for a while." Mrs. Hunter brushed off the bedspread before taking a seat beside Adeline. "When my husband died, it felt as if I had fallen out of the world and everything had stopped. But, I could not hide. I had three children who now had only their mother. It was a battle every morning to stand and dress, but I carried on because I had to, because there was something beyond myself to care for."

Mrs. Hunter rose and held out her hand. "You must find your own motivation. Might I recommend the choice to not let Mr. Westengaard win even after he has been defeated?"

Adeline's hands clutched her bedspread as she took several deep breaths. Taking Mrs. Hunter's hand, she slid her feet to the floor.

Once Adeline stood, Mrs. Hunter said, "Based on what Miss Quinn has told me, we have much to discuss, but first—"

She touched one of the wisps of Adeline's hair before whistling. Adeline glanced in the mirror, watching as Mrs. Hunter's magic swiftly braided her hair back, finishing with a stylish bun.

With a tight smile, Mrs. Hunter said, "Now, there's the Miss Winkleston I know."

She led Adeline into the sitting room, now empty except for the fine furniture and a few landscapes hanging on the walls. It was a far calmer space and eased Adeline as she joined Mrs. Hunter at the dining table.

"Where is Serena?" Adeline said.

Handing Adeline a plate of still-steaming chicken and roasted vegetables, Mrs. Hunter said, "She looked exhausted, so I sent her home to rest in her own bed."

Adeline's eyes lowered. Serena had spent three full days here. Of course she needed rest.

"She'll be back for dinner." Mrs. Hunter pulled a worn notebook from her handbag. "I wanted a few hours to talk freely."

Adeline chewed slowly on her chicken, half-hoping it would delay Mrs. Hunter's soon-to-come questions. Though she had sent for her, facing Mrs. Hunter's scrutiny would be hard.

"I do think you put too much trust in Mrs. Dolan," Mrs. Hunter said. "However, without her, you will need help managing things. The Bradford School is closed for the summer, so I have time to help you as best I can. You also have Serena, but the pair of us have our own affairs to manage and cannot do everything.

"Your father would be a great help, if—"

Adeline shook her head. "No. He—I'm not ready."

Mrs. Hunter's lips pressed together before nodding. "When you are ready, I will send for him. For now, is there anyone else you can fully trust?"

All of the balls and extravagant parties from the past year ran through Adeline's mind. There were hundreds of faces, many with names, but the conversations had been light and empty. She thought of Helena Velis, but quickly dismissed the notion. She and Helena only ever discussed their dates and dresses.

She pushed back further, to friends in college and from the Bradford School, to the women who always asked after her at the Sandarian festival she went to with Rompell every year, to her father's neighbors.

Her chest panged and a tear fell. Months ago, she would have turned to Bronhart, but their romance was a hollow memory. Now, only one name remained, and even that was more of an acquaintance.

"Just Officer Kingston," Adeline said. "We are not close, but he has been a great help, and—"

"Both Mr. Kingston and his brother Henry are honest men." Mrs. Hunter nodded. "In these matters, integrity may matter more than friendship."

Jotting in her notebook, she said, "I'll invite him to join us for dinner. In the meantime, I'd like to make a list of everything Mrs. Dolan did for you."

Adeline's heart sank as the list quickly lengthened. No wonder the woman had treated her as little more than a doll to pose in front of society.

After an hour, Mrs. Hunter set aside the list and helped Adeline sort through a basket full of letters and invitations. The "decline" pile quickly towered, including several marriage proposals. The "possibly accept" pile was slim, and the only invitation she accepted was for lunch with Peter Talbot and Flora Primrose. He was a kind man and they had done much to help her escape Westengaard.

As they neared the bottom of the pile, Mrs. Hunter frowned. Using her handkerchief, she pulled out a midnight blue envelope with gilded edges. Adeline scooted back as twisted, dark magic emanated from it.

Tossing it onto the serving tray, Mrs. Hunter whistled, lighting it on fire. Adeline jumped as it lit into blue flames, sparks flaring up.

"What was that?" Adeline said.

"It seems you've caught Madame Blue's attention." Mrs. Hunter glared at the envelope's smoldering ashes. "You must be careful."

"Who is Madame Blue?" Adeline rubbed at the goosebumps along her arm. The dark magic was lingering longer than she liked.

"You will never hear of her directly in the papers, but many of the magic crimes Inspector McCay investigates are done by those in her employ. I have thick charms on the Bradford School to hide my students from her attention."

A chill settled on Adeline's skin. "What would she want from me?"

"Everything."

"Why haven't you mentioned her before?"

"If you keep your magic quiet and mind your own affairs, she and her network will rarely notice. However, she is why I taught you protection spells."

Adeline sat back, wondering how much more lay in the world of magic beyond her knowledge. She rolled her fingers, sending a ball of light across them. Did she even want to know more?

Mrs. Hunter set down the basket and lifted a blank envelope. Enclosed was a brief note wrapped around another envelope. Mrs. Hunter took in a breath before handing Adeline the note.

> *I will be sending a trunk of your childhood things. I found this letter from your mother's sister in your drawer and thought it would bring you peace when I can do so little to help you.*
>
> *I do not deserve your forgiveness, but I hope you remember my love for you, Little One.*
>
> *Your Papa*

Adeline's throat clenched as she closed the letter, hiding her father's words.

Mrs. Hunter's eyes narrowed as she analyzed the enclosed envelope. "You never opened it."

Adeline stared down at her hands. "I was preparing to marry Bronhart and didn't want to look to the past."

Sliding over Adeline's aunt's letter, Mrs. Hunter said, "Perhaps it was not the time to read it yet." She seemed about to say something more but stood instead. "I think it best I go manage a few business matters. I'll be back within the hour."

Adeline looked up, her eyes pleading. Mrs. Hunter glanced at the envelope, a tightness in her jaw. She left the suite, leaving Adeline alone with the letter.

Her finger pressed to the cursive letters reading *Arastella Dumond* before opening the envelope. She swallowed, trying to quiet her heartbeat. Unfolding the paper, she frowned at the few sentences on the page.

Dear Adeline,
I'm not one for writing down words, so I've sent you a message in
the song below.
I wish I'd found you long ago, but I'm glad we might meet soon.
Aunt Stella

Raising an eyebrow, Adeline skimmed the lyrics paired with a line of music notes, looking for hidden meaning in the simple words.

Open the window and, carried by the wind,
I will come and sit by you there,
Listen to my heart and uncover my mind,
Sing these words and I will be near.

She frowned while singing the first line. Magic surged through her. She shouted and dropped the paper. The magic ebbed away.

She hesitated before lifting the paper and singing again. The magic was strong but had a sweet gentleness. Across from her, the image of a woman formed out of light. As Adeline finished the last word of the song, the image came into focus and she stared at a projection of her aunt.

Arastella Dumond was not what Adeline had imagined.

She wore a long duster coat over a pair of over-sized pants and a red gingham shirt. A pistol rested at her hip and her pants were tucked in a pair of boots splattered by mud. Her blonde hair was streaked with gray and pulled back in a loose braid. Her face was tanned by years in the outdoors.

Her eyes, though, were the same blue as Adeline and her mother's.

Adeline found herself walking toward the woman. Her hand reached to touch Arastella's arm, but it passed through.

As she pulled her hand away, the projection of her aunt said, "It's hard to begin these things." She patted her hands on her legs. "Well, I'm your aunt Arastella, or just Stella. Your mom is my younger sister

Mariana—I always called her Ana. And you're her Adeline."

Tears fell down Adeline's cheeks as she dropped into a chair. She stared up at her aunt, watching the glint of tears in the woman's eyes.

"I spent—" Stella turned her head away. "It took a long time for Margaret Hunter to reach me. My mother, your grandmother, was hurt badly when Ana ran away and she burned the letters Mrs. Hunter sent before I saw them.

"Before we met yesterday, I thought—" She blew out some air and used her thumb to brush away a tear. "Well, let me go back a bit.

"Times were already hard before your mom left. No magic can keep crops growing if there's no rain. Then, my mother tried to lock Ana into what she saw was a proper marriage. I'd been locked into one of those myself, and when Ana came to me I had to help her get out.

"From the day she got to Pippington, she wrote me every week." Stella smiled.

Adeline's breath stilled as long-forgotten memories from her childhood came, of hearing her mother in her bedroom, talking to someone who wasn't there.

"She told me about falling in love with your dad and about you being born."

Stella pulled a photograph from her coat pocket and held it out. Adeline leaned forward, staring at herself as an infant. She pressed her lips together, holding back a sob.

She had only one photograph of her and her parents, and it was hidden in her mother's box. Every now and then, she pulled it out to look at it, but sad memories came and she shut it away.

"I wept when she told me Conrad had died, and then the letters stopped coming," Stella said. "I knew something was wrong. I didn't have much and it took me a few months to raise the money to buy a train ticket to Pippington. I left my own children in my sister-in-law's care for almost two months, but I had to find my sister and her girl.

"I went straight to the last address Ana had sent. Some slug of a man answered the door and said you and her were—" Stella swallowed as she looked down. "That you both had passed on.

"I found Ana's grave, but I couldn't find yours. I used every trick and spell I could, but I couldn't—" She took in a wavering breath. "I'm so sorry, Adeline. Part of me kept saying, 'She's all right. Just keep looking,' but I thought—I thought you were dead.

"And just yesterday, I'm down the hill at the market, and I overhear your friend, Mrs. Hunter, mention Ana. We talked and she showed me your picture—You look so much like your mom.

"It's been over 12 years, and there you are, doing so well." Stella grinned. "Mrs. Hunter says you were raised by a good man, that you're getting an education, and you've got a nice young man you're likely to marry."

Adeline pressed her hand over her mouth as she cringed. She wished she could go back to those simpler days with Bronhart, before her wealth.

"I don't know what I can offer," Stella said, "but I'd like to see my sister's girl—my niece. I'll wait to hear from you, but I'd love to show you where your mom grew up, have you meet my three brothers, and all your cousins. There's so many cousins to meet." She sighed. "And if you can't come here, then I'll find a way to head out there. I don't much like the train ride, but I'd go for the chance to meet you.

"There you are, Adeline Dumond Winkleston."

Stella's eyes raised in thought. "I think I know what I can give you. There should be enough magic left for that."

She raised her hand as she sang out a few notes. The room disappeared and Adeline found herself sitting in a forest, massive pine trees rising around her, a soft sunlight peering through. A deep stream flowed nearby and a pair of teenage girls sang together as they jumped from rock to rock.

Adeline's heart stilled as she stared at her mother's youthful face, bearing a mischievous smile as she sang. The song was one Adeline and her mother had sung as they had tidied their small apartment, her mother using her magic to send the broom dancing across the room.

Mariana jumped to the next rock before turning her hand, sending water splashing up at what must have been Stella. The older sister gasped as water drenched her skirt and Mariana bent over laughing. Stella's face scrunched in determination and she pushed both of her hands forward.

"No! Don't!" Mariana shouted as water swelled toward her. The wave hovered for a second before crashing over her.

She shouted before jumping and shoving Stella into the stream, falling in after her. They splashed in the water before crawling onto the muddy shore.

Both of them panted as they lay on the bank. Stella turned her face toward Mariana and grinned. Mariana smiled back and they both broke out in laughter.

The forest faded and Adeline found herself alone in the hotel suite, the image of her aunt gone, only the letter in her hand.

She sang the song again and Stella's form appeared, repeating exactly as before. The message led to the memory, and then ended far too soon. She sang two times more, enjoying the warmth of her aunt's smile, wondering what the names of her uncles were, and what her cousins were like. She found herself laughing with her aunt and mother as they splashed each other, and she hated the emptiness that came each time everything ended.

All of this had been in her drawer for nearly a year, but she had been too consumed with ignoring her magic, with marrying Bronhart, and then her life as an heiress.

She went to the window and looked out over the city. Lake Chalice lay in the distance, rows of mansions between her and its shores. Visiting the mansions once she gained her wealth had felt so exciting, but standing here, holding a letter connecting her to so much beyond herself, felt more full.

The door opened and Mrs. Hunter quietly took a seat at the table.

"I'm sorry," Adeline said. "I didn't know how much you did to get this to me. I wish you had told me."

"When I gave it to you, you were busy trying to fit yourself into a life you thought you wanted," Mrs. Hunter said. "I knew you would open it when the time was right. I just wish it had been sooner."

"What is she like?" Adeline joined Mrs. Hunter at the table.

"She is a hard-working and generous woman," Mrs. Hunter said. "Though, less refined than I'd expect, given your grandmother's obsession with your noble lineage."

"You've met my grandmother?"

Mrs. Hunter shook her head. "She would never see me. In her eyes, I am a mixed breed and far below her."

Adeline leaned her head on her palm. "My grandfather threw out my father for marrying my mother. My mother—she never talked about her family, but I always hoped her parents were kinder." She sighed. "It seems my grandmother might not have approved of my father."

Mrs. Hunter poured room temperature water from the teapot into a cup and held a pair of fingers on the side.

"When Mr. Rompell brought you to me, and you told me what families you are from, I was quite shocked." The water in her cup boiled and she set a teabag in. "Both families have a long tradition of being highly respected in their communities. The Winklestons have long had monetary wealth and the Dumonds, while financially poor, have an inheritance full of magic." She glanced at Adeline. "You inherited both sets of riches."

"I'd rather have neither."

Mrs. Hunter slowly stirred her spoon in the cup before saying, "You've said that often about your magic. But, taking your magic from you would be like—like removing a string from a violin. It can still play some music, but something would be wrong."

"But, I've lost control many times." Adeline placed her hands on the table. "And, it's part of why Westengaard—"

"Once he knew Mr. Rompell was your father, you would have been his target, even without your magic." Mrs. Hunter hesitated before placing her hand on top of Adeline's. "I fear, if you hadn't had your magic, we would have lost you completely."

Adeline's eyes met Mrs. Hunter's. "Thank you. I—"

She thought through everything she should thank Mrs. Hunter for, for letting her into the Bradford School, for teaching her about magic, for advice given so quietly over the years, for helping her with so much.

Mrs. Hunter pulled away her hand and picked up her teacup. "But, now you are safe, and there is much to manage." She gestured at the stack of invitations to decline. "Miss Quinn and Mr. Kingston will be joining us soon. I suggest we have them tackle that first."

Despite Adeline's exhaustion and the pain deep within, she let a small smile form. Touching Mrs. Hunter's arm, she said, "Thank you for caring much more than you pretend to."

A smile briefly crossed Mrs. Hunter's lips. Sitting up, Mrs. Hunter set her notebook on the table. Adeline leaned forward as she and Mrs. Hunter discussed the next task to manage.

Chapter 29

The next morning, Mrs. Hunter gave her a salve bearing magic to heal the burn on her arms. Though the pain left quickly, leaving pink splotches on her healing skin, no salve could quickly heal the pain in her soul from Westengaard's cruelty.

She spent the rest of the day in her suite, keeping herself in motion. As long as she kept on, her sorrow and worry drifted to the edge of her mind. She had to trust Inspector McCay and ignore Westengaard's voice haunting her.

Serena quickly took on the work of clearing Adeline's social calendar and managing future appointments. Jack still had a bewildered expression from being told the day before, "I need a circle of people I can trust. Will you help me?"

His answer had been a quick yes, and he steadily ran errands to retrieve information or deliver messages. Whenever he returned, his presence brought an easiness, his good humor lightening the room.

After two days, stacks of account ledgers filled the spaces where flowers had been. Adeline tried to tackle understanding the financial reports, using the small bit of accounting she had studied at the college. As she tossed away a stack of papers in frustration, Jack said, "Do you need help looking through those? My brother Henry's a sharp man with finances."

With Mrs. Hunter's support of the recommendation, Henry Kingston joined the small circle. As he entered, limping with his cane, his face narrow and serious, she could hardly match him as Jack's brother. However, he quickly proved himself as he sifted through page-after-page of quarterly reports, explaining how the ledgers were set-up and what to look for.

In the afternoon of his second day, he laid out a series of pages next to each other and walked her through the numbers. At the end, he explained, "Most of your wealth is locked into businesses and other investments. Your cash income has been lower than your expenses for months, even without considering the costs for—"

He coughed uncomfortably, and she finished, "For the wedding." Her heart sank. "And Westengaard's embezzlement."

Henry nodded. "It's a good thing you own the hotel. Otherwise, you'd be living here on credit." He pointed to a smaller ledger. "Which, speaking of, Mrs. Dolan has three seamstresses on retainer for you, as well as a number of other services."

"Cut everything you can, except the servants from the mansion," she said. "There's no need to leave them on the street."

"I am only a consultant, Miss Winkleston. My role is to only—"

"Then I hire you as my business manager." She glanced at him with a frown. "I can do that, can't I?"

Henry raised an eyebrow. "Of course, but I would recommend someone with more experience."

She shook her head. "I need someone I can trust. Mrs. Hunter says you are good enough."

"I was only a gardener when I worked for Mrs. Hunter."

"I am hiring you, Mr. Kingston. You may set whatever salary you think is fair."

Henry rubbed his forehead as he blinked. "I suppose I accept, though you'll have to announce me in person to the board. I don't think they'll believe me."

Adeline's stomach tightened. She had faced the board for her businesses only once, just after she had inherited her wealth. During the meeting, she barely listened, her mind drifting off to the dress she was going to wear to a gala that night. Afterward, she had left board meetings in Mrs. Dolan's care.

She ran her hands over her face before saying, "Then call a board meeting and I'll announce you."

Henry scheduled the board meeting and Adeline marked one week from her disastrous wedding by sitting for hours in the hotel conference room, surrounded by the board members managing her businesses. There were moments she worried the meeting would fall apart, but Henry glided around the obstacles, his firm, honest nature guiding the conversation.

A few female members sat among the board, but the majority were older men in suits, giving her condescending looks as they said, "Now, young lady."

After a third man repeated the phrase, Henry said, "Miss Winkleston is the owner of your company, sir. I ask you to address her as such."

One of many rounds of grumbles passed through the room, but the board members called her by her name.

When all was completed in the late afternoon, Henry escorted her back to her room, a pair of McCay's officers a few steps behind.

"How much did you choose as your salary?" she said.

Henry stated an amount slightly more than what she had been paid at the Bradford School.

Her eyebrows raised and she said, "That is far too low."

"You need to cut expenses, and I don't—"

"I have millions that I don't know how to manage. I need your help, Mr. Kingston, and you should be paid fairly."

"I'll see what you can afford," he said.

Reaching her door, he twisted his cane on the ground before saying, "Miss Winkleston, you are aware I am friends with Mr. Bronhart?"

The mention of Bronhart's name brought a heaviness. The

busyness of the past few days had helped her quiet thoughts of him, yet worry over him still hovered in the back of her mind.

Forcing herself to keep her eyes level, she nodded.

"How is he?" she whispered, unsure she wanted the answer.

"He appears well, but I haven't spoken with him in a few weeks." Henry's eyes narrowed. "How much is he aware of the magic involved in this whole affair?"

Her eyes widened and she whispered, "You know of magic?"

"I know more than I'd like." He adjusted his spectacles. "But, Mr. Bronhart—If I had lost my Evelyn as he lost you and found out it was all based on—" He rolled his eyes. "Hypnosis or some spell, I—" He waved a hand. "I would have gone to her immediately."

"We had an argument just before—" She swallowed, trying not to remember that night. "And had gone through several disagreements before that." Pressing her lips together, she tried to hold back tears. "I don't think he'll come."

"Have you asked?"

She shook her head. "He doesn't know anything about my magic. He wouldn't understand."

"You would be surprised how much a man is willing to understand when he is in love." He raised an eyebrow. "Although, I am only the expert on myself."

Henry's words lingered with her as she entered her room and Serena joined her for dinner. Looking to her friend, she said, "I'm thinking of writing to Nathaniel."

Serena sat up. "Part of me hoped you already had. He must—I can't imagine how he felt when he read the paper and learned the truth." She took a breath. "He either thinks it's a lie or feels guilty for not seeing the truth."

Adeline spent the evening pacing, her mind churning through a thousand scenarios. Still unsure of her action, she sat at the desk and wrote,

Nathaniel,

*If you are willing, I would like to speak with you. There is too much
to explain in a letter.*

She sealed the envelope before she could change her mind and
handed it to Jack as soon as he returned from his patrolman duties.
Once he stepped out, she collapsed onto an armchair. Serena sat beside
her, gripping her hand and whispering, "Whatever happens, you have
done the right thing."

Sunday morning, Adeline lingered in her room, sitting on the edge
of her bed as she listened to Stella's letter again. Watching it for at least
the twelfth time, her eyes traced the threads of magic forming the
projection of her aunt. If she pulled at it enough, she might be able to
learn the spell and send her own projection back. She had asked Mrs.
Hunter about the spell, but the headmistress said, "It is beyond my
capabilities."

Adeline had already sent a letter, but it would take weeks to reach
Stella. Sending a version of herself would mean so much more.

The room turned to forest again as the memory with her mother
played. Adeline leaned against the bedpost, looking up at the trees.
One day, she would walk through the forest herself, smelling the same
earthy scent her mother had, feeling the same breeze. For now, she
would enjoy the brief glimpse of her mother.

She frowned as a fog cast over the image, clouding out her mother
and aunt. As if rising out of a deep pool, the image of Westengaard
formed, his clothes torn and his face dirty and scratched. She shrunk
back on the bed as shock held her still. He held his hand out to her,
his blue eyes pleading with her. Even as her heart pounded, shouting

for her to run, she found herself raising her hand toward his.

Almost as if a light flicked on in her mind, Adeline realized what she was doing. She crushed the letter in her hand and the image disappeared. Gripping the bedpost, she stared at where the phantom of Westengaard had stood.

Her hands shaking, she spread out the letter, staring at her aunt's handwriting. A fury filled her. He had already stolen her mind for so long, and now he broke the refuge of her aunt's letter.

Mrs. Hunter had sat with her for at least an hour each night for the past week, trying to find a way to break Westengaard's ties. The connection had seemed to be weakening, but now, she could feel his power growing.

Adeline jumped as someone tapped on the door.

Mrs. Hunter entered, her face grave. Sitting up, Adeline waited for Mrs. Hunter to confirm her worst fears: that Westengaard was free and seeking her.

Instead, Mrs. Hunter said, "Mr. Bronhart wishes to speak to you."

Adeline let out a pent-up breath and pressed her hands to her cheeks. Those were not the words she had expected, though Bronhart's presence sent off a whole other set of nerves. However, facing him felt far less frightening than the thought of Westengaard escaping.

"Are you all right?" Mrs. Hunter frowned as she walked toward her.

Adeline swallowed before holding out the crumpled letter. Tears came as she said, "I just wanted to see my aunt and mother—and—he appeared."

Mrs. Hunter drew in a sharp breath. "Inspector McCay said the spells were strengthened this morning. He shouldn't—" Her fist clenched. "I'll go myself and check." She glanced at the door. "Should I send Mr. Bronhart away?"

Adeline pressed a hand to her breast as she focused on breathing.

She wanted to send him away, to hide and not face him while panic built up. However, if she declined his visit, there was little chance he would come again.

She had to face him, no matter the consequences.

"No," she said. "Tell him I'll be out in a moment."

Mrs. Hunter touched her hand briefly before leaving the room.

Adeline folded her aunt's letter and slid it into her pocket.

Glancing in the mirror, Adeline whistled a spell to smooth her hair. She straightened the sleeves on her pale blue dress, the color complementing her eyes and lessening the paleness of her face. She pinched her cheeks, hoping the pinkness might stay and he wouldn't see her fear. There was already enough to untangle with Bronhart.

Adeline's heart jumped as she entered the sitting room. Bronhart stood near the window, his dark, tailored suit complementing his tall frame. Serena chatted at him, trying to fill the nervous air.

Seeing Adeline, Serena smiled at Bronhart. "Here she is. As I said, I really should be going to my appointment."

As Serena exited through the suite's front door, she gave Adeline a quick, encouraging smile. Adeline nodded back, trying to show as much courage as she could.

Crossing to a maroon armchair, Adeline felt Bronhart's troubled stare follow her.

Unable to meet his gaze, she kept her eyes down and said, "Thank you for coming."

She motioned for him to sit across from her and he approached the chair. However, he stopped beside it, pressing his knuckles against the back.

Adeline gripped her armrests. The innocent hopes and thrills of their early courtship ran through her mind, but they felt as if from a distant lifetime.

"I've spent the last week trying not to believe what the paper's said about what happened to you." He shook his head. "Because, if it's true, that means—" He punched his fist against the chair. "That means I failed you, and—"

"You had no reason to see the truth," she whispered.

"I had every reason," he said. "You were not yourself, and your father came to me the next morning. He told me something was wrong." His fist clenched. "But, I was so angry. And then that night, when you came to me." A heaviness lay in his eyes as he looked at her. "I thought you were merely drunk, and I let myself believe that until yesterday, when I was at Peter Talbot and Flora Primrose's wedding."

Lowering his head, he said, "At the reception, I was sitting alone and Flora came to me. She said—She told me—" Bronhart rubbed his neck as he paced. "She told me how Westengaard had hypnotized her too, using her to escape some prison out in the Surris Mountains. Listening to her, hearing her tell of his control, and abandoning her in some meadow—"

He stopped and looked at Adeline.

"What have you suffered because of him?" He took a breath. "And what could I have done to stop him, if I hadn't been so angry that night?"

She wished she were the same girl as a few months ago. Then, she would bounce from her chair to seek rest in his arms, hoping to comfort his guilt. That girl, however, had been innocent and willfully ignorant of the darkness lying in the world.

Instead, though the words weighed as heavily as rocks tumbling from her mouth, she said, "You could have done nothing to stop Westengaard."

"I should have fought harder," Bronhart said. "I should have seen through how much you changed those few months before. Looking back, I'm sure he started controlling you at that dinner at the Ophombauch's, didn't he?"

Adeline stared at him, wishing this were the simple truth of what happened. The actual truth, however, drove deep into her breast and stung.

Her mind ran through the argument that night at the Morveaux. She could almost hear herself as she insulted Henry's future wife, mocking the best gown the woman could probably afford. She wished her words could be blamed on Westengaard, but they were hers alone.

Tears broke down her cheeks and Bronhart knelt beside her. He took her hand between his.

"It's all right, Adeline. I'm here now." He brushed away a tear from her cheek and gave her a sad smile. "Whatever has broken between us, we can mend."

Pushing his fingers away from her cheek, she breathed, "That is not the truth."

Bronhart's smile faltered but he kept hold of her hand.

Looking him in the eye, a pressure built in her chest. Her mind sought words to explain, to capture everything she had hidden and everything Westengaard had done to her. There was so much he deserved to know.

"My father once asked you what makes me most unique," she said.

Bronhart's eyes narrowed. "That was only a trick question."

Adeline shook her head. "He meant this."

She raised her palm. Weaving together a few threads of magic, she formed a spark which quickly became a flame. She let the fire hover there, twisting and turning.

Bronhart's brow furrowed as he stared. "I've never seen your father do that trick."

She shifted her hand, changing the flame from orange to green. With a whistle, she twisted the flame into the figure of a dragon circling over her palm.

Bronhart rose, his eyes wide and face pale.

"That day, when you took me to ride the dragons, a spell I used set them off." She closed her fist, making the flame disappear. "The morning after my birthday, everything was broken in the house because my magic flared out." A tear fell. "The day we met, the girl was on the roof because of magic and I used a spell to help her get down."

Bronhart fell into the armchair across from her as if someone had punched his chest. His mouth opened and closed several times.

"Magic is real?" he said.

"Yes." Adeline's lips pressed together. "And—" She choked on the words, but forced out, "And Westengaard—his magic—"

She covered her hand over her mouth as a sob came, followed by heavy tears, the terror of his touch filling her. Her fist clenched as she felt his pull on her. She was supposed to be free, but she was still trapped.

"Westengaard used magic to control you?" Bronhart said.

Adeline wiped her cheeks with her handkerchief as she tried to gain control and find the right words.

Bronhart ran his fingers through his hair before rising. "If I had known, I would have fought to protect you."

"He is powerful." She took in a steadying breath. "Even Mrs. Hunter can't break his spell."

He frowned. "Mrs. Hunter has magic? Anyone else? What about Serena?"

"Serena doesn't know anything, but Papa—" She shook her head. There was already too much to explain and Rompell's secret needed to be kept.

"Of course he knows." Bronhart grunted before flexing his hand. "Because magic is real."

With his voice quiet, as if he wasn't sure he wanted to know the answer, he said, "When—when did you fall under Westengaard's spell?"

Adeline swallowed. "That night, at the Morveaux, just after we fought."

Bronhart's jaw tightened. "Nothing before that moment?"

"I was fully myself." Adeline cringed, wishing this weren't the truth.

Bronhart's brow furrowed as he paced the room. "Would you have ever told me about your magic?"

Adeline shook her head. "I hated my magic. I thought I could hide it and just have a normal life with you."

Bronhart paced before stopping at the window. Leaning against the windowsill, he said, "A normal life?" He glanced at the room. "Adeline, even without magic, your life has never been normal. You were taken in and raised by a kind stranger, and then inherited such immense wealth—" He shook his head. "Your life is one others dream of having."

"They may have it," she whispered. "I'd rather just go back to being a schoolteacher."

Bronhart looked out the window overlooking Pippington. Adeline followed his gaze along the skyline and the cranes marking buildings rising in the heart of the city.

"But, we can't go back, can we?" he said.

Clutching her handkerchief, she replied, "No."

He reached into his pocket as he walked toward her. Her breath stilled as he held out the simple diamond engagement ring meant to bond them months before. She cringed at her giddiness when, under Westengaard's full control, she had placed the ring in an envelope and sent it to Bronhart.

"I came seeking the girl I had given this to," he said, "hoping to find her now that Westengaard is defeated. But, I lost her long ago, didn't I?"

Though her arms shook, Adeline forced herself to stand. "I may have lied about my magic, and gotten caught up in my wealth, but I did love you."

"And now?"

His words pressed in around her as she looked in his eyes, hoping to find the answer there.

She remembered the warmth of his proposal as she lay exhausted and recovering from her birthday. The excitement and promise of their future had clouded her pain as she looked into his eyes, so full of hope and devotion.

Today, she sought for that spark of love. There seemed a dim ember, but it was shadowed and she didn't know if she had the strength to help it grow.

"I don't know," she said.

"Neither do I, but—" Bronhart raised her hand and placed the ring on her palm. "If you are willing, I think we can find our way to each other again."

Part of Adeline wanted to collapse into his arms, to weep on his shoulder and renew what had been lost. But, once he left the room, she knew her sorrow would return. Leaning on him would not heal the hollowness within.

Her throat clenched before she said, "I wish I were ready, but I need time."

His eyes remained on hers as his shoulders sank a little. He seemed to fight for what to say before he whispered, "Then time is the gift I will leave you with."

He touched her elbow and kissed her cheek. The brush of his lips was gentle, yet she shuddered as it brought memories of Westengaard's kisses. A tear fell down her cheek as she wished she could simply accept Bronhart's kindness.

Stepping back, he seemed about to say something more. However, he turned away and left the room, leaving Adeline alone.

Chapter 30

A sob broke through Adeline and she let herself collapse to the floor. She hadn't realized how much strength it had taken to stand before Bronhart. Curled up on her side, she cradled her head in her hands, letting herself cry.

She wept for the life she could have shared with Bronhart. She wept for Rompell, for the trust that had broken between them. She wept for the lost days under Westengaard's power. She wept for her parents and what her life would have been if they had lived.

Would she have met Aunt Stella long ago? Would her grandfather have forgiven her father and restored his wealth? Would her father have accepted his inheritance?

And who would she have been if born into wealth?

This realization struck the deepest.

Westengaard was to blame for his spell, for controlling her. But, things with Bronhart were broken before Westengaard had captured her at the Morveaux.

She yelled as she remembered that night. The glamor around her had been so empty, and yet, she had wanted to be the best of it.

And it wasn't just that night.

Her thoughts, her words, had been so disdainful for the world she had come from. Sitting among the upper class, she tried to hide what she saw as her rough edges. She dismissed people like Mrs. Frizban and Jack, good people who had always been kind to her.

All of the layers of finery and jewels were peeled away and she couldn't recognize the girl underneath. Who was she without her wealth, without her pretended place in society? Who was she as simply Adeline?

She was an orphan, adrift and without her papa.

With a yell, her power throbbed out of her. As she cried out, vases shattered throughout the room. The couch somersaulted, the cushions flying and smashing into glass tables. An armchair lit on fire.

She pressed her hands to the carpet, letting the cloth smolder beneath her fingers. She wished she could turn back time, return to being a child, innocent and ignorant of the traps lying in the world.

Her magic quieted as she sobbed again. She sat up, resting her head against her knees.

"Papa," she whispered. "What have I done?"

Her fingers rubbed together as she pictured the coin with his face on it. The coin lay in her jewelry box in her childhood bedroom on Nightingale Lane, but, perhaps, thinking of it would have the same power.

Just as she had as a child, trapped in a ditch with no hope of escaping, she whispered, "Rompell, Rompell, Rompell."

She rocked, waiting for him to appear, to kneel before her, saying, "What is your wish?"

However, the only sound was the wind whistling through a broken window.

Raising her head, she cupped her hand in front of her and conjured fire. The flame formed into her mother and father dancing together, laughing in silence as they twirled. She watched them turn slowly, shivering as she remembered that night in the snow, believing no one would come.

But, Rompell had saved her.

She drew in a shaky breath as she wished he were here, that she could lean her head on her father's shoulder, and he would speak, wise comforting words.

Footsteps crunched on glass. She didn't dare look up as she hoped her wish had conjured him.

"That's beautiful," Jack said as he crouched in front of her, watching the dancing figures.

She closed her fist, ending the flame's soft dance.

Though Jack was now a friend, he did little to ease the longing for her father.

"I heard a lot of noise and wanted to make sure you're all right." He glanced at the overturned couch, broken vases and tables, and half-burned chair. "I think we'll say a horde of wasps came in the window and we had to fight to get them out." He scratched his head. "That should explain most of it."

Raising her eyes to face him, she said, "Why are you helping me?"

"I'm an officer of the law," he said. "That's what I do."

"You've done more than your job."

"Well, you've been given a poor hand these past few months, and—" He shrugged. "I hope, by now, you see me as a friend."

She rubbed her cheek. "But the way I used to treat you—you were always kind to me and I always turned you down."

"You always just said you were busy." He gave her a brief, sly smile. "I saw the men you went with and I knew all they wanted was to parade you around.

"And knowing you—" He lowered his eyes and tossed a piece of broken porcelain between his hands. "Over at the Bradford School, I'd watch you laugh and sing with the girls, help them pick themselves up and dry their tears when they scraped a knee, and then, there was the day in the greenhouse, where you snuck a bit of magic to fix a girl's flower."

He pressed his lips together before saying, "I kept thinking you could do better than the shallow blokes you went with, and I was glad when you met Bron—" He stopped as he glanced at the broken furniture. "I'm sorry things haven't gone as you hoped."

"There may be a chance," she said, "but, I'm not that girl anymore."

"We all change." He raised his eyebrows. "I've even been transformed into a frog twice, but each time I was still myself."

She frowned, wondering about the full story of those transformations.

Jack grinned at her as he went on, "It's like my dad often says, 'As far as we might wander, there's always a true part of ourselves we come back to.' And, Miss Adeline, I think, underneath it all, you're a good one."

She wished she could see herself as Jack did, with such simple hopefulness.

Rising, Jack carefully brushed broken glass and porcelain off his pants. "Earlier, Miss Serena and I were talking about how to best help you, and it occurred to us that you've not been outside in days."

Her chest tightened. "Once I go outside, everyone will be watching me."

"Miss Serena and Mrs. Hunter've driven off most of the onlookers, and I'm sure Mrs. Hunter's got a spell or two to manage the rest." He jerked his thumb toward the window. "It's a beautiful day and some fresh air will do you good." He shrugged. "And, Miss Serena's downstairs with Mrs. Hunter, with a picnic already put together. Seems a shame to waste it."

The way he spoke made picking up all the broken pieces of herself sound so easy. It would be long before her sorrow would quiet and become a dull pain. Yet, looking around at the chaotic room, she knew there would be no peace here.

She took his offered hand and stood.

Walking out in the sun, sitting at a park overlooking the shore of Lake Chalice, Adeline could almost forget Westengaard's appearance and then turning down Bronhart hours before. She smiled a few times, but still couldn't bring herself to laugh. Not even when a band played at a nearby gazebo and Jack convinced Mrs. Hunter to take a turn around the dance floor with him. The headmistress was stiff, and Jack was smoother than expected. When he returned, he took Serena on a second round.

They talked and laughed as they danced. Adeline knew the glint in Serena's eye as Jack led her in another twirl.

"How are you doing?" Mrs. Hunter sat beside Adeline.

Adeline looked out at the expanse of water. "I wish I could be at peace."

"That will take time," Mrs. Hunter said. "But, you will find it."

Adeline took in a breath and tears formed. "How? I gave up Nathaniel, and then Westengaard—"

"Let Inspector McCay worry about Westengaard," Mrs. Hunter said. "We've added more protections and officers from the capitol are coming for him tomorrow afternoon. We must trust you will be free."

"And then, there is Papa." Looking out over the lake, the answer came to her. "Perhaps, after lunch with the Talbots tomorrow, I will go and see him."

"I think it will be good for both of you." Mrs. Hunter squeezed Adeline's shoulder. "Do you need me to come with you?"

Adeline shook her head. "I need to do this alone."

Mrs. Hunter sat for a moment as the wind drifted over them. "Never think you are alone, Miss Winkleston. There are always friends to help you."

That night, Adeline hardly slept as she played out speaking to her father a thousand times. In some versions, he slammed the door shut. In others, he threw the door open, took her in his arms, and they wept together.

Whatever came of it, she had to face him. She had to make peace.

On the drive over to Peter and Flora Talbot's, she was glad Jack was assigned from McCay's squad along with Officer Hanson. It was good to have a friend close as each street brought flashes of memories from the wedding.

Peter and Flora had been as hurt by Westengaard as she was. Today's conversation might be hard, but she would pull through.

Jack and Officer Hanson took their post beside the Talbot's apartment door and she knocked.

Flora threw the door open and grinned. "I'm so glad you're here."

Adeline tried to smile, but her muscles were stiff as she entered.

Flora danced across the room, almost as if floating. "Peter! She's here!"

A series of clatters echoed from the kitchen before Peter stepped out. He grinned.

"Thank you for coming, Miss Winkleston. We're honored. Quite honored—uh—" He rushed to the dining table and pulled out a chair. "Not used to guests yet."

Adeline set her handbag on a side table before taking the offered seat.

Flora and Peter were a flurry of motion as they finished setting the table, both of them stopping to say things like, "Sorry we're not ready," or, "I do hope you like biscuits." Adeline leaned her elbow on the table and rested her chin on her palm as she watched them. On their way in and out of the small kitchen, Flora snuck kisses on Peter's cheek and his face turned pink as he beamed at her.

A light sweetness filled the air. Adeline had always longed for a romance full of the torrents of emotion she had read about in books.

Now, she had achieved such a romance and found herself wishing for the ease and joy Peter and Flora had.

The roasted chicken was dry, the biscuits hard, and the vegetables wilted, but Adeline enjoyed the meal. Peter talked about some of his latest shoe designs and Flora bounced out some ideas.

As the meal neared an end, Flora said, "Peter and I asked you here because we were sure you might need a friend. While I was at the Morveaux, I overheard—" Her face paled.

Adeline found herself tensing.

"Well, I heard your mother was a Dumond."

Adeline sat up. "She was."

Flora smiled. "I am so honored you are willing to sit at my table. The Dumonds—I don't know if there's a greater family in the Surris Mountains, with so rich a—"

"I am honored to be here," Adeline said. "Based on what Inspector McCay said, if it weren't for you and Mr. Talbot—" She swallowed. "The wedding would have been far worse."

"I didn't mean to make such a show," Peter said as he pushed at the husk of his biscuit. He looked across the table, a sweetness in his eyes. "I only wanted to make sure Flora was all right, and, I'm glad I could help you. What that man did to both of you, stealing control of your minds, using you to get what he wants—it's just not right."

Adeline found herself smiling broader than she had in days. Peter had always been a gentle, kind man. She was glad he and Flora had each other.

"Peter told me you're adopted," Flora said. "And that you've never been to Surris."

"I have not." Adeline smiled sadly, thinking of Stella's letter. "But I would like to go."

"Wonderful." Flora grinned. "Peter and I are going in a month or so to see my family. I—" Tears fell down her cheeks and Peter squeezed her hand. "I was transformed into a flower for nearly ten years. I'm sure your mother's family misses you as well."

Adeline blinked back her own tears. To be a flower for almost a decade, waiting day after day to be rescued—Adeline could hardly imagine what Flora had gone through.

All at the hands of Westengaard.

Pushing aside a spike of anger, Adeline smiled at Flora.

"I would be honored to join you," she said.

"And your father, Mr. Rompell, he would be welcome as well," Peter said.

Adeline's fist closed around her armrest and she forced her smile to stay. "I will ask."

"Mr. Rompell came to me one night at the Morveaux," Flora said.

Adeline sat up, her smile disappearing.

"He promised to help you and me escape Westengaard." Flora touched Adeline's arm. "When you see him, please thank him for me."

"I will."

Staring down at her clenched hands, Adeline tried to keep her face calm.

She had been so focused on herself, on her own pain, on why Rompell hadn't saved her sooner. Yet, there were so many things she hadn't considered. Flora and the danger she had been in was just one. She had thought of Hidaya and Rompell's sons, but she often forgot to think of them as living people. They appeared as only statues, but Rompell had known them, had held them close in their true form. Staring at their still faces for fifteen years was a heavy burden.

She needed to speak with Rompell immediately. She needed to be near her papa.

Rising, she said, "It has been an excellent visit, but—"

The door burst open. Flora and Peter rose. Adeline turned toward Jack as he panted, all color gone from his face.

Jack pulled in air before saying, "Westengaard has escaped."

Chapter 31

Adeline froze in place, the world dark for a moment. How could she not have sensed his escape? She flexed her fingers, feeling for his magic. The ties remained, but he was pulling very little.

He must have figured out she could still sense him. Or, he had been using her as a decoy.

She heard voices around her, but none of the words made sense. Flora clung to Peter, her face matching the same terror rising in Adeline. Jack took Adeline's arm and lead her out of the apartment and down the stairs, leaving Flora and Peter in the care of Officer Hanson. He led her past her own vehicle to a black motorcar and helped her inside.

"How is this possible?" she said as Jack started up the engine.

"Seems he weaved spells in his books," he said as he sped down the street. "This morning, a mob of women under his spell stormed Cordson's Department Store. While Inspector McCay was out investigating, someone snuck into the station and helped Westengaard escape." He shook his head. "He's been missing for hours and they just figured it out."

Adeline gripped his arm. "Where is Papa?"

"I'm sure McCay's sent officers to take Mr. Rompell to safety."

"We must go to him."

Jack glanced at her. "That'll be one of the first places Westengaard will look."

"I need to see him."

"My orders are to get you to a safe house."

"Take me to Rompell first." She swallowed. "I need to know my father is safe."

Jack cracked his neck before jerking on the driver's wheel. "All right, but, it'll have to be quick."

"Thank you," she said as she kept hold of his arm.

Her heart raced along with the motorcar. She forced herself not to imagine Westengaard melting Hidaya and the boys.

Jack skidded to a stop in front of her childhood home on Nightingale Lane. Adeline bolted from the motorcar and ran to the door. She pushed her hand forward, forcing the door off its hinges and sending it flying in.

There was no time to be careful.

"Papa!"

She ran through the familiar rooms on the first floor, but there was no sign of him. His study was empty, the stacks of books gone and the desk clear except for an envelope bearing her name.

Her hand shook as she lifted it. She skimmed through the letter apologizing for not protecting her, speaking of his love for her. On another day, she would read the words. Today, she needed to know where he was.

At the end, he wrote, *I am taking Hidaya and my sons with me and closing my affairs in Pippington. I am leaving my properties in your name. I think it best you are protected from my past.*

She held her hand to her head as she looked through the letter again, searching for any clue of where he might be. There were tracking spells she could use on the letter but they were unreliable. Instead, she ran out of the room.

"McCay's other officers must have already gotten him," Jack said as she sprinted past him and up the stairs.

She went to her room and grabbed her jewelry box. Tossing bracelets and earrings across the bed, she sifted through the contents.

Her fingers wrapped around the coin Rompell had given her the night he had lifted her from the snow. Shutting her eyes, she whispered, "Rompell, Rompell, Rompell," pouring her own magic into the coin.

Raising it, she could see the lines of magic forming the wavering blue light.

For the first time in so long, her choice was clear.

As she marched down the stairs, she wondered if Rompell had any weapons left hidden in his study. However, physical weapons would do little good against Westengaard. Besides, she had no training and would look a fool with a sword.

Walking toward the motorcar, Adeline said to Jack, "Can your pistol do anything against magic?"

Jack frowned as he hurried to keep up with her. "There's a spell in the bullets that'll cut through some magic." His eyes widened and he grabbed her shoulder, stopping her.

"What are you thinking? It took McCay's whole squad plus Peter Talbot's hammer to stop Westengaard at your wedding. You can't—"

Holding out the coin, the blue light shining, she said, "We need to find my father."

"Give that to McCay and she'll find your father." He jerked his thumb toward the motorcar. "My job is to keep you safe."

"Then I will go alone."

"I'll arrest you if I need to."

Adeline looked him in the eye. "Did my father tell you what the statues at my wedding were?"

Jack's face paled as he nodded. "His wife and sons—cursed by Westengaard." Jack gestured toward the car. "I'm sure McCay has sent officers to protect them."

"Papa took them with him." She held up the letter. "He needs to be warned."

"What if Westengaard's already tracking him?"

"Then we need to make sure we get there before Westengaard."

Jack held her gaze, his jaw tight. Throwing up a hand, he said, "We should at least get help. Maybe Mrs. Hunter—"

"There's no time." Adeline strode to the motorcar.

Taking his place in the driver's seat and starting the engine, Jack said, "All right. Where do we go?"

Adeline raised the coin, laying it flat on her palm. The blue light was fainter than she would like and invisible to Jack's eye, but the direction was clear as she gave Jack instructions and they drove out of the city.

Rompell kept his truck in a low gear as it chugged up the hill. Given the wheeze of the engine, it might seize up and die at any moment. Carrying three pure gold statues in the crate strapped to the back would be too much for most vehicles. However, he couldn't risk leaving the crate out of his sight. Not even riding in a train would be safe.

Reaching the top of the hill, he pulled over to let the engine cool. He got out and leaned against the truck, resting his gloved hand on the crate.

Though he had saved Adeline, he had lost her.

He knew that the moment he had entered her room at the hotel and she had turned away from him.

He had failed her just as he had failed Hidaya and his sons.

Over the past week, he had quietly settled his affairs and signed his buildings over to Adeline's name. They would be a small addition to her immense wealth, but she would protect the widows and poor who lived as his tenants.

Now, his life in Pippington was finished. He wasn't sure where to go next, but, wherever he ended up, he would begin a new anonymous life. As long as no one knew him, he could keep others safe.

He leaned against the truck and looked out at the ravine ahead, the afternoon light brightening the pine and aspen forest.

"I wish you could see this," he said to the statues. He smiled sadly, picturing how wide his sons' eyes would be, looking at such tall trees, so different than anything in Sandar.

There was no chance of his family being restored, but he was still husband and father.

He drank from his canteen before climbing back in the motorcar and starting up the engine. The truck rumbled forward and he kept the gear low as he went downhill toward the ravine and the stone fence beside the bridge.

Halfway down the hill, tires screeched behind him. He glanced in the mirrors.

A motorcar skidded down the hill after him, swerving erratically. He pulled toward the side of the road and pumped on the brake. His brakes squealed, the truck hardly slowing.

Prickling ran along his arm and a chill followed down his spine just before a flash of bright light shot out from the vehicle behind him.

The ground exploded in front of him.

The truck's front tire hit the small crater and the truck fell onto its passenger side. The windshield cracked and the truck skidded down the gravel road. Flecks of stone pelted Rompell through the broken windshield.

The truck smashed against the stone fence, crushing part of the roof. Rompell ducked back, his head narrowly missing the dent. He kicked at the driver's door as footsteps ran toward him, the glow of blue light shining as magic formed.

Cursing under his breath, he made a final kick and the door flung open. Ignoring the bruises on his arms and legs, he pulled himself out of the cab and climbed on top.

Looking down, Rompell's eyes met Westengaard's. His old enemy smiled at him as he gathered power around his hand.

Somehow, Westengaard had unlocked more of his magic. He was still not at his full strength, but the pistol hidden in Rompell's jacket was nearly useless.

Still, Rompell pulled out his pistol and fired. Westengaard jerked his arm forward and the orb of magic blasted out, burning the bullet in its path. Rompell slid down the truck's crushed roof, letting the pistol fall from his hand. The truck lurched as the magic blasted into it.

Pulling off his gloves, Rompell hurried as Westengaard gathered his magic again. With only a portion of his power, it should take time for him to prepare a blast. Rompell needed to keep him busy and distracted.

He curled his bare fingers as he looked down at Hidaya, a corner of her face visible through a hole in the crate. Making a silent prayer he could return for her and their sons, he pressed his hand to the truck, turning the truck gold while the crate remained wood. The gold should repel some of Westengaard's magic.

Sprinting into the forest, he tucked his gloves in his coat pocket. The air was warm, but he pushed his speed. His lungs burned, reminding him he wasn't a young man.

He grabbed several stones, feeling their weight increase as they turned to gold, and slid them into his pockets. Skidding to a stop, he grabbed a thick stick and hefted it as it transformed. It would be heavy enough to do some damage.

Ducking behind a tree, he stilled his breath and waited.

He wasn't sure how Westengaard had escaped, nor how he was going to stop him. However, he would fight till the end.

Adeline rubbed the coin in her hand as Jack kept his foot hard on the pedal, pushing the motorcar's speed. The vehicle shook and she cried out a few times as they swerved around carts in the road, narrowly missing oncoming vehicles.

They stopped only once in Cragsville to refuel the motorcar. Then, they drove beyond the small town, past farms, and into the forest.

The hours went by in silence, giving too much time for Adeline to think.

How was she to fight Westengaard?

She didn't know how much power had been his and how much had been hers. What if he had broken his shackles further or stolen power from another?

Even if her power was greater, his skill was better.

She stared at her hands.

So much of her training with Mrs. Hunter had been with teacups and simple spells. Her mind raced through the hours Westengaard had spent training her, teaching her to see each filament of magic, how to feel her way through a spell. The training had been meant to give her the skills to unlock his hidden shackles. There had to be something she could use against him, some way she might have a chance at winning.

She glanced out the window as they passed pine and aspen trees, rising up into the low mountains far west of Pippington. Compared with the giant trees shown in her aunt's letter, these trees were small. Yet, they were much larger than the trees back home.

Jack placed his hand on her shoulder. "We'll find your father and he'll be just fine."

The churning in her stomach and the brief surges of Westengaard's power pulling on hers told her he was wrong.

They reached the top of a hill and Jack lowered the gear as they began going downhill.

Adeline's heart stopped a beat as she stared at the golden truck lying close to the ravine below, another motorcar beside it, blocking the path to the bridge.

Jack slammed on the brake pedal, swerving the motorcar around a small crater in the road. Gravel kicked up as Jack brought the vehicle to a sliding stop.

"I think we found them," Jack whispered.

Adeline threw open her door and jumped from the motorcar. She slammed the door and sang out a long note before he could get out. She spread over Jack's motorcar a spell Mrs. Hunter had taught her to seal a broken window for a few hours. Spread out over so large a surface, it would hold for less time but it would keep Jack inside and safe.

"Adeline!" He fought with the door handle before slamming his elbow against the window.

She ignored his yells as she ran toward the overturned truck. Westengaard's magic was thick in the air, almost sickening her. Black marks scarred the sheening gold along the truck's side. She reached the wood crate and used her magic to blast aside the lock. The door slammed open.

Hidaya and the boys were inside, remaining whole statues.

At least Westengaard had not reached them.

The echo of an explosion boomed from the forest and she jumped back. She scanned the dense trees in front of her as she twisted Rompell's coin between her fingers.

What was she doing?

That night at the Morveaux, she had tried to fight, but Westengaard had blocked every attempt. She felt more connected to her magic now, but much of her magic was still tied to him.

Her heart thudded as another boom echoed. There was no time to hesitate.

She closed her hand around Rompell's coin as she gathered her skirts with her other hand. Though she shook, she marched toward the forest.

Rompell dove behind another tree right before the one he had been hiding behind exploded into splinters. He had lured Westengaard close only once, bashing him with a thick golden stick and pelting him with several golden stones. That trick hadn't worked again and Westengaard seemed as strong as ever.

He knelt for a moment, letting himself pant as Westengaard wove the next spell. Blasting things took less focus and power than transformation or other spells. As long as he could keep Westengaard distracted, he might have a chance.

Rompell touched his bare hand to the tree and threw a hefty rock toward the closest set of bushes. Dirt flew up as Westengaard blasted them. Rompell took the distraction to sprint behind another set of trees.

He crouched, listening for Westengaard's footsteps, watching for the next movement.

Westengaard seemed to appear in front of Rompell. Before Rompell could dodge, Westengaard's knee connected with his jaw, sending him flying onto his back. Rompell's head rang and his jaw ached as he tried to roll to his feet. Westengaard kicked his heel into Rompell's shoulder, knocking him back. Before Rompell could rise, Westengaard bent down and planted his knee on Rompell's chest.

Wheezing for breath, Rompell grabbed a handful of dirt and threw it. Westengaard spat and wrapped his fingers around Rompell's neck, squeezing hard. Rompell kicked and twisted, shoving Westengaard's jaw, his fingers digging in and making red marks.

His neck muscles flexed, fighting as Westengaard's grip tightened. Spots were filling his vision, but he kept shoving on Westengaard's jaw as his free hand felt in the dirt for anything he could use.

"And just think," Westengaard snarled, "what I will do to Adeline when I return to Pippington."

Rompell grabbed a rock in his fist and swung it toward Westengaard's head. Westengaard whistled. An invisible weight dragged on Rompell's arm, pulling it down.

His legs thrashed, but the world was becoming less clear.

As his lungs ached, begging for air, a vision rose of Adeline running toward him, her face pale and full of panic. She yelled and shoved both of her hands forward. The air rippled, sending dirt and pine needles flying. Westengaard glanced to the side just before the force of her spell knocked him back.

Rompell gasped in breath, wishing Adeline were only a vision as she ran to his side.

"Go," he panted. He reached to push her away, but stopped and closed his bare fist.

A wall of light flashed out from Westengaard. Rompell jabbed his elbow into Adeline's chest, knocking her out of the way. He shut his eyes, waiting for the blast to hit him.

Adeline felt the surge of energy even before Westengaard launched the spell. Her heartbeat pounded in her ears as she turned her head. Rompell's elbow rammed into her chest, knocking out her breath and shoving her back.

Westengaard's spell rushed forward, singeing trees and burning scattered leaves as it approached. Humming a low note, she raised her hand, using the traces of her power in Westengaard's spell like a magnet to draw it toward her. She swung her arm, sending the power into a tree behind her. The tree cracked in half and fell.

Holding up a hand, Westengaard gave her a devoted look. "You don't understand, my love."

Adeline felt a pressure on her chest, traces of false adoration prodding her.

Anger rushed through her as every touch, every caress, every kiss from Westengaard sped through her mind. Her power swelled within her like heat rising, burning away the tendrils of Westengaard's spell.

His pretense of devotion fell from his face and he glared. "Should have killed you at the wedding."

He swept his arms in a precise motion, light gathering around them. Adeline sang out and shoved her palm forward, sending a line of fire rushing at Westengaard. She spread her arms, sending the fire in a circle around him. He twisted his arm and brought a rush of air, extinguishing the flame. Adeline shot several orbs of fire in rapid succession. Westengaard chopped his arm, as if drawing a vertical line in the air. The orbs of fire split around him, landing in tree trunks and leaving black marks.

Westengaard drew a circle in the air and a series of green spheres formed along the path. He shoved it forward, the spheres swerving in the air. Adeline whispered a protection spell, bringing up a shield of air in front of her. The spheres exploded against it in rapid succession, sending her a step back for each one. She glanced back. She was getting too close to the ravine.

"He doesn't have his full strength," Rompell said as he reached her side, bent over as he forced in breath, red marks along his neck.

"He has more skill," Adeline said. She whistled and raised her hands, blocking another barrage of energy.

"Keep fighting." Rompell ran toward the forest. "He's getting tired."

Adeline didn't believe Rompell as she shot back waves of energy, sending fireballs and walls of air, and everything she could think of. Westengaard blocked each with a whistle or wave of his hand and sent matching spells of his own.

She was sweating, her body aching as she bent the magic around and within her. Her anger was helping fuel it, but she couldn't keep this up forever.

Rompell returned to her side, holding a narrow, golden stick nearly his height, the end pointed.

"Can you distract him," he said.

Adeline grit her teeth as she gathered air around a tree trunk. With an extra push of her power, she hurled it toward Westengaard. The warlock waved his arm and the trunk burst into flaming splinters, sparks scattering across the forest floor.

As the sparks flew, Rompell ran forward and launched his make-shift gold spear. Adeline's heartbeat quickened as she gathered air around it, pushing its speed.

It struck Westengaard's thigh, the force knocking him to his knees.

Westengaard yelled. Adeline took a deep breath as she gathered a protection spell. He punched his fist into the dirt and the ground rumbled as his energy tore at it. Adeline reached for a tree branch as she lost her balance. With another shout, Westengaard waved his hand.

The ground caved apart as Adeline fell. The rush of broken earth caught her and dragged her toward the ravine.

"Adeline! No!" Rompell yelled as he dove toward her.

His bare hand grabbed her arm.

Her slide stopped and she looked up at her father. He stared at her, horror in his eyes.

A numbness spread along her arm, swiftly reaching her fingertips. Keeping hold of where the gold had already spread, Rompell pulled her to safety.

With her safe, he held his hands to his head, tears falling.

Adeline stood as the gold ran its way toward her shoulder. She had thought it would hurt more, but, instead, there was a nothingness where her arm should have been.

"You didn't mean to," she whispered as her own tears broke.

Biting her lip, she stared at her golden hand. She could see the weave of magic around it, the threads rising to her shoulder. She could sense traces of Westengaard's magic mixed with something unfamiliar and ancient.

Her breath became shallow as the gold spread toward her chest.

Wheezing, she held her hand over her golden arm and sang out notes. The threads of light bent with her music, twisting together.

The numbness advanced down her right leg, nearly breaking her focus.

The spell was similar to the ones shackling Westengaard's magic, the ones she had spent so many hours trying to unravel. She didn't have much time, but she had to try. Westengaard had already taken too much.

Choking in another breath, she pushed harder against the spell. Threads broke apart, unraveling, slowing the spread.

Rompell held his fists to his chest as he whispered, "I'm sorry, Little One."

"This turned out better than I hoped." Westengaard limped to Rompell's side, leaning on the gold spear, blood stains spreading from the wound on his leg. "Perhaps I should let you live."

Rompell jumped to his feet and punched Westengaard's face, knocking him back a step. Westengaard pressed his hand to Rompell's chest and shoved him away with a spell. Rompell's back hit a tree.

"Why do you try to fight?" Westengaard glared at his long-time enemy.

Adeline kept her eye on the spell. The threads were breaking apart, but there were too many remaining to pull and unravel. Both her legs were gold and soon she would have no air. She needed more time.

"I found the spell decades ago and spent years twisting the magic, trying to understand it." Westengaard smiled at her. "When I realized I couldn't recreate it, I gave it to my dear old friend, to see what it would do." He bent down, bringing his face close to hers. "There is no cure."

The gold spread up through her neck, cutting off her voice.

Westengaard cupped her chin and brought his lips to hers.

Rage fired through what little was left of her. Moving her hand that hadn't turned yet, she grabbed his arm. She pushed the spell from her, binding the threads she had broken to his magic, the lines of his power now too familiar.

Westengaard's eyes widened as he jerked back, trying to break her hold. But, her hand was gold and frozen on his wrist.

Her right eye went dark as the gold spread, but she used what small part of her remained to tie off the spell. Somehow, she could reach beyond herself and bind the final threads together.

Gold spread along Westengaard's arm as he pulled and fought. Adeline gasped in breath as her neck and chest were restored. She forced herself to concentrate even as her heartbeat returned and she could feel the wind on her skin once more. Somehow, this was working and she needed to keep fighting.

She filled her lungs before singing out a loud note, pushing her power into the bound spells. Other threads of light and magic seemed to appear, tied to Westengaard. Power rushed along the lines, speeding the gold's spread through Westengaard. As she collapsed to her knees, the spell's final thread left her and absorbed into Westengaard.

He shouted, but the sound cut-off, leaving his face frozen in gold, his eyes wide with horror as he stared at his raised hand.

She shuddered as she dropped her hand from his wrist. Though exhausted and aching, she stepped away and turned toward her father.

Rompell stood several paces away, his hands shaking as he stared at his palms. He clasped his hands and shut his eyes. Taking a trembling breath, he pressed his bare palm to a tree trunk. Adeline gasped as nothing happened.

"The curse—" She shivered as she glanced at Westengaard's statue. Small filaments of magic came from trees Rompell had turned gold. As the magic absorbed into Westengaard's statue, the trees returned to their natural form.

She frowned as she tried to understand. Tying the spell to his magic appeared to have drawn the rest of the curse like a magnet, pulling the fragments to him. If she was right—

Her heart skipped a beat as she faced Rompell. His eyes widened as he ran his hand along a low branch, brushing the pine needles, staring as they remained green. He grabbed a handful of pine cones and then ran his hands through the dirt.

Rising, he faced Adeline. She held out her hand to him.

He stepped back. "No. We can't risk—"

She ran the few steps between them and grabbed his bare hand, keeping a tight hold.

He collapsed against her as he broke into sobs. Her own tears came as she wrapped her arms around her father, holding him as he had held her on nights when she had cried from heartache. He raised his hand and touched her cheek. She placed her hand on top of his as she smiled.

"You are free, Papa."

His fingers brushed back her hair before he kissed her forehead and pulled her into a tight embrace. She pressed her face against his shoulder as they cried together, their tears falling for joy and for the pain his curse had brought for so long.

After a while, he pulled away, but kept his hand wrapped around hers, his skin soft, his grip strong.

He seemed about to say something, when his eyes turned toward one of the trees behind her. With a gasp, he grabbed her shoulder.

His eyes widened as he said, "Hidaya."

Rompell let go of her and sprinted into the forest. Adeline's heart stilled as she realized what he meant. Gathering her skirts in her hand, she ran after him.

A lightness quickened her step and she smiled. Finally, all would be made right.

Chapter 32

The edge of the forest seemed too far as Rompell sprinted, jumping over fallen branches and bushes. His feet skidded in the gravel as he reached the road.

His breath stopped as he saw Hidaya.

Her face was full of confusion as she stared at Jack and his wild gestures. The young officer was trying to explain circumstances despite speaking no Sandarian. Jabir and Amal clung to their mother's side, their eyes wide with fear.

Rompell's tongue clamped to the roof of his mouth and he felt the same fear as the first time he had seen her after his fall from being emperor. There was so much to explain, so much to tell her.

But, she was here, as beautiful as ever.

"Papa!" Jabir ran forward, Amal following close after. Rompell knelt and caught both his sons in his arms. His hands shook as he held onto them and kissed their cheeks.

"It's all right," he whispered, a smile forming. "Everything's all right."

"Where are we?" Hidaya stood in front of him, her robe curving around her figure. Setting down his sons, he faced her.

"Barthan." He stepped toward her. His fingers hesitated before wrapping around her wrist and pulling her close. He embraced her and pressed his head against hers, taking in the sweet scent he had dreamed of for so long.

Placing her hand on his cheek, she looked into his face, her brown eyes full of worry.

"What happened?" Her finger traced the crow's feet around his eyes and one of the streaks of grey in his goatee.

"Stiltsken," he whispered. "He—I fell for his curse."

Her eyes widened. "Where is Tamina?"

"She is safe. With my brother Solvan in Sandar."

"What?" Anger shaded her face and she bit out, "Where is my daughter?"

"I lost you for fifteen years." His throat tightened as he kept hold of her. Tears fell as he said, "She is grown, almost a woman—"

Hidaya fell against him as if hit in the stomach. She gripped his shoulder. "That's impossible."

He thought through how to explain. He had never imagined this day would be real and had never considered how lost she would be, waking years later in a strange land.

To Adeline, he said in Barthanian, "Watch my sons, please. Hidaya and I—She needs to see—the statue."

"Be careful," Adeline whispered.

In Sandarian, he said to Hidaya, "This is Adeline. She is—" He frowned, wondering how Adeline looked to his wife. He still saw her as the small child he had raised, but Hidaya only saw her as a beautiful young woman. "Like family. She saved you. She will watch Jabir and Amal while I show you something."

Hidaya eyed Adeline, mistrust in her eyes. "They should stay with us."

"I am friend," Adeline said in her limited Sandarian.

Rompell wished he had pushed her to learn more than the bits she picked up from him switching to his native language or visiting other Sandarians.

"You can trust her." He squeezed Hidaya's hand.

Hidaya gave one last suspicious glance but let Rompell lead her toward the forest. As he guided her, his heart pounded as he sought what to say. Before he explained anything, she needed to see.

They reached the clearing, cluttered with splintered trees and small craters in the ground from Westengaard and Adeline's battle. He led Hidaya to where Westengaard stood, frozen forever in gold.

She gripped his arm tighter as she glared.

"This is what happened," she said, pulling away from Rompell, "to Jabir and Amal—" She looked down at her own hand and Rompell cringed at the memory of her transforming to gold. "To me."

Rompell's head hung as he nodded. "I was trying to save us. He offered me a potion—"

"He gave it to you at Periv, didn't he?" She slapped his chest. "And, you hid it from me?"

She stormed across the clearing and sat on a fallen tree trunk. Holding her hands to her face, she said, "Walk me through everything. Help me understand."

Rompell rubbed his forehead as he paced. There was so much, but she was willing to listen. She deserved to know everything he could explain.

He began from the moment he lost her, tears falling down his cheeks as he described lifting Tamina so frail and small. His words carried across years of pain as he and his brothers fought to defeat Westengaard, and then Westengaard's capture and Rompell's exile.

Dusk settled over the forest as he told her of finding Adeline in the snow and taking her in.

"And she is the young woman watching our sons?" Hidaya said. "She is your adopted daughter?"

Rompell nodded.

"You said she saved us and broke the curse."

"Yes," Rompell said.

Hidaya let out a breath before standing. His heart quickened as she walked toward him, the rising moonlight highlighting her face. Her throat flexed as tears filled her eyes. "Only a few hours ago, Tamina was a child in my arms."

"Solvan has sent me letters every year since I left Sandar," he whispered. "I have kept them safe and he has protected her. She has a good life with him and Briya. Their children are her brothers and sisters and she is nearly a young woman."

"I want to see her," Hidaya said.

Rompell opened his mouth to tell her he was exiled, that he and his brothers had agreed his presence as an unpopular, supposedly-dead emperor was too dangerous in Sandar. If found out, it would undermine their position and risk his death. But, even that was not enough of an excuse to keep a mother from her daughter.

Stepping toward her, he said, "We will find a way."

Hidaya kept her eyes on his as she took in his words. "You should have known better than to trust anything from Stiltsken."

Rompell's head hung and he turned his face away.

"But, then I think of the fifteen years you have carried these burdens."

He dared raise his head.

"It will take time for me—for me to accept all of this, but—" She rested her hand on his cheek and looked him in the eye. "But you are my husband, and the prince I was foolish enough to fall in love with."

"I am sorry," he said, "I wish—"

"I once thought you were dead and would never return to me," she said. "I cannot imagine how much you suffered, losing Jabir, Amal, and—" She swallowed. "And Tamina."

"And you," he whispered. "Every day—I—"

He stopped as she placed her other hand on his chest and leaned close, pressing her lips to his. Tears broke again as he pulled her against him, his lips pressing harder. He knew her kiss did not mean full forgiveness, that each day he would strive to build a better life for her, to make this a new home. But, with her kiss, the heaviness of so many years fell away and a lightness he hadn't felt in so long filled him.

Here she was, his wife, soft and warm and real.

Their lips parted and she rested her head on his shoulder. He rubbed her back and they held onto each other.

An orb of light glowed from Adeline's hand as she entered the clearing.

"Papa, it's late," she said, "and we have far to travel."

Rompell kissed Hidaya's cheek. "Let me take you to our new home."

Hand-in-hand, Rompell and Hidaya followed Adeline to their sons and the motorcar that would take them to Pippington.

Chapter 33

Adeline held a hand over her mouth as she tried to hold back a laugh. Rompell stood with a mock-serious expression, holding up a dark sheet. Amal crawled out from underneath and Jabir poked his head out, whispering to his brother in Sandarian. Hidaya sat on the couch beside Adeline, giving Rompell an amused expression. She snapped at Amal and gave him a quick, commanding look. His eyes widened and he crawled back behind the cloth.

"As I said," Rompell announced to the small crowd in the sitting room, "where there were two, now there will be none."

He dropped the sheet and Jabir and Amal hid behind a makeshift curtain strung between two chairs, except where Amal's feet stuck out.

Rompell rubbed his jaw to hold back his own smile before raising the sheet once more.

"And now, they will return."

He said some words in Sandarian before sweeping back the curtain. Jabir and Amal stood beside each other, their arms raised as showmen.

"How lovely," Mrs. Frizban said as she clapped. Serena gave false gasps of amazement. Mrs. Hunter gave a polite clap before returning to her tea. Amal ran over and climbed onto Hidaya's lap. She kissed her son's forehead and spoke compliments in Sandarian.

Adeline grinned at her father, a warmth in her breast. He gave her a wink as he smiled back.

Serena and Mrs. Frizban had quickly accepted the lie they concocted of Hidaya being the widow of a soldier from Rompell's days in the Sandarian army. They had written to each other and Hidaya and her sons had come to Pippington, where she married Rompell.

Hidaya had taken the most convincing as she repeated, "But he is my children's father and my husband."

The argument had ended with Hidaya giving up and saying, "You have a backwards country."

In the nearly two months since, Hidaya had settled in as well as she could, quickly picking up Barthanian words, but still wearing Sandarian clothing. Adeline was trying to learn more Sandarian than she had gained growing up with Rompell. Most of her attempts led to Hidaya giving her a wry look followed by a laugh.

There were moments, as Adeline helped them settle in and introduced the family to Pippington, that Hidaya's eyes would grow distant, a sorrow in her face. Adeline would give her a sad smile, acknowledging the pain Hidaya must feel at being so far from home and to know her daughter knew little of her.

Still, Hidaya carried on, showing a strength that helped Adeline keep going. There were days when the memories of the past year weighed on her. She often wished she could turn back time and stop herself from becoming so vain or from falling to Westengaard.

At least Westengaard's statue had been taken by the Surris Rangers and locked deep in the Culparr Mines. There had been a debate about melting, but that risked undoing the spell binding him.

It was better to be sure he would stay a statue and she would remain free.

A knock on the door brought Adeline to her feet. She stopped as she smiled at Serena. "Could you get the door?"

Serena raised her eyebrow, clearly suspecting Adeline's intent.

Adeline batted her eyes innocently.

"I don't remember Rompell teaching you any magic tricks as a child," Mrs. Frizban said.

"She was too busy learning to be a lady," Mrs. Hunter replied.

"And what a fine young lady." Mrs. Frizban grinned and squeezed Adeline's arm. "Look at how you've grown from that little ragamuffin girl." She sighed. "We'll miss you."

Adeline returned Mrs. Frizban's smile.

Standing in this room, it was hard to imagine leaving Pippington for the Surris Mountains and living there for the next few months. Yet, as she went to her offices and checked finances with Henry or attended the few social engagements she accepted, she would be glad to be gone. Sitting among those she had once hoped to impress left her wondering how she ever found this fulfilling.

And, there were still so many whispers, so many rumors.

Based on her letters with her aunt, Surris would provide a grand escape from such pressures.

"Jack!" Jabir ran toward the latest guest.

Still in his patrolman uniform, Jack caught the boy in his arm and swung him around. Jabir spread his arms out, laughing as he pretended to fly. Amal ran over and Jack grabbed him. He swung the boys over his shoulders, both giggling as they hung upside-down.

"Sorry about being late." With a wink, Jack added, "Had to save the city."

A pang hit Adeline's chest and she winced. The day after Westengaard's defeat and the return of Rompell's family, McCay had set Jack on probation from her squad and sent him off for six months as a full-time patrolman. Ever since, he had been given poor assignments like rescuing cats and managing traffic. It was an unfit reward for a man willing to help Adeline face a warlock.

When she had gone to McCay to speak on his behalf, McCay had held her gray eyes on Adeline and said, "Officer Kingston disobeyed clear orders." She jabbed her finger at Adeline. "And you, Miss Winkleston, should be more careful."

Even though she had slowed his career, Jack acted as if it were nothing. Over the past two months, he had come over at least twice a week, checking on how Hidaya, Jabir, and Amal had settled in. Sometimes, he brought Henry with him and Adeline would arrive and find Jack and her business manager fixing a pipe or helping move furniture. Jack usually stayed for dinner while Henry went home to his wife.

The nights Serena joined them pleased Adeline the most. Adeline would linger in the corner of the porch, smiling as Jack and Serena carried on an easy conversation.

"Jack brought this for you." Serena sat beside Adeline and handed over a box wrapped in plain brown paper and a blue ribbon.

Adeline unwrapped the box. Inside lay a plain, bronze compass. Engraved on the back was written, *May you find your way home.*

"That's very sweet," Adeline said.

"Isn't it?" A giggle burst from Serena and she clamped her lips together. Adeline laughed as she bumped Serena with her shoulder.

Watching Jack and Serena's budding courtship almost made it easier to forget her failed romance with Bronhart. Her hand went into her pocket where she held the letter Bronhart had sent her a few days ago. It was a simple set of words, merely asking after her and congratulating her father on his supposedly new family. Yet, even after talking the letter over with Serena and then Rompell, she hadn't decided how to reply.

The conversation carried on through the night, with Adeline moving between each of the friends gathered. Jabir and Amal groaned as Hidaya ushered them to bed. Even after they were tucked in, they reappeared for glasses of water or forgotten toys. On Jabir's fifth attempt at escape, Adeline guided him back to his room. As she pulled his covers over him, he said, "Don't go, Addy."

She kissed his cheek. "I have to, but I'll send you a wonderful present."

"What will it be?"

"It'll be a surprise." Leaning close, she whispered, "If you shut your eyes and dream, then I'll be able to find just the right thing."

She rose and turned to leave. Hidaya leaned against the doorway, a sad smile on her face. She stepped out of the way, letting Adeline close the door gently behind her.

Touching Adeline's arm, she said, "They—I—" She frowned, her eyes distant as she sought to translate her thoughts. Meeting Adeline's eyes, she pressed a hand to her own breast. "You are part of our hearts."

Adeline smiled and squeezed Hidaya's hand. In her stilted Sandarian, she said, "You are in mine too."

Hidaya laughed at their broken words and embraced Adeline. Arm-in-arm, they returned to the sitting room.

Within the hour, Mrs. Frizban filtered out followed by Mrs. Hunter. As Adeline walked her to the door, Mrs. Hunter touched Adeline's elbow and said, "I am glad you are going. Your aunt is very excited."

Adeline squeezed Mrs. Hunter's hand. "Thank you. For everything."

Mrs. Hunter gave her a small smile. "You have grown up quite well, Miss Winkleston."

Adeline returned the smile and then the headmistress was gone.

The evening wound further toward its end and Serena yawned before saying, "I really should be going."

Jack jumped to his feet and said, "I'll walk you to your motorcar."

Holding back a laugh, Adeline walked them both to the door. Once on the porch, Jack gripped her hand and gave it a firm shake.

"I hope you find everything you're looking for in the Surris Mountains," he said. "If anyone gives you trouble, you let me and

Henry know." He smiled. "Though, I think your father'll manage things before we can."

Adeline returned his smile. "Thank you, Jack. I'll remember that."

Jack left the porch and waited at the bottom of the steps, leaving Adeline alone with Serena. Adeline hugged her friend tightly.

"I'll write every day," Serena said. "Still, I don't know how I'll go on without seeing you."

"I'll be glad to hear from home." Stepping back, Adeline raised an eyebrow. "And let me know when Jack finally asks you on an evening out."

Serena glanced away as she blushed. "We're going to the Dragon Races Saturday."

Adeline pushed her friend's shoulder. "Why didn't you tell me?"

"He—We didn't want to distract you while you were getting ready to leave." Serena grinned. "And, I wanted to save it as a surprise for my first letter."

With a laugh, Adeline hugged her friend once more. "I'd rather hear it from you, but I can't wait to read about it."

As they pulled apart, Serena's smile faltered. "And, if anything happens with—whatever fellow comes your way, you'll tell me, won't you?"

"Of course," Adeline said, "Though, I'm still not sure what to say to Nathaniel."

"You'll find the right words." Serena kissed her cheek. "I'll count the days till you come home."

Adeline grinned at her best friend and squeezed her hand. She leaned against the porch post, watching as Jack helped Serena into her motorcar and then linger a few minutes, their laughter bubbling together. Finally, he stepped back and Serena drove away. Whistling, he crossed to his bicycle. He gave Adeline a final wave before climbing on and riding off down the street.

Lingering, Adeline pulled Bronhart's letter from her pocket and read it once more. How could such benign words leave her stomach in such knots? There was still so much to heal between them, and here was her chance. Yet, she hesitated.

"Have you written him yet?"

Adeline spun around to face her father as he leaned against the doorframe.

"No. I'm not sure what to say."

"One letter doesn't need to hold much, and you'll feel better once you're done."

A prickling ran across her chest as what to do became clear, but her throat clenched at the answer.

"I will be gone for many months." She raised her eyes to meet her father's. "I need to set him free."

Rompell walked over and took her hand.

"If you and Bronhart are meant to be, then you will find your way back to each other." Squeezing her hand, he added, "If not, the right man is worth waiting for."

She smiled sadly. "I don't know if I'll ever find a love as great as yours and Hidaya's."

"I hope your life will at least be simpler."

He led her to the porch swing and they sat together, her arm linked with his.

"I'm glad you have your family," she said. "Leaving is easier knowing you won't be alone."

"My life will be full," he said, "but a piece of myself will always wander with you, Little One."

Her lips pressed together as her throat clenched. She glanced at her father, her heart warm as she thought of everything he had given her, from providing her a home as a child, to seeking to protect her, to nights like this, where his wisdom gave her comfort.

Of all she loved in Pippington, he would be the hardest to leave behind.

She leaned against his shoulder and he put his arm around her, just as he had for so many quiet evenings on this porch. A tear fell down her cheek, but Rompell wiped it away. Shutting her eyes, Adeline drank in the cool evening air, enjoying being merely a daughter sitting with her father.

THE END

Author's Note

The seed of Adeline and Rompell's tale came from a question by a friend, Vanessa Haggard, after she read an early draft of The True Bride and the Shoemaker (The Pippington Tales – Book 1). If you haven't read it yet, The True Bride and the Shoemaker culminates in Adeline's disastrous wedding to Westengaard from Peter Talbot's perspective. Westengaard's accusations led Vanessa to ask, "Is Adeline a witch?"

My answer was, "No."

At this point, Adeline was just a minor character in Peter's adventures and meant only to be a silly young woman who becomes Westengaard's pawn.

However, the question, "But, what if she did have magic?" lingered.

From this grew The Matchgirl and the Magician and other "what if's" took shape.

- What if Hans Christian Anderson's Matchgirl was rescued and lived?
- What if the tales of Rumplestiltsken and King Midas were combined?
- What if a young woman with great powers grew up in a world that doesn't believe in magic?

Now that the story is fully formed, I would say Adeline is still a silly young woman for most of this book. However, what makes her compelling is when she must face her magic and grow. As I have gotten to know Adeline, I have realized there is much more to her story than I realized.

For the four years since that seed was planted, this story has traveled with me as I have moved between three states, started and completed graduate school, moved to a new city for a new career, and published the first two Pippington Tales.

Over time, the story changed. At first, Rompell was a milkman trying to help a widow and her child. Then, he became the mysterious vagrant, but had a romance with Adeline's mother, Mariana. While Mariana is a great character, her part of the story took away from the core father-daughter relationship, and also became a problem once I discovered Rompell's romance with Hidaya. So, Mariana had to pass away before the story began, leaving Adeline an orphan. One day, I might tell the bittersweet tale of Conrad and Mariana Winkleston.

As this story has developed, the world of Pippington has grown. I am excited to share future stories of the frontier and magic of the Surris Mountains, of the criminal underworld led by Madame Blue, more of the world of mermaids, of the behind-the-scenes adventures at the dragon races, and more of Adeline's journey as she matures and her magic grows.

Oh, and of course, to resolve her future romance.

I hope you enjoyed this journey through the world of Pippington and hope you will come back for many more.

Acknowledgements

First, to my readers who have joined me in traveling through Pippington. It has been fun to share this world and watch as other people enjoy discovering its hidden corners and wonders.

Second, thank you to my editor Tara Newland for your hard work, excellent revisions, and being an excellent friend. You are a great companion on the journey through Pippington.

Third, thank you to my writers group – nominally, The LDS Beta Redears Writers Squad of Doom. Thank you to the various members who remain and have passed in and out. This includes Alicia Dawn, Simon Driscoll, Benjamin Hewitt, Britney Mills, Kathryn Olsen, Tanisha Rene Hayes, and Caitlin Jacobs. You are all fantastic writers who challenge me and push me to be a better writer.

Fourth, thank you to my beta readers – Jenny Flake Rabe, Lily Taylor, Danielle Thorne, Anita Dean, Annie Malekzadeh, Adria Cavenaugh, Lisa Stasforth, Vanessa Haggard, Rachel Hawks, Carolyn Young, Cassie Rowse, Alicia Dawn, Cathrine Bonham, Sara Roring, Miranda McClean, Naomi Cohen, Brent Longstaff, Michelle Algood, and Heather Davis. Your constructive feedback and support was essential for polishing this story.

Fifth, thank you to Seedlings Designs for a fantastic and gorgeous set of covers. It has been exciting to see my design dreams come true.

Sixth, thank you to Paul Bishop. You've been a great mentor in the writing world and I appreciate your support as you've helped me polish blurbs and navigate the strange paths of publishing.

Seventh, and finally, thank you to my family and friends. Together, you have been incredibly supportive. There are a lot of you and I could probably fill this page with thanking each one of you. I especially want to thank my sister Natalie for the many times I've said, "Hey, what do you think of this idea," and she's patiently provided feedback. I am fortunate to have a great family and many fantastic friends.

To everyone listed here and anyone I may have missed, a final big thank you. I am sure we will journey on to many more tales in the world of Pippington.

Other Works by L. Palmer

The True Bride and the Shoemaker

The Pippington Tales Book 1

Welcome to Pippington, where motorcars bump down old, city lanes, elegant shoes appear by magic, and an ordinary shoemaker can become a hero.

Peter Talbot could use a little magic. Cheap factory-made shoes are putting his shop out of business, his nagging sisters will never let him rest, and his efforts to find true love are constantly thwarted by worldly fickleness. However, the gift of a wild primrose and a shipment of rare griffin skin are about to change everything. When beautiful, handmade shoes begin appearing in his shop every morning, Peter is determined to find his secret helper. What he finds introduces him to adventure and the hidden world of magic in Pippington.

The True Bride and the Shoemaker is the first of The Pippington Tales, based on The Elves and the Shoemaker and other fairy tales.

 To read a preview, visit tinyurl.com/truebride

The Lady and the Frog

The Pippington Tales Book 2

Welcome to Pippington, where motorcars bump down old city lanes, frogs transform into men, and mermaids just might be real.

Evelyn Havish is through waiting for Henry Kingston to look up from his ledgers and propose. But, when Henry's brother Jack is transformed into a frog and trapped in a well, Evelyn must join the rescue. Armed with her training as a lady and a solid punch, Evelyn must outwit a scheming heiress, wrestle an octopus, and kiss far more frogs than a girl should be expected to. As she dives deeper into a hidden world of magic, she discovers Jack may not be the one who needs saving.

To read a preview, visit tinyurl.com/ladyandthefrog

The Mermaid's Apprentice:

Book 1 of The Pirate and the Mermaid's Tailor Trilogy

Mabel Sinclair never planned to become a pirate.

All she wanted was to escape her dull life as a debutante and conquer the world of fashion. One fateful night at a ballroom ends when Mabel's foolish brother is kidnapped and transformed into a toad. To save him, Mabel makes a bargain with a mermaid and travels with her to an unexpected realm of magic. Once there, Mabel must choose between being imprisoned by cruel merfolk or joining pirates.

Antonio Cortez never planned to fall in love with a pirate.

A sailor who dreams of returning to his quiet life as a tailor, Antonio's plans are knocked off course by a chance meeting with the dashing pirate Mabel Sinclair. Antonio bonds with Mabel over their love of fashion, only to become a target for Mabel's growing list of enemies.

Fighting for their lives and their future, Mabel and Antonio find they have only one ally to turn to: the treacherous mermaid who Mabel bargained with in the first place.

The Mermaid's Apprentice is an epic tale of pirates, mermaids, and adventures in high fashion.

To read a preview, visit
tinyurl.com/mermaidapprentice

About the Author

In between exploring the hidden magic of Pippington, L. Palmer works in public service and lives in San Antonio. She is an award-winning speaker and has presented on various topics at writing conferences, studied English and Film at The University of California Santa Barbara, and has a Masters in Public Administration at Brigham Young University. She developed her imagination and adventure skills through growing up in Girl Scouts, working at resident summer camps, teaching high school English, and reading great books of fantasy and magic. While she doesn't typically host tea parties, she does enjoy hosting some for dragons on Tuesdays. For the latest news, visit: lpalmerchronicles.com

To explore more of Pippington, visit:
lpalmerchronicles.com/pippington_tales

To sign-up for L. Palmer's Newsletter, visit:
lpalmerchronicles.com/about

For updates and free bonus content, visit:
lpalmerchronicles.com/exclusive-preview

If you enjoyed this book, please take the time to leave an honest review on Goodreads, Amazon, or the bookseller site of your choice.

Follow L. Palmer on social media:

- Facebook: facebook.com/lpalmerchronicles
- Instagram: instagram.com/lpalmerchronicles
- TikTok: tiktok.com/@lpalmerauthor1

Printed in Great Britain
by Amazon

32268032R00229